MW00527875

ONE OF MANY

by

B. M. J. GATT

ONE OF MANY

Copyright © 2015 B.M.J.Gatt

All rights reserved by the author according to the Certificate of Canadian Registration of Copyright Section 49 and 54 of the Copyright Act. No part of this book may be reproduced, lent re-sold, hired out or circulated in any fashion whatsoever without the explicit prior consent in writing of the author.

Whilst some of the events and the actions of some individuals described in this book are based on actual events, the characters in this book are fictional and are derived from the author's imagination.

Cover design: Sarah Kuehn

Interior design: John Breeze

IBSN : 978-0-9937755-0-5

Manufactured in the United States of America

Author's Note

One of Many was essentially born during my attempt to become a writer. Told to *write what you know*, unseen voices spoke to me. *Tell our story*.

A child growing up in England, I knew nothing about Jamaica's history or my ancestry. A mother, I became interested in tracing my ancestry. My eyes opened to the rich history of Jamaica. Throughout my research and whilst trying to write my first novel voices spoke to me from the past, peeking over my shoulder; they told me what to write.

I first began to write in an "English" voice, but could not get into the characters' heads. The writing was all wrong. My problem was putting on paper what I heard in my head. When I read through the chapters I wanted to hear the rich, raw Jamaican voice. It was not there. I finally threw away the first few chapters and started over—typing away in pure unadulterated raw patwa, whatever that is. The words flew off the pages. Often typing away during the day, or late at night, the characters told me what to say. Many times I had to stop and laugh out loud, other times felt deep sorrow for their suffering. In all, I was heartened by the resilience of the characters. They taught me that in spite of hardships their spirit for survival was solid as a rock. They introduced me to the Jamaican "wicked sense of humour".

Dedicated to my father and mother
and to the untold "one of many,"
to whom I am eternally indebted.

"When me t'ink on me sweet Jamaica, water come a-me eye."

- *Jamaican calypso*

TABLE OF CONTENTS

PROLOGUE

Notting Hill, West London, 1958

They studied the slim-bodied coloured with his head bowed. Some heard tell that Clifford Webb was a nice, respectable man. He was married to a good-looking, clear-skin woman, and he had three pretty *pickneys*. He was hard-working, with no scandal to his name. He was a Jamaican man.

Clifford raised his heavy head. The eyes bored into him. A woman coughed. Touching her lips, she stifled another. He pulled off his grey hat and cupped it over his trembling knee. Leaning forward, he felt his body shudder.

He was no talker. Johnny Walker was the only thing that loosened his tongue. Johnny Walker gave him courage. He licked his dry lips, pushed himself onto his weak legs and sucked deep at the hot, musty air. He must untangle his tongue. It felt like a pound of salt fish in his mouth. His head thumped. Struggling for sensible speech, the faces swam before him—like *janga* in a stormy river. Even his mum-ma's face joined them. He fumbled with his hat and placed it on his head. Was this the obeah Mum-ma had predicted when she prophesied he would go foreign? What else she had said, he couldn't remember. He parted his lips into a sarcastic curl, and miraculously, words flowed. Free, not stumbling, but thundering and forceful, like Dunn's River's mighty waterfall.

"Dem charge us double. Fe rent dem stinking place." His voice was raw, his patwa harsh. "Double me a-say. Wat choice we 'ave. But fe pay. Force us fe sleep two. T'ree. Four to a room. An' dem condemn us. We labour 'ard. Do widout. Save. Buy our own place. Still dem condemn us. Saying to us. 'So. How come you West Indians come a-England an' live like kings?'"

His words rumbled, roared. They filled the club with power and vindication.

"Only work *us* gets. Is wat whites no want dutty dem hands on. Dem a-say. Is all *us* coloureds fit for. Still dem condemn *us*. Now." His dry tongue lashed out in harsh mockery, like a whip flaying a bare backside. "Now dem a-say. Dey a-coming. Fe kill *us*. Burn *us* up. Mash *us* up. Grind *us* up like cornmeal. Drive *us* out-a-England. Eh, eh. Well."

A heavy sigh echoed. It was a sigh that said, "Enough. Time come!"

Now they finally understood. This Jamaican had plainly stated one fact: Britain had abandoned them to her bullyboys.

"Enough me a-say," cried Clifford. Knees dipped, he threw out his arms in anger. "Dis wickedness *must* end. West Indians *must* now protect demselves. De only time English police rouse dem white backside. Is when black man fall dead on English pavement. Britain no care rawted 'bout us.

Teddy boys an' such say. Dey is coming. Fe kill. Burn *us* out. *Us* say. Beat dem back. *Us* say. Prepare. Now!"

Rawted teeth sucking and *eh-ehing* filled the air as heads nodded and shoulders stiffened in vexation, sorrow, and determination.

When Clifford said "Me never come a-England fe see murder done to me family," the room held its breath. "Is criminal wat is 'appenin'. White yard boys tell us. Dem is coming! Fe burn down me house. House me an' me wife bust our backside fe buy. An' law. As usual. Gwan stand by. An' do not'ing? How we fe let dat 'appen. Dis no America. Wid lynching. An' de Klu Klux Klan. Dis a-England! Our mother country. We her people. Good as any white!"

"See 'ere," Clifford continued, stabbing his smoke at the sombre, staring eyes. "Show a hand all dat Jamaican." Fifteen brown hands flew up. He glanced around. "Trinidadian?" Five shot up. "Barbadian?" Three more. "Rest a-Small Island?" As he counted three more, a sweet peace claimed his soul.

"We come England. Fe a new life." His words were sorrowful, guttural, and slow. "A better life. Fe our children. An' ourselves. An' dis how Britain treat *us*? *Us* dat fight fe give dem freedom? *Us* dat fill dem coffee cups. Sweeten dem tea? *Us* dat mak' Britain rich. Fe centuries. Wat our reward? Fe all a-dat? Closed doors. Turned backs. Nasty sour faces. England no 'appy wid only beating *us* wid iron bars. Cutting *us* up on dem streets. England is coming. Fe finish us off. England is coming. Fe burn *us* down. In. Our. Own. House. Batter. Kill *us*. Well. *We*. Say. Enough. *We*. Say. Now we mean business. *We*. Say. Now *we* prepare."

BOOK ONE

Webb Hill, Jamaica

Clifford Webb lay flat on his back staring dead eyed at the *duppy*-like shadows flittering across the wooden walls of the small bedroom. Outside an owl hooted in the sticky heat. Insects scurried in the thick bush land that surrounded the two-bedroom house nestled at the heel of the hill. Perspiration oozing from his half-naked body, he shifted his bottom, sighed deeply, and brushed sweat from his forehead with the back of his hand. Head tilted back, he watched slivers of dawn light peep through the dips in the corrugated tin roof resting on the house's wooden boards.

Fast asleep, and unaware of her husband's worries, Clara turned towards him and sighed contentedly. *How she sleeping so fine*, he wondered. *She no sense me restlessness beside her? No understands wat been lately 'appenin' on Webb Hill?*

Clifford's blood and history was here. She had heard some of this history but didn't know everything that had happened years back.

All that lived round about knew this was his land. Pappy gave it to him when he married Clara Bennett. Pappy got the land from his own pappy, and so on before he was born. How was she to know all of this if she was not from here?

Though not one to *labrish* or talk big-mouth talk, his ears had tingled with his brothers' deceit and lies. They were like poisonous pus that refused to heal on an old sore, and his nose holes were full of their stink.

Exhausted from nights of fretting, his head pounding and begging for sleep, he turned his back on his wife.

Yellow Bird was already pecking for food on the roof. Clifford closed his eyes as a brooding sadness settled upon his soul. Today he must face trouble alone. Today he *gwan* die. Why was it always this way? No matter how hard he tried to avoid trouble, it always tracked him down. The cockerel's call in the yard depressed him further. Easing away from Clara, he pulled himself to the edge of the bed and sat up, gripping the side. *Another sleepless night*, he thought. *Another workday at de bush. If only me can stay 'ere. Once me leave de house, it no turning back.*

He pushed himself wearily to his feet and went to the chair by the window. After pulling on the banana-stained nylon shirt and faded brown trousers he had draped over the back of the chair, he placed his sweat-stained brown hat upon his head. Leaving Clara to her dreams, he went into the yard.

Once he had saddled the mule and loaded her back with two crocus bags of yam and coco heads, Clifford pushed his tools between the bags and left for his field. Selecting the overgrown weedy area beside his banana grove to plant the heads of coco and yam, he pulled out his tools and began his steady toil—clearing weeds and brambles, turning over the rich soil and raking it. Deep holes dug, he dropped the heads inside and covered them with mounds of earth for the Good Lord to water and nourish for a plenteous harvest. The sun ripe in the sky, he straightened up, walked to the mule, and unpacked salt fish fritters and sorrel punch. He ate and surveyed his land.

Clifford Webb was the youngest son of Samuel Webb and Mary Carr. Slight bodied and five foot ten, Clifford had a long face and high cheekbones with an aquiline nose that flared slightly at the tip. Small ears and a high forehead gave his face an honest, open look. Gentle and quiet by nature, he kept his thoughts to himself and avoided crowds.

For Clifford was a small settler and land was life. Land was better than money. Land grew crops for the belly. Land fed his animals. Because his land was vital for his family's survival, what had happened since his pappy's death not only robbed him of sleep, but also his peace of mind. How were his head and heart to understand that his own flesh and blood was doing this to him? They knew this land was his lifeblood. It alone sustained his family. His mum-ma's words thundered inside his head: *"You know not you own!"*

Before Clifford built his house, he and Clara had lived under his pappy's roof. The day he brought Clara to the hill, he and Pappy entered into a strict understanding: this fertile land was his inheritance forever.

That second night on the hill Pappy had called him and Clara into the eating area. He told them he would give them the section of land over the pass, boards also to build their two-bedroom house below his own. The land was fertile and rich. Mature mango, pimento, coconut, almond and other food-bearing trees grew there. Several streams and a narrow trail led to it. If only he had put the gift in writing.

Clifford now knew that long before Pappy died, snake hearts must have been plotting for his prize section. Now that Pappy was dead, how could he concentrate on his fieldwork when day and night, his brothers' betrayal screamed in his head?

He bit into a fritter, gazed at his inheritance, growing in abundance in the distance and a searing pain struck at his heart. It was as if he had been stabbed by a friend. To think he might lose all this, his coconut, pineapple, gynep, sowersop and naseberry—his land. Overcome by a deep sadness, his fist tight around his mug, he strode to the mule, opened the saddlebag, and pulled out the bottle of Johnny Walker he had packed with his food. He uncapped it; half filled his mug, and began to drink.

Heavy heat hung on the hill like a harbinger of doom when Clifford arrived home and unsaddled his mule. He entered the house and went to his small, shuttered bedroom, where a thin ribbon of light sliced through the joins of the boards. Drunk, slightly swaying, approaching the three-drawer mahogany bureau, he yanked the top drawer forcibly; it shot from the stops and fell onto his feet.

"Backside," he cursed, dropping to his knees. He searched though the scattered underwear. Flinging a vest across the room, he muttered, "How me fe find it in all dis blackness? Rass, where it be. Me know it 'ere. Remember." Finally finding what he had hidden from Clara, he muttered another slurred "Aho," clutched the side of the bed, and pulled himself upright. Feet parted, body firmed, he studied the object in his right hand. He turned it over. Fascinated, flicking back the lever, he peered inside the chamber and mumbled, "T'ree bullets. Aho. Eh, eh. One sting. Dead. Bite like black widow. Plenty bullets fe wat me want fe do. Machete no man fe dis. Since dem brand me weak. Mak' dem bring dem rawted self. Fe t'ief me land. Den dey gwan see. If. Me still weak."

His drunken mind satisfied, he snapped back the lever, jammed the gun inside his trouser belt, and waddled unsteadily from the room.

* * * *

Tilda's eyes were like two full moons watching the disappearing back of her dada from under the bed. He did not know she was hiding there. In the whole of Jamaica, she loved him the best. Her mama caused confusion in her head; she felt timid around her. Her feeling for her big sister, Missy, was muddled and mashed in her head. Only Dada pulled the pink-and-yellow Paradise Plums from his pockets to push into her hand. Only he made her happy and content in the house. But, *not* today. Today she felt strange. Today things did *not* feel right. Today even the house smelt wrong. There was no familiar scent of fresh mullet seasoned with thyme, or the rank odour of green bananas as they rolled in hot, salty water. Fiery peppers in garlicky rundown; coconut milk simmered with scallions and salt fish. Today, even dada did not seem like dada at all.

Missy was with friends at the gully below the house. With no one to play with, Tilda felt an odd unsettledness. Forgetting her mama's warning, "Me room a-no pickney play place," Tilda decided to play in her parents' room. She checked to see if anyone was watching, crept in, and walked towards the mahogany wardrobe. As she trailed her fingers along the side of the bed's dark, wooden, headboard, the door flew open; she panicked and slid under the bed. Her belly flat on the dusty boards, her nose itching, she stifled a sneeze. A man muttered curses. They drummed at her heart like a funeral march. Confused, trembling, and afraid even to breathe, her mind advised her to stay hidden under the bed until he left. But, how to not let him see her? Easing onto her elbows, she stealthily shuffled backward. Her heels touching the far corner of the wall, she crouched up like a crab to wait.

It was some time before the room grew quiet. Inching forward on her belly, she peered out. He had left. The room empty, she quickly shuffled out and hurried to the window and pushed aside the shutters. Climbing onto the ledge, she jumped to the grass outside. What must she do next? Go back inside where all was peculiar and unsettled? Her head a muddle, she turned towards the veranda and was about to enter the house again when she heard raised voices coming from inside. Her dada and mama were warring. Heart pounding with fear, she turned and ran.

The House

The gun tight in his trouser belt, Clifford lumbered into the kitchen where Clara, pregnant with her third child, was suffering greatly in the heat. Hands in a bowl of water and sweating, she heard Clifford's staggered steps and turned to greet him. When she saw the gun between his belly she cried, "Clifford! Why you got gun?" Wrinkling her nose at the nauseating stench of Johnny Walker, she said, "An' man. Why you a-drunk dis time a-day? You know how me a-stay. Is throw up you want me do?"

"Woman leave me be, you hear." Clifford flicked his hands wildly at her. "No tangle wid me today. You hear! Today me ready fe de rass clawt' t'ieves. Today me no care a backside wat gwan 'appen to me."

Surprised by his unusual show of temper, she waddled up to him.

"Clifford. No do dis t'ing. Dem kill you fe sure." She touched his arm to try to calm him down.

"Wat me care 'bout dat." He pushed at her hand. "'Cause me always been quiet. Dem t'ink dem can t'ief me property? Is not'ing you want me fe do?"

Clara thought that this new Clifford Webb must have been gnawing over troubles with his people. His bloodshot eyes told her he was stone drunk. No reason would budge

11

him. But, drunk and with a gun... ? She began to panic. That he was angry was a fact. But something else was in his eyes— a deep despair, some torment she did not understand. "Clifford, me a-beg you. Wat dis madness you planning? Whe' you gwan do?"

That first time on the hill, she had tried to fit in with his family. But, her looks and high-minded ways and breeding was one dish his family would not swallow. Her man was not their donkey, or unpaid yard boy. Nor was she fresh, seasoned mullet for his brothers to lust upon. She had kept secret his sisters-in-laws' jealous, sly insults. To unburden them to Clifford would only have boiled up bad blood. Now that they had shown their true selves, why should she keep their dislike a secret from him?

That their youngest brother owned such a prize for a wife had stuck in their craws. The conniving thieves even now were plotting to drive him from his land. Clifford must think she was some fool-fool jackass not to see any of it. She saw it all but glued tight her mouth to keep the peace. Her easy, pleasing man never realised this had started her first day on the hill. It was only now that the facts were spitting in his eyes that he saw it clear as glass. But, the gun. What was he planning?

Somehow, she *must* try to distract him. Get the gun from him. But how? Almost in tears, she decided to release the hurts she had carried since the first day of their marriage.

"Clifford Webb, you learn not'ing, nuh? You people never care fe me. De day you bring me to de hill. Is de day you rub salt on dem open sore. You family never care 'bout me."

"Hush you mout' woman." He stabbed his right index finger at her. "Wat you fe do wid dis?"

When she flinched at the venom in his voice, he softened his tone. "Me know is a-fact-you a-say, woman. How it must a-burn dem bad. Dat dey youngest brodder gets handsome woman fe a wife. When it come time fe christen our childs. Wet dem head a-church? Eh, eh." He chuckled and tested his words upon his slack tongue. "Dem examine. Is anxious. Wants fe see if us baby 'ave natty bump head like dem own babies! Breed pickney wid fair skin an' smooth hair in Jamaica. Stand you in a good stead. Youself know it how Jamaica a-operate. Dat an' Pappy's property is wat-a-eat dem up. Dat wat dem want fe dig out me eye for."

"Aho," she said, her head nodded in mock agreement. Finally, he acknowledged. His family were wicked.

She must get the gun. Vengeful and drunk, he might accidentally shoot her. Desperation caused her to throw out her hands and beg, "Is widow woman you want mak' a-me, Clifford Webb? Say dem dead you up? Who you childs fe call dada? Clifford. No do dis t'ing. Me no use to dis sort a-life, you know. Is grave you want go? Lawd-a-massy." Groaning, bent forward, and cradling her bulging belly into her arms, she wept. Clifford still showed no mercy. His next words bounced off the wooden boards of the kitchen and pierced her heart.

"Hear so, woman. Me mind no turning. All a-dem want fe t'ief me place Pappy give me. It me land. Even if Pappy no give me piece a-paper fe prove it. Pappy word been always law in 'im house. Now 'im died. Dem want tak' it from me. Well." He pulled the gun and waved it at her. "Today it me or dem. Mak' dem come kiss me bare backside. Dis gwan settle dem!"

13

Tilda

Sometimes a faint memory of an old man entered Tilda's brain. She was behind the big house. Her dada and uncles were lowering the wooden box into the deep red earth. Afterwards grand-mama's house swarmed with people, like red ants after honey. Rum bottles clinked. Tipsy people talked all sorts of fool-fool nonsense. Laughter and the pungent odour of curry goat and rice and peas filled the house as if some big celebration were happening. But all Tilda could think on was that wooden box buried in the deep dirt, behind the house.

As far back as Tilda's young brain remembered, people had always died. Women had wailed. The nauseating odour of cedar coffins made her stomach churn whenever Mama mentioned a relative had died. She was glad her grand-mama Webb was not dead. Whenever trouble hit her, she could run to the big house that sat at the top of the rise and find comfort.

Small-boned and slim, Tilda was what Jamaicans termed a "*marga-foot gal.*" She had brown eyes, and freckles dusted a smaller version of her dada's nose and cheeks. Her nature, reflective, a dreamer, Tilda preferred her own company. Perhaps it was her sensitivity that made her sense that her mama disliked her. Why else would Mama push out her mouth at her? Kiss her teeth and shoo her away, as if she were some bothersome blue bottle fly?

When Tilda woke, she usually rubbed sleep from her eyes, pulled on her frock, and ran outside. Scurrying onto the little humpbacked rise that separated her house from the big one above, she would place her bare feet into the dewy grass, squat, lock her fingers behind her neck, and allow the weak morning sun to caress her back. High on the hilltop, alone in her little world with only the vast expanse of sky for company, she sometimes followed the flight of a bird, wishing she too could soar freely over the gully, way up high, then perch contentedly on a branch of the almond tree. Lost in her serene and contented make believe world, if her belly growled for food, she would hurry home for her cornmeal porridge. Today, she did not visit the mound. Disturbed by an unknown tension in the house, she fled to the big house above.

An Argyll Scot
Jamaica, 1855

Tilda's great-great-grandfather, Samuel Webb—the fourth mulatto son of an Argyll Scot, James Webb, and his Negro housekeeper, Sally—built the large square timbered house that squatted like a fat bullfrog on the rise. Facing the full sun, it viewed its domain like a king.

The sturdy, three-bedroom house had been built for strength and endurance. Six thick, wide concrete slabs steadied the base to the earth. Inside, two long, narrow bedrooms ran parallel left of the eating area. A dark, tight passage sliced its way to the third bedroom at the back. Here, a small parlour and veranda overlooked lush, dense, vegetation where every imaginable shade of green sloped towards the distant horizon below.

When James Webb drafted his will in 1855, he must have been acutely aware of the racial divides that still existed in Jamaica even if slavery had been abolished in 1834. He willed that upon his demise, three thousand Jamaican pounds be distributed immediately to each of his four sons. A provision also declared that each son should receive five hundred Jamaican pounds per year until the age of thirty. These bequests were both rare and generous for the time. Not only was Jamaica a fertile ground to amass great fortunes, she was also a harem for white males to liberally scatter their seeds among their female slaves. Unfortunately, the latter was the sole legacy these white males left their numerous mulatto children. Abandoning them to Jamaican's harsh climate, they purchased sumptuous estates, or titles, in their native lands.

James Webb was not of that ilk. He bequeathed unto Sally peaceful habitation of his house until death. She also received a life interest of twenty pounds Jamaican currency per annum. Sally's tenacity for survival and James's Scottish thrift, fierce independence, and work ethic embedded in Samuel a proud legacy.

Samuel did not wish to be classed "a lazy, illiterate half-cast mulatto." Most of these wasted their lives carousing or sponging off relatives. His father shipped him to England at age eight. Boarded out and educated, he returned to Jamaica at age eighteen as neither fish nor fowl. It did not take him long to feel like an alien. White society shunned him. So did the true Africans in a Jamaican culture governed by strict divisions of race and skin colour. Whites would not acknowledge this educated mulatto upstart whose schooling and refinements far surpassed theirs. He was not of them. Although Samuel dearly loved his mother, he no longer had things in common with the slaves, nor with the various dilutions of colours on the island. After sober thought and due consideration, Samuel concluded that he must branch out on his own.

One morning whilst reading the newspaper an advertisement for the sale of a well-stocked property in the far-off parish of Portland caught his attention. Although the journey would be arduous and long, he decided to investigate. He packed provisions, tools, a change of clothing, and, before the sun rose on a clear morning in May, saddled his horse and rode off.

He had heard that wild hogs roamed that part of the island but saw none on his journey. Nearing St. Margaret's Bay, at the mouth of a dense thicket, he nudged the mare into a brooding forest. Sparkling brooks trickled beside vibrant moss. Ferns clung tenuously to gigantic, mouldering tree trunks that seemed as though they had lain for centuries on the forest floor. Lima ropes dangled eerily, as if suspended from heaven. Every living thing seemed to draw nourishment from the forest. The land rose sharply, the mare slacked her pace. All appeared asleep.

Two hours later, bending over the mare's neck, Samuel urged her up a summit that left them breathless. The cloying forest suddenly released them onto an area of land overlooking the brink of a gully. He slid from the mare, stretched his aching muscles, and patted her neck.

"Good lass. Good. We here," he cooed in his half-Scot, half-Creole tongue.

To his right, lush grass covered a small humpbacked rise. Where the land levelled, a rickety, hut-like structure hid between a thicket of trees and bushes. His father's legacy would give him this. Here he would build his house. Here he would raise his family.

Help

Her bare feet racing to the big house above, Tilda went in search of her widowed grand-mama Mary Webb who lived alone. Thick, long plaits swinging around her neck, she ran up the wooden steps, calling, "Grand-mama, grand-mama."

Gasping, she craned her neck and called again. When no one replied, she jumped off the steps, swerved right and raced to the back of the house, calling again. Still getting no reply and beginning to panic, she heard a sound to the far right of the veranda and dashed towards it.

Behind the house, the land dropped sharply, levelled, and then rose to the same height as the house. This small section of land appeared as if it had been deliberately flattened to look like a *V*, with a handle to its right. Perched on top was a cookhouse. Small and wooden, this orphan house had a dirt path leading to its door from the main house. Years of trampled feet had worn away the grass to leave small flat tufts around the edges of the gritty red-dirt path.

Whenever Mary Webb worked in her kitchen, the planked door was always open. Swinging back and forth, it allowed for the free passage of air. When absent, to keep out stray animals, she always secured it with a piece of crocus string.

19

Here she cooked nourishment for her family. Whites boiled in a large pot of soapy water, thick black coffee brewed, and hot, potent cocoa drinks laced with rum and nutmeg. In the middle of the dirt floor was a circular coconut mat. The two front legs of a crudely fashioned plank-backed bench touched its edge. Facing the bench, a glassless window gave a picturesque view of a forest of trees descending into the gully below.

Mary Webb was five foot four, stocky; she stooped slightly when she walked. Today, her frizzy grey hair, parted down the middle, was in two plaits and pinned at the nape of her neck. A sun-bleached cotton apron protected her blue, patterned frock. Her husband's dusty, lace-less black shoes on her bunion feet made a *slip-slap* sound when she walked. Apart from a few wrinkles at the corners of her eyes and mouth, her medium-brown face was smooth, her nose short. Dark, piercing eyes and a firm, fixed mouth sealed in her secrets. Not pretty-pretty, like the *dry-land tourist* type, Mary Webb was termed "comely." But what was extraordinary about Mary Webb, was her hands. Huge and powerful as a man's, they lay like dinner plates on her lap. Hard work kept her aged body durable. Whenever alone, her countenance took on a troubled, fretful expression.

After her husband died, she sometimes allowed her mouth to slide with her grandchildren. "You grand-pappy never choose me fe me looks. But fe bear pickney. An' work like donkey," she would say.

Her back hard against the planked bench, Mary Webb deliberated on her life. Lonely and feeling the blues, she glanced absentmindedly at the charred Dutch pot on the wooden table by the window, then at the three battered pans hanging from wire hooks on the wall. Settling upon the crocus bag under the table, with its few pieces of yam and dasheen, she released a slow, regretful sigh and allowed her aged body to wilt on the wood. *How come time a-fly so fast,* she pondered. *How come. Wid all me childs now big an' wed. Old age a-catch me so quick? How come. All dese years. Me dat t'ink me so wise. Never see dat dis day gwan come.*

Memories swirling around her head, hearing Tilda's urgent call, she paused in her deliberations and called back, "Child, me up 'ere. Come up nuh."

Fifteen minutes before, heat had been giving her aged legs hell as she hauled a pail of milk up the hill. Securing it onto the mat, she had buckled onto the bench to rest and was pondering when Tilda raced into the kitchen as if chased by a *jumby*. Glad to see her grand-pickney, she moved the pail to the side of the bench and glanced up. Tilda's troubled face told her something was wrong. She gently touched her grandchild's shoulder, and said, "Child. Wat ails you? Today, you frisky like pony!"

Mary Webb did not wait for a reply. Knowing that whatever had brought the child would soon slide out; she flapped her hands at Tilda, motioning for her to wait. She went to the wooden table wedged against the wall, bent, removed a handful of sticks from underneath, snapped them into small pieces and laid them criss-cross under the cooking grid. Dry twigs added, she struck a match and pushed it between the sticks, then placed another lit match to the pile. Arching forward, lips pursed, she blew, checked if the fire had caught, and blew again. Unhooking a small bamboo fan from the wall, she placed the pail on top of the grid and fanned until a fierce flame licked the side of the pail.

"Soon heat up an' ready," she said, straightening up. "Want some? Fresh today," she added, her brown eyes twinkling.

.

21

Tilda nodded. She knew Grand-mama was knowledgeable. She had good obeah and could fix anything.

Mary Webb eased onto the bench and patted the space beside her. "Come. Child. Come. Sit beside me, nuh."

Tilda sat.

"Dem plenty today nuh," said Mary Webb, shooing away a fly. To lighten the sad look on the child's face, she chuckled and said, "Like dem want fe *nyam* us up. Eh, eh." Her body snug against the bench, Mary Webb searched the small troubled eyes gazing into hers.

"Wat a-troubling you today, child?"

Tilda blinked, slid close to Mary Webb, and said softly, "Grand-mama." And, as if she were telling the wind a secret, she quietly and timidly said, "Dada got a gun. 'Im. 'Im. An' Mama a-quarrel. I fear!"

Although Mary Webb's ears were sound as a bell, she thought she had misheard the child. To true up the facts, she cocked her ear close to Tilda's mouth.

"Eh. Wat. Wat you a-say child? Talk up. High. Wat dat you a-saying?"

Tilda bowed her head. Now she had Grand-mama's full attention. Her eyelids twitched. She gulped nervously. Swallowing her dry spittle, she shuffled so close to the old woman that Mary Webb felt Tilda's small, hot body against her hip.

"Dada. Got gun, Grand-mama," Tilda whispered, so quiet, so close that her lips almost kissed Mary Webb's ear. "Say...he gwan shoot somebody, an'... an'—"

Her voice froze. Her throat corked up, petrified, her tongue refused to release the raging emotions that were strangling her heart. She shook uncontrollably. A mournful wail burst from her paralysed mouth. When she slid under the bed and hid, hearing her dada and mama warring, running to her grand-mama's house, raging rivers had swept her along. Now she was drowning—sinking into a dark, deep pit. Babbling madness, she flung her head up and stared at Mary Webb.

"Oh Grand-mama," she sobbed. "Dem fight. In kitchen. An' me come. 'Cause. Me know you mak' it right. Mak' it right, Grand-mama. Me a-beg you. Mak' it better." Weeping bitterly, Tilda buried her head into the old woman's belly.

Mary Webb's eyelids jiggered. She was sure madness were upon her. Lips pursed, she gathered the child into her arms and rocked her gently. After a short silence, she said, "Hush puppus. Hush. You too small a-pickney fe carry big people's worry 'pon you head." Rocking and cooing at the trembling child, her troubled brain tried to find sanity in the jumbled babble. *Suppose pickney mak' dis up? Suppose. Listening to big people's hotness. Cause confusion fe cloud pickney mind? De way some Jamaicans calculate dem t'inking. Two an' two no always mak' four. An' dis pickney got enough imagination fe de whole a-Jamaica.*

Trying to soothe the sobbing child, Mary Webb pondered. Her last boy must be in some grievous badness. Always one to keep worries to himself, he never let out steam. He would stew them over and over until they burned up crisp. Then only would he take to the bottle, and then all hell would let loose. She cupped the small chin in her hand and searched the wet doe-like eyes.

"Child, answer me true-true. Is wat you a-say a-gospel. It dat you a-preaching?"

Tilda sniffed, blew her nose into the apron, and stared back at Mary Webb. "It true-true Grand-mama. Me see de gun."

The fire hissed, and Tilda laid her burden into her grand-mama's apron again.

Mary Webb sat in silence for a while, then, glancing over Tilda's head and seeing milk escaping over the rim of the pail, she kissed her teeth in vexation. Releasing Tilda, she stood and muttered, "So," to no one in particular. And, "Trouble a-come a-Clifford. If dis child a tell truth. Better hurry 'im place quick." She lifted the pail, placed it on the table, and covered it with a banana leaf.

Dis no look good at all, at all. Dem all a-fighting fe land. Wid dem glasses a rum an' smoke? Well. Mak' her pickney buoys laugh an' boast over wat dem pappy leave. How many a-Samuel's pickney been plotting an' conniving fe 'im land? At Samuel time. Even de daughters a-come last. Now man dead. Wid no will fe divide up 'im land. Trouble a-breed like neyga woman on heat. Man musta t'ink he gwan live till judgment come. Maybe de years dem been wed. Man been trying fe kill her wid work. So she dead before 'im. She living. An' must deal wid 'im pickneys. An' dem greed.

Samuel had not been long dead when she heard the labrish start flashing from their mouths. All of them wanted to play boss man on Webb's land. As if the land belonged to any of them. Her own mum-ma had a saying for this: "*T'ieves never prosper.*" Mum-ma had been wrong. *Plenty a-t'ief a-prosper in Jamaica like mosquitoes.*

She knew they wanted her and Clifford's land. How she tried hard to put some fight into Clifford as a small boy. Try as she might to starch up his backbone, his nature would not turn. Soft, with a woman's heart, he was "*always de one fe get de last coco from de crocus bag,*" as the island proverb said. Clifford had always been the underdog of the family. Once only she had glimpsed his strength.

He was about nine. His pappy had dragged a runt kid from its mum-ma's belly and left it for dead under a susumber bush. Clifford rescued it and nursed it on cow's milk. It grew strong and virile. Every day when he came

24

home from the bush, he would call his kiddie and it would run to him. Then one day, he called and not a bleat. He searched the whole hill and gully for his kid without success. Nearing the house after a fruitless search, he smelt curry goat. That day, Mary Webb witnessed a madness she had never seen before. The boy seemed to turn lunatic. His brothers had laughed. Told Clifford they had killed and cooked his kid. He rushed into the house and grabbed his pappy's cutlass from behind the door. She had to call Samuel, who wrestled it from Clifford. From that day on, he was never the same; he was withdrawn, quieter inside and out.

Now things were different. Now they were no longer pickney boys but grown men with greed in their hearts. She blamed Samuel Webb for dropping dead without making provisions to settle his land.

She *must* see her boy.

"Come. Tilda. Child, follow me," she said, working her mouth into a hurry-come-now frown. "Wat you a-say is no good, at-all-at-all. Best fe leave milk. Dem pappy was alive. He control dem. Dead now. War a-*bruck* out on Webb land. Hum," she muttered shaking her head. She stared through the glassless window at a mango tree in the distance. "Which a-dem land belong to? Eh! Eh! Tell me dat. Which a-dem. Lawd-a-massy on us all. You dada de littlest a-dem. An' dey want fe *nyam* 'im land from 'im like when rats a-gnaw cheese."

Tilda did not understand one word of Mary Webb's jumbled patwa but she was happy. Grand-mama would make things right.

Mary Webb doused the fire, bunched her frock with one hand and grabbed Tilda's hand with the other. Ignoring the unfastened door, she said, "Come child. Make haste."

25

Her shoes *slap-slapping* on the dirt track, she hustled down the hill to her house while her head buzzed with what her own mum-ma's said about the ungratefulness of children. *Kill pickney give Mum-ma. Mum-ma no gwan eat. But kill Mum-ma give pickney. Pickney gwan eat.* Reaching the bottom step, panting, she paused, said to Tilda, "Stay still. Changing clothes. Soon come," and bustled inside.

A quick glance around the eating area, she hurried along the dark, narrow passage and entered her shuttered bedroom. Her husband's shoes made a hollow *clank* on the dark boards when she kicked them off and eased into the mahogany chair beside the four-poster bed. As her body sagged into the dark wood, she waggled her head and a woeful dread settled on her heart.

"How me fe bear dis trouble?" she moaned. "Dis time dis trouble may kill me dead. Trouble. Trouble. Always it a-trouble. Even now Samuel dead. 'Im legacy still a-haunt me like jumby."

She sighed deeply, closed her eyes, and tried to rest both brain and body. Yet, try as she might, her feverish brain would not allow her body rest. For wisdom said "Worries no gwan chase trouble away." She knew she must stop worrying and do something. She pushed herself up, bustled to the large mahogany wardrobe at the far side of the bed, pulled open the double doors, and caught her breath. An overpowering odour of mothballs gushed into the suffocating room.

Four plain cotton frocks, guarded by mothballs tied into small calico squares on wooden hangers, hung inside the wardrobe's dark interior. She tilted her head left, scrutinised the frocks and a bitter sound slipped through her lips.

"Hum."

26

Those long wedded years. Not once had Samuel Webb asked if she needed clothes for her back. He installed her in his house and she became his slave. Not once had he thought that she, his woman, needed nice things to pretty-up-herself. Necessity must have forced him so she not disgraced him to sometimes buy a few yards of cloth for her to sew into dresses for church and special occasions. No sooner did she return to the yard, she changed into her work clothes.

The man was like a wild hog that second day of their marriage. His kindness turned into sourness for his children and those under his roof. She bore it as his wife. Duty demanded she did when she wed Samuel Webb. That loving she had inside to give him that first year of the marriage vanished like dew on grass. So it stayed until that day he dropped dead in the yard.

Plain, simple, and serviceable, the dresses mirrored her life. No frills, flounces, or ornaments to show a man's love for his woman. "Hum," she muttered again. That first day she inhabited his house, he had made her understand one fact: he had married her so she had better be grateful he had hauled her up the mountain. Like his house, land, and children, she became his property.

She grabbed the rose-coloured frock from its hanger and draped it over the bed, bending before the wardrobe, pulling out a large round box from the back; she took out her black straw hat and stood. To see better, she opened the door leading to the veranda.

Her apron and frock off, clean white drawers pulled onto her plump backside, her frock over her head, she buttoned the front. A white belt buckled around her broad waist, her hat firmed onto her head, she pinned it into place. A glance at her feet, her stockings pulled over each knee and secured into place with a large black button, she slipped her feet into her only pair of low-heeled black shoes. Viewing her reflection in the small mahogany-rimmed mirror, reassured she would do, she hurried through the eating area and back into the hot sun.

Tilda turned when she heard the door open. Her mouth opened in surprise. Her grand-mama was dressed so fine.

Mary Webb did not join her. Instead, she said, "Wait. Soon come," and hurried back inside. She returned clutching a crocus bag.

Mary Webb was no fool. She saw the question mark on Tilda's face. Her motto was, *"When trouble hit you. Pickney shirt fit you."* If trouble came her way, she would dress for it. Trouble would *not* find her body in *dutty* work clothes. Suppose—suppose some day, someone boxed her down and she was as helpless as a newborn babe. Suppose—suppose people hoisted her up—dragged her tired old body down the gully—clear past Master Brown's backyard—to the hospital. What would feisty neyga people think when they saw her wearing the very same clothes that she had been wearing to feed her goats or pigs? Suppose, just suppose, when the nurse pulled down her *baggy* to jab an injection in her *batty*, she witnessed *tear-up* drawers on her backside. How was she to live that down? Her wrinkled, bamboo legs sticking out-a-patched-up drawers. Jamaicans loved their labrish. They had wicked, waggling tongues. Long before they heaved her down the gully, the breeze would have blown her shame through the parishes: Portland, St. Mary, and St. Thomas, even clear to Kingston Town. She could see it all. Dipping their green bananas into their *run-down*, pushing them into their mouths, licking their oily fingers, island people would laugh at her shame. That she, wife to respected, big property man Samuel Webb couldn't even afford to buy decent baggies for her batty. *Never* would she bring such scandal on herself or her family. Appearances counted in Jamaica. Wear tear up, dutty clothes—even holey *marenas* in one's yard. If stepping from the yard, it's dress-up time. She *always* dressed for trouble.

✳ ✳ ✳ ✳

Mary Webb had not always been kind or understanding. In her sixty-odd wedded years, she had steeled her backbone and silenced her lips. She obeyed what the Good Book preached about obedient wives, cowered down to Samuel Webb and never showed a feisty puss-like face when he played big-man in the house. She even endured how he treated his pickneys. That was what the Good Book said obedient wives do. Nobody had to tell her what was in the Book. Sunday school and solitary readings had taught her well. Many times when grievous hurts entered her heart, she would remember parts in the Book that she had never experienced in her married life: the parts about love and kindness. Other parts that said softness should exist between a man and his woman. But she placed her trust in the Almighty, with hope. He would help her endure to the end. It came. Her life of hell ended the day Samuel's coffin descended into the bowl of the earth behind the house. The day they lowered him into Hell thunderous rain fell. Since then, she never once visited the grave.

She recalled the black frock she had worn on her back, the one she had sewn in secret. The one that kept her strong so she didn't turn lunatic. She would wait until he left for his field, and then draw the black cloth from the back of the wardrobe. Using an old frock as a pattern, she cut out the pieces. In this stolen time, she would sit and sew with a smile and think about the day she would wear it. That last time

29

when she stared at his face through the black net, the black dress formed around her body like any skilful dressmaker's fashion piece.

Eyes dry as bramble, she never cried. What good was crying? She might as well have howled at a mongoose. Crying never worked with him. A workhorse was what he had wedded. His mule tied up at the yard got better treatment: rubbed down, good food, and a handsome saddle.

Suppose 'im no dead. Best man stay where dey place 'im, she would think after he died. People who asked why she never visited the grave were told, "It grieves me bad fe see 'im lying in de dirt back a-yard." So, it had stayed to ease her pain.

Samuel was dead, but still stink lingered on the hill. His pickneys had inherited his wicked legacy of greed.

Betrayal

Her left hand clutching the crocus bag, her right Tilda's, Mary Webb made for Clifford's house.

Tilda's heart felt lighter. Grand-mama would fix things. Life would return to normal.

A lopsided fence sitting in a wilderness of weeds separated Clifford's house and the one on the rise from the gully below. This gully led into a dark, weepy cavern. Originally built to keep out stray animals, and long fallen into disrepair, the fence caused much contentious teeth sucking whenever visitors living on the other side of the gully tried dipping underneath to get to either house.

As Tilda and her grand-mama neared the fence and a susumber bush, she cupped her right hand, fixed it against her brow and saw something that stopped her in her tracks.

A youth in a sun-bleached blue shirt and brown, banana-stained trousers tied at the waist with string leaned against one of the thick fence post. He held his head high, proud and tilted, making his long, broad, hook-like nose appear sinister in the brilliant heat. The angle of his head gave the illusion of the curved beak of a John crow. Woolly, untamed hair sprang from a raw-boned head. He reminded Tilda of the wild bushman she once saw when she accompanied her dada to his section of land. His right fist clutched a cutlass. When he saw Mary Webb and Tilda approaching, he propped his cutlass against the post, threw out an arm, and began taunting Clifford, who stood a little distance away.

"Old man," he yelled, pulling an earlobe, he stabbed a chicken-neck finger at Clifford. "See dat little piece a-dirt. Back-a you-yard? Is all you gwan get. Not'ing else."

As if he had dusted his business with his uncle off his hands, the youth bent and bunched his trouser legs inside black galoshes that looked too big for his feet.

Clifford who stood bareheaded in the sun felt as if his brain was fried. He had been alone in the house during a heavy drinking bout when he heard someone call outside the house. Walking onto the veranda and seeing the youth in the distance, he flicked his hand wildly and ordered him to "tak' his marga backside from his yard." Getting feistiness back, and fearing his brothers were following, he touched the gun at his waist and went into the hot sun. Stone drunk and disorientated, all he had wanted was to crawl into bed and let dark consume him. It was too late now. Eyes shaded with his right hand, he studied his nephew. Why had they sent Joseph's boy? He could see his brothers on their veranda laughing at him while sucking a mango seed. Well, let the jackasses laugh. He was no coward. In the dark black night, he had decided. It was he or them. Now he must finish it.

He opened his mouth to talk, but jumbled words trickled onto his thick tongue.

"You pup-pa an' de rest a-dem. A-bush t'ieves," he said, his body swaying. "Hear wat me a-saying, buoy? Bush t'ieves. Dem t'ieves dat wait fe people fe leave dem land. Den crawl a-people place fe t'ief dem. Pappy place is fe all-a his pickney."

Not only did they plan to steal his birthright, but sent this *dry-foot* boy to face him? This ultimate betrayal pounded in his hot, pain-filled skull. He squeezed tight his eyes to try to silence his tears.

"All-a-you musta t'ink me soft. Easy fe pacify. Even dem own mum-ma dem want fe drive from her place? Wat sort a John crow is you all?"

His own flesh and blood was doing this to him. From the time he was a baby-boy, he shied away from face-to-face trouble. That they sent Rufus boiled at his gut. "Buoy," he cried drawing out the word. "Shame tak' dem up? Dat why dem send dem yard boy to me place?"

Rufus scowled and lowered his head. He hadn't expected any backside trouble from his uncle. The brothers wanted Clifford's land. Rufus's father, the eldest had sent his most volatile, short-tempered, and sinister son to deal with Clifford. Rufus had fired many wars in the district. He spelt danger! If his father had disputes with others, his son was sent to settle it.

The youth cocked his head. He seemed to be trying to decide how best to tackle Clifford. Callous and warp minded, never bothered by his conscience before, his head did reason. This was his pappy's little brother. He did merit some respect. But no sooner did the thought came, greed plucked it from his head.

"Answer, buoy," Clifford cried. "Is shame dat a-tak' dem up? Is shame dat a-stop dem from coming? Is shame dat a-stop dem from facing dey own brodder?"

※ ※ ※ ※

Mary Webb shivered. She knew Clifford's silent steel. Her pickneys would try to take her land. Samuel may be

33

dead, but she would *not* sit at her house like some hatching hen, *not* let her pickneys thief her place from under her backside. *Rough life mak' fe a tough wife.*

She was about to firm down her hat to go deal with the *rank-foot* boy when a bellyaching moan erupted beside her. Glancing down, she dropped the crocus bag and shrieked, "Stand still, pickney." Seeing Tilda was about to run to Clifford, she grabbed her hand and shook it. When Tilda whimpered and shrank back in terror, Mary Webb softened her voice. "'Dis t'ing a-no picnic, child. So. Stay still. Me a-say!"

Sweet Saviour, she thought, dropping Tilda's hand. *Why Joseph 'ave fe send dis trouble a me yard? De buoy's nose shouldn't be in dis t'ing. Samuel childs alone 'ave claim on 'im land. Did Joseph send Rufus? Maybe buoy come fe some'ting fe 'imself? Whatever kind a-hurricane a-blowing. Me must settle it before blood spill on Webb land.*

She left Tilda whimpering and went to the fence.

"Buoy," she said bitterly. Head tilted, she stared at her grand-boy. "Why you want bring dis disgrace to de family. Fe land? Land belong to any a-you? You too faas! Galang a-you own yard. Leave dis business fe odders. Land once was you many times over great–grand-pappy. Forward 'im an' so on. Hear you name mention in any a-it? Buoy. Answer me dat."

Although her tongue spat nastiness, Mary Webb's head reasoned. *No God-fearing woman should even t'ink. Much more speak such unchristian-like t'ings. Yet. Wat left fe me fe do when wild hog charge onto me place a-wanting fe root up me good victuals. On top a dat hog mess. It want fe kill me dead inside de bargain. When all me a-do. Is try fe drive 'im off?*

She flicked her angry hand at Rufus and kissed her contemptuous teeth and cussed him to "tak' 'im *marga* backside back to 'im own yard." She thought she detected fear flickering across his face. But when he sneered, sucked his teeth, and jammed both hands onto his hips and said, "Go 'bout you business, old fowl", murderous ideas ignited in her head. The rancid-mouth boy had no respect for her age or station in life. If only she had brought Samuel's cutlass. During her marriage, many venomous thoughts had filled her head to use the cutlass on Samuel. She had resisted the urge and pushed it deep inside her belly. Now this rank-foot boy resurrected the putrid vomit in her mouth. "You dem chief t'ief?" she cried, itching to box the smirk from Rufus's face.

Rufus pouted. This type he had never tackled before. He rarely had to deal with his pappy's mum-ma. Her squawk unsettled him. Head lowered, he stabbed a vicious kick at the weeds flourishing around the fence. He was mulling over how best to deal with her and did not see Clifford approaching.

Mary Webb did.

"Me buoy," she wailed grabbing at Clifford's arm. "You is one alone. Go back-a-you yard. Let de ignorant bush hog stay, nuh. Clifford. Me buoy. You child. She over dere." She jabbed a trembling finger at a terrified Tilda—she looked as if she would collapse onto the grass.

It was difficult to say if Clifford had heard her or not, for his drunken brain ignited in anger when Rufus snorted and said, "Old woman. Me no takin' no rawtedness from you. Go you house. Leave dis business to me. Or me chop you up too."

Never had a pickney or grand-pickney of Pappy ever showed disrespect on Webb Hill. De backside buoy brought shame an' disgrace to Webb Hill. Vengeance pounded at Clifford's skull. A wild, destructive madness seized him. He shoved his mother from him, rooted his feet into the ground, and yanked the gun from his waistband.

"Blood clawt," he said, slurring his words. The gun in his right hand, he waved it at Rufus. "Bring you marga backside a-me place?" He steadied the gun with his left hand. "Want t'ief me land?" He stepped forward two paces. "Gwan finish it now." He aimed the gun. He pulled the trigger.

Tilda felt like a spectator in a nightmare. The single shot missed. The sharp crack echoed in the gully, blasted like a stray firecracker. Nesting birds scattered. Squawking, they fled to strange shelter.

Rufus raised his cutlass—Tilda sprang forward like a bullet from the gun. Mary Webb quickly grabbed her frock and hauled her back. "Stay, child!" Then to Clifford, "Buoy, look out dere—"

Clifford's hands trembled. He dropped the gun.

The old woman and Tilda's tussle distracted Rufus, when he pulled down the cutlass; it missed Clifford's head and sliced into the fence. Clifford made a desperate grab for the gun but did not see Rufus quickly seize a stout stick. It struck his shoulder and levelled him to the ground on top of the gun.

Tilda's heart almost hurtled into her mouth. Dada was dead. "Dada," she screeched, weeping uncontrollably. She flung herself on top of Clifford's seemingly lifeless body. "You dead me dada. You *hasounou*. You dead me dada!"

Not once did Rufus glance at Tilda, nor showed her pity. He kissed his scornful teeth, leisurely snatched up his cutlass and carefully examined the blade.

"Man no dead." Rufus glanced at her and smirked. "But mak' 'im try dat again an' me finish 'im wid dis." He shook his cutlass at her.

Clifford was neither dead nor unconscious. Weakened by Johnny Walker and the sweltering heat, the stick had merely clipped his shoulder.

* * * *

Eyes dry and wild, Mary Webb stared at her son. A primitive urge tugged at her womb—to go and box down the boy. Again, her galloping old heart spoke wisdom. *Old age finally jump onto you back. A-wanting fe grind you to you grave.* Yet, although a part spoke so, the other rebelled. *Old age 'ave 'im use. Sixty-odd year's a-wedded hell. 'Ave welded you endurance. You earned you courage.* Armed with righteous determination, she stooped, seized the crocus bag, hobbled to the fence and opened its mouth. Her hand pushed inside, fist firmed around the handle, she hoisted it high in the air. She studied its white, wide, sturdy hips—winking in the brilliant heat, with regret—it was empty.

The sudden sight of the chamber pot startled Rufus. What was its significance? Unused to civilized reason, he furrowed his brow and mocked her.

"Old woman," he said, "wat you gwan do wid dat? It you weapon? Gwan box me down wid you piss pot?" Overcome with laughter and watching Clifford trying to stand, Rufus said, "Backside. Boss man. Boss man. You. You. Send de madwoman. Wid piss pot. Fe fight me?" What did he care about the old woman and her crazy ways? He had boxed down his uncle.

Mary Webb stepped forward and rammed the chamber pot onto the post.

Rufus straightened his stringy body and wiped his gleeful eyes with the back of his right hand. Scowling, he studied the chamber pot. His thick, fleshy lips slackened into a slow show of surprise. His crinkled brow suggested confusion. *Is dis some trick a-de sun?* he wondered. *Some deep obeah magic? Some madness a-de old crow?* He glanced at Clifford, still trying to stand, and at the flush-faced fowl, still clutching the crocus bag in her fat fist. *Wat de old bird hatching? Wat she planning wid de piss pot she put on de fence?*

For the first time in Mary Webb's life, she felt her age. Her body sagged. Her heart felt mashed up. Beaten to a pulp, she craved death. Again wisdom spoke to her. *Wat de use you be to de living if you dead?* She again, heeded its counsel.

"Buoy," she cried, waggling a crooked finger at the chamber pot on the fence. "See chamber-pot over dere? See how you strong now. Got you vigour. T'ink you is some big man. An' me is a dried up old crow. But, you just *wait*. Eh, eh. Wait."

Her mournful cackle punctured the sky. It echoed in the gully below. The clarion call roused the first Samuel Webb, and all the ancestors buried deep in Webb's red dirt. Way up on this breathtaking summit of gullies, woodland, lush bush land where sultry caverns wept. Sparkling brooklets, streams, cascading forests, and an everlasting abundant greenness must bear witness to her cause. This day, she summoned up a curse. One that only a great sorrow could release. A curse deadlier and darker than Jamaica's own obeah. She demanded Haiti obeah!

Her tongue felt fat, heavy, like it was covered in a cup of thick black molasses. She saw into Rufus's evil heart. He may play the big man now, but one day someone *gwan* box him down. Sauce his batty good and proper with hot-pepper-sauce. She kissed her teeth in scorn.

"Jamaicans 'ave a-saying: *'De higher monkey a-climb. De higher monkey a-expose.'* You. You dat know not'ing since morning. Life gwan b-o-x you down. Gwan lick you marga batty. Till you head get 'tunted. You gwan beg fe mercy. See me 'ere." She stabbed her right thumb into her chest, and then ran her rough tongue over her rusty teeth. "Since den. Remember wat me a-saying. Till you dead."

Rufus did not fear her, but like most Jamaicans, he was very superstitious,. He knew obeah's evil power. African slaves had brought voodoo spells and sinister traditions to the island. Witch doctors and obeah women still practiced the old customs. People would often slink off in the dead of night to visit an old obeah woman or a witchcraft man to put a spell on an enemy. He had heard of a woman who had stolen another's husband. The slack jezebel went blind for no sensible reason other than the wife bringing home an obeah doll and stabbing pins into its eyes.

He glanced behind him. Every tree and blade of grass seemed to vibrate her words: "Till you dead." He viciously kicked the fence again and almost pitched off the chamber pot.

The witch had planted bad seeds in him. A fear festered that he had never experienced before. He knew he should have left after he boxed down his uncle. Why he stayed, his head did not say. Before, when Grand-pappy lived, trouble never came to the hill. To still his unusual disquiet, he threw the old bat a challenge.

"Old woman, I no fear you."

Mary Webb's head jerked backwards. *Never* had she ever swallowed disrespect from any pickney boy. This piss-foot boy, who was like a tree that marga dogs cock their legs against to piss, would finally make her settle a duty she felt bound to perform. She must cut the umbilical cord. Lips puckered in distaste, sorrow stabbing at her heart, she said, "Buoy. Since you show you is devil man 'imself. Me curse you. Hear wat me a-saying to you, buoy? Me. You pappy own mum-ma is placing obeah 'pon you head." She balled her right fist, and, gazing at Heaven, shook it at him. "De Good Book it a-say, 'Dem dat live by de sword. Shall die by de sword.' Remember. Buoy. It gwan 'appen to you." She pulled hard and long at her dry throat and spat at him.

Rufus saw the slime flying towards him. Jumping away, he kissed his teeth and sauntered off.

Mary Webb waited until he disappeared. She stooped and picked up the crocus bag. The chamber pot would stay on the fence to perform its obeah. Trudging sorrowfully up to the big house, she left Clifford stumbling towards his, followed by Tilda.

* * * *

Clara had no notion of what had happened between Clifford and his nephew. When Clifford refused to listen to her and made it clear that he was determined to seek vengeance, she decided to visit her sister. Time would settle his temper. She had called outside for Missy and Tilda to come into the house. When only Missy replied, and several attempts to find Tilda proved futile, she and Missy left the hill. She knew that Tilda would return home when she was hungry.

She slept fitfully beside her senseless husband that night after hearing that war had broken out on the hill.

The following morning, gloom permeated the house like a black shroud. Clifford seemed preoccupied at the breakfast table. He ate his porridge in silence, went to his bedroom and dressed for visiting. Grey hat on his head, he returned to the kitchen with a small suitcase.

"Going to Maggoty Point. No know when me coming back. Day or so" was all he said, then left.

Tilda did not see him go. She and Missy had kept to their room. When she finally crept out and hurried to the front of the house, her dada was gone. So was his grey hat.

Her dada owned two hats—a sweat-stained brown one he wore around the yard or at the bush and a grey one, that had a darker grey ribbon around the crown. It matched Clifford's grey suit and shiny grey shoes. Tilda could tell where her dada was by his hats. If he wore the grey one, he usually came home smelling of liquor.

When five days passed without a sign of Clifford, Tilda began to pine for him. Would she see him again? Though she often wanted to question her mama when he would return, she silenced her lips. Asking would get her a tongue-lashing. Since dada left Mama always looked miserable and hot tempered. Once, thinking she heard his voice, racing to look, realizing her mistake, she changed directions and slid under the house. Her body low, shuffling along the dirt until she reached a supporting beam, she rested against it.

Her original plan had been to hide under the house from her mama scolding and then return to the house when her temper cooled. The underbelly of the house was dark, dusty, and still. Cocooned in its musty, warm blanket, Tilda's eyelids drooped. She slept, and the minutes flew.

She heard voices, opened her eyes, saw total blackness, panicked, threw out her hands, jumped up, banged her head on the boards above, and fell flat on her face. Sneezing, and spluttering, and rubbing her mouth and face with the back of her hand, she carefully eased herself onto her bottom. Where was she? She smelt goat urine. She was under the house. Here was where the goats settled at night.

She heard voices again. Crawling towards them, collecting tar-like goat droppings on her hands and knees, when near the voices, she squatted down to listen. Her

41

mama and grand-mama talked. Grand-mama asked Mama when Dada was coming back and if Mama had heard about Dada's war with Rufus. Mama explained Dada had left for Maggoty Point without saying why. She did not know when he would return. Tilda heard something about how Dada's family treated him. Hunkering into the dirt and craning her neck, she heard teeth sucking. A pull on the veranda's rail signalled Grand-mama was now on the veranda. The voices became as clear as if both stood before Tilda.

"Hear Tilda witness dem wickedness?"

"Clifford never say much, Mistress Webb. Little is all 'im a-tell. Youself know 'im never one fe talking much. Say Tilda witness it?"

There was another clicking of tongues. The wooden rail creaked.

"Poor pickney. Shake her bad when de slack-mout' boy almost dead Clifford. Certain she no say not'ing?"

"No. But she one pickney dat always peculiar. Never understand she."

"He come back. Say me got some business me want fe discuss wid 'im. Hell's wat's playing at de brodder's yard." There was a thump. Grand-mama must have stepped onto the grass.

Two days later, Clifford returned late in the evening. He went straight to bed.

The following morning, smoking at the kitchen table, Clifford stretched his legs underneath, raised his hand to take another drag of his smoke, and noticed his nicotine-stained fingers. *How many Albany me smoke since morning*, he wondered. *Two. Dis must be me fourth. Pappy is at fault fe me addiction. Ordering me an' brodder Lewis fe tak' care a-'im tobacco field. Young buoys'll try any'ting. Getting dem fe look after 'im tobacco field was like releasing a mongoose inside a chicken coop. How me fe forget de day*

42

Pappy catch me sitting on mango tree branch, puffing away at dem mak'-do smokes. Pappy pulled off 'im leather belt. Caned me an Lewis backside real good. Couldn't sit down fe a week. Cured Lewis. Never smoke since den. Never me. "Why you want fe burn good money you no good neyga buoy" is wat Pappy would say to me now.

Knowing he must tell her, Clifford took a final drag and mashed out his smoke. "Clara. Decide fe leave de hill. We'll rent a place at Maggoty Point. Can't stay 'ere now."

Clara had just finished drying the dishes. Hands full of crockery, she turned, and the plates slid from her hands. They broke on impact. She stood still, stricken eyed, staring at the white shards skidding across the dark wood. They scattered like shredded strands of coconut. She bent dreamlike and scooped up the broken crockery into a dishcloth. Throwing them into a bucket in the yard, she went to the table and sat.

"Hear wat me a-say?"

After some time, she said, "We leaving de hill, you say?" Her speech was slow, almost a whisper. "We leave hill you a-say. How den we gwan live. Eh. Answer me dat, Cliffford Webb. From Webb Hill, how we gwan live."

He too had questioned his decision to leave Webb Hill. Moving to Maggoty Point was no easy solution. Yet, what other choice did he have? One thing was fact: staying on the hill was impossible. Those that thought him weak hadn't glimpsed what was in his heart that day. He had been drunk with Johnny Walker, which was why the boy had boxed him down. He recalled aiming the gun—nothing else. Except...righting his hand and pulling back the trigger. He had been certain his aim was true. Then a shot—something else, he couldn't tell what, boxed the gun out his hand. This fact his mind had puzzled over and over from that day. *Backside! Did me imagine it? Did Johnny Walker 'tunt me head like some jackass so me couldn't t'ink straight? After. Me remember. Tilda bawling on me belly. Rawted! Wat me care? Let dem t'ink wat dem want. Clara may no like it. But me is leaving. Dat decision is final.*

"It true wat you saying, Clara. Our home is 'ere, on Webb land. Land dat been in our family from way back as me can recall. 'Ere is where me heart and soul is set. But see 'ere." He rose and went to her. "All dis was dem plan. Long time. Fe t'ief me land. Drive me from me place. Now dem gets wat dem want. Dem a-laugh at me. You want me fe stay an' eat crow bait? Dat you want?"

She searched the troubled eyes and haggard face of her man. She knew it was a hard, hard thing for him to admit that his family was wicked enough to thief his house and land, his family's lifeblood.

A few clouds hung in the unusually cool morning sky. Soon refreshing rain would relieve the heat. As if smelling change, the goat had bumped and bucked under the house all night. Soon Clifford would have to run the goats down the gully for feeding.

"You family live round 'ere, Clifford. We leave, wat we eat? How we live? Wat gawn 'appen to us?"

He brushed the flat of his hand across his damp, worried, brow. "Me know life's hell fe us now. Me know Maggoty is an uncertain future. Day an' night me head tell me so. Yes, me family 'ere. An' yes, it me home. But which a-me relative you see run a-me yard fe help me? No worry you head. We make out a-Maggoty. If dat's wat a-trouble you. Find some'ting fe mak' us live."

So he could not see her tormented eyes, she turned her head from him. His land was his life. Her man had never raised a wicked word or hand to her since they married. All this nasty suffering came from his greedy family. She tried to visualise a future for them away from the hill but could not. Bitter accusations against his family burst from her lips.

"Can't bear it, Clifford," she cried, thumping her fist on the tabletop. "Can't. 'Ere. Is. Our. Life!" *De backside shame. De scandal. De disgrace. To t'ief 'im inheritance. To drive 'im from de hill?* His family had mashed their future into nothingness. She flung her head into her arms and howled. When her eyes had finally drained, head raised, she said, "Me hate dem. Hate every marga backside one a-dem."

Leaving The Hill

The decision to leave the hill final, Clara prepared. The hard part was leaving her security on the hill. Moving morning dawned bright and no clouds threatened. Clifford carried two cases, Clara one, Missy and Tilda a small bundle each and six of Clifford's male friends and three mules all trudged down the gully. They arrived at Maggoty Point three hours later.

The night before the move, Clara had settled the children in bed, checked the cases, cleaned the almost-empty house, and fallen exhausted into bed. On his back beside her and unable to sleep, Clifford had stared blankly at moonbeams pushing through dips in the tin roof. He checked his head. *Goat sold. Buoys coming fe help in morning. His family!* "Rawted," he cursed quietly through clenched teeth. *Since de ruckus. Which a-me people come fe see how me is? Dem scarcer dan trying fe find teeth in a newborn babe. It's as if me dead an' buried.*

His mind spinning like a pickney's gig, Clifford turned onto his side. *Like me want see any a-dem. Cha. Leave all you t'inking man. You t'ink too much. It settled. Finished. Clock can't slide back now. Boat at sea. If fierce wind a-blow. It only life.*

Head deep under the sweat-soaked pillow, he tried to clear his mind, to sleep, but the thought of losing his ancestors' land chased sleep away. Easing from Clara, he went to the kitchen, found a crocus bag, dropped two heads of yam and a hand of dasheen inside, and twisted the neck. He went into the yard, where a myriad of insects scurrying in bush land serenaded the moon. Stars sparkled in the blue-black sky like uncut diamonds. The sack over his shoulder, he followed the silver globe to the big house above.

In this night of shadows, a lone, single-wick kerosene lamp glimmered in the dim eating area where Mary Webb sat on one of the hard wooden benches at the family mahogany table. Ghostly shadows flittered across the wooden walls where deep secrets lurked, ready for the telling. Moths dancing frantically around the lamp, Mary Webb willed her eyes to stay awake.

She never locked her door. For which fool-fool jackass of a-somebody would wander clear up the mountainside at night to thief her? Detecting footsteps on the wooden floor, she looked up and was startled when Clifford entered, dropped the sack at the table leg and sat opposite her. She reached over and pulled the lamp closer.

"Leaving early morning, Mum-ma," he said, rubbing his slender hands together.

She did not immediately reply. Instead, she searched her son's sensitive face, then dropping both hands onto her lap, knew she must accept the few crumbs that life threw at her. Not only had wedded life grieved her but so had her pickneys. Clifford, her only salve among her litter was also leaving.

"So," she said finally. Lifting her right hand, she batted a moth from her hair. "It's come to dis. You leaving de hill. Me t'ink somebody must-a put obeah on dis place. Else, how dis t'ing 'appen 'ere? When badness comes Jamaican's way, dem a-say, '*One day, one day, hold ya mak' me cut!*' to ease dem hurts. Dey know dat no matter wat kind a wickedness evil-

47

minded people a-do. One day t'ings gwan turn right. But," she added, oiling her tongue with spittle, "dough meself has always advise so. Never in all me born days did me ever t'ink dis t'ing gwan 'appen at me own yard."

His eyebrows arched in puzzlement, he bowed his head and stared at his hands. She had always been so solid, strong and immovable, like the soil that nourished his crops. That she was opening her heart to him disturbed him plenty.

Her head tilted, she savoured his silence, then, like a cockerel inspecting a hen, she made a cackling sound with her tongue. "Eh, aho. Clifford buoy. Lately t'ings been 'appenin' dat surprise even dis old woman dat witnessed plenty in her life." Her bright, birdlike eyes studied his when he raised his head.

"Want fe see some'ting?" she said suddenly. She smiled a secret smile.

Her movement was so quick that he had no time to turn away. Peeling away the left sleeve of her frock, she bared a deep purple scar that sliced her upper left shoulder. The scar bypassed her bosom to disappear under the brown, wrinkled creases of her armpit.

Clifford drew in his breath and stared at the disfiguring scar.

"Cha," she said, rolling back the sleeve as quickly as she had peeled it away. "Me remember like yesterday when it a-'appen." She wiggled her head as if the scar was the one trophy she had to show for her hard-hard life. "Crossing field. Down gully. When me get near a mango tree. Beside Mass Crawford place. A bull spy me. Set chase. Me young den. But still me no swift enough fe beast. Blood! Larks! How me bleed when de devil finally 'ave 'im way wid me. Me survive dough. Lawd Almighty, He alone knows how me survive. It 'appen now. Fe sure me a-dead. You pappy in 'im grave. But me 'ere still."

She grew sorrowful; her mind seemed in some distant place. Perhaps recalling happier times when the threads of her life were not so tangled. Memories confirmed that she more than her husband deserved a resting place in the grave.

The wick shimmered, enfolding mother and son in its dim glow, her brain festered with recollections. Never one to rattle idle words, and fearing people's pity might blight her; she had kept silent about her troubled marriage. She trained her heart to bear its silent sorrows and had locked them away for safekeeping with the Almighty.

Her childbearing years—dropping a pickney every year like a bitch—Samuel Webb still demanding she work like his donkey without assistance. Now that her last boy was leaving, the time was fully ripe for her to unlock some of her life before she died.

Clifford grew uncomfortable. Deeply embarrassed and desperate to leave he forced himself to soak up what she released of her slave-wife existence under the dominance of his pappy. He recalled all of them sitting at this very same table, respecting. No one skylarked in Pappy's house. All obeyed. Mum-ma would read from the family Bible—telling tales of Brer Anancy's antics, and share terrifying jumby stories before bedtime—how they terrorised their young hearts. The stories kept them awake in the pitch-black, sweltering night. Eyes terrified, hearts thumping, they kept watch in case the duppy or the Rolling Calf came to thief them. He remembered how his small body quivered and cowered under the sheets. *Why*, he wondered now. *Why in Dicken's name. Did older heads t'ink it dem duty fe fill poor pickney head wid fool-fool supidness. So dem wet dem beds?*

"Hear wat me mum-ma an' pup-pa, Winston an' Eleanor Carr, say de first time dem clap eyes on you pappy?"

49

she asked, jiggering her shoulders, and recalling happier times. 'Nice complexion. No too black. Or pretty-pretty. Quiet. Speak well. Respectable looking' was wat me pup-pa let slide when Samuel mount 'im horse fe leave."

She chuckled at the memory of Samuel's well-seated backside on the saddle. "Me mum-ma partial to 'im, Clifford. She warn me dough. She advise me too. She say, 'Once a man marries, Mary, dem start getting above dem station. T'ink dem nice. Eh, eh. Dem go looking fe a new fowl fe get fresh wid. Cha! Plenty flighty marga-foot woman out dere dat gwan swarm round a husband. Like flies after bad meat. Dem no got not'ing better in dem head dan getting sweetness from man. Bring plenty trouble fe de wife, Mary.'"

She related her youthful courtship in that sober way of hers that reminded Clifford of how she rarely showed her emotions. His boyhood memories of her were blurred. She had simply been there. To be used. Like the old dresser behind him. Never asked her opinion, she gave none. Acknowledging this family fault brought a strange emotion into his heart. Apart from the incident at the fence, never had he heard her once raise her voice. Pappy had brought her to the house like a prized heifer. This fact shamed him, head bowed he endured her pain.

"You pappy greedy fe land, Clifford. If somebody owe 'im. He gets payment in land. Land an' more land. Same t'ing dem a-fight over now."

He wanted to mention that her parents had made a bad judgement about his pappy, but kept silent. Looking behind him, he saw that nothing had changed since his boyhood. The same family Bible was on the same mahogany dresser. The same ornate gold mirror hung above. The narrow, pitch-black hallway led to bedrooms with small cots on wooden floors that she still scrubbed, on her knees, every Friday morning with her coconut brush. Painful memories flooding his head, he stood.

"Early morning leaving, Mum-ma." He gazed at the comb lines parting her grey hair.

The lone flame blinked; eerie shadows caressed her face. She reached for his hand, pulled him down, and flapped her right hand at him.

"Wait nuh," she said. "Some business fe finish before you go."

He sat.

She took his right hand and enclosed it in her thick, clammy fingers. He shivered. Webb people *never* touched. His fingers felt like icicles against her hot, imitate flesh. He stilled his body while she slowly peeled aside each of his trembling fingers, like she seperated a hand of ripe bananas.

"See 'ere," she said, squinting down at his outstretched palm. "Look. 'Ere." She tapped her index finger at the dark, jagged grooves running down his palm. "See. Dis you future. Know wat me a-see?" Shifting her bottom on the hard bench, she searched his troubled face. "Travel. See it. Buoy, you gwan travel." Satisfied at her prophecy, she smacked her lips.

A bird cooed in the eucalyptus tree behind the house and broke her spell.

"It foolishness you saying, Mum-ma."

She fixed her provoked eyes on him and clamped her thick fingers over his wrist. Shaking her head, she said, "Cha, buoy. I no mean Maggoty Point. No man. No mean Maggoty. Abroad. Abroad wat me seeing. Jamaica can't keep you now. Foreign parts is fe you."

He knew he had vexed her.

Her vision ended, she released his hand and searched his troubled face. "Me buoy, dem may try fe drive you from de hill. But you fast-fastened in me heart. Dem seem fe forget de saying: *'Wat sweet nanny goat, gwan run 'im belly.'* It tak' a long time fe river fe flow before it a-reach dry land you know, Clifford. Same way de Almighty works. He gives us experience wid life. Evil people gwan reap wat dem a-sow. Some'ting fe you." She turned her back abruptly and began to unbutton the bodice of her frock. Her hand pushed inside, she quickly worked around the brassiere pod supporting her shrivelled breasts. Pulling out a small bundle, she re-buttoned her frock and placed the bundle on the table.

"Fe you," she said.

"Wha—!" Stunned, he stared at the small calico bag.

"Some'ting fe you an' you childs. Been saving since Samuel dead."

The dim, shadowy room crackled with sorrowful goodbyes. When would he see her again? When would he ever set foot on Webb Hill? His weak legs tingled. To not let her see his trembling lips, he bowed his shamed head and did not see her push the bag at him.

"It all right me buoy. Tak' it. You future is good. Go where de Good Shepherd a-tak' you. No worry you head 'bout me. Me heart tell me fe do dis. So no deny me it."

He took the calico bag and pushed himself slowly to his feet. He stood awkwardly before her.

Satisfied that she had unburdened part of her life to him, she too stood, went to him and pulled him close. His head nestled next to her clammy carbolic scented chest, she finally released him and watched him walk to the door, open it, and disappear into the dark, lonely night, where the lone moon and stars followed him to the two-bedroom house below.

Maggoty Point

Maggoty Point district rested between two hills that had formed when a ferocious storm flayed the east side of the island. When the residents woke on the fifth day of the storm, their town had sunk hundreds of feet below the road. Muddy trails and weeping streams merrily trickled over uprooted trees and dead animals.

Before the storm's devastation, a good road had serviced the daily lives of Maggoty Point's residents and country people who transported their produce and animals into town. Before the new road was constructed, the only reliable way in and out of town was a narrow dirt road sandwiched between a peak to its right and a steep gully to its left.

Whenever Maggoty Point's older heads thought on the wicked breeze, the one that wrecked the good road, they sucked their teeth scornfully and said, "Only tak' de treacherous, narrow road wid de gully below in an' out a-town. An' never ever drive more dan one donkey 'round dat steep bend at de same time." They advised that taking any other route to town was asking to be dead.

Like many of the fabricated Anancy stories that had sailed into existence, a story began circulating around the district. A white man once came from Panama and bought land in the district of Maggoty Point. His intention was to make a big profit from bananas and coco. He had heard the warning of the narrow, treacherous pass but ignored it. It was purely neyga people's ignorant labrish, he thought with scorn. He planted crops, harvested them, and loaded them onto his donkeys.

Beasts bred around Maggoty Point knew that the pass was dangerous. They also knew to never, ever travel side by side along the trail. To do so was unprecedented and unheard of. The foolish man loaded his produce onto his donkeys. Burdened and weighted down, bumping and braying side-by-side, the donkeys approached the perilous precipice and froze. Sensing danger, they dared not place one hoof further. Stinging whip lashes on their backsides made them lunge forward to their deaths.

That was in Maggoty Point's past. When Clifford rented a two-bedroom house, half a mile from the town's centre, a reasonable trail meandered towards the main thoroughfare. The house looked as if someone had scooped out a bowl of earth below this dirt road and dropped the house inside the dip. Teak-boarded, as most in the district, it sat on six square wooden slabs. Wooden shutters protected each window from the fierce sun. Five red concrete steps, brightly polished, led to a veranda where a door opened into a small parlour. At the rear of the house, the kitchen faced a large backyard, where a mature mango tree provided shade from the sun. To the right of the kitchen, a door opened into the children's bedroom and another into Clifford and Clara's bedroom.

A community standpipe above Clifford's house supplied water to the residents. Abundant vegetation, banana plants, mango trees, susumber bushes, and gungu peas surrounded a sprinkling of houses. Except for the government buildings, no buildings in Maggoty had electricity. Three months into their move to town, Clifford's family became the first to enjoy the benefits of electricity.

For some time Maggoty Point's officials had sent letters of complaint to the government officials in Kingston. Why, they had asked, must Maggoty Point's country folks drive their donkeys from market, in the dead of night, with only a broken down *rucka-rucka* road and the naked moon and stars to guide them home? Why did government people not provide Maggoty Point with electricity?

Kingston officials ignored the first crop of letters. Maggoty Point's second crop was not as polite. These letters brazenly accused—was the government trying to kill off Maggoty Point country people by denying them electricity? Did the government not understand that country people paid taxes just like those in Kingston? Did the government want country people to *bruck dem necks* down a gully at night? When a government official in Kingston tore open the letter, she rolled her eyes, kissed her teeth and then gave it to her superior.

As was his custom, he quickly scanned the missive for money or other bribes. Finding none, he mashed it in his fist and flung it at a bush outside his window. This war of words continued to rage between Maggoty Point and Kingston until, finally, news came. Britain, the mother country, was sending aid to Jamaica. Part of Maggoty Point would get an improvement grant, and electricity would be part of the bargain.

One thing about the electricity business mystified Clifford—why were they placing some of the poles above his house? Was it the best place? Years later, Clifford still could not fathom their motive.

It was a sweltering hot Monday morning when a noise clamoured above the house.

Jamaicans have a peculiar custom: hire one man to do a job and not only must he be paid, he must also be supplied with one bottle of rum. Hire six men to do a job, and six bottles of rum was a must.

Tilda was in the back yard when she heard the commotion at the front of the house. She ran to investigate. Six men haggled on the rise. Curious, she bent low and skirted behind a bush to watch and listen.

A quarrelsome, reed-like neck man, in a sun-bleached khaki shirt and trousers stood beside a small, thickset, man, in a knitted multicoloured hat and almost knee-high black galoshes. The thickset man pulled down his hat and said, "Me say it 'ere dem say it fe go." He pointed to a place below his feet. "Dis de place. 'Ere is where we put it."

"Certain 'bout dat?" replied his companion in a whining singsong voice. Feeling the steam of the morning heat, he questioned his stout companion's choice of footwear.

Six men had come to install the poles. While the two argued, four idly waited. Common sense told the four that the headmen were working up to a butt of horns, and standing in the heat was plain stupidity. Kissing their teeth, they sauntered to a shady tree and dropped under it. Lounging onto their elbows in front of poles, digging equipment and six bottles of rum, they labrished and shot the breeze while the headmen settled the business.

"Me say it 'ere. Where else dem fe go?"

"'Oo appoint you boss man 'ere?" demanded the thin man. He jammed his right hand onto his bony hip. The stouter pulled a crumpled paper from his shirt pocket and smoothed it out.

"'Ere, 'ere it fe go." He jabbed a calloused finger at the paper. "Man you own eye no see it? Why you a-question, question so-so? We got job fe do. Day soon dry."

Reedy-neck stared at the paper and then reluctantly nodded. He flapped his hands at the four lazing under the tree. "Come. We settle t'ings. Come."

Tilda checked their progress from time to time from behind the bush. Six weeks later, they finally left, and evening became her favourite time of day. She would stand on the veranda and wait for the electric bulb to illuminate the rise above her house.

* * * *

Clara did not miss the hill. At first worried that Maggoty Point would not suit her; several trips to town convinced her, town life was better than the isolation of the hill. Her third child dropped, she could now sport her three-inch red shoes. No longer must she guard against stepping into chicken filth or goat droppings. Most important, Clifford's family no longer watched her.

There was one thing however that troubled Clara. A month after their move, Clifford began coming home late and smelling of alcohol. One evening, hearing a clatter outside their bedroom door, it swung open and Clifford staggered in. Hat on his head, he fell fully clothed onto the bed. She tried rousing him; all he did was grunt and slept. Three straight weeks this happened. One night it came to a head. He came home drunk, fell onto the bed again and started snoring. She tried waking him, to get his dutty shoes off her sheets. She pulled off his shoes in vexation and even flung them savagely onto the wooden floor, in hopes that the ruckus would wake the man. All he did was mutter that mosquitoes were biting and snored louder. She unclipped his belt and yanked it from its loops—lifted his heavy legs, pulled off his trousers, and dragged off his shirt. About to hang his clothes in the wardrobe, something dropped with a clank onto the wooden floor. Arching forward, to see what had fallen, she cried out in alarm. "Backside! Wat man doing wid dis." She nudged the gun with her toe and pushed it under the bed.

During her husband's many, midnight, drunkenness, Clara had kept silent. The following morning, she decided to question him about it. She found him reading the Gleaner in the parlour. Hooking her right arm onto her right hip, she said, "Clifford. Why you carrying gun?"

Clifford was suffering from a slight hangover and had no recollection of the previous night, he reluctantly dragged his red-rimmed eyes from the newspaper, squinted in puzzled pain at her, and said, "Wat dis you saying, woman?" He shook the paper and dismissed her.

The section in the newspaper that had caught his attention was a report on Jamaica's economy. Slowly reading, painfully assessing the island's problems, his brain made its own editorial comments. *De same damn stale news. Island still in trouble. Prices still rising wid no relief in sight fe de poor. Now dat Britain done a-bleeding Jamaica dry, she buying less an' less from her.* He turned the page. *Same blasted t'ing 'ere too. Jamaica economy a-going into depression. Paper full wid not'ing but depression, oppression, an cricket. All same damn reason why neyga people-a-chop each odder up. Why paper no report some good t'ing? Only blasted sensible t'ing in paper is de comic strip!*

He smelled food, stood and ignoring Clara, folded the newspaper and followed her vexed hips to the kitchen. Plantain, ackee and salt fish lay on a white tablecloth.

Clara sat. She forked a piece of fried plantain and a wad of ackee and salt fish into her mouth.

Clifford placed the newspaper beside his plate, raised his fork, and continued to read.

Three mouthfuls later, unable to keep silent one moment longer, Clara pushed aside her plate, linked her arms high onto her chest, and said, "Still you no answer me, Clifford Webb. Up hill. You say you get rid a-gun. Still it in de house. As me a-say. You a-lie to me?"

Clifford closed the newspaper, pushed away his food, placed both elbows onto the white tablecloth, and studied her. "Woman! Me no some pickney child dat you fe question you know. Gun me business. So, no worry 'bout me, you hear?" He pinched the restricting cloth of his trousers between his crotch and pulled it towards his belly in a show of vexation.

"Fe pity sake, woman. Hush up, nuh. Let a-hungry man eat, nuh?" He picked up his fork and scooped ackee into his mouth.

Heat flooded Clara's neck. Her indignant lips trembled. All she was asking was for the man to calm her worries. When they left the hill, she thought that their troubles had stayed on the hill. Why was he carrying a gun? Was he expecting more trouble? Too much was on her brain for him to try and whitewash the truth with his words—try and convince her that this was not important. Before, on the hill, when he finished his work, he came home. Now loose mouths were saying that he had taken up with no-good policemen.

"Me worry 'bout you, Clifford."

"Who ask you fe worry? Can tak' care a-meself."

"But gun..."

"Dat. Me. Business. Woman."

"Eh, eh," she said, temper reddening her cheeks. "So." She pushed herself clumsily to her feet and glared at him. "Since gun you *own* business. Me asking you dis. It also you *own* business. Fe stagger home drunk? So me undress you?

An' put you a-bed. Like you some pickney child? Eh. Answer me dat. Clifford Webb."

Clifford stared at her in surprise, lips parted. He grinned, threw back his head, and laughed.

"Clara Bennett," he said, brushing a fist across his wet eyes. "You one feisty woman. Only late me realise me marry a feisty woman!"

"Still you no answer me?"

"Jumby slide it inside me pocket. When me no looking. Satisfied?"

"T'ink me is some fool-fool duppy, Clifford Webb?" she cried indignantly. She knew he was sidestepping her questions.

His face fixed into a serious mask, he stood, marched to the parlour, grabbed his hat and workbag, and left.

Sonny Ford

Clifford and Clara had not been long at Maggoty Point when one of Clara's numerous relatives, who worked at the Revenue Office, recommended that Clifford work at the office as a Revenue runner. He would collect taxes from the local people and those living around Maggoty Point.

At first glad for the job, Clifford soon found that the pay just about supported his family. On Webb land, he had owned his house and grown his own victuals. In town, he had to pay rent for the house and buy food from a store or the market. He had tried to cut down on his Johnny Walker and Albany smokes, but reasoned, what good was a man's life if he could not jingle a few coppers in his pocket to buy his cigarettes? Clara was a good seamstress and sewed most of their clothes; he wanted to give her more than *hen scratching*. Plagued by money matters, he kept his worries from Clara and drowned them in drink.

History recorded that the Revenue Office was once an elegant building owned by an Englishman, Sir Nicholas Boone. A wealthy Jamaican planter, Boone made plenty of money from slaves. Crop records and various indentures and historical titbits showed that Sir Nicholas amassed an enormous fortune; abandoned his numerous mulatto children, left his plantation in the capable hands of an overseer, and retired to a life of ease and plenty on an estate in Bath, England.

Those that knew Sir Nicholas during the years he profited from slavery heard he had one wish. Before his final cut with Jamaica he desired to have a brick-and-mortar edifice built to his honour in Jamaica. One that would stand the test of time: be a constant reminder of his great wealth and influence in Jamaica. The white Creoles living in Jamaica at the time wrote long letters of his dealings. Packet ships ferried gossipy epistles between England, Jamaica, and America. These described how, on a splendid spring afternoon in London, when daffodils were in full bloom, Sir Nicholas alighted from his elegant coach, sauntered across Duke Street's muddy puddles and entered the doors of Dawson & Dawson. After instructing the good men to draw up immediate plans for a monument to honour his name in Jamaica, he handed over a handsome note of credit.

If it were at all possible to ask Sir Nicholas Boon's abandoned half-caste children or their slave mothers whether he knew Jamaica well, they would have replied in the affirmative. As for the men at Dawson & Dawson, later events would attest to the contrary. Not one of these Englishmen had ever so much as placed one pink toe on the island. Nor did they know her culture or climate.

The plans finalised, the site selected, ships hastened diagrams and instructions to Jamaica. An overseer employed masons, carpenters, and gangs of slaves to feverishly finish the building. When completed, the native Creoles of every colour and creed praised its magnificence and grandeur. Unfortunately they foresaw its future—a fate many buildings of its ilk suffered in Jamaica. Her storms, hurricanes, constant sweltering humidity, her insect life, and ever-creeping jungle-like vegetation, and slave uprisings, would, eventually, mash it up.

* * * *

After a fatiguing day of trying to squeeze taxes from poor people, Clifford sauntered across the cracked black and white tiles of the Revenue Office and entered a sweltering spacious area dominated by two massive circular columns. Rising from ground level, they clutched at a discoloured white ceiling where a tired fan slashed aimlessly at insects. Elaborate balls, sumptuous gatherings, and ruckus carousing had once graced this large area that had descended to the title of Maggoty Point Revenue Office.

Clifford pulled his hat, waved it across his hot face and scanned the handful of workers idly lounging behind crude wooden desks. Spotting a woman beside a column, he approached her and placed his black satchel onto her desk. The sudden *thwack* pulled her from her nail inspection. She looked up, slackened her contentious, thick red lips, and sighed heavily.

"So, Mister Webb," she said, sighing in refined patwa. Her shiny, mamba-like arms reached for the bag. A fat, blue-black fist clutched it and unbuckled the front straps. She peered inside, tipped the contents onto her desk and dropped the satchel at her feet. She did a wiggle with her broad backside and, like a hen pecking corn from dirt, slowly separated the coins into piles of pounds, shillings, and pence with blood-red fingernails. Nodding, she grunted, counted, and wrote in a black book she had pulled from a side drawer. She removed a silver coloured tin from the same drawer and scooped the coins inside before returning the ledger book and tin to the drawer. To show that she, Clifford's superior, had concluded her duty for the day, she again wiggled her fulsome backside, and, lifting a heavy hand, caressed the stiff, crimped hair that stood like train lines upon her scalp.

"Last time collection more," she drawled, patting the train lines again.

Clifford was desperate to go home. When her flat nose flared, as if she had sniffed bad fish, he saw a warning. He must throw the fowl some corn.

"Is all dem can pay, Miss Lewis," he said.

Blessy Lewis was in no mood to tolerate feistiness from this yellow-skinned man. Though new to her job, she knew that Clifford Webb was friend to the Deputy of the Revenue. She also knew other feisty ears listened. Friend or no friend to the deputy she would let Clifford Webb know *she* was his boss. She straightened her thick neck and flared her nostrils again.

"Maas Webb," she said, dividing her lips in a false smile. "People like dese slack tax payers hide more dan dem pay Revenue. Next time dey can't pay. Get dem fe sell some'ting, nuh?"

Satisfied that she had convinced Clifford Webb that she, a neyga woman, would take no excuses from neyga people, and knowing she had the power to fry him with the other Revenue thieves, she broadened her nose and continued.

"Dese people musta t'ink Revenue a-run on charity? Tell dem. Dey no pay. Lose dem land." She fluttered her sparse lashes above her small black eyes, a challenge for the yellow-skinned *sambo* to disagree with her. When Clifford stared blankly at her but remained silent, she grunted, grabbed the satchel at her feet, and almost threw it at him.

This was Clifford's first encounter with the frog-faced vixen. The man who usually took his collection must have been promoted. Yet, Clifford reasoned, surely as a woman, she must have some womanly feelings for the poor. He felt that in years past, her type would never so much as get her fat backside inside the Revenue. Her kind of ugliness once cut cane under the whip of a gang headman. He knew that whether in the cane field, Revenue Office, or wherever, *dis kind a-cornmeal* never changed. Evil-minded people like this always ignored the sufferings of others. He felt sure that some relative of this *blow-fire-a-bush* woman must have fixed the job for her. His uncharitable thoughts disturbed him. Once, such unkindness never entered his head. Should she read his mind, he silently chastened himself to endure her feistiness. The Revenue job was his bread and butter. Masking his face, he hooded his eyes and smiled like a puss.

"Yes, Mistress Lewis. Me tell dem wat you a-say."

He left her. Hurrying to the exit, a hazel-eyed, honey coloured man hailed him.

"Clifford. Man. Glad fe see you. When you come in?" The man threw out his hand, grabbed Clifford's, and pumped it vigorously.

"Sonny," said Clifford, glad to meet a friend after the bullfrog woman.

"How you been, man? Long time no see. Hear you voice."

Sonny Ford was Clifford's school friend, and they were the same age. At sixteen Sonny had left the countryside for Kingston, where he finished his education. He knew the Maggoty Point district and easily got the position of deputy to the head of the Revenue Office when he applied. Sonny was also a distant relative of Clara. He had put in a good word for Clifford when the Revenue runner position became available. The men were different in both lifestyle and temperament. Good-looking Sonny Ford liked to dress stylishly and pay particular attention to his appearance. He enjoyed his single life and said he was too young to die yet. His short-sleeved blue shirt was paired with gabardine trousers and his dark brown hair was plastered flat onto his skull.

"Hurrying, man?" asked Sonny.

"No so you t'ink. Clara wants me home. Since we move 'ere. Worry if me late. Can't t'ink wat lately tak' up de woman's head. But, so. Wat you want?"

There was a lull in the talking around them. Sly eyes stole curious glances at Maas Ford, wanting to know why he was talking to Clifford Webb, who was fresh at the Revenue.

"Only labrish. Follow me," said Sonny, walking towards a door left of the spacious area.

They entered a small, cluttered space where a long electrical cord dangled from a high ceiling. Clifford waited while Sonny moved stacks of files and papers from a chair and dropped them on the floor behind his desk. After sitting, Sonny leaned forward and said, "Well man. Tell me. How you doing? How's job? Life?"

"Busy man. Busy. Move. New child. Dis job. All a-keep me out a-circulation."

"Congratulations. So you is father again?"

A fly circled Sonny's head. He bent, grabbed a bamboo fan, and attacked the insect. He missed with each swat. Clifford grinned when the fly abandoned its victim to fly onto the lightbulb.

"Nasty t'ings Clifford. Can't keep dem out. Look at dis." Sonny pushed an ink-stained file at Clifford. "Full wid people dat can't or won't pay."

Clifford eyed the file. He repeated the same sentiments he had voiced seconds before to the sour-faced woman. "Hardness a-hitting Jamaicans, Sonny."

Sunny narrowed his eyes at the unjust censure.

"Me no stranger to wat you a-saying, you know. Clifford me know 'bout hard times. Cornmeal porridge an' green banana is wat sustain me fe a long time. Me know so. So no say so to me. Rawted man." Sonny softened his voice. "Dem no pay taxes. Me job gone. So it a-go man. Why you t'ink me get dis position. Banishing me to Maggoty brought me no favour." Frustrated, he arched forward and widened his intelligent eyes. "When I get dis job, dem instruct me fe use rawtedness on tax t'ieves." He flattened his fists onto the wooden desk and soured his lips. "Dem tell me so. If country people t'ink de Revenue gwan turn blind eye on dem. It dem backside mistake. Say to me. Colonial days long over. It a long time since white man was a-boss in Jamaica. Neyga man now a-rule. An' neyga man no gwan tak' no backsided excuse from no neyga people. Harshness is wat we gwan use on dem. Dem no pay. Tak' dem land. Cow. Horse. Fowl or mule. Sell dem livelihood. Even dem wattle house. But get de taxes! Dat's de advice me get when dem offer me dis job, Clifford."

Clifford heard a whine, then felt a nip on the back of his neck. "Rawted," he cursed, slapping his neck and killing the mosquito.

"T'ink we should hire dem kinda bloodsuckers fe collect taxes, Clifford?" said Sonny, chuckling at the battle between man and insect.

In spite of his worries, Clifford relaxed in his friend's company. Lately life had been hell; Sonny's light-heartedness cheered him.

An odour of rum and stale tobacco permeated the small, shabby office. Flaking, mildewed cement grinned from the once-white walls that resembled something a dog might throw up after trying to eat a bullfrog. An army of ants emerged from a crack at the base of a wall. Marching

67

upwards, they disappeared through another crack, where the wall met the ceiling. Behind Sonny, loose-leaf files lay in dusty, haphazard mounds for insect fodder. Slapdash neglect festered everywhere. No one cared. The hands of the ancient clock still registered the same time as they had when Clifford entered. Time and dust seemed to stand still. Why had his educated friend allowed this slackness to happen? Had the ignorant Revenue people broken his spirit?

As if Sonny had read Clifford's mind he said, "Clifford, man. Dis no life fe a single man like me. Wid no responsibilities. Wat 'bout you? How you survive if dem let you go 'ere?"

The unexpected question startled Clifford. He lowered his head so as not to show his worried face. What would happen to his family if he lost this job? Already the underbelly of his shoe grinned for mending. He might complain about the work and pay, but Jamaicans had a saying: *"You never know de use a-you backside till boil tak' it up."* He took the revenue job for granted, but at least it fed his family. With no job, how would they survive?

"No know, man." Clifford was brooding over the question with his head bowed and did not see Sonny get up and approach him.

"Man. Why you no go England?"

Totally baffled, Cliford raised his head and studied Sonny's face. "England? Wat England fe do wid me?"

"Plenty." Sonny eased the side of his bottom onto the edge of the desk and studied his friend.

"England our mother country, man. Hear wat a-'appen over dere?"

When Clifford still looked puzzled, Sonny continued. "Mother country in big trouble man. Wid war over. Plenty of her men dead. She need us. Crying out fe workers. Our

68

duty fe help. When I hear 'bout it. Mak' enquiries. Answer come. Dis week."

He lit a smoke, gave one to Clifford, and said he wanted more than Jamaica offered. Island people were suffering. Still single, he would try England.

"So. Decide already!" said Clifford, smiling. He admired his friend's adventurous spirit, and was glad he had seen him before he left Jamaica. "When you sail?"

"If plans run smooth. Next month." Sonny hooked his finger at the closed door. "Revenue knows. Glad fe go. Why you no come too? Island can't feed all her people."

"Me?" Clifford widened his eyes. "You joking man?"

Yet, was Sonny's suggestion such a jackass thing? Could he really go? What would happen to Clara and the children? It sounded like one stormy river he did not want to cross. "No know 'bout dat, man. Got big responsibilities. England one big proposition fe tak' on. It not fe me. But me glad you gwan better youself. T'anks dough. Keep it in mind."

He stood, extended his hand, gripped Sonny's, and shook it.

"Tak' care a-youself man. Write. Let me know how de Mother Country a-treat you."

Mangoes

Now five years old, Tilda still missed the hill. She missed the rank odour of the goats that scampered and bucked before settling under the house at night. The old mango tree down the gully, where she would often hide and dream: and squatting on her mound, with only the blue, untroubled early morning sky for company.

The property at Maggoty Point that rested on red dirt had no private place to dream or be alone. One day, longing for her grand-mama's thick, curdling milk and her home on the hill, she was listlessly wandering through the house when she bumped into Clifford.

"Sorry, Dada," she moaned, dropping her head. Clifford paused. Her mournful tone startled him. He had been so consumed with his own worries that he had forgotten that she, more than anyone he knew, had feelings he did not understand.

Noting her sad eyes, he said gently, "Come. Come outside wid me." He took her hand and led her down the steps into the backyard. They passed a papaya tree bursting with buds. At the mango tree, Clifford forced a weak smile and pointed at the thick branches stretching heavenward.

"See dat, Tilda? Come June, July, full wid mangoes. You like mangoes?"

Tilda knew no mango tree could lift the heavy load from her heart. Yet, to please him, she cupped her right hand to shield her eyes, craned her neck, and studied the knobbly branches. Dark green leaves cradled pale pink blossoms. A faint exotic perfume wafted into the sweltering heat. He took her hand again, led her to a guinep stump, and placed her on top.

"When me little, Tilda, me pappy got plenty mango trees on 'im property. Which you t'ink was me best?"

"No know, Dada," she said sadly. She did not want to hear or talk of happy times.

"Beefy, Tilda. Beefy. Dat me best. De flesh, eh, eh." He chuckled, screwed up his lips, and smacked them in false pleasure. "Fleshy. Sweet. Lawd. Man It sweet, Tilda. Mout'-a-water just a-t'inking on it." Forehead crinkled, eyes rolled in mock seriousness Clifford seemed to consider the merits of the different types of mango.

"Plenty different mangoes in Jamaica, you know, Tilda. Let me see." He cocked his head left, pretending to think deeply. "First, dere's Stringy. Stringy OK. Ever eat one?"

She shook her head.

"No, well. Stringy OK. But is as its name. Eat OK. But got plenty string in it. Bind you teeth up. If it false, eh. Den. Number 11, Bombay, Black Sweetie. Name dem all, me t'ink. Soon it be mango season. Den you try dem all. Not too many dough," he warned, playfully wagging his index finger at her. "Eat too many. Gets bellyache. Belly run. Flies get fat up. Eh." His white teeth flashed a crooked smile. "Me glad tree 'ere. Me favourite."

He grew silent as he studied the tree and recalled happier—freer times—away from his pappy—working on the land he loved—the hot sun scorching his body—all that empty space freed his soul. He moved close to the grassy

71

stump, leaned against it, and thought on the peculiarity of his two pickney girls. Missy hadn't said much about the move and settled in quickly at the new school. But this one was strange, sensitive. Felt things more than Missy did.

"See section below." He pointed to the land sloping below the house, where the sun flickered through giant umbrella-like branches. "Bush land now. Soon me cut it back. Plant a few victuals. Coco. Yams. Dasheen. Not like de hill dough, eh? But wat we fe do eh, Tilda?" His voice grew melancholy. To say the small scrub of dirt below was better than the hill would be merely showing a false face to his second child. They both knew it was all foolishness.

Later, alone and smoking in the parlour, he tried to read the newspaper, but memories took him to the hill again. He was fifteen, and Pappy was a prosperous man, respected and well liked in the district. Pappy's public face was that of a pious, good Christian. Reverent and God-fearing, Pappy often preached from the pulpit.

Dawn came early on Webb Hill on Sundays when all things holy was strictly observed in Samuel Webb's house. Dawn found the boys up, dressed, and rounding up stray animals. The girls milked the cows, tidied the house, and prepared breakfast

Pride was paramount to Samuel Webb. Pride was his buckler, his shield against an ever-shifting world of backsliding, disobedience, and wantonness. Supporters of his public face were his family.

Samuel Webb would wear a black suit, highly polished black leather boots (up to his knees), and a black hat on Sundays. He inspected his family for flaws before departure to church. Mounting his mare as an emperor, he flicked the animal's rump with his whip, and called, "Gee up, girl," and then descended the gully without a backwards glance.

A black straw hat covered Mary Webb's wiry, plaited hair on those mornings. A black handbag hung from the crook of her arm. The other clutched a small Bible. Her plain, cotton frock swished against bushes and brambles as she meekly walked behind the brown backside of her master's mare.

Four demure daughters, in sensible frocks and hats, traipsed behind. Birds warbled merrily. Six handsome sons, in starched white shirts, ties, dark trousers, and trilbies, guarded the rear. Three things only disrupted this reverent Sunday morning caravan: death, storms, or hurricanes. If it rained, which was frequent, up went umbrellas, and on the caravan trudged.

Arriving at the church, Samuel Webb would fling the animal's reins to Clifford and order, "Tie up beast till service over, nuh." Then, climbing the steps he raised his hat and acknowledged fellow worshippers before entering the sunlit church. From the hill, down gullies, over banks and beside streams and bush land, they made the treacherous, winding, dirt trek to church, and back, every Sunday.

Clifford folded the newspaper and placed it on his lap. Never would he treat Missy, Tilda or little Roy like how his pappy treated them.

Miss Marcy

Six months after meeting Sonny, Clifford came home one day, dropped his work satchel in the parlour, crept behind Clara, circled her in his arms and planted a hot, wet kiss on her moist neck.

"Clifford!" she shrieked, jabbing her elbows into his ribs. "Why you a-frighten me so? You no see me busy wid food, eh." Though she was displeased that he had surprised her, she smiled, glad that he still loved to play with her.

"First t'ings first. When food be ready? Hungry like mangy dog." He sniffed the air and released her.

Clara dipped the spoon into the soup and stirred. "Soon." She pushed a sprig of thyme into the thick, dark, brown liquid. "Is gungu soup. Miss Marcy come a-market from country. She pay me visit. Bring us few yams an' peas. Say how bad weather a-lash dem up-country."

His mind ran to the cantankerous, broad, batty woman. Entering their house, she would sniff like a mouse after cheese. He scrubbed his moist neck with the flat of his hand.

"Mak' dem keep dem bad weather up-country. No want it down 'ere," he said. He knew Miss Marcy only visited to suck gossip from Clara. Before reaching her house, clear up Simons Hill, she would have passed their business on to others. "Is rain all she a-say dat a-'appenin'?"

"Clifford!" cried Clara, gluing her lips in false displeasure. "You self know me no 'ave time fe neyga people's labrish."

Not wanting to further dutty up the woman's reputation, he kept silent, instead he rolled his eyes in disbelief. He knew, as sure as Jamaica was hotter than hell, tongues rattled when women met. Countrywomen were the rowdiest rattlers of all. They spread gossip faster than *wash-out* medicine.

"Since she no say not'ing. An' dat me no believe. Wat else she tell you den? She ask 'bout you darling Clifford? Eh? She mention me? Eh?" he said teasingly.

Clara, who always took her cooking seriously, was reluctant to discuss the woman's visit with him. She must always watch the pot or her food might burn. Also, she must administer the exact amount of seasoning; else the soup would taste insipid. Her rule for cooking: taste, add a pinch more nutmeg, a sprig of thyme, and taste again. Salt more, or drop in a few more pimento berries. Stirring the soup, some instinct warned her to watch what she said. Else, she might spoil his happy self that had been so touchy-touchy lately. She gazed into the pot and remembered that the moment Miss Marcy waddled into the kitchen, she began to suck on Clifford's name, as if sucking on a mango seed.

"'Bout you she no say much," she said at last.

"An'?"

"She, she," Clara stammered while the soup gently bubbled inside the Dutch pot. "She enquire if you OK. After we move 'ere. Concerned fe know if you settle good an' tak' to Maggoty."

Her stiff neck and tight lips told Clifford she was whitewashing the woman's actions.

"Eh, eh," he said, watching her closely. "So. Miss Marcy wants fe know if me 'appy. Eh? Wat fool-fool t'ing you is saying, Clara Bennett? Dat woman need fe sniff news like neyga man hooked on ganga. Youself know she only want fe poison me name. Visiting," he said with a sneer, his voice hard, "pretending concern. De woman no care one backside 'bout me."

Clara's belly muscles tightened. Lately her man had been changing. Lately he had taken to strange thinking. It seemed that lately the devil had placed hardness in his heart so that only nastiness slid from his mouth. He was more sensitive with people who wanted to faas in his business. When he asked "It only dat she ask?" how could she tell him the rest? How could she say that as soon as the woman squatted her batty into a chair, she widened her eyes and began to inspect what was inside the house?

Miss Marcy had blown into the kitchen like a bad wind. She had unpinned her hat, fanned her face with it, puffed out her plump cheeks, and said, "Larks, Clara. It hot, hot, hot. Like de living hell. Heat a-boil up me body. Eh."

How could she tell him that even before she said she needed a glass, Miss Marcy had flown like lightning to the parlour so she could inspect their property and broadcast it up-country?

The woman had worn Clara down with her visit. She soured her lips and eyeballed her hostess until she grudgingly placed food before her. After she had eaten, and only then, did the woman hoist her hefty breasts with her right arm and declare she was taking her leave. Dragging her feet to the kitchen door, a coconut basket dangling from her right arm, she descended into the yard. Her sudden hustle and haste was all pretence and show. For as sure as St. Thomas Parish rivers flooded when it rained plentifully, Miss Marcy would leave a parting gift. What good was only visiting for a little victuals for the belly. Victuals soon passed through her system and dropped down the latrine. Juicy gossip was far better. Juicy gossip got her into houses, got her free food.

Her right foot fast on the bottom step, Miss Marcy looked up and waggled her head. "It vex me bad Clara. Wat country people a-labrish 'bout you," she said. "Say. Say disgrace drop 'pon you head. But me"—she tilted her head like a mongoose— "dough dem drop you disgrace in me ear. Me gum up me mout'. An' say. You 'appy wid wat life a-hammer 'pon you head."

Miss Marcy and "hoity-toity Clara Bennett," as she called Clara, had a history. They had studied at the same school, and Miss Marcy had fixed her eyes on Clifford as a suitable husband. She never forgave Clara for thieving her man. A frustrated spinster, she would pay a visit, feign friendship for food, and, on leaving, slice her hostess's character like a cutlass on sugar cane. Her periodic visits were made out of pure spite. She wanted to find flaws to use as weapons against Clara and Clifford.

The full sun licking her moist face, Miss Marcy shifted her basket and looked up. "Face look marga since me last glimpse you, Clara. Sickening fe some'ting? Pickney big up you belly again?"

Clara had fully expected the woman to bare her teeth before leaving. When Miss Marcy snapped viciously at her ankles, she sucked in air and stiffened her back against the doorpost. With a flushed face and crinkled forehead, Clara said slowly and deliberately, "Meself hear when people 'appy. Dem got sleek, slim body. Meself also a-hear. Dem dat faas in odder peoples' business. Bloat up like bullfrog. It only wat me a-hear. Meself no know if it true-true or no. It only wat meself a-hear."

Clara waited.

The woman's eyes enlarged like two cannonballs. Her nostrils flared, she lowered her head and hid her face under her broad-brimmed straw hat. As Miss Marcy's body wobbled with temper, Clara knew she would receive her parting gift.

"Hear also 'ow you is offish, Clara Bennett," said Miss Marcy, lifting her head she glared at Clara. "Stuck up. High-an-mighty. T'inking you better dan us up-country. It also wat. Me. Hear." She sniffed and jiggered her body like a scandalised fowl fluffing its feathers. Tugging at the belt around her broad waist, she said, "Gwan leave you now, Clara Bennett," and flounced off around the side of the house.

Clara tilted the pot slightly left and dropped four pieces of yam inside. She would never tell her man the true nature of Miss Marcy's visit.

* * * *

Clifford wandered to the table and sat. Flies droned over slices of bread, melted butter, and ripe bananas protected by a mesh. It had been some while since he enjoyed his favourite soup. Although only a small piece of meat floated around the peas in the Dutch pot, he was better off than many who owed taxes.

Five in the morning, the Wednesday before, he had left the house after only a quick bite of breadfruit and coffee. Nothing passed his mouth until he returned home that night.

Four hours he and the mule climbed the height of Come See Me Mountain to find a man who owned unpaid taxes. His throat dry as cane trash, the scorching sun beating his body, he rested on a rock. The steep gully below hid caverns and dark weeping secrets. Should he pitch below no one would find him.

He continued up to a flat, grassy area of land extending towards the horizon, then falling sharply. In the distance a woman was bent over a bucket, her ebony arms deep in water. She scrubbed on a wooden washboard. Unaware he watched her scrawny body bobbed back and forth like a rudderless boat. She pulled an article from the bucket, twisted it, and dipped it into another pail. Swishing it around in the water, wringing it, she shook it vigorously, and then threw it over a nearby bush to dry. The impatient mule snorted, she spun around, almost knocking over one of the buckets. Straightening up, she grinned, brushed a hand across her brow and deposited small clusters of bubbles onto her dark skin.

"Maas Webb. No see you. Busy washing!" she said, her black eyes twinkled, lightening up her smooth, mahogany face. A loose, sun-bleached homemade frock hung around her bony shanks encased in a pair of tongue-less men's boots. Grey, wiry hair peeped from a green tie-head. Although she appeared malnourished, Clifford knew she was strong as an ox. At first he was puzzled that she knew his name, but then he remembered everyone knew Revenue runners. They were branded bad men in the district. He looked around, seeing no one else but the woman, reluctant to bring up the unpaid taxes with her, but knowing he must, he pulled his hat, and said, "Good day, mistress. How you be?"

"Fairing, Maas Webb. Fairing. Eh, eh. Wat else poor neyga woman fe do, eh?" She grinned again, stooped, grabbed the bucket of soapy water, and flung it at what looked like straggly callaloo plants and a gungu bush beside the hut that served as her house.

A cool breeze brushed his hot cheeks, reddish glints of the retreating sun blazed from mountain peaks in the distant horizon. He did a quick check in his head. *Cooper. Husband. Henry. Wife. Eunice. Land. How she fe manage fe pay de tax?*

Revenue runners saw many like this family. They survived on scraps of sections clinging to a mountainside. If sold, the land and ramshackle bamboo hut would not fetch much. "Mistress," he said, coming to a decision, "you man home? You childs?"

"Man long dead, Maas Webb. Lightning kill man dead. Months gone. 'Im coming over de pass. From Fast River. Lightning strike 'im dead. No hear a-t'ing 'bout 'im till preacher come say 'im a-dead. John crow belly full a-'im. Before dem haul 'im carcass home." She shook her head and kissed her teeth, accepting her hard life as the Almighty's way of tenderising her for salvation.

"Picknies? All a-Kingston, Maas Webb. Come visit me soon dem say. But. Larks. Never glimpse one a-dem dese six months gone. So dem stay, Mass Webb. Soons as town life claim you childs dem forget 'bout us up-country. So"—she jiggered her shoulders—"'cept fe old hen an' nanny goat down gully. Only me you see. But me manage. Somehow. De Good Lawd. Mak' me manage."

"Sorry fe hear you man's dead, Mistress Cooper." What else could he say?

Dusk drew closer. Puffy, blue-grey clouds began to settle overhead. The air grew cooler. She approached him, a bucket clanged against her legs.

"Wat you come see me fa', Maas Webb?"

Her serene acceptance of her pitiful life touched him deeply. Could Clara consider hiring her for a few hours a week to earn a little money? Things were tight with them, but "Every-mikkle—mak'-a-mukkle" was what Jamaicans said. Any little they gave her would help.

"No, mistress. Just passing. Resting me body. Just passing. Sorry fe tak' up you time. But now, me bid you good day." He touched his hat.

She stood clutching her chipped white enamel bucket while he unhitched the mule and disappeared down the gully.

The long, lonely journey down the mountainside made him understand one fact: each had a heavy cross to bear in life, and it was only lifted when someone lent a helping hand. Island people had a saying for this, *"One eye man king in blind man country"*. Things may look bleak for him, but there was always someone else worse off than him. Arriving home, he opened the top drawer of his bureau and removed six shillings and ten pennies from his savings. He marked the Coopers paid.

Letter from Sonny

Clifford rarely received letters. From habit, each Monday morning, he strolled towards Maggoty Point's drab post office and entered the low wooden three-roomed building. He approached the counter and politely asked the light-skinned woman the same question: "Any letters come fe Clifford Webb, mistress?"

The woman would silently study him with brown inquisitive eyes, as if bursting to question him with "Who gwan write you?" She would then drag her feet to the back of the building to return empty handed; always with the same reply: "Not a-degge-degge-t'ing, Maas Webb."

On this particular Monday morning, Clifford asked her the same question. She, after giving him her usual feisty stare, traipsed to the back of the building and, to his surprise and her astonishment, returned clutching a small blue airmail letter. She did not immediately give it to him. Instead, clutching it close to her chest like a lover, she studied him with an unusual excitement in her normally hostile eyes.

"One fe you, Maas Webb," she gushed. Still clinging to the letter, she licked her dark purple lips. "From abroad. England. Never know you know somebody a-England, Maas Webb," she twittered. Licking her lips again, she widened her eyes like a fowl spying a fat worm.

Clifford's eyebrows shot up in surprise. Who was writing to him, and from England? The woman was talking fool-fool nonsense. The rare letters he did receive were Jamaican, official, and demanded money. He eyed her hand suspiciously. Why did she not give him his letter? Although always reserved and polite, Clifford still knew the score in Jamaica. Post office people usually *duttied* things up. They were often accused of winkling money or news from letters before handing them to the addressees. The woman must have detected that this yellow-skinned man would *not* play cricket with her, she grudgingly thrust the letter at Clifford.

He turned the letter over, silently read the name on the back, and whistled softly. "Sonny."

She immediately bustled up to him; standing on tiptoe, she peered over his shoulder. "Is yellow man Sonny Ford?" She warbled like a tropical bird. "'Im dat one time work a-Revenue? Dat tak' 'imself a-foreign? 'Im a-writing from England? Say how 'im be?"

Certain that a worker had already steamed it open, sucked out the juice, and glued it back, he slid the letter into his breast pocket, smiled, said, "Good day, mistress," and left.

He followed a narrow, meandering trail between palm trees and bushes to an area where large concrete blocks formed a barricade along the seashore. Dusting a slab, he pushed back his hat, took the letter from his pocket, and slid open the seal with his fingernail. The date told him it had taken over a month to reach Maggoty Point from London. The different inks used told Clifford that Sonny had made several attempts to finish it.

> *Clifford,*
> *Sorry man I never write sooner as promised. You know writing and me never agree. I must tell you straight, Clifford,*

83

*me glad me decide to come to England. There's plenty of work
here. It like ripe mangoes dangling from tree ready to pick.
Found meself a fine job that pay plenty times over what me
earn in Jamaica. Clifford, why don't you come, man? Money
easy to save. From what me hear from relatives about
Jamaica's work situation, me no going to hurry back home.*

Clifford could picture Sonny hustling to make money on
London streets. A breeze ruffling his shirt, he folded the
flimsy-three-sided, blue letter and returned it to his pocket.
He removed his hat, fanned his face, then laid the hat on the
slab. In the distance, the sea's gentle waves glided over
warm, golden sands, then pulled back their powerful wings.
He heard a sound and turned. A woman balancing a basket
of oranges on her head was disappearing between the trees.
Soon that was what he and Clara might be doing if their
situation did not improve—selling bananas and such at the
market to survive.

Countrywomen rose early on weekends. They trudged
down gully banks. Many crossed streams. Some took boats to
get their produce to the town centre to catch the early
morning Kingston truck. Bananas, dasheen, coco, pimento
berries, cassava, mangoes, and such like loaded onto the
open-backed truck, they sat beside their produce. Muscular
arms clutched the sides of the truck as it swayed and pitched
with every bump and rut in the mashed-up road. At
Kingston, amidst noisy hagglers pushing carts loaded with
bottles of cream soda, crackers, and peanuts, the women
scurry over rotten fruit and vegetables to find a pitch.
Spreading their goods onto crocus bags, perching atop
wooden stools or upturned buckets they flash brown arms at
buzzing blue flies or scavenging dogs. Black metal scales
attached to a hook hoisted high, they weigh ackee, pimento
berries, gynep, or shelled gungu peas, to drop inside coconut

84

baskets or sheets of newspaper. Only when the true daylight faded, and evening beckoned, did the women collect unsold goods and return the way they came.

Unless Jamaicans had land, money, or a good job, most sold produce or goods to survive. For this reason, Sonny Ford had sailed to England.

Clifford opened the letter again.

England need us, Clifford. The country is mashed up bad. You wouldn't believe some of the things me witness here. Man, parts a London so bad, it need fixing up. Come man, come help build up the mother country.

He smiled remembering Sonny's infectious laugh. Stuffing the letter back into his pocket, he grabbed his hat.

The Suitcase

Three months after Miss Marcy's visit, Clara was dusting the dresser in her bedroom. Moving around the bed to straighten the sheet, her toes touched something underneath. Curious, she stooped, threw up the sheet, and pulled out the suitcase that was usually on top of the wardrobe. She laid it on the bed and clicked it open. Neatly folded inside were Clifford's grey suit and a shirt. She wrinkled her brow and flopped onto the bed.

So! Now she knew. It was not all falsehood. What she had long suspected was true-true. The times her man came home late, she had believed he was on Revenue business. If she tried to question his lateness, she got his sour face. Too timid she had been to say what she feared. It was some slack woman. If he was not fooling around with some slack, black woman, what other reason was there? Why else would he be acting so snakelike? Why else would he pack his *grip* and hide it under the bed? Married men having badness with other women was not strange in Jamaica. Such badness was as regular as a heartbeat on the island. Heat seemed to steam up passions. The suitcase underneath the bed was evidence enough. Her man was unfaithful.

Chilled at her discovery she hugged her chest with her hands and rocked back and forth like a rudderless boat. She must still her suspicious heart. Stop incriminating thoughts from infecting her head. But tried as she did, they multiplied.

Facts said, Jamaican men did not have it in them to stay faithful to one woman. Facts said, Jamaican men were pent-up tomcats that ran from puss to puss. Facts said, most of Clifford's married friends had plenty of pickneys with different women. As these facts pounded at her skull, she glared at the damning grip. Was Clifford a shallow stream like those wanton men? Had he forgotten what they had faced to marry?

When single, suitors had sniffed after her like bees after blossoms. Blue Mountain honey dripped from their lips when they promised her the moon, the stars, and the whole galaxy. Being particular, she never favoured one of them. Not once did she allow one to hug her, like that Chinaman who brought her the sweetest Cuban cane. The first time she spied Clifford, she knew. He was for her. The way he talked. And he treated her as if she were a queen.

Samuel Webb never took to her. That first time Clifford dragged her up the hill and introduced her to his pappy, the man looked her over as if he were inspecting a heifer for sale. Her skin crawled, as though infested with red ants. Mary Webb had stood silent, staring, saying nothing. Clara, used to skylarking and gaiety, not knowing how to respond to this strangeness, shrivelled up inside. Quiet as always, Clifford said nothing at first besides the introduction. He then told his pappy that he intended on marrying Clara Bennett of Red Haysel. His bride was not from the Webb side of the country. Not of their breed, she was an outsider, and of a higher colour. Clara Bennett looked as if she had been born and bred in Europe. His pappy had wheeled around but kept silent when Clifford said no matter what Pappy felt, this time he would choose his own wife. So, up the hill Clara went.

Loving gaiety and tomfoolery, up the hill she learnt to, *"talk an' taste her tongue"*, she leant to keep silent. Think hard before she said anything to his family. And, up the hill she stayed until greed and envy drove them off.

A hard life she could bear—Clifford with another woman? That she would never bear.

If he left her, how would she manage with the children? Beg relatives to care for them? Her mother could not assist. A sister could house them for a season. But *"Come see me an' come live wid me a-two different t'ings"* is a true-true Jamaican saying. Live with relatives for a while, and they soon curdle on you. Troubles soon boil up when relatives overstay their visit. Her eyes tearing up, she tightened her arms around her body and willed her brain to empty its pain. Still stormy weather threatened.

Was Clifford like the no-good tomcats? The rum-soaked wedding cake barely dry on the lips, they start roaming the district for women: *"Sweet t'ing. Hey. Se-se. You niceness."* She twisted her disgusted lips and snorted. "Hum." No sooner did a tomcat get what he wanted and the puss dropped a few pickney, he jumped over the next fence to tell a new puss the same lie.

Her dead pappy was also so. Handsome as hell, he had straight, black hair, sky-blue eyes, and clear, fair skin. He owned plenty of land and money. It was well known throughout the district, and told to her by her own mama. Edward Bennett had married Dora Small, but she could not quench his passionate thirst.

She had heard of a time when a bad breeze hit the island and almost mashed it up. The storm forced the thieves, fornicators, adulterers, whoremongers, and all those bound for Hell into serious reflection. Perhaps the Almighty was about to chasten them. Not wanting to roast with the simple sinners, her pappy had hustled to church. He begged the grateful minister to hear his confessions. The entire church overfilled with backsliders. They trailed behind the joyous minister for miles to the roaring river to be baptised. When the storm ceased, and the sun dried the earth, the newly baptized returned to their usual riotous living

Her pappy she felt sure populated many in the district with different women. They loved his generous self. "Hum," she muttered again. What had the doctor put on his death certificate? She felt certain it was some sexual disease. He used it so much that it shrivelled up in shame! Men!

She rose, closed the suitcase with a snap, and pushed it back under the bed. At the window, she searched the yard above. Hardship she would endure if Clifford was faithful.

✳ ✳ ✳ ✳

For three days Clara kept her suspicions silent. On the fourth day, her raw emotions overrode her good intentions. When Clifford came home she would confront him with her fears.

Her back stiff as a washboard, she placed a jug of water and glasses on the table, and picked up an orange and a knife. The blade curving around the fruit, she furrowed her brow as the orange zest stung her eyes. *A man was a man. But is Clifford like dem Monday an' Tuesday men? Dem dat stop wid one woman one day an' is gone wid another woman de next day*? She now understood some of her own mum-ma's mutterings: *"If young wives knew wat old wives know, dem be in no haste fe wed."* Did me own mum-ma 'ave dis sort a-worrying an' sufferings? She dropped a perfectly coiled orange skin onto a plate, poked a thumb through the middle, separated the sections, arranged them on another white plate, and picked up another orange.

Clifford walked into the parlour and craved liquor courage. A finger of Johnny Walker poured in a glass; he took it to the kitchen and added water. He sipped and immediately his anxieties floated away. Pulling a chair and sitting, he laid the glass on the table and inhaled deeply.

"Clara. Got some'ting fe say."

Clara tightened her grip on the knife. She would tell him now.

"Me leaving. Me can't stand it no more."

The knife slid from the orange and sliced into the soft flesh of Clara's thumb but she felt nothing. Numb and in shock, she stared at the blood dripping onto the yellow segments of the orange and a mournful sound pushed out of her mouth. "Backside! Look wat me do." She dropped the knife, clamped her fingers over her thumb, and ran from the kitchen. Entering her bedroom, she nudged the door shut with her leg, wrapped the bloody thumb into a white handkerchief, and flopped onto the bed. Her marriage was over. Her man was leaving her. Her chest heaved; it would split. She dropped her thumping head into her hands and bitter tears trickled through her fingers. As she wept, she heard the voice of Enid Mason. Through the window floated her neighbour's whiny rendition of "Rock of Ages." And, in spite of her pain, she silently mouthed, "Dat woman still can't carry a tune."

Enid Mason

Clara had lived in Maggoty Point for some time before she met Enid Mason. She was standing at the entrance of the Methodist church with Tilda when a medium-brown-skinned woman in a wide-brimmed black hat bustled up to her.

"Me is Enid Mason," said the beaming, oily faced woman as she closed in on Clara. Almost mashing Clara with her fulsome breasts, she added, "You carry a tune?" As Enid edged nearer, Clara felt she would faint. The woman's hot body belched Khus Khus perfume. Clara stepped backwards and was about to reply politely when the woman cut her off.

"Maggoty Choir a-short-a-singers," she gushed.

This unwelcome friendliness perplexed Clara. Had she met the woman before? She was certain she had not. She fanned her hot face with her hand.

"Me...well," said Clara, blushing from heat, embarrassment, and too much Khus Khus. "Me name is Clara Webb. Sometime me sing. At me house." Clara started retreating.

Tilda, who had patiently endured the interaction between her mama and the woman, and who felt duty-bound to defend her mama, said, "Mama got a-pretty voice. Mama always a-sing."

Enid turned to Tilda, glowered as if she had spotted a pesky blue bottle fly, and dismissed her. She turned back to Clara.

"Dis you pickney?" Enid asked. "Well, Mistress Webb. Since you fresh-fresh to Maggoty. Choir need pretty voices. Hear we also a-near-by neighbours? Eh, eh. Not so far me live from you. Me choir mistress you hear. Run choir practice. Every Wednesday. You come join," Enid said. "Fe sure you gwan like it."

Enid Mason, her husband, and her three sons rented a house about three mango trees from Clara's place, along a rutted, potholed road infested with every insect invented to torment man. This road led to Maggoty Point's town centre. When it rained, which it did constantly, pockets of water settled inside the numerous dips and ruts in the dirt road. The town officials' advice to sanitise all still water was ignored. Heat boiled the still water, and mosquitoes multiplied into the thousands.

The following Wednesday evening, deciding to investigate the choir, Clara tidied herself and strolled to the church. Enid welcomed her and introduced her to the anxious-looking choir. She understood their apprehension when practice started. Enid not only threatened with her mouth, she bullied with her breasts. Her Amazon-like arms vigorously keeping to the beat, if the choir hit a wrong note, she cuss at them, "You all a-mak' noise like when pig a-squeal over dem victuals." Singing "Guide Us, O Thou Great Jehovah" was rather a grievous task when patwa cuss words filled their heads.

When she first arrived at Maggoty Point, Clara heard that the Reverend Charles Sinclair had not long been the church minister. Plenty of labrish about the reverend had spread through the town like flies on cow filth. It was rumoured that the parent church, in some foreign place, had deliberately misled the reverend. No one had informed him of the full weight of the cross he would bear in Jamaica. No sooner had the good man placed his shiny leather shoes onto Maggoty soil than his steps faltered. But rallying, he reminded himself, *what greater cause is there than saving souls in this primitive vineyard of the Almighty's?*

His first day at Maggoty Point had been in the full heat of the sun when, hastening to the church, boxing away a fly; he glanced at the exterior of the church. Mopping his flushed face with a white linen handkerchief, he strolled towards the weathered teak door, pushed, entered, and looked up. Shock and disbelief registered on his face. The brilliant blue sky winked at him from holes in the roof. That first day in Jamaica humbled him. It taught him humility and the *real* meaning of sainthood.

Weaving through the long, crude benches he approached the pulpit where an old fowl dozed. Hearing the crunch of shoes, she opened an eye, squawked, flapped her wings, and raced helter-skelter over the benches. The reverend eventually released her outside.

From that day, duty buckled his knees in fervent prayer onto the coconut mat. Duty drove him to cry mightily to the Almighty daily for patience, fortitude, and endurance to submit to his cross. Perhaps, had he met Enid Mason that first day, he might have lingered longer on his knees. If not for his saintly wife's constant reminder of duty, months later, the broiling heat, tormenting insects, and backsliding congregation would have driven him back to Scotland.

A week after his arrival Enid had charged into his sanctuary and demanded that Maggoty Point Methodist

Church have a choir. She assigned herself as its mistress. Startled by her forceful declaration, the meek reverend raised his clammy bottom from the wooden chair and politely acknowledged her presence. Rigorously fanning his right hand in front of his flushed face, he declared in his soft Scottish lilt, he would be *verry* gratified, highly delighted, and eternally indebted if Mrs. Mason took on that task. If the reverend had known what grief she would cause, he would never have been so trusting of Enid. Some days later, safely ensconced under a mosquito net, his sweltering brain cooled by a sweet Jamaican evening breeze; had cause for sober reflection. Had he been too hasty? Should he have delegated the choir's management to such a forceful woman? Whenever he spied Enid's bobbing, white-feather hat at church, he quickly sought the safety of his office.

There was one particular Sunday that the Reverend, Clara, and Maggoty Point's residents would never forget. Reverend Sinclair had given a rousing sermon. He spoke on how the spirit could move an individual. The congregation echoed its agreement with more "amen's" than usual. That was when Enid decided to demonstrate how *really* moved she could be. She had been sitting betwixt twenty sweating sinners. Earnestly listening and vigorously fanning her face, she heard the Reverend's call for a mighty repentance. She jumped up, swayed from side to side like the waves of the Caribbean Sea, threw her arms heavenward, and cried, "Praise de Lord."

Dissatisfied with this miniscule offering, Enid shuffled along the bench. Bumping knees and mashing toes, she eventually reached in the aisle. To the amused astonishment of the congregation, she twitched, jerked, and stomped her feet in a devilish dance. Hands thrown out, head flung back, she cried in joyful abandonment "Hallelujah, hallelujah!"

The swift backwards flick of her head threw both her hat and wig behind her. The hat catapulted onto the lap of an old woman who was praying. Roused from her meditation, the old matron opened her watery eyes, twisted her chicken neck and tried to detect the hat's origin. The flying wig landed on top of an elderly man's head. To his delight, he had regained his full head of hair.

* * * *

Nursing her bloody thumb, Clara though, *Why t'ink on dat idiot of a-woman now?*

The door opened. Clifford entered. "Clara," he said, walking towards her. "Since me leave de hill, me never 'appy."

"Clifford...you—"

She tried to rise, but he waved her down with his hand. He wanted her to listen good and well.

"Woman. Mak' me get it out nuh. So no interrupt. Dis, dis place"—his hand circled the room, as if it were roping a stray calf—"Outside. Not much land fe grow food fe us. Revenue runner no pay much. Me proud. Stubborn too. No gwan ask people fe feed me family. Rather starve. You know so Clara!" He stared into her sad, upturned face and demanded understanding. "Youself know how Jamaica life a-harsh fe poor people. Widout good job or money. Jamaica life is all distress. How me fe stand by an' mak' you an' me childs beg. Or sell items a-market fe sustain us. Before me do so. Me bust me backside from sundown to sunup. An'. If island can't maintain us. Me must tak' drastic action. Even if it a-mean me leave me sweet Jamaica."

He sat down beside her on the bed and told her that Jamaica had conceived him.

When he was a youngster he told her, his grand-pappy had told him some of the island's history. The Tainos, or Arawaks were the first people to populate Jamaica. Spanish invaders, who had brought black slaves to the island, tried to enslave the natives without success, and eventually killed them all. Unsure what to do with the land, Spain kept only livestock and a few soldiers on her. The Spanish named her "Jamaica," the old Arawak word for "Land of wood and water."

"Clifford," his grand-pappy had said, all those years ago, "Britain heard how Spain was out fe conquer de world. So wat you t'ink she do? Her lord protector, Oliver Cromwell, send out William Penn an' Robert Venables to sea. It was dey dat stumble on Jamaica an' surprise der old enemy Spain. Fight tak' place. Britain beat Spain. An' she fly off. Abandoned dem few African slaves. Dat escape into de hills."

"Eh, Eh," the old man continued. Grinning, he slapped his machete-scarred knee. "No brodder. Dem tough African warriors secreted demselves in de hills." Excitement filling his eyes, he stabbed a crooked finger in the air. "Dat wat dey do, Clifford buoy. Hide fe years. In Cockpit Country. Use superior warfare. Against dem Redcoats. Backside." Chuckling mischievously, arching forward, he mashed his flabby belly with a fist. "Dem neyga men trickify, you see. Lick all dem Redcoats!"

"So, wat you t'ink next 'appen?" He twisted his John crow–like neck and insisted that Clifford uncork his ears and "listen good." "British had to surrender from chasing dem. Had to mak' a treaty wid dem. Give dem der own government. Name demselves Maroons. Only section a land in Jamaica dat Britain never controlled, Clifford. Someplace Maroon blood a-mingle wid ours. Our black side come from

96

some Maroon woman. Scottish an' Maroon is one powerful mix, fe stubbornness an' pride." He leaned forward and stared at Clifford as though they were two conspirators in an adventure. "Clifford buoy. A stubborn man. Is one dangerous man. Remember dat."

His grand-pappy had told him that when Britain grabbed Jamaica from Spain, it was sparsely populated. Then she called her white sons and daughters from all over to come to Jamaica. Seduced by promises of land and adventure, plenty of whites rushed to the island. To escape from the controlling clutches of the British government, English, Scottish, Jewish Welsh, and Irish people were only a few who came for land and freedom. It was even rumoured that Britain sent hundreds of Irish maids to Jamaica to be wives for her single white sons.

"Eh, eh. Wat-a-t'ing-a-dat, Clifford?" He gazed at memories long past and tried to dislodge wisps of history his own father had told him.

"Clifford. No t'ink it only neyga man dat be slave 'ere. Plenty sort was banished in Jamaica dat disagree wid Britain's politics an' religion. Pope people. Quakers. Jews. Jacobites. Such like reach dese shores. De yellow an' putrid fevers dead many a-dem. Jamaicans is one hot pepperpot mix, Clifford."

He reached for his clay pipe, pulled a stub of tobacco from his leather pouch, stuffed it tight into the bowl, struck a match, and lit it. Sucking at the stem, he hoisted his legs onto the wooden bench and threw back his grey head. Wisps of smoke rose from the clay bowl.

"Read dem history books, Clifford. Read wat white men write 'bout Jamaica. Plenty is left out a-dem books. 'Bout de black man's burden. Since me born. Me never read one degge-degge t'ing 'bout one black man dat give 'im life fe

Britain. Not'ing is in dem white-man book. Dat say it neyga man's sweat an' blood dat mak' Britain great. Which page give praise to any black man?"

His frustration heating, he shifted on the wooden chair and clamped his stale teeth onto the stem of his pipe.

"Aho," he cried, waggling his head. "Sometimes being born black. Is one grievous business, Clifford. But. More grievous. Is how Britain treat de black man. As if. As if we no matter. As if our blood-no-count one backside to dem."

Clifford's grand-pappy never tired of telling Jamaica's history. Once agitated, he would suck greedily at the clay pipe. An odd expression in his eyes, head tilted to the right, he would mutter and totter and grieve for all who had suffered the cruel whip of the slave master. Kissing his scornful teeth, he would knock ash from his pipe and grab his glass of white rum to ease his hurt.

* * * *

Clifford sat beside her while she nursed her thumb. This was the first time he had shared his grand-pappy's tales of Jamaica's bygone strengths and sorrows. These tales had been sunshine in his dark, growing-up days. He missed the old man more than he missed his pappy. Once when grand-pappy was strong in his liquor, he told Clifford how his Scottish great-grand-pappy had taken up with a good-looking black woman. Unable to marry her, she became his housekeeper and the mother of his sons. This was how the colours mixed on the island. The long-ago ramblings helped Clifford understand one fact: all Jamaicans were colonizers. All came from somewhere else. All had been dumped onto this little piece of paradise.

When Clara sniffed but kept silent, he touched her hair gently. "Me can't beg, woman. Youself know how me proud. Grand-pappy cussed me once when he witness Pappy's lickings on me backside. He say, 'Buoy, you too proud fe you own good.'"

He rose and went to the window. Turning, he said, "Not much fe show fe our life, eh Clara? 'Ave money, buy you best."

The sadness in his voice and his unexpected words confused her further, and she widened her eyes. "Clifford Webb. When since me ask you fe money? Is money me want? When since me ask you fe even a-quatty?" Lips trembling, she wondered why he could not understand. If he were faithful, even Jamaica's *quatty*, the least of her coins, would bind her to him. "Still you no understand. It only you an' de children me want."

She wanted him to tell her now, not to punish her with all his talk-talk. If he was leaving her for some slack, black, woman, he must tell her now.

When he turned to her and said "Listen nuh", and she shook her head and bowed it, he grew perplexed. Why was she acting like a rebellious pickney who had had her backside whipped? He puckered his lips and sucked long and hard at his teeth. Clifford made the famous Jamaican *Kiss Me Teeth*— that sneering, rawted expression that meant different things when a person is faced with a hell-full of provocations. Sometimes it meant: you hard a hearing? T'ink me care? Galang 'way because me no gwan pay you no mind. Move you rawted backside 'way from me. Else me gwan box you down. Or, the feistiest of them all, "Kiss me bare backside!"

In this case Clifford meant, "Why you no listen to wat me saying woman."

99

"Chu, Clara Bennett. You is one hard a-hearing woman fe understand, you know. How me fe leave. If you gwan act like a sulky-sulky pickney? Well. I decide. Can't stay in Jamaica an' eat flies. England wants workers. An' England wants me!"

Clara's head jerked, her lips slacked, eyes widened, disbelief shook her. Her mouth opened. She stuttered, "Aho," then trembled. Head lowered into her arms, she howled.

Experience had taught Clifford, if Clara act like so, don't touch her. Just talk in case she felt to listen.

"Sonny write me. Letter come fe some time. Wat 'im say mak' me t'ink hard. Promise he'd write when he gets a-England. Cause he always a-skylark, I never put 'im on practice."

Clara howled on.

"Say he knows our situation. Write say England need us, Clara. England pay me well fe help build her up. Mak' me decide. Try fe us. Eh? Wat you t'ink Clara? Wat you t'ink?"

Clara howled louder. Now she knew. When she threw her body at him and knocked him backwards onto the bed, she knew. When she hugged him up, she knew. He was not leaving her for a slack black woman. He was leaving her for England. The mother country would give him a good job so he could work hard and feed his family. The mother country would let him draw back a little of what she had taken from Jamaica.

Clifford's Journey

When Clara learnt Clifford was not leaving for some slack, black, woman, her relief was overwhelming, soon that relief evaporated. He would leave soon for England. How would she manage without him? Since they married, except when he went to America, they had rarely been apart. Now he would be gone for months, if not years. Life was one mashed-up mess. But, her mum-ma had once wisely counselled, "*Wat can't be cured must be endured.*" England was the only answer for a better life. Clifford had explained that he would go ahead, find work, and save up to send for her and the children. It would not take long. Sonny had written that plenty of work was awaiting him in England. He would do as the saying advised, "*Hog say de first dutty water me catch, me gwan wash.*" So why wait? Sonny's letter had convinced him that he must seize this opportunity now. Go ahead and prepare a life for them in England.

Tilda had heard the whispers between her dada and her mama. She had also seen their worried and anxious faces. Her dada was leaving again and her heart was heavy. In bed and unable to sleep, staring in the dark at the roof, Missy on one side of her and Roy on Missy's side, she never felt so alone. Why did her heart still beat when it pained so much? Her dada was going someplace far away—over the sea. To a place called England. The day Dada told them, she had followed him around like a lapdog, watching, wanting to soak up all the memories she could of her beloved dada. His lilting voice, the way his gold teeth flashed when he smiled.

The night before Dada was to leave, Mama told them to go to bed. He hugged all of them up and said when they woke the following morning, he would be gone. She had clung to him, wanting to remember his smell, tobacco and Johnny Walker.

In bed, the hours ticking by, her eyes drowsy, Tilda knew she must stay awake. All she had to do was to focus her eyes. Keep them open, listen to their whispers and footsteps in the kitchen and the night would last forever. Dada would still be here. Morning would never come. Tilda did sleep. Morning came. Her eyes opened, she sat up in bed, jumped off and ran to her dada's bedroom. The door was locked, mama was crying.

* * * *

Clifford woke after a long sleepless night. Heavy hearted, he could not look at Clara. The pain was too much for them. Clara's sorrowful eyes would have finished him. He would unpack his suitcase and stay. The night before both had said all their goodbyes. Now at raw dawn, still drowsy, he made coffee in the kitchen and sat at the table.

Also awake, Clara immediately made cornmeal porridge. That was all that she or Clifford could stomach. Anything else would have stuck in their throats. Since she married Clifford her life seemed to be always changing with never a safe harbour. First he left for America and then they moved to Maggoty Point, now England. Her man said this was for their future and their childs. He would go ahead to England, save up and send for them.

Clifford kissed Clara goodbye and left carrying one suitcase to the bus depot. He took the bus for Kingston and stayed overnight with relatives. The following morning, he boarded the ship for England.

On board the ship now, his grey trouser legs flapping against his shanks, like flags in a storm, Clifford watched Jamaica's peaks disappear.

Years back, during the Second World War, he had boarded a boat to America to grow crops for starving Britain. Missy was not long born when he heard good paying work was plentiful in America. He asked around. Some said go. Others said it was all idle labrish. Wanting to better his situation and not be like *"salt fish dat sit 'pon counter an' wait fe bread an' butter"*, he decided to try America. Not wait for luck to drop in his lap.

He went.

Cha man! What a fool-fool jackass he had been. High wages for easy labour—all were seductive false promises. It had been long, intensive, backbreaking labour. It almost crippled his young body. Yet, what did it matter? He learnt fast. Jamaicans had a saying: *"Fool monkey once, you no gwan fool 'im twice!"*

With little money to return home, he had endured his long penitence under the hot American sun. He visited American towns on the weekends and saw the *real* face of America. He had heard a little in Jamaica of the way America treated her coloured people. Never had he seen the "Whites Only" signs before coming to America. He wondered at this peculiarity. How was it that he, a coloured Jamaican, could freely visit places barred to coloured

Americans? *Wat sort-a poppy show an' slackness was dat,* he wondered?

America called herself the "land of the free." He wondered which part was free. He never saw any of her freedom. Jamaica was freer. Island people could roam like stray calves clear to the seashore if they had a mind to. Nobody cared a damn if you drowned in the warm blue sea. Returning to Jamaica, he decided, no amount of money would ever induce him to set foot in America again.

Jamaica's coastline slowly fading, a sad, soulful loneliness settled around his belly line. When would he see Clara and the children again? How could he live without them? The soft breeze kissing his cheeks, he turned and listened to a man walking along the deck singing the haunting, Jamaican calypso.

> *When me t'ink on me sweet Jamaica, water come a-me eye,*
> *When me t'ink on me sweet Jamaica, water come a-me eye,*
> *Come back Charlie, come back gal, water come a-me eye,*
> *Come back Charlie, come back gal, water come a-me eye,*
> *When me t'ink on me sweet Jamaica, water come a-me eye.*

BOOK TWO

Life Without Clifford

Soon Tilda would attend school for the first time and, to Clara's vexation, she learnt schoolchildren no longer wore their mum-ma's homemade uniforms, they now sported store-bought ones. She had already let down the hem of Missy's school skirt, and worried, if she made her pickneys wear homemade uniforms, shame and scandal would fall upon their heads. For, were Jamaicans not quick to labrish and badmouth her pickneys, even if they glimpsed a peculiarity in them? Clifford in England, money was scarce. How could she hide her lack of money? How could she prevent her scantiness from being broadcast out of doors? She emptied the contents of her purse onto the kitchen table one evening and checked and rechecked her shillings and coppers. The money still added up the same. Later that night, worrying in bed, she turned over, sucked her teeth, muttered, "De Good Lord will provide," and slept.

Mitchell Mercantile was the largest retail store in Maggoty Point. Pins, needles, ribbons, gaily coloured bolts of fabric, hats, socks, handbags, shirts, suits, and ties groaned from its long wooden shelves and floorboards. Merchandise was stuffed in every nook and cranny. The store boasted, "If one could not find an item in Mitchell Mercantile. Order it from our catalogue."

Clara left Roy with Missy and took Tilda to town. A quick glance at the pricy items displayed in Mitchell's window, she hurried inside with Tilda, and marched towards the uniform section.

Girl's school uniform was black shoes, navy blue skirt, white blouse, and white ankle socks. Boys' were khaki shirt and pants. Selecting a suitable uniform for Tilda, Clara did what most town dwellers did: asked to pay on trust—pay a little each week until the debt was paid. The manager agreed.

Her shopping completed at Mitchell; Clara entered Bata Shoe Shop next door. She told Tilda to sit while she looked for an assistant. Spotting a slim, yellow-faced young woman, she beckoned with her hand and pointed at Tilda. She told the young woman her daughter needed black lace-up school shoes. The assistant gave mother and daughter a quick look, marched off, and returned with a wooden foot measurer. She measured Tilda's feet, and then gave her a pair of shoes. They fit perfectly. Clara disagreed, saying they were too tight.

The perplexed assistant shrugged her shoulders, re-measured the slim, small feet, and informed Clara, in her best Jamaican English, that the measurements were correct; she also added for good measure, that Bata's store policy was to satisfy its customers.

The assistant hurried away, brought another box and dutifully slid the shoes onto Tilda's feet. Clara was not satisfied. This to-ing and fro-ing went on for some time, until the young woman's once-helpful mouth grew pinched and tight. Fatigued and now sweating a river, her *speaky-spokey* English slid into aggrieved patwa. Struggling with another shoe box, she threw aside Bata's policy of satisfying customers, kissed her vexed teeth and muttered, "Wat wrong wid de wo'man? Wey she no a-mak' up her mind? Is want she want I a-stay a-de store till moonshine come?"

She dragged her sore feet to the back of the store again, then came back and flung down another pair of shoes. Tilda tried them on. Her feet sat in them like a sailor in a rowboat. Clara calmly said, "Me tak' dem."

Tilda curled her toes in the shoes almost the size of her dada's. She was about to tell her mama this truth when Clara hissed a warning in her ear. "Seal up you mout' an' no contradict big people in public place. Else you gets box down when you gets home."

Tilda sealed her lips.

"Me say, shoes fit right," Clara told the now desperate-looking, sour-mouthed assistant who, observing that Clara was finally making a move to leave, stopped her mouth from saying, "Pay fe damn t'ing an' get out a-de shop."

"Me fix extra-ness in shoe when me reach home," Clara sweetly told the assistant, who was ramming the shoes into the box. Grabbing the money from Clara's outstretched hand, she marched away.

Clara quickly left the shoe shop with Tilda clutching the shoe box. Money worries had made her vulnerable and vexed. Tilda's school shoes would eat into her precious food money. At all cost, she must never show her scanty money face in the shoe shop. She must play act with the Bata assistant—not disgrace herself in front of *faas* mouths. Pickney feet grow fast. Just like Missy's, Tilda's feet will soon grow into the shoes. Clara's wisdom was, *"better big shoes fe wear a-school, dan no shoes at-all."*

Hair

Monday morning, her first day of school, Tilda ate her cornmeal porridge and orange. She was dressing in her new uniform when she heard her mama call. She must hurry. It was time for her hair to be combed.

Tilda had big hair. Contrary, wild, and wiry, it could provide a roost for an entire family of fowls. Hurrying to the kitchen she found her mama sitting on a low stool—in her hand was a yellow comb, at her feet, a large jar of Vaseline and a tin mug of water. She was timidly approaching her mama when Clara grabbed her arm and yanked her forcefully onto the bare floorboards.

Clara missed Clifford dreadfully. The little money he had sent from England almost gone, she took out her vexations on her second daughter. Tilda had always been peculiar and secretive. Missy was open and never a bother. Whereas Tilda…well she was so much like Clifford. The mere sight of her provoked Clara. She clamped Tilda's head between her knees, grabbed a hank of the dark brown, coconut bark-like hair cascading over her lap, and began combing. She teased, pulled and sliced the yellow comb through the thick hair, until Tilda's scalp and forehead screamed in agony. The torture was so unbearable that, raising a timid hand, Tilda tenderly touched her hair. A sharp *thwack* stung her knuckles.

"Sit still nuh," Clara cried, flicking the comb. She tugged at the wild hair again. "Else how me fe finish hair if you a-pull-pull 'way so? You no seeing time a-passing?"

Tilda withdrew her hand, squeezed tight her eyes, and tried to control her tears. The pulling pain intensified.

"Mama, mama. It a-pain,: she said. She heard teeth sucking over her head.

"Why you a-fuss-fuss over not'ing?" said Clara, whose straight, long hair had only a slight wave. "Long an' wild is you hair. Too much fe a little pickney like you," said Clara. "Never inherit it from me side a-de family. Not one neyga strain in me hair!"

If Tilda could nod her head, she would agree that her mama had spoken a fact. Hair washing for her mama was easy. She would cut sections of thorny aloe from a nearby plant, soap her hair, rinse, scrape the slimy, opaque juice from the prickly plant, daub it over her hair, and rinse again.

"Get natty part from you dada's side a-family."

Desperate not to complain, Tilda winced but kept silent when another tug stung her scalp. What did she care if her hair was not straight like her mama's? Kink or nappy, she was glad her hair was like her dada's.

Clara tied the last ribbon onto the end of a thick plait, opened her legs, and released Tilda.

"No bring lice home wid you." She pulled strands of thick, bushy hair from the comb, rolled them into a ball, and scrunched it into a piece of newspaper.

"It no pay fe expose you hair on de ground. Wind blow it where it a-please. People peculiar," Clara muttered, pushing herself to her feet. "Burn later. You may be little pickney, but wicked people may still use it fe obeah."

Maggoty Point School

Maggoty Point School was about three miles inland. A dilapidated, rusty iron fence at the back separated it from the Methodist churchyard. Like most buildings on the island the school was square and elevated on short, thick concrete blocks that allowed violent downpours to flow underneath. The inside was large and open and divided by a walkway in the centre. The south end had a raised, wooden, platform used for assemblies, or whenever the headmaster or teachers needed to instruct the entire school. The school concert was performed here each year. Below this raised platform, a low, wooden, fencelike barrier, divided the seniors at the south end from the juniors at the north end. Right of this platform a door opened onto the schoolyard. Six wooden steps, north of the building also descended into the playground.

When locals learnt plans were a-blowing to build the school in such a peculiar place, the elders scratched their heads. They knew their wisdom far superseded the young jackasses at the town office. Seventy years plus of life had taught them, *"de older de clock, de faster 'im wind."* Aged like mature mango trees, wisdom taught these old islanders that what these dry-foot officials planned was all foolishness. Tottering and sucking their teeth they flung shame and disgrace onto the young cockerels' heads, "Wat backside t'ing a-dis. Way dem want fe place a-pickney learning place beside a-duppy house?" No one listened to their wise counsel and no official ever gave a sensible explanation as to why the school was build next to a *jumby* house. Eventually the elder's wisdom prevailed—the town officials must have gotten the land cheap.

There was one other factor that these officials had not considered. Island people, ripened on hurricanes, storms, thunderous lightning, hunger, and plenty of grievous hardship, feared two things: obeah and graveyards.

Legends abounded on the island that graveyards nightly released jumbies and the dreaded Rolling Calf. A heavy, dangling chain around its neck, the demon calf rose from earth's womb with jumbies, in the dead of night, to haunt the unwary, superstitious, and wicked. Eyewitnesses trembled. They told horrifying tales. Their own eyes had beheld their dead and buried relations returning from the grave. These apparitions came back to haunt them. Fists shaking at a backsliding relative, they warned, "Repent, or Mr. Satan man is a-coming fe haul you to hell."

* * * *

Although the sun was young in the sky, Tilda's armpits were wet as a fish as she tramped the three miles to school beside Missy. Kicking a pebble, she dragged her feet and frowned, marring her usually serene face.

The night before, she had tossed in bed. Missy, who laid next to her, and who had felt the heave and throw of the mattress, had hissed at her to settle to sleep or she would wake Roy, who slept on Missy's side of the bed. Tilda had mournfully released her worries to her big sister and, during the long, sweltering night, Missy educated her in whispers.

Now, in the sober light of a clear morning, Tilda's head hammered with Missy's graphic midnight explanations. Her belly churned with worries. She felt she would vomit her cornmeal porridge over her new uniform. When she spied the school through the trees, she said dully, "School big."

Missy only half listened to Tilda. Anxious to meet friends, she brushed aside Tilda's anxiety as timidity and newness. Yet, Missy's lips did part into a mischievous smile as she reviewed what she had told her sister the night before. How the timid puss trembled. How she hugged up close to her, as if she had seen the Rolling Calf. It had not been her intention to be bad minded or feisty, but, well, it was just...well, school life could mash up a cry-baby pickney. Tilda needed a warning. Missy dropped her school bag at the base of a tree before the school's entrance, grabbed a thick branch and swung four good swings. Her skirt ballooned in the breeze. She dropped to her feet, picked up her bag, and walked on.

Tilda wondered if what Missy had said the night before was true-true. Nervous and biting her lips, she was following Missy when she felt her arm grabbed.

"See wat me mean," said Missy, pointing ahead.

Tilda looked. A short dumpling of a girl had just yanked another girl's hair and run off. "Watch out. Dem wicked a-school," said Missy.

Missy took Tilda to her classroom, told her she would see her at recess, and left.

Unable to find her sister at recess, Missy hurried to Tilda's class and found her sitting alone on the third bench of the twelve in Tilda's class. When the school benches were first fashioned, splinters and nail heads covered the boards. Over the years students' backsides had smoothed them out to a shiny finish. Tilda's back against the wall, Missy asked her why she was hiding and had not come outside to play. Tilda mulishly shook her head, lowered it and told her sister she would not go outside to get boxed down.

Missy could not believe her ears.

"You can't act so-so a-school," she said, rolling her eyes. "Like you some shamy darling." Her sister was just like Jamaica's timid green fern that grew low on the ground. If slightly touched, the fern enfolded its leaves as if ashamed or frightened. "Get outside. Learn fe stand up fe youself. Get tough quick!"

"But," mumbled Tilda, shaking her head again, "Youself a-say dem-a–wicked-a-school."

Missy screwed up her mouth in vexation. "Why you a-always acting like some shy baby Tilda. You know me no see me friends since school break up. How me fe play wid dem if me have fe look after you all de time."

When Tilda brushed her sweaty palms over her skirt and refused to budge, Missy knew she had to do something drastic to rouse her. She slid along the bench until her shoulder touched Tilda's.

"First time me fresh a-school," she said, "one try fe box me down. But me learn quick fe tak' care a-meself. Never bother me much now."

Tilda smiled weakly and hugged her chest. She turned her back on her sister. Missy was only trying to *courage-her-up*. Tilda had never needed to fight or biff anyone before. Wasn't the first time getting boxed down always the worst time? She would make certain she was never boxed down, first or last time.

"You saying so, Missy, 'cause it easy fe you. You big. Me only small fly at cow's backside." Whimpering, she stared at the wooden wall.

Missy blew air out of her hot cheeks and snorted her disgust. She wanted to say, "Who protect me when me new a-school? Better you hurry fe tough-up youself. 'Cause me no gwan always be around fe protect you." Instead, she said, "All start fresh a-school, Tilda. It how it a-go. You lucky. 'Ave me a-school. When me start fresh. Nobody help me. You no worry."

When Tilda still refused to budge, resisting the urge to box her sister herself, Missy decided to drop the vital ingredient for survival in the schoolyard into Tilda's ear.

"Tilda. Wat me a-say a-dis. Watch out fe de older pickneys dat 'ave years a-practice dan you. But"—she dropped her voice to a whisper—"sometime even younger pickneys get lucky. Can lick down a bigger pickncy. Boy or girl. It no different. All fight de same. Only, only..." Missy paused, she studied Tilda's thick, long plaits, they almost reached her waist. "It only dat. Girl pickney got plenty more hair dan boy pickney."

What Tilda *did* learn was, her pigtails were her weakness. If what Missy said was true, she knew she was in for a tough time at school.

Mrs. Beryl Reid

Sweaty, lethargic, and hot, Tilda shifted on the wooden bench, leaned forward and tried to filter out the drone of her strict and feared teacher who talked too much, sounded like a mosquito, and should release them outside to breeze their bodies? She raised a limp hand to scrub her damp neck and was jerked from her daydream. Her teacher rapped her ruler loudly on her desk.

"Attention please. Children. Attention. Now." Body stiff like a sergeant major, the teacher glared over the rim of her round spectacles. "A few of you may already know that next month is our school concert. I want you all to pay attention."

The sleepy bodies rustled with just enough heat for the teacher to see that they were paying attention to her.

"It is my wish that you all be involved in this year's concert—individually, as groups, or as a class."

The class whispered and giggled. Girls nudged each other and craned their necks. At last *some'ting* exciting was coming that would break up the teacher's continual drone. *The cat sat on the mat. Repeat after me in perfect English please, and do not, I repeat do not, say, "De cat a-sit-a-de mat." That will not do. Not in my class.*

Although the girls in Mrs. Reid's class were excited about the coming concert, the boy students "calypso" to a

116

different tune. They covered their mouths with their hands, kissed their teeth, and grinned sheepishly. Teacher or no teacher, they were *not* going to make jackasses of themselves at the concert.

Tilda heard the word "concert," dragged her eyes from her inkwell, raised her limp hand, and volunteered to participate.

Mrs. Beryl Reid was fair-skinned; at one time she would have been called a mulatto. Brown haired and hazel eyed, she had a splattering of freckles across her plump cheeks. Round spectacles on a dainty, turned-up nose, helped her keep a watchful eye on her class, like a chicken hawk. Conservatively dressed, she shone as one that kept strictly to her calling. A long wooden ruler was forever it seemed glued to her right hand. This she used to instruct and disciplined her class. For, she often reminded herself, she was from the school of, "Spare the rod and spoil the child."

What her class dreaded most was spelling. If a student was given a word to memorise, he or she must stand and spell it, exactly, or down came the ruler onto knuckles— hard. She taught the basics: reading, writing, arithmetic, and spelling. Also some nature study, a little sewing, and, if time permitted, a splattering of geography.

Places outside of Jamaica.

England.

She taught the class that England's climate was different from Jamaica's. England had something called snow. It was white and icy cold. Similar to the round iced treat that Jamaicans called *suck-suck*. The only difference was that England's snow fell from the sky and was *not* covered in red syrup. English winters were cold and damp. A miserable grey wetness seemed to forever cover the entire country. Sometimes it was difficult to see one's hands. This dreadful

117

grey wetness was called fog. England's Queen was also Jamaica's Queen. She lived in a place called Buckingham Palace.

She also introduced them to an exotic, Far East country called China where people had skin the colour of ripe bananas. She even made them recite a damn-fool rhyme about a child named Ah Foo and his sister Si Ling.

Once, a few hygiene people came to put on a slide show at the school. They demonstrated the proper way to clean teeth with a toothbrush and toothpaste. What these enlightened people did not seem to grasp was—Jamaican country ways were different from theirs. Jamaican country folks would *never* waste good money on foolishness like toothpaste and toothbrushes! What was the point? A few dabs of toothpaste onto the toothbrush, and the toothpaste vanished like *Anancy's magic pot*, especially if it tasted like peppermint sticks. Wise, seawall people knew the best thing for teeth cleaning—Jamaican *chewstick*. Jamaican chewstick was ideal for healthy white teeth. It grew freely in the bush. Rise early, go look for the vine, slice it into small pieces, stick it in the mouth, and chew. Keep chewing—a whole lot of spittle would foam up in the mouth and then dig in the teeth with the chewstick. It was far superior to any toothpaste and toothbrush. The hygiene show was very enlightening though. It cemented in country people's heads one fact they already knew: they were not the only ones with dutty teeth.

Mrs. Reid loved the written word. Knowledgeable and cultured, she craved all forms of art. Her lifelong crusade was correct English diction. Her teaching career began when she took an English degree in Kingston. Having surplus funds after her degree, she decided to "go foreign",—tour Europe for a year—soak up museums, theatres, and lectures with one ultimate goal: attain, if feasible, a teaching post in

England. When her numerous applications in England were rejected, she sailed back to Jamaica determined to keep her flame alive. Accepting a teaching post at Maggoty Point School, she vowed, with the intensity of her idealistic heart; carry out her crusade. Always speak and teach perfect English diction in the classroom.

She was not long at Maggoty Point School when the first flurries of disappointment lapped at her boat. Undaunted, she sailed onwards with rose coloured glasses—eliminate patwa from her students' unruly Jamaican tongues. Unfortunately, though well rounded, talented, and highly educated as Mrs. Reid was, she simply could not grasp one fact: Jamaican pickneys were rebellious. What Jamaican pickney ears heard was not always what Jamaican pickney tongues said. And so, she was reminded of the story of Mr. Jamaican Crab.

❊ ❊ ❊ ❊

Mr. Jamaican Crab had always accepted his fate. He was a crab. Yet, as he grew older, one thing vexed him: never would he be like the other sea creatures. They darted and swam gracefully. They jumped and performed all manner of wonderful movements. His friend Mr. Fish darted back and forth. So did Reverend Shark. Professor Stingray and Doctor Jellyfish moved whichever way they wished. Yet, no matter how hard poor Mr. Jamaican Crab tried to straighten his legs, they always shuffled sideways. As the seasons of his life passed, he grew crabbier and crabbier. His dream to be like the other sea creatures would never be realised.

On his fortieth birthday, it finally dawned on Crab— what was the use of feeling sorry for himself, he now understood the wise saying *"when coco ripe, it must bust"*. He must make a change—act now, before it was too late. First he consulted Professor Stingray, tried his psychology, but saw no improvement. His next stop was Doctor Jellyfish. The doctor's numerous natural sea potions did not work either. It was only whilst conversing with a passing hammerhead shark that Crab grew excited. Hammerhead told him of a fantastic cure. Above the sea on dry land, said Hammerhead, whenever earth people sinned, they followed a process to become new creatures. They attended church, repented, and miraculously changed into upstanding citizens.

Crab was ecstatic. The mere prospect of becoming whole and upstanding made him giddy with delight. Always a cautious creature, Crab first did some investigating. He wanted to know whether this upstanding business was a ruse. He pressed Hammerhead further. Were these land mortals the very same sinners who held revival meetings? Were they the very same ones known to jump *poco*, the ones that were called *Pocomania People?* Crab stressed that he would have nothing do with such uncouth individuals. He desired reverence and deep devotion.

Hammerhead soon put Crab straight on the subject. If reverence and deep devotion was what Crab desired for his cure, the Methodist church was for him.

Sunday morning dawned bright and clear. No cloud marred the bright blue sky. Mr. Jamaican Crab dressed in his best suit, hopped onto dry land, and shuffled to the entrance of the Methodist church. No sooner did Crab's crabby legs touch the first step of the church, they straightened out. He strolled upright into the church and met the minister. He sang and praised the Almighty as any upright Christian would. Before his departure, he shook hands with the minister at the church door. As soon as his straight legs touch the dirt outside, they buckled sideways, and stayed sideways for the entire week. Undaunted, the following Sunday, Crab returned to church, walked inside and his legs straightened out.

And so it was with Mrs. Reid's class. No matter how often her tongue chastened her class, no matter how often she raised her voice and slammed her ruler onto knuckles, once her students left her class, their stubborn Jamaican tongues slid back to patwa.

"Class," Mrs. Reid demanded. She rapped her ruler onto her desk and peered over her spectacles to silence the discord. "We shall practice our concert song. Let us learn the words to perfection." She threw out her hand and vigorously batted the air. "Ready, class. Eyes on me. One, two, three."

Hark! the vesper hymn is stealing,
O'er the waters soft and clear;
Nearer yet and nearer pealing,
Soft it breaks upon the ear,
Jubilate! Jubilate!

On and on the class blissfully sang. They had finished the last "Jubilate" and were about to begin the final "Amen" when Mrs. Reid slammed her ruler violently on her desk again.

"Stop!" she cried. "Stop immediately, I say. At once, I say."

She trembled with outrage. Her eyes bulged like a bloated bullfrog through her spectacles. She had broken her vow. Never lose her temper with her students.

The students froze in surprise. Their mouths snapped shut. Heads bowed, they nervously waited. *Who mix up de word a-de song? Who Teacher gwan blame? Who Teacher gwan box down wid her ruler?*

Mrs. Reid gulped three short, heaving breaths and tried to subdue her temper before she spoke. Her cheeks ballooned like a sail in a mighty wind.

"If. If I hear," she spluttered. "If. I. Ever. Hear. One. More. 'Jumby-batty' from *this* class, instead of 'Jubilate,' I shall, I shall..." Unable to swallow her students' audacity, she smashed the ruler hard onto the desk. It snapped in two. She stared at it, straightened her neck, glared at the bowed heads, and hissed through clenched teeth, "If I ever hear the use of that word again, I shall use"—she grabbed half of the ruler and stabbed it at them—"this on someone's batty. Do. I. Make. Myself. Clear?" Fixing a false smile onto her face, she said, "Now class. Remember. Practice makes perfect. So let us resume and try once more."

Hark! the vesper hymn is stealing,
O'er the waters soft and clear;
Nearer yet and nearer pealing,
Soft it breaks upon the ear,
Jubilate! Jubilate! Jubilate! Amen!
Farther now and farther stealing,
Soft it fades upon the ear.
Now like moonlight waves retreating,
To the shore it dies along;
Now like angry surges meeting,
 Breaks the mingled tide of song.
Jubilate! Jubilate! Jubilate! Amen!
Hark! again like waves retreating,
To the shore it dies along.
Once again sweet voices ringing,
Louder still the music swells;
While on summer breezes winging,
Comes the chime of vesper bells.
Jubilate! Jubilate! Jubilate! Amen!

On the summer breezes winging,
Fades the chime of vesper bells.

School Concert

Moneyed Jamaicans were the only ones who could *nice-up* themselves and attend the theatre or other refined enjoyments in Kingston. If country dwellers could scrape up a few shillings to attend such cultured events, they came in *rucka-rucka-transport*—an almost-broken-down bus. Since distance and expense made it almost impossible for country folks to enjoy such pleasantries in the capital, the older heads of country parishes invented the concert. Concerts to Jamaicans meant rude walking, skylarking, and patwa talking.

The day of Maggoty Point school concert finally arrived. The Friday afternoon recess over, the teachers threatened their students, "Behave or else," and marched them to the top end of the school. On the platform, hands at his sides, back ramrod stiff, the vexed headmaster silently endured the unruly students pushing and jostling to get a seat. Unable to endure the rowdiness on minute longer, he flung out both hands and bellowed at the top of his voice, "All a-you. Stop dis ruckus. Settle down so we start. Cha!"

The hall immediately hushed. He pulled a handkerchief from a side pocket, vigorously scrubbed his neck and face, and stuffed it back in.

"It concert time again," he said, sounding bored. Heat belched from the furnace of bodies staring up at him. Desperate to hurry through his part and get off the platform, he said, "An'. Since all a-you want fe be a movie star like Harry Belafonte—"

Raucous clapping drowned his words. Allowing for some whistles and teeth sucking but knowing that "*if you allow monkey licence, 'im want fe drive*," he quickly silenced them with his hands.

"Mrs. Reid gwan introduce who will perform. So clap up. Show dem you glad dey doing dem t'ing fe you." He looked to his right to check that Mrs. Reid was ready to deal with the stupidness he had to endure every year.

Like most Jamaican men, the headmaster liked a skylark. However, familiarity with pickneys was not his tonic. He was Maggoty Point School headmaster; its authority and its disciplinarian. In the many years he and his wife, Tunkus, had been loving, never once had they dropped a pickney. If they had, perhaps he would have *petti-pattied* it to make it thrive. Perhaps he would have learnt more tolerance. His curt introduction over, he marched off to join his staff.

Tilda hid behind her teacher at the side of the platform. Why had she volunteered to take part in the concert? She lightly touched her hair and tried to calm her bawling belly and cork her bladder so it wouldn't leak into her baggy. Soon she would perform, and anxiety was already tripping her up.

Her head still stung from her mama's morning head combing. Clara had plastered Tilda's hair with water and Vaseline, then twisted sections into perfect mattress-coil ringlets, she had placed Tilda's concert dress inside a white pillowcase, to keep it clean and told Tilda, "It you Sunday best. So, no fool-fool wid it an' mess it up, you hear. Eh."

Clara then hesitated, pushed the sack at Missy and told her to carry it. "Else, Tilda spoil it." Missy had stared at her mama but said nothing. She did not know why she should carry Tilda's dress, which was much nicer than what she had to wear.

Mrs. Reid marched onto the platform, positioned her feet centre stage, and surveyed Maggoty's youth.

"School. Students," she said, clearly and precisely, her words sounding strange and foreign amidst the hall full of patwa ears. "May I have your attention, please?"

The school settled. A few whispered. They were glad they did not have the stiff-backed, stern-faced speaky-spokey and precise-English-talking woman for a teacher.

"Those who will perform for us have worked very hard and diligently. I hope you will be impressed with their efforts, as I am. So, give them your encouragement. Clap after each performance. Our first act will be Dunkie Brown."

The eyes swung left. When Dunkie Brown did not appear, whispers blazed through the students like wildfire on sugar cane in a drought. *Wey Dunkie Brown de? Did de Rolling Calf t'ief 'im?*

Mrs. Reid was also curious. Not one minute earlier, she had left the eager youth awaiting his performance. She strode to where the performers waited and found the smirking boy leaning against a wall labrishing with a girl.

"Dunkie Brown. On stage at once," she ordered.

Eleven-year-old Dunkie Brown was short in leg and plump. He wore a short-sleeved khaki shirt and khaki shorts that ended at his kneecaps. He lumbered onto the stage, grinned like a nervous melon, and flashed brilliant white teeth. Gulping in a few short breaths, he took two timid steps forward, extended his arms like an eagle swooping above the sky and then shifted from foot to foot as he sang,

126

Me step-e come over,
Me step-e come over,
Me step-e come over
De bright dutty water,
Oh, oh, oh, oh, oh, ratta,
How you come over. Wait!

Dunkie squatted, twitched like a rat, froze, glanced right, glanced left, then rose.

Me put me right foot so,
Me put me left foot so,
Me put me right foot so.

Wobbling and twitching, he demonstrated a cautious rat trying to cross a rough body of water.

Oh, oh, oh, oh, oh, ratta
Dat how me come over. Wait!

The wailing serenade became too much for one senior male student. "W'at sort a-song a-dat?" the boy cried, jumping up. "Rat Boy," he shouted. "Oh, oh, oh. Is you got de bellyache, sah?"

Dunkie ignored his taunts.

De bright dutty water,
Oh, oh, oh, oh, oh, brodder
Dat how me come over.

"Boo-boo head boy," yelled another senior male student through cupped hands. "Move youself from dere. Get you big fat batty off, Rat Boy."

Ignoring all rude interruptions, Dunkie courageously finished his performance before running off towards the back of the platform.

127

Mrs. Reid was not pleased. Indeed, she was furious. Chest heaving, lips pursed, she marched onto the platform.

"Silence," she cried, waving her new ruler at the students. "Students, silence I say. Now." She sympathised with the brave youth. It was outrageous for him to suffer the torments of those who thought it beneath them to perform. "Silence at once I say." She stabbed her ruler at a group of rude senior boys at the far right of the hall.

"May I remind you all. This is not a brawl but a school concert. The performers are doing their best to entertain you, so please do not embarrass them by behaving in such a disgraceful manner, or else this will be the last school concert. Ever." She touched her heaving chest and adjusted her eyeglasses, which were sliding off her nose. Peering at a group she would deal with when the concert ended, she added, "Please give due attention and your best behaviour to our three girls. Give them a welcome by clapping, please."

A timid trio, Missy and Tilda on the outside and Zelda Moore, Tilda's fair-skinned friend in the middle, nervously shuffled to the far back of the platform.

"We singing," Missy began shyly. She glanced at Tilda and Zelda, who had sidled up to each other for protection. Noting the three were petrified, Mrs. Reid tried to encourage them to move closer to the front. The terrified girls did not budge an inch until she gestured with her ruler.

"Girls. Move forward," she hissed.

The three shuffled as far forward as their nerves dared them to. Missy gulped nervously and whispered to Zelda, "Now."

Zelda Moore, the palest and most confident of the trio, took the cue. She stepped right, raised a pale, slender arm, fingered golden ringlets tied with a perfect blue bow and sang,

I'm a white girl with me curly hair. Zelda swayed her hips. Her pale yellow lace dress, nipped at the waist with six-inch blue ribbon, swayed back and forth like a gentle sea breeze. Zelda looked like a perfect Dresden doll amongst heathens.

Next was Tilda. Left hand on hips, she nervously patted her coiled hair with her right hand and sang, *I'm a brown girl just de same.* Tilda's role was to tell her audience that although she was brown skinned, she was just as worthy and presentable as Zelda. Tilda ended her line, shuffled backwards, and joined her hip to Zelda's.

Missy fixed her eyes onto the wooden floor and did exactly what her teacher had taught her. She bewailed the hard life of a neyga woman.

But me poor black gal—

The hall zinged. It was as if lightning bolts had zapped the school. Whistles shrilled like piglets fighting for scattered feed. The entire building was suddenly in an uproar. Handclaps drowned Missy out. Thinking she was getting the same disfavour as the rat boy, she stepped backwards in terror. When the students remembered the speaky-spokey teacher's warning, they settled just long enough for Missy to push her trembling fingers underneath the white tie-head covering her hair. She scratched her scalp, slid sweaty palms down her shapeless, crocus sack frock, sang, *But me poor black gal,* and was again interrupted. A boy leapt up and flung out his arms. "Se, se. Come 'ere ya sweet t'ing," he yelled between cupped hands. "Wa' me give you some'ting fe 'appy-up-you-face?"

Another shouted. "Wey you get dat dress? You mum-ma t'ief it from market woman when she a-turn her back?"

Missy legs felt weak. They would buckle under her. She gulped nervously and continued. *But me poor black gal, wid me natty bump.* She paused for effect, stared piteously at the upturned faces, raised her right arm, and yanked off the tie-head. Ten tight, twisted clumps of hair that resembled porcupine quills stood upright on her head. She was about to end with the punch line, but the entire school, knowing the song, stood and thundered, *But me love it just de same*.

How well the school understood Missy's rendition of the lot of a poor neyga woman.

A Blue Airmail Letter

A month after the school concert Tilda came home from school, run into the kitchen, and heard her mother singing, "Oh happy day, when Jesus wash our sins away." Now, sucking pea soup from her spoon, she eyed the letter on the table.

Missy was gulping mouthfuls down as fast as she could— she was going to meet school friends. Four year old Roy was scraping thick brown sludge into a mound in the centre of his plate, flattening it with his spoon, he repeated the process. Clara, who always insisted on good table manners, was eating absentmindedly.

"You dada write from a place call Shepherd's Bush a-England," Clara said. She signed; pushed aside her plate, picked up a banana, pulled back the skin, and nibbled daintily.

Roy, glad for any excuse not to put what looked like dog's mess into his mouth, asked, "Dada live a-bush a-England?"

"Me no know, Roy. But it seem peculiar to me. Dat you dada leave Jamaican bush. Fe England bush." Clara finished the fruit and placed the skin on her plate.

The idea that his dada lived where the Baby Jesus and shepherds lived intrigued Roy. He wanted details.

131

"Mama," Roy said. He scooped a wad of the sludge and plonked it onto the plate. "Is dere shepherds dere too? Like dem in de Bible. Dat visit de Baby Jesus?" He whacked his spoon on the edge of his plate.

"Cha," Clara snapped, her temper heating. Her lathargic hand rose to box her son's ears, but remembering what was in Clifford's letter, she pulled it down and said instead, "Such t'ings me no know."

It was one of the hottest days of the summer. Even the flies lolling on top of the cupboards refused to buzz. Soaked in sweat, Clara pinched the bodice of her frock, flapped it, and tried to find words to explain something even she did not understand. She wiped perspiration from her nose.

"If you dada say. It a-bush 'im live at. It must mean it a-bush 'im a-live. An'"—she blew out of her hot cheeks and hoped her explanation would satisfy them so they would leave her in peace to figure out how to get them to swallow what she must tell them. "'Im write from Shepherd's Bush. So shepherds must live dere too."

Later that night, unable to sleep, Clara took Clifford's letter to the kitchen, turned up the wick, and read.

> *Darling Clara,*
>
> *You wondering why it take so long to write, but to find time to write is difficult with me working shift work. So I hastily write this. When I leave I say I'd send for you and the children, but me never expect such harshness here. England have jobs. But soon as you earn your little money, pay rent and eat, expenses eat up the rest.*
>
> *Little by little that's all a coloured man can do in white man's country. I miss you and the children.*
>
> *I have good news at last...*

She scanned the letter again under the spluttering wick. "Clifford understand not'ing," she muttered, shaking her head. "Else why 'im place dis burden on me head?" The letter folded, she doused the wick and went to bed.

The following morning, knowing time was quicker than a blink, she decided to tell the children. But before she did, she would cook something special to sweeten the coming disappointment.

The crocus bag by the door held four dry coconuts, two plantains, a hand of dasheen, and five roots of coco. She squeezed the brown-crusted dasheen to check for disease, and placed it on the table to cook with fried chicken, rice, and peas. The two coconuts cracked in the yard and grated, she squeezed out the milk, simmered it in the Dutch pot, and then skimmed off the oil for frying the chicken.

Victuals might pacify pickney but they did not always make them happy. Clifford always carried *stagaback*, peppermint, or Paradise Plums in his pocket. Clara could live without sweetness. Before telling them what their dada wrote, she would make a special treat. She cracked the remaining coconuts, sliced them into tooth-like pieces for coconut cakes, and simmered it in water with grated ginger. When tender, she added a good portion of brown sugar and allowed it to simmer again. The mixture thick and sticky, she spooned batches onto a wet banana leaf and left them to harden.

Later that evening, having chewed their last chicken bone, the table cleared, Clara gave each child a coconut cake and read them Clifford's letter.

> *Little by little that's all a coloured man can do in white man's country. I miss you and the children. I have good news at last.*

I save just enough for you to come to England. I know it will be hard on the children to leave them, but what me to do?

So I enclose the money for you to book your passage. See if you can find somebody you trust to mind the children till we both save to send for them. The passage will cost...

No worry about the children, we send for them soon. Just get the papers ready. Me sending postal order for fifty pounds to cover expenses.

A suffocating lump formed at the back of Tilda's throat and struck her dumb. When it finally began to dislodge itself, all she could cry was, "Mama. Wat's gwan 'appen to us? Wat's gwan 'appen to us?"

Loretta Price

Maggoty Point's main traders were Mitchell Mercantile, Bata Shoe Shop, Sinclair Grocery, and Chin's Jerky Joint, which sold jerk chicken, curry goat, rice and peas, and Red Stripe beer. Campbell Bakery touted *hard-dough bread*, flat, round *bullas*, *grater cakes*, fiery *patties*, and other floured delicacies. Next to Campbell, but separate from it, Mrs. Claris Beauty Parlour straightened the nappy hair of beauty-conscious women.

Along a curving sidewalk, tie-head women in brightly coloured clothes squat over baskets of oranges and grapefruits to sell goods. Hagglers peddled fried fish fritters, cassava, and grater cakes before shop fronts. Hawkers, baskets full of homemade stagaback, stretcher, peppermints in twisted greaseproof paper, and coloured hair ribbons, called out to passers by, "Buy some'ting, nuh." A dreadlocked men sipping Red Stripe beer grinned from a sun-bleached advertisement nailed to a wooden wall. A balloon sprouted from the mouth of a busty woman in a faded floral frock and jaunty pink hat. She invited the living to step inside Marcy's Funeral Parlour and "Make Marcy Funeral Parlour give your dead loved ones a good send-off."

Finding a cool spot, near the bus depot of a busy intersection to leave Tilda, Clara ordered her to wait there until she called her. Missy, she explained, needed new school shoes, and too many pickneys would overcrowd the store.

"First t'ing," Clara said, "stay still 'ere. Second t'ing. No talk to people you no know. Else dem t'ief you." Dropping these unreassuringly words into Tilda's ears, she hurried into the crowded road with Missy and Roy.

Shielding her eyes with her right hand, Tilda followed Clara until she disappeared into the bustling crowd.

A woman guiding her donkey caught Tilda's eye. Two large open-weaved coconut baskets, overloaded with green bananas, bobbed at the animal's side. Her right hand balanced a basket of ackee on her head; the other clutched the animal's lead. As the crowd thickened around her and her donkey, she tugged its lead to draw it closer. This unjust censure seemed to irk the donkey; it reared back its muscular neck and stopped. The basket almost pitched from the woman's head. She did a quick body sway, steadied her basket and turned and cursed the animal. Its large scornful nostrils widened, ears flicked back, it twisted its stubborn neck and studied the jabbering humans sauntering in the blistering heat.

This, it seemed, was Donkey's first trip to town, and, like a man new to drink, it drank in the scene deep and full. Pulling back thick, fleshy lips from mammoth, stained teeth, it brayed at the hot humans. Donkey wanted them to understand. *Dis fool-fool woman musta t'ink she control me. When it me pleasure fe carry her produce a-market.*

A cry of *"T'ief, t'ief!"* startled Tilda. Turning, she saw two men hurtle out of Sinclair Grocery and race onto the sidewalk. Diving into the road, they weaved and shoved through the crowd as they tried to catch a woman escaping with her stolen prize.

Above the commotion and the screech of calypso lyrics, *"Give me back me shilling wid de lion 'pon it, de lion 'pon it,"* from a nearby shop, Tilda heard her mama call and ran across the road.

When she reached her mama, Clara was with a stylishly dressed, pale-skinned woman who had light brown hair. Tilda could tell from her mama's pinched mouth that she did not like the woman in the blue frock and matching hat holding a white lace parasol above her head. Seeing Tilda approach, the woman smiled mischievously and said, "Dis you odder daughter, Clara? Larks. She a small sin'ting', dough?"

Clara had just completed her shopping when she had "the monkey's luck" to bump into the woman coming out of Bata Shoe Shop. Hot, irritable, and tired, head throbbing and throat parched as dry brambles, the last thing Clara wanted was to deal with this big-mouthed woman.

Her mind wandered to a time on the hill. It was early morning. Hitching up her skirt she stepped onto the flat grass with her wattle basket in hand. "Come wid me," she said to Tilda, who stood at the rise watching red ants scurry out of a hole. As they walked, Tilda softly hummed, *"Carry me Ackee go a Linstead Market, not a quattee wud sell."* Reaching a clearing, Clara stopped beside a tamarind tree, placed the basket on the ground, and tugged at a low branch. Pulling at the brown pods, her hands full, she said to Tilda, "Hold up de basket," and dropped the pods in. Arms aching with the weight, Tilda held the basket until it was half full and her mama's arms could no longer reach the rest. She followed Clara home and helped her peel away the thin, dark brown brittle shells then scoop away the sticky brown tamarind from the seeds. Clara added brown sugar, rolled them into balls and placed a few into a jug. She then mixed it with more sugar and a scoop of baking soda. It fizzed into a refreshing drink.

She wished she could sip some now, along with the cool sorrel drink she had made that morning when she picked the dark pink flowers that grew beside the naseberry tree. After pouring hot water over the leaves and adding grated ginger, she had left them stewing before straining the liquid and sweetening it with brown sugar.

Some people were either hard of hearing or born with a crocodile skin—Clara had given Loretta every hint that she was hot and weary; Loretta ignored every one.

"Dis me second child. Tilda."

Loretta blew out of her flushed cheeks.

Clara and "hurry-come-up" Loretta Price, as she referred to the woman, had grown up together. Compared to Clara, Loretta looked a cool fashion piece in her three-inch-heel blue shoes.

"Larks, Clara," twittered Loretta, her blue-grey eyes twinkling. "Me never remember if you introduce me to you childs before. So. How me fe know all a-dem? Youself know how me is partial to pickney childs. Especially pretty pickneys like dese."

Roy had spotted a scorpion on the ground and was giving it a good mashing with his shoes when he felt his shirt neck yanked, pulling him to his mama's side.

"Larks, Loretta. Hotness bad wid me today, you know," said Clara. "Excuse me manners. Dis Missy, me eldest. Tilda. Me boy Roy." She gave Roy a slight shove in the back. "Childs. Dis me cousin Loretta Price. On me mumma's side-a-family."

With the same power to raise the hairs on Clara's neck that Loretta had possessed since their schooldays, she parted her lips and released that slow, lazy drawl of hers.

138

"Cha, Clara. Why you so formal like? Ever tell dem how we know each other? From way back?"

Clara fanned her face vigorously with her hand. "'Ave one more business matter fe settle before night catch me a-street corner, Loretta."

If Loretta had heard Clara, she made no sign of it. "How Clifford, eh? Hear lately from 'im? Hear some big scandal 'appen up de hill. Dat reason you leave?"

Clara had had enough of Loretta's gloating haughtiness. She grabbed Roy's hand and snapped at Tilda and Missy to follow.

"In bad rush, Loretta. Business waiting," she said, and left Loretta smiling that same superior smile she always hated.

A Painful Visit

Having decided to leave her children with her mother when she left for England, a week after her encounter with Loretta Price, because the children barely knew her mother, Clara decided to take them for a visit.

Dora Small Bennett was a thin, dried-up fire stick of a woman who lived in a small wattle house. A wire fence protected it from cows in the adjoining section. Almond, mango, and pimento trees sheltered it from the fierce heat.

The third in a brood of twelve Scottish, English, and African mixed-blood children, at her husband Edward Bennett's death, his plantation divided between his legitimate and *flyblown* children, Dora received a small section of his land.

A month after her husband died, Dora's children, except Clara, had gathered around to discuss her future. "Come live with us," they begged. Fiercely independent, she refused. She asked instead that they build her a small, bamboo, wattle, house on her section—just big enough for her aged body to roam on. They chortled and derided her nonsensical notion. Her eldest boy, a big-time lawyer in Kingston, owning a big showpiece house, servants, and yard boys, had turned his serious, light-skinned face upon her. Did his own mama want people to know that she lived in a bamboo house? She shamed him even to think so. The very idea!

"Mama," he gently chided, carefully rubbing his well-tended hands together; he tried humouring her in the lawyer-toned voice he always used to seduce clients into being reasonable about his hefty bill. "You can't live in a wattle hut. It's not civilised."

Dora bristled. Her hackles heated. She cocked her head like a nanny goat being goaded by a ram. She glared at her impertinent pickney. Could this be the same boy, she wondered, whose batty she had not long ago wiped?

"Gallang 'way buoy," she cried. "Gallang youself. Go live in you big fancy piece of a-house. Get me wattle one. Fe breeze up me backside. So me sleep good sleep. None a me backside pickney gwan turn me mind 'round."

From their pickney days, their mama had been as stubborn as a mule and had stayed stubborn into old age. Defeated, they agreed, with one stipulation: should she change her mind, she would come live with one of them.

Dora had lived contented in her neat, cramped bamboo house among bush land until Clara and her children crawled under her fence.

When Clara told the children that they would live with the shrivelled up woman, Tilda could not remember seeing her before. Missy showed her emotions, she silently plucked at her lace frock and stared dry eyed at her mama. Roy kicked a chair legs until Clara slapped his hand. Tilda sat still, silent, eyes like hot ashes, dead inside. She wanted to lie down, to sleep forever. Why was mama leaving them with the old witch they barely knew? What was happening to her world? Everyone she loved, every place she had lived, was disappearing. She longed for the safety of the hill and the mango tree down the gully.

Before Clara left, she rented a squeezed-up, one-bedroom place for her children and mother.

The day she left them with Dora, an intense loneliness plagued Tilda into adult life and fused into her character. She daily mourned the loss of her Grand-mama Mary Webb, the safety of the hill, and her Dada. Her fragmented world was as fleeting as morning dew on grass. Yet, with Mama and Dada gone, each day the sun still shone. Every morning, birds warbled sweetly outside. People still laughed. Why was it so?

BOOK THREE

Auntie

Dora Small Bennett had been reared in a culture of unquestionable obedience to parents, elders, and the Good Book's doctrine "Spare the rod and spoil the child." It cemented her character into flint. This old-school mentality of absolute obedience ensured sanity, respect, and order in her house with fourteen children. Her last child long married, she rarely dealt with children. Faced with guarding a new generation of children now, the constraints of her aged, arthritic body severely curtailed her ability to enforce her creeds. If she tried to do so, Missy, Tilda, and Roy simply feigned ignorance, pretended they did not understand her.

"Auntie, wat dat you a-saying?" they would ask, using the name she had ordered them to call her and faking frowns. Constantly using this ruse to question her orders, they raised the old woman's hackles and blood pressure.

Dora had taken ten of her teeth into old age—five evenly scattered on the top and five on the bottom. Clara had taught her children to show respect to elders. Whenever Dora's mouth sucked and sprayed spittle over their faces, they tolerated it, wipe the slime away and never complained. To whom could they complain?

Sometimes Dora would reach out an arm to strike an offender. This was like trying to catch a janga in a swift, muddy river. Her grand-pickneys simply slid away, ran outside.

Old age might have slowed down the contrary Jamaican matron, but she still remembered her own mum-ma's wisdom: *"Dere's more dan one way fe catch a monkey"*.

She too began to feign ignorance when the children were disobedient.

"Roy," she cackled, "youself know how you old grand mum-ma a-hard a-hearing, nuh. Eh. Eh. Buoy. Come closer beside me, nuh." Unaware of her intentions, Roy would sidle towards her pained-up knee. She bore it valiantly, the hot stab of pain when he fastened his body against her arthritic limb. Asking slyly, had he taken that extra cornmeal dumpling, or that missing piece of grater cake, should Roy's mulish mouth tighten, his head droop, or he refused to reply, she would press him for honesty. Did he know what Devil Man did to sinful boys, she would ask? Should he mutter a quiet something, or tried to run off, she would quickly grab his arm, haul him back, nip, twist, or wring his arm, backside, cheek, or any other place on his body that her bony fingers could reach. She once pinched Tilda's arm so hard, that her eyes watered. Tilda refused to cry. Her tears had died that day her mama sailed for England after her dada.

The itty-bitty cramped bedroom and eating area they had previously shared with their mama was a palace compared to the tight, shell-like rented room and derelict three-sided tin-roofed cooking outhouse that Tilda saw on their first night with Auntie. She thought it was an animal pen. That first black night, Auntie had called out for them to go look for wood. They thought she was, as Jamaicans said, "*playing de fool fe cetch de wise*". But then they saw her sour, puckered lips, they knew she was serious. They grinned sheepishly and asked where.

"Go look any place," she said, rolling her exasperated eyes, swinging her chicken neck to heaven, she seemed to ask the stars for deliverance. "Road. Under de fence. People place. Down gully because"—she stabbed an arm at some distant horizon while her almost-toothless gums sloshed and spat—"de pot can't cook wid'out fire. An' fire can't blaze wid'out wood."

Not understanding, and never gone searching for firewood in the dark before, they stared at her in bewilderment until she sucked in her lips like a babe at its mum-ma teat, "You all stay de," she sloshed. "Eh, eh. Soon hard life gwan bite you batty. So learn fast."

Missy, the oldest and the bravest, led them between dark, dense, forbidding bushes; they cowered, clutched each other, trees shivered, crickets chirped, leaves rattled and tree toads croaked. They quickly grabbed scattered sticks and ran back.

Returning with their offering and expecting cooked food on the table for eating, they showed Auntie their pathetic piles. She hooked her finger at some mysterious place and told them to follow. She would show them fire lighting. They giggled. Surely Auntie was funning.

Auntie was *not* funning.

"All a-you t'ink you some sort-a-lord an' ladies. An' me is you servant? Better you all learn quick. Once only me gwan teach you fire making. After dat. It you dat making it."

Auntie ambled to the half shell of a hut, stooped, formed four large stones into a square on the dirt, broke twigs, and laid them on the stones. Easing dry grass between the rocks, she placed the twigs on top, struck a match, pushed it at the tinder, and waited. When a faint light showed, she said to Missy, "Gal. Bend an' blow. Blow till it light good. Hurry nuh."

Missy watched the fire building with dread. She bent almost low as the old woman, extended her youthful bottom, puffed out her cheeks and blew. Huffing and wheezing she blew ashes over her face and hair.

"Cha pickey. Blow de fire nuh. No de ashes," cried Auntie. Pained at Missy's puny effort; like a saint enduring a great trial, she sucked her teeth and said, "Before we eat. We must cook. Before we cook. We must light fire. Now you live wid me. Remember dat."

As did many of Auntie's sage sayings, these words, uttered on that miserable of first nights with Auntie stayed with Tilda for the rest of her life: "Before we eat we must cook. Before we cook we must light fire."

Milk and Cheese from England

Tilda had just celebrated her eighth birthday and Missy just ten when, as part of her drive to assist her malnourished colonial children Britain sent assistance to Jamaica's schoolchildren. She shipped powered milk and cheese to Kingston; it was then trucked to each school district and on to each school. When Maggoty Point school received their quota of shiny tins they stacked them in the school kitchen beside the school.

There then followed heated discussions and teeth sucking between the headmaster and the teachers. How would the milk and cheese be given to the children? Who would do it? The headmaster asked the teachers of the older students to select three sensible senior girls for this task. Missy was one of the three selected.

Early in the morning, on the day of the planned distribution, as they travelled to school Missy told Tilda to hurry to the school kitchen as soon as her class was dismissed at recess. Tilda must not tell anyone.

At recess, as directed, Tilda ran to the kitchen where Missy and the girls guarded a table piled with the tins. Pulling Tilda to a corner, Missy told her to stretch out her right hand. She spooned a portion of milk powder into her sister's cupped hand and told her to taste. Tilda opened her mouth, touched her pink tongue to the creamy powder, and felt heaven tickling her tongue. She licked her palm clean and opened it again for two more scoops.

Next was the cheese.

A yellow sliver of cheese in her palm, Tilda daintily pinched a piece, pushed it into her mouth, and worked her tongue around the tangy morsel. It tasted much better than the sweaty, bad-smelling one her dada had once brought home. She raised her arm and studied the yellow blob on her dirty palm. How mama would cuss and scold her for not washing her hands before she ate. Mama was not here. Mama was in England. She was in Jamaica. She was hungry. What was the use of clean hands if there was nothing in them to eat?

Each time Auntie opened the blue airmail letters and read them, she would tap her dry, crooked fingers along the edges. "Dem send dem regards," she would say to the children, fixing her watery eyes upon their anxious faces. "Say dem soon send fe you." If Auntie noticed their disappointment when the letter returned to her apron pocket, she never spoke of it. "Cha, Missy," she once said when two months went by without a letter from England. "No mak' up you face so. You lucky. Got dada an' mama a-England fe send some'ting fe you. Look down road," Auntie said. Sucking her gums, she pointed at some unknown place behind her. "Plenty a-pickney like you a-starve out dere."

148

Ironing

Tilda often wondered whether Auntie's grey hair and scant-toothed mouth was the reason she messed up her clock times. What other explanation was there? Why did Auntie always confuse her daytime hours with her night-time hours? Why did she always start her daytime work just when she, Missy, and Roy wanted to drop exhausted into bed?

Nearing midnight, the room a sweltering oven, Auntie would gather the week's washing. A single-wicked kerosene lamp flickering in the dark, jumby-like shadows flittering across the bare, wooden walls, Auntie would shake every item, dip her fingers inside a can of water, sprinkle the clothes, and roll.

Missy would make a fire in the outhouse and place the iron on top. While Auntie waited for the iron to heat up, she would hum her mindless tune.

Tilda believed this was Auntie's punishment for evading her stinging pinches. Roy also stayed awake in case firewood needed fetching. Missy would bring in the hot iron; grasping it with knotted fingers, Auntie, lift, press and chant, *Since Jesus came into my heart, since Jesus came into my heart*.

On the floor, her back against the hard wooden wall, eyes heavy for sleep, Tilda pulled her thin nightie over her

149

knees, aired her underneath, and Auntie turned up the volume.

Anybody 'ere who loves my Lord?
I want to know, oh, I want to know,
Do you love my Lord?

Auntie was like a bat that livened up at night. *Slamming* and *bamming* the hissing iron over the clothes in the sultry, dark night, her loose shift flapped around her bony shanks.

Sing it in de valley if you love my Jesus,
Sing it in de valley if you love my Lord,
I want to know, oh, I want to know,
Do you love my Lord?

The only time Auntie paused in her fervour was when the iron cooled. "Tilda," she would call. "Tak' iron. Set on fire, nuh. An'. Mind it hot-hot, eh." Easing into a chair, shaking her grey head, she would close her eyes. "Bones getting old an' worrisome fe dis sort a-t'ing. But. Since de Good Lawd commissioned me. Fe do 'Im bidding. Who a-me fe argue wid 'Im." Ballooning out her cheeks, she would seal her lips from further complaint.

One night, a small pile remained to be ironed when Tilda carried the iron into the star-studded night. Afraid that the dreaded Rolling Calf or jumby hid behind a bush to jump on her, she hurried to the makeshift hut and placed the iron on the dying embers. Checking for wood and finding none, she knew she had to go look for more in bush land. Ghostly shadows surrounded her. Trees took on the guise of *duppies*. Jumping at a deep chortling croak, she grabbed the warm iron and ran inside. "More still left fe iron, Auntie?" she asked, trembling.

150

"Larks, pickney," said Auntie, pushing herself up and mopping her moist face with the flat of her hand. "Two t'ings only left fe finish."

Without testing the iron for hotness, Auntie took the iron, smoothed out Tilda's school blouse and Missy's skirt, placed the iron on the table and told the exhausted three to go to bed.

Christmas 1954

Two months after Tilda's eighth birthday a round cardboard barrel arrived from England for Christmas. Auntie hoisted it onto the table, undid the strings, and wound them around her fingers. She eased away the paper, smoothed it out for later use, and laid it aside. The letter taped inside the barrel read, she pushed it into her pocket.

"You dada an' mama say dem miss you," she said to the solemn, staring faces. "Send Christmas barrel fe you all."

She peered inside the barrel, removed a flat box, read the name written on it and gave it to Tilda—colouring pencils. Her mama and dada had remembered she liked colouring and did not own any coloured pencils. She also received a fair-haired doll in a blue frock and a pair of black patent shoes.

There was a small black purse for Missy, a green cotton dress, black patent shoes, and a silver bracelet; Auntie allowed her to slip on her wrist to admire before taking it for safekeeping.

Roy squealed with delight when he saw his red train. He later tormented his sisters with his *fe-fee whistle*. He also received new shoes.

Auntie showed them her two cardigans and the tube of ointment for her arthritic knees but quickly folded and put away the four pairs of bloomers and vests. The barrel finally empty, Tilda was still admiring her colours.

"No tak' dem school," Auntie warned. "Else t'ief gwan t'ief dem, child."

Tilda was not listening. Tenderly touching the crayons, she could almost hear the envious squeals of the girls at school.

"Come from foreign," she would boast. "Me dada an' mama send dem all de way from England fe me."

Christmas dinner would be special, Auntie told them. Their dada and mama had sent extra money for it.

The table set, the children waited and waited for Auntie, she had been a long time cooking dinner in the outhouse. Missy finally decided to go see why she was taking so long. Nearing the outhouse, she found Auntie flat on her face in the dirt. Mosquitoes, droning flies, and an army of ants were devouring their Christmas dinner.

"Lawd-a-massy," moaned Auntie as Missy helped her to her feet. "Look wat tribulation fall 'pon me head. Look wat me a-do." She shook her head. "Food fall," she wailed. "How it a-'appen? Me no know? Backside, wat we fe eat now?"

Stumbling towards the house, leaning on Missy's arm, she mumbled, "All me a-do is turn fe check fire when me toe buck on stone. Food fling from me hand."

Christmas dinner with Auntie was quiet and sombre. They nibbled slices of bread and butter and washed it down with bush tea.

Minna Thomas

Tilda had adjusted to school life and had made some friends. Despite Auntie's warning, to not take her colours to school, after the Christmas break, she hid them in her school bag and sneaked them to school.

Anxious to show her friends her colours, she fidgeted and shifted on the bench. Dismissed at last, she raced to the almond tree in the schoolyard and showed her crayons to a few girls. News spread fast, like scarlet fever. *Tilda Webb got a colouring box from England. Come fe see.* Girls scurried and gawked; they oohed and aahed—except for one sour-faced girl.

Minna Thomas had disliked Tilda at first sight. A known bully, she previously had no reason to trouble Tilda's world. Two inches taller than Tilda, and twice as stout, Minna's broad chest and muscular arms strained against a white blouse stuffed into a pleated skirt.

"Humph," Minna said, she jabbed her elbows into the ribs of a tittering girl admiring Tilda's colours and blocking her view.

"You's a-liar, Tilda Webb," Minna said. Her fists fixed onto her hefty hips, she funnelled her mouth into a piggy snout. "You daddy no send you dem colours. T'ink you thief it!"

The other girls' mouths snapped shut. Unafraid, yet wary of the bully, they moved away from Tilda as Minna bustled up to her.

"T'ink you's special, Tilda Webb?" Minna sneered. Her small, rat-like teeth bared, she fanned Tilda with her stinky breath. "Well, Mistress Tilda Webb. All me a-say is dis. You's one natty-bump-head pickney. An' a dutty liar." She flung out her right arm and slapped Tilda's hand. The crayons rose in the air and then fell to the ground.

Tilda's mouth opened wide into an *O* when Minna raised her right foot and stomped on the crayons.

The right heel of her shoe on the crayons, Minna ground them into the dirt.

"Dem no so pretty now. Mistress Tilda Webb."

Tilda felt as if she were in a dream. Her head exploded like an over-blown balloon pricked by a sharp pin. Her fists automatically clenched hard as cricket balls. Right arm jerked backwards, she rammed it into Minna's belly, the girl toppled backwards onto the ground.

Minna quickly scrambled to her feet; Tilda Webb must have had a lucky punch. She dusted grass and dirt from her skirt and matted hair, crouched like an enraged bull and sneered, "You's dead, Tilda Webb. Gwan box you redibo head offa you redibo neck." She made a fat fist, lunged at Tilda, and rubbed a sweaty *ratta* fist onto Tilda's nose.

Tilda had a peculiarity. Whenever threatened or under stress, her head took her to another dimension—usually a place of safety, other times a dark, vengeful hole. Minna's sweaty, stinky, fist, hard on her nose pulled Tilda to that dark vengeful hole. Her mind flew to the hill—Rufus boxing down her dada—his land and house that his brothers had thieved. Injustice and rage spiking her veins, she quickly sidestepped the girl, slugged a right into her belly; Minna

155

slumped forward; she shook her head like a wounded gladiator.

When a right uppercut stung Tilda's cheek and flung her backwards, she squared her fists, protected her face and threw another wicked right at the bully. Then, possessed by a demon it seemed, she rammed punch after punch into Minna's belly. Her legs buckled and she fell like timber onto the ground. Fists clenched, her thin arms throbbing, her breath sharp and short, Tilda leapt onto Minna's back, grabbed a tuft of her hair, and yanked back her head. A blood-curdling screech splintered the air as Tilda rained blow after blow onto the girl's back.

Missy heard the uproar from another area of the playground; she raced to see what was happening. She pushed through the cheering bodies. Her shamey-darling sister was beating the daylights out of a girl almost twice her size.

"Tilda, stop," she cried, unable to believe her eyes. She lunged forward, tried to pull Tilda's flailing arms away from the girl, Tilda shrugged her off and kept up the battering.

"Tilda. Me say stop," begged Missy, now almost in tears. "Stop nuh. Gal bawling. Stop. Tilda. Please. Me say stop. Else you kill de pickney."

Tilda did not seem to hear Missy. Still fisting the girl, Missy finally grabbed her arms and pulled her off Minna.

Mr. Conrad Greaves

Maggoty Point School headmaster, Conrad Greaves, had an interesting history that the older heads labrish to every resident and greenery that rattled with insects.

It was said that the birth woman who had cut his umbilical cord had laid him between his mum-ma's breasts and prophesied, "Pickney puny. Soon dead." The woman had pulled hundreds of *sicky-sicky* pickneys from their mothers' wombs; she had also witnessed plenty of them placed in the ground in small boxes. Death to her was closely linked with birth. Eight bare-backside pickneys already ran wild in their mum-ma's yard. Her reckoning was, should this pickney died, it was one less mouth to feed.

Her ordeal over, the mum-ma wrapped her tiny weed into a piece of raw calico and nursed him on every bush herb in Jamaica. Still a runt at six she heard of an obeah woman with a good cure for puny pickneys. She dragged him through cane pieces and bush land into the woman's dark, latrine-scented, evil-feeling wattle shack. Infested with bones, bullfrog carcasses, chicken feathers, and lizard skins, he ran outside and vomited. His mum-ma pulled him back inside the shack.

His head against his mum-ma's hip she labrish with the hag who gestured wildly with her arms. They jabbered things

157

he did not understand. It seemed that a bargain had been struck for his mum-ma's hand reached inside her crocus bag to pull out a not-long-dead chicken to show to the tie-head, yellow-faced she who puckered her sour lips and waggled her head, tinkling her plentiful earrings. *Bam, bam* went his mum-ma's agitated hip against his head when she again dipped inside her sack. Ugly woman's eyes rolled excitedly. She peeled back her lips from her almost toothless gums, grabbed mum-ma's Captain Morgan rum and the chicken with blood-coloured claws, pulled mum-ma closer and whispered in her ear.

His visit to yellow woman shocked him so much that he never remembered leaving her shack. Back in his own yard, his mum-ma said to him, "From 'ere, no move you batty. Soon come."

She cleaned the old tin bucket by the door of the house with coconut husks and ashes and then disappeared. The hot sun almost *crisped him up* before she finally returned.

"From 'ere, no move you batty," she said again, hoisting him in the air she dumped him inside the bucket. "Soon come." She left. Wilting and sweating, the midday heat and sun cooked the sticky stink inside the bucket, it rose to his nose. He wiggled his toes and sniffed the hot putrid slime.

Pig poop.

His own mum-ma had placed him in pig poop— exchanged her good chicken and Captain Morgan rum so he would grow in pig poop? He almost fainted from the heat. The stench almost killed him dead. Knowing that mum-ma had plenty of pickney and couldn't always watch over him, he pulled up his right foot to escape. A sharp slap struck his batty. Howling, he cursed his mum-ma. She got bad advice for her good rum and chicken. She didn't listen.

"From 'ere, no move you batty. Soon come," she said. Arms akimbo, she stared hard at him like a mad dog.

The town folks broadcast that a truly peculiar thing happened—Conrad Greaves never moved his batty from the pig poop; he sprouted like a tall weed.

✳ ✳ ✳ ✳

The headmaster's office was small, cramped, and hot. Two tarnished metal frames displaying his certificates clung to rusty nails on a wall. Directly below these, a shabby three-shelved wooden cabinet housed weevil-holed textbooks, ink bottles, pens, and school implements. Locked inside were slingshots, knives, a cutlass, and sundry confiscated weapons. On the third shelf of a small bookcase near the window, a well used, dark brown, leather strap, curled its tail. A shuttered sash window at the rear of the room allowed a hot breeze entrance. Only three chairs could fit into this small office—the headmaster's in front of the window, and two strategically placed before his desk. This small, intimate, wooden, haven was Conrad Greaves refuge. Here he hid from the tribulations of school life. He would lock the door, prop his feet onto his desk, close his eyes, and vegetate for a while. Enjoy his midday feast; prepared the night before by Tunkus, she had lovingly packed it inside his work bag.

Conrad Greaves had just pulled the side drawer of his desk, opened up the salt fish, ackee, and boiled green bananas, about to dip his finger into his victuals when the door handle rattled. A woman bawled for him to come quick.

Sparse eyebrows arched, he raked the two over with his eyes and frowned. He pushed aside the books at his elbow and hugged his body against the hard wooden chair. Conrad Greaves sucked his teeth. He was vexed.

These two pickney had the backside feistiness to disturb his afternoon rest and food. *How long dis gwan tak'*, he wondered. *Why must school pickney be so aggravating?* Why he had become a schoolmaster, he didn't know. He supposed his mum-ma had known what she was doing when she set him in pig poop. *Day been long an' vexing. Better get it out-a dem quick.*

Here was another peculiarity of Jamaicans. No matter how well educated, stylish, or travelled they might be, whenever stressed or agitated, Jamaicans always reverted to raw, unadulterated patwa. "Wat dis me hear 'bout you fighting?" He pulled himself close to the desk, to show them he was vexed. "Both a-you hard-a-hearing? Dis sort a-t'ing me no allow at me school, you know? Cha!"

Tilda's eyelids flickered. The headmaster was talking patwa. Her teacher's ruler licked the knuckles of those who talked patwa in her class.

Conrad Greaves waited for an explanation. When both heads drooped, and the mouths stayed mute, he hit the desk with his fist. "Reasons give me when me ask misses? Whole day long. Me no 'ave."

Tilda's legs twitched nervously. She slyly eyed her enemy from under her lashes. When she got home Auntie would certainly give her a-lick-batty. Even worse, Auntie might write a blue airmail letter to Dada and Mama in England, saying their daughter had disgraced them at school—even though it was Minna's fault for boxing her colours out of her hand. Minna had mashed them like cow *poo-poo* in the dirt. As she considered this damning evidence against Minna, her conscience quickly corrected her. *Eh. Eh. It you dat disobey*

Auntie. You dat tak' de colours a-school. Dat de reason you gwan gets lick batty from Headmaster. An' from Auntie.

Minna was the first to speak. "She...she...she." Rearing back her defiant head, she locked eyes with the headmaster. When his eyes narrowed, and his mouth puckered as if he were sucking a lime, her explanation dried up. Lips glued together, she turned her head from the headmaster so he could not see her eyes.

Proud that her mama had always taught her to tell the truth, Tilda saw her chance to speak. "She, she call me a...liar."

"You's. Me, me..." Minna blustered interrupting Tilda. She must immediately enlighten the headmaster. She was not to blame for the fight. "Master Greaves. It no me dat fe blame fe de fight. Tilda Webb dat-a-start it. Tilda Webb it be dat a-box me down. An' Tilda Webb it be dat try fe bald up me head."

The headmaster knew he could no longer look at the wispy hair, puffy eyes, and dust-covered face without bursting into a backside laugh. He swung to face the window.

Me must, he thought, trying not to laugh. *Must. No matter wat. Silence de rawted tickle. A-threatening fe mak' me bust out laughing. Me must face dem wid me serious face.* He quietly groaned, "Rawted. No. Dis no funning situation. Mak' me hear de rest a-de lies." He firmed his lips into a hard line and turned.

Minna's fables enlarged. Pausing in her ramble for air, trying hard to avoid eye contact with the headmaster, she glanced at the strap straddling the shelf. Had she enough to sting the batty of *redibo* Tilda Webb? If not, when the headmaster released her, she would salt it good and proper. She dragged her eyes from the belt and clenched her backside in anticipation.

Well, thought Tilda, *me no letting de liar get away wid dat.* Minna Thomas was one big liar. The barefaced coward was pretending innocence. The instant Missy dragged her from the *dutty* liar, her mouth had stayed frozen—because, schoolyard said, "Wat a-'appen in de schoolyard a-stay in de schoolyard." Minna had changed the game with her Anancy story.

"She. She call me. a natty-bump-head pickney," Tilda said, galled that her enemy had used this degrading Jamaican expression. She was not a dunce whose hair flaked off, no matter how much Vaseline was plastered on it. "Liar too she did call me. Say. Say me dada never send me colouring box from England. Say me t'ief dem. Den box dem from me hand. An' mash dem wid her dutty foot." Her heart heaved like the waves of the sea. "Also. Push her stinky mout' in me face. A-saying she gwan box me down."

The girl sitting like a stone at the riverside while Tilda's accusation washed over her, knew her only salvation was denial. She shook her head. "Never! You's. Me. Never!"

Vengeance fuelling her veins, Minna turned to Tilda. "You's...you's de liar, Tilda Webb."

The quick scrape of the headmaster's chair on the wooden floorboards echoed in the small space. Strong, stringy arms grabbed Minna off her seat and rammed her down—hard.

Conrad Greaves was deeply vexed when he sat back down. Maggoty Point School harboured every problem under the heavens. What to do with these two. He recognised flimflam when he saw it. Was one punishment equal for both? His fingers drumming on the desk, he glanced at his watch and turned to the window again. *Only*

162

one o'clock. It still hot like hell. When a determined fly squeezed through the shutters and zoomed above his head, he wondered if it was worth killing. *Dese two! If me allow me guard fe slide now. Give way to de bubbling backside laugh still t'reatening fe erupt. Wind gwan whirl its dust fe plenty teeth kissing 'bout me slackness. Me is de headmaster. Terrifying dem is me duty.* He hardened his face again and turned.

Tilda Webb. Father. Clifford. Mother. Clara Bennett. Sweet, sweet looking woman. Both a-England. Decent family from wat me hears. His eyes went to Minna. *Dis one different. Bully some a-say. Hear her name plenty a-time. Connected wid trouble. First time afore me dough. Expect it no be her last. Wat fe do? A slap on de face, a fist in de back a-one t'ing. But dem two last year dat bring knife an' bottle glass to school fe fight. Dat some'ting different.*

Tilda was easing her bottom from the piece of wood sticking through the chair when Conrad Greaves swung back.

"As me a-say. Both a-you know me no allow fighting." He suddenly remembered. Wasn't his darling Tunkus's mother some relative of Clara Bennett? With all the mingling in the district, he could never place who belonged to which family. What would his sweetness say when he told her this? She would say, "Pickney must protect demself a school. Schoolyard is one dangerous place." He glanced again at the time. *Tree more meetings fe go before me going home time.*

"Get up," he barked, coming to a decision. The startled two jumped up. "Push out you hand," he said, looking at Minna. He pulled the strap from the shelf and lashed three good licks onto Minna's outstretched right hand. "Now. Gallang. No mak' me catch you 'ere twice."

Head bowed, Minna rubbed her stinging palm down her skirt, shuffled out, and closed the door.

Tilda's lips quivered. Now she would get hers. Eyes squeezed tight, she extended her right hand and clenched her teeth.

"Come 'ere, Tilda Webb."

She opened her eyes. "Miss," the headmaster said, scowling at her. "Wat punishment you t'ink you deserve?"

"Me no know, Mister Greaves." Head bowed, she studied her shoes.

A thin smile hitched up the sides of Conrad Greaves mouth. "Must 'ave discipline in me school? Let me see dat hand again."

She trembled. Extending her hand she closed her eyes.

"If me wife Tunkus wouldn't give me hell when me gets home," said the headmaster, his voice echoing in the room, "you'd feel de sting a-dis!" His strap lashed onto the desk.

Tilda smiled nervously when she closed the door.

Tilda and Coolie Girl

At recess one day, Missy tried to cajole Tilda into playing jacks in the graveyard behind the school. Tilda shuffled her feet in the red dirt and shook her head. She would not visit the jumby house, even in daylight. Missy puckered her lips in disappointment, opened her hand, and showed Tilda her jacks. Plenty of her friends were already playing there, so why was Tilda always such a shy baby she had asked. Tilda scrunched up her mouth and dragged her feet after her sister to the tumbledown fence at the back of the school that divided it from the Methodist church graveyard. They dipped under the wire and followed the bushy path that led to the neglected, weed-infested burying ground where schoolchildren only visited in daylight. The marble and concrete headstones were a favourite to play jacks and marbles.

Monuments for Maggoty Point's former citizens had once populated the Methodist church graveyard. Years of hurricane and storms had unearthed most from their resting places to deposit at tree trunks, roadsides and fields. Some clung precariously against cliff sides. Overtime creeping vegetation eventually suffocated them from memory.

Tilda reluctantly followed Missy who was hurrying through the slumbering dead to find the best smooth surface on which to play her game.

"Look Tilda," said Missy, darting between two graves. "Dere. Come." She pointed, raced towards a beautiful specimen, and plonked her bottom onto the edge of a marble square. Her jacks spread out, she turned to see if any of her friends were also playing.

"Wat she doing 'ere?" said Missy, scrunching up her nose in distaste.

"Who?" Tilda swung her neck to look.

"She," Missy yelled, wanting the other students to hear. "Coolie. Why she 'ere?" Missy pointed to a girl.

Missy might not care if the girl heard her. Tilda did. Embarrassed that her sister had caused the other students to stare at them and the girl, Tilda bowed her head and sneaked a long look at the girl.

Head bent, a slight, dark-skinned girl was intent on her solitary play. She threw a tiny ball into the air. Before it fell, she quickly plucked each metal jack with delicate fingers. She never looked up once. Thick, rope-like plaits tied with narrow black ribbons swung from a scrawny neck. Tilda knew that her hair swarmed with lice. Remembering her mama's warning, she scratched her head. The girl lifted her head and looked towards Tilda and Missy. Her huge, solemn black eyes stared at them for a while, then, lowering her head; she scooped up her jacks, dropped them into her skirt pocket, slid off the slab and hurried through the graves towards the fence.

"Coolie. Coolie," cried Missy, jumping on top of the gravestone and yelling at the girl. "Dirty lice-head coolie."

"No say so Missy," said Tilda, pulling at her sister's skirt. "It's wicked. Why you a-call her a coolie?"

166

"How me fe know?" said Missy. "It's just wat dey call dem."

Tilda did not understand. How could Missy dislike a girl she barely knew?

"T'ink she hear you, Missy?"

"Me no care."

Tilda cared. Her marble pinging on the gravestone, a sad feeling fluttered around her belly button. She felt bad for the dark-skinned, black-haired, curry-and garlic-scented people that Jamaicans called "*Coolies*." The few at the school kept to themselves. Other students avoided them and called them names. Years later, Tilda better understood this childhood incident. Coolies were bonded East Indians who had come to Jamaica to work on the plantations after emancipation. A grey-haired Clara told Tilda that when she was a young woman, Coolies lived near her home in long, low hutlike buildings.

"Dere," cried Missy, triumphantly slamming down the marble just as the school bell rang.

Wash Day with Auntie

A wash day with Auntie meant an early morning wake-up and an arduous, long walk dragging dirty clothes to the riverside. In time, Tilda believed that Auntie's late-night ironing and dawn clothes-washing was her way of trying to beat the rooster—a competition to see who could wake first and go to sleep last. Though her young brain often pondered these perplexities, it never received a sane answer.

"Wake-up time," Auntie trumpeted at raw dawn.

"Auntie. It no school day," said Tilda, rubbing her eyes. "Why we wake so soon?"

"Gwan wash clothes a-river, pickney," Auntie replied. She never wavered, nor once pitied them. Why should she? Who else was their protector? Who else must teach them respect, obedience, and life's harsh lessons?

The week's dirty washing stuffed into pillowcases—down gullies, through bush land, and over fields they trudged. Finally pushing through a brambly clearing, they faced the thunderous foam of the Rio Grande as it tumbled and roared down the mountainside.

"Over dere. Tak' dem over dere," Auntie pointed, her voice shrill above the deafening roar. Straining with her bundle over rocks and stones to a calm spot on the riverbank, she settled her pointy bottom on top of a large flat stone. The pillowcases emptied and sorted into piles, she clutched the bar of soap with her rheumatic fist, plunged it into the river, and lathered each item. Rubbing, scrubbing and rinsing, and finally twisting, she called, "Hang on stone or bush fe dry, nuh."

Only Roy loved wash day. Only his legs sliced the clear sparkling water in search of crabs and janga among the weeds and rocks. Sometimes he found the small, black, hard-shelled barnacle-like crustaceans Jamaicans called *busu* that clung to the side of rocks. Prying them from their sticking places, he dropped them into his tin can for Auntie to boil-up. Tilda, who was always hungry, hated them. She had tried them once then refused to eat the things that looked like fat black ants and tasted like grit.

Auntie never allowed them to lather the wash. Pickney would waste good soap, she said. Sometimes she threw a few articles into the swirling water for Missy or Tilda to swish and rinse. Once, after giving Roy's clothes a good scrub, she decided to cool her arthritic legs in the river. When she glanced up, she flapped her arms in alarm. "Run, Tilda! Pickney! Missy, run! Run before river drag de clothes away."

Skirts bunched in hands, legs flying over the clear water, Missy and Tilda chased the disappearing clothes. Spluttering, panting, drenched from head to toe, they frantically tried grabbing shorts, baggies, and vest before they floated away like a convoy of ships.

Water was plentiful and free, but riverside washing could be hazardous. A stone must always anchor down the washing, or the swirling water would drag it out to sea. Rafters taking tourists down the Rio Grande often fished out articles of clothing with their long bamboo poles.

Running, wet to her skin, water stinging her eyes, birds darting overhead, Tilda wondered if her dada and mama in

England knew they chased washing down the Rio Grande. Paddling to a shallow area, she bent and searched in the river for the small shrimps Jamaicans called "*janga*." Spotting a quick flash of silver, she plunged her hand into the water. Like the memory of her dada and mama, the small shrimp vanished. Did she really have a dada called Clifford? A mama called Clara? Did they really leave for England? Were they really like the janga in the river, just a fleeting flash in her memory?

Change 1955

To enlarge and expand her great empire, in 1655, Britain sent Admiral Penn and General Venables to the New World. They mishandled an attempt to seize Hispaniola from Spain; instead they attacked Jamaica, one of Spain's weaker islands, and seized it on May 10, 1655.

Three hundred years later, in 1955, Jamaica prepared to celebrate Britain's victory over Spain. Haiti's president, General Paul Magloire, was to attend the anniversary celebrations. As part of her Caribbean tour, Princess Margaret Rose, Queen Elizabeth's glamorous socialite sister, would also visit. The governor of Puerto Rico, Senor Luis Munoz Marin, would open the Agricultural Fair at Denbigh. Important as these upcoming events were, they did not disturb the lives of Missy, Tilda, Roy, or Auntie. From daybreak to the close of her eyes on her pillow at night, Tilda endured a hard, relentless life of survival.

The day Auntie sliced open the airmail letter that would change everything and read it to them, they showed no emotion. Had they not heard the same promises many times before? "Soon we send for you," yet they still lived with Auntie who, like an old hen, scratched for food to keep them alive.

If a child left in the care of relatives in Jamaica took sick, the letter notifying the parents in a foreign country would often arrive *after* that child had died and been buried. Parents working in foreign places did not have the money or means to visit sick children, much less their graves. In time, that child would become a memory.

When Auntie re-read the letter, they still kept silent. Tilda had learnt the saying *"First time you see monkey, 'im ugly. Plenty time you see monkey, 'im pretty."* Abandoned, the children blew fire, accepted their fate, and adjusted to what life threw at them. They survived. Their former life with their dada and mama was a memory. Auntie was their reality.

"You no hear wat me a-saying," Auntie cried, scrunching up her lips and kissing her vexed teeth. "Dem sending fe you! Eh, eh, pickney. Hear wat dem is saying?" She tapped her fingers against the thin blue sheet and read again.

> *We are sending for Missy, Tilda, and Roy. In the letter, we send a postal order for forty pounds. Cash it at Maggoty Point Post Office. Make sure them no thief you. Buy clothes, shoes, hat, and anything they need. Passport picture and the rest. We will send more money soon next time we write.*

The children did not respond, silent and motionless, Auntie pushed the letter to Missy. "Read fe youself. See if it no true-true wat me a-saying."

Missy glanced at her, pulled the letter towards her, scanned it, pushed it to Tilda, and ran into the yard.

A Royal Visit

Six weeks before the celebrations Mrs. Reid placed her pen on her desk and closed her textbook. Her bottom snug into the hard wooden chair, she scanned and considered the sixteen girls and fifteen boys in her class. Like a John crow devouring the putrid flesh of a four day dead cow, she dissected each child, row by row. Had she wasted her teaching time on them? A titter from a troublemaker left of the room alerted her to misbehaviour. Arched forward, hawk-like, she glared over her spectacles at the disruptive boy who had *jucked* his elbow into his neighbour's ribs.

Muffled sounds echoed in the large, sweltering space. Heads bent, pens dipped into inkwells, her class scrawled lazily. Some blotted their exercise books. If a slight doubt still lingered in the far regions of her brain, it never marred her ability to sensibly reason. Her duty was clear: try to pry open her students' contrary Jamaican skulls and inspire them to do great things once they left her class.

She thought deeply, at the same time quietly admonishing herself to cast aside all the uncharitable Jamaican patwa that was trying to invade her selection process. Hard as she tried, some *did* slide in. *Cha. 'Im not'ing but a-coco head an' green banana water buoy. Soon as dat gal leave school. She gwan drop a few pickney. Dat buoy always a-looking fe put*

173

up a fight. 'Im, 'im gwan roam town wid a cutlass looking fe chop somebody up. Wat chance 'ave she. Wid twelve pickney already at her house. 'Im show promise. But can 'im mum-ma an' pup-pa lend 'im attention?

No sooner did she vent than she repented.

She sat stiff and upright, back hard against the chair, like a three-times-starched doily. Mr. Greaves had consulted all the teachers about the tremendous event. A prominent person of great importance would be visiting their town. Excitement boiled from the headmaster like Jamaican pepperpot soup. Maggoty Point School would perform before this person of importance, the headmaster said to his staff, mopping his flushed face. All the teachers except Mrs. Reid broke out in patwa. Which class? Who would decide? What would be performed? When Mr. Greaves turned to Mrs. Reid and said she would organize everything for their school's performance before the Princess, even more patwa voices rang out. When complaints of favouritism were brandished about, the headmaster stood firm. Mrs. Reid, he said, had the experience. She had been to foreign countries. Seeing Paris, Rome, Italy, and England, made her no dry-land tourist, but a true tourist. She and only she would make Maggoty Point School proud. The patwa grumbles dried up. It was settled.

Her choices were few. Who could quickly absorb instructions and then carry them out to perfection? Time was short. The elections over, a glorious event would burst forth on Jamaica. She never dreamed such an event would ever happen in her lifetime. The headmaster had advised her to prepare immediately. Time was of the essence. The ones chosen must never say, "Mum-ma sick an' me can't come." Or, "Too far fe walk." Or, "Pup-pa want me a-bush." These images were too painful to contemplate. Her selection must be both sensible and reliable.

Tilda carefully dipped her pen into the inkwell. Desperate not to blot her work, she slowly wrote in her exercise book *Jamaica is an island.*

"Tilda Webb. Come forward."

Tilda jumped. A large black blot of ink splashed over the word *Jamaica.* Her belly lurched; she nervously glanced towards her teacher. Why had she called her? Her belly tight with nerves, she laid down her pen and dutifully slid across the knees of the sniggering students. Ignoring whispers that teacher was going to serve Mistress Hoity-Toity Tilda Webb hot sauce on her batty; she approached her teacher's desk.

"Call me, Teacher?" she said, looking up.

Mrs. Reid looked down and saw fear on her pupil's face.

"Do not be alarmed, Tilda. Nothing is amiss. Mr. Greaves has informed me that our Princess, Princess Margaret of England, will soon visit Jamaica. As part of her visit, she will come to Maggoty Point. Our school will perform for her. Mr. Greaves has asked me to select eight students for the performance. You and seven others will dance for our Princess. Would you like that?"

Tilda's mouth swung open and then snapped shut. "A wat dat you a-sayin, Teacher?" said Tilda in raw patwa. She stared wide-eyed at her teacher.

"Are you deaf, Tilda Webb?" Mrs. Reid's neck jerked back sharply. She shook her irritated head. "I sincerely hope my selection of you is not a mistake?"

Tilda felt she was drowning. No one was saving her. Her knees knocked together like cymbals. The only bright light in the dark cesspool sucking at her head was the fact that Auntie had forced her to change her baggy that morning before she left for school. If she fainted, clear onto the floor, in front of her teacher, at least her baggy would be clean. "A...a wat? Me no understand Teacher. Wat you a-saying Teacher."

"Tilda Webb," said Mrs. Reid, sighing at the grating patwa. "Have I not taught you—"

"Enough!" she cried, turning to her class and glaring to extinguish further giggles. "Silence. I *will not* tolerate discord. I have not finished speaking. Now." She returned her attention to her stricken-eyed pupil.

"Tilda Webb. I believe I have taught you well enough, instructed you tolerably in the Queen's English, made you understand that I do not tolerate patwa in my class." Like a general unwilling to surrender absolute defeat to an enemy, she stiffened her shoulders. "I understand, from what I have been told, that soon you will leave us to join your parents in England. Do you wish, the instant you open your mouth in England to sound like an illiterate buffoon? Before leaving us, you must try to cultivate their language. Understand?"

Tilda did not understand one word but dutifully nodded her bewildered head and stared up in silence.

It was then that Mrs. Reid detected terror in her young student's eyes. The child did not comprehend the rare honour being bestowed upon on her.

"Well, enough. As I said, Tilda," she said, slowly and deliberately to try to calm Tilda's fears, "Princess Margaret will soon be here. We shall perform a dance before her." Mrs. Reid became lost in her daydream. Her eyes glazed over. She purred and savoured every word, as if licking honey from a spoon. "An evening of entertaining and celebration will be held in Princess Margaret's honour. Our school will entertain royalty."

Tilda's heart clanged against her chest. *Teacher a-just talking stupidness. Why pick me?* Heat flooded the back of her neck and armpits. Her head felt funny.

"How me gwan do dat, Teacher?" She grabbed the edge of Mrs. Reid's desk to steady her shakes. Then, remembering the admonition to talk speaky-spokey English, she quickly corrected herself. "How will I do that, Mrs. Reid? Who will teach me?"

"I shall, Tilda," she said, ignoring the patwa slip. "I shall be delighted to teach you all."

Though Tilda's head throbbed with *All me gwan do is mak' a poppy show a-meself in front a-de special Princess from England. England is where Dada an' Mama is. Maybe dem come visit me wid de Princess*, she obediently nodded her head and said, "Yes."

"Excellent. You are very lucky." Mrs. Reid smiled a rare smile, softening her usually stern face. Her pupil did not yet fathom the great privilege offered to her. It was obvious that her declaration had confused and distressed Tilda.

"To be selected is a rare honour, Tilda. Mr. Greaves believes you, with others not yet chosen, will do very well. It is indeed wonderful and rare for a child like you to have an opportunity to dance before a princess. It is something you will treasure and remember forever."

Mrs. Reid liked the child and hoped she would make something of herself when she sailed to England. She pursed her lips and crinkled her eyes. What she would give to be Tilda. The coloured fabrics and dance steps floated before her. The calypso.

She would make Jamaica proud.

૪ᗡ   ᑕᱺ

Telling Missy

Her teacher's words jangling in her head, Tilda could not concentrate on Missy's labrish as they trudged the long journey home. Biting her lips, brow crinkled, she tried to think of how to tell her sister what her teacher had said. Finally, remembering that her class was certain to scatter her scandal, and wanting Missy to hear what Mrs. Reid had told her first, Tilda shyly told her sister the news.

"She a-say a-wat?" Missy shrieked, squinting at Tilda. She stopped abruptly in the middle of the dirt track.

"Dance, me a-say. Want me fe dance before de English Princess." The instant she said it, she regretted it. Best to have let Missy hear it at school.

Missy smirked and screwed up her face in astonishment. Tilda knew her sister did not believe her. Missy asked Tilda to explain slowly, no crying or stuttering. When she had wrinkled the crab meat out of Tilda, Missy twirled and chuckled on the dusty road, like a drunken man in a brewery. She giggled. The idea—her timid shamy darling of a sister prancing and dancing before the princess. What a backside joke.

Tilda shrank inside her skin. It wasn't right for Missy to act so—laugh at her like a jackass. All she had done was explain, in the best way she could, what had happened in the classroom.

"But, why you?" asked Missy. She now stood completely still, no longer giggling. "Plenty better an' prettier dan you a-school."

Missy's barefaced honesty wounded Tilda more than Mrs. Reid's patwa chastisement. Fists jammed onto her slight hips, she said, "Me no know why Teacher a-pick me fe de dance. But it no right fe you fe tell me shame to de wind."

Missy whacked her school bag against a bush. "You feared?" she asked feeling, just a little contrite. "Glad it no me. Else me brain gwan boil wid worry morning till night time. Mak' me wet me baggy." Missy giggled at her joke. *Imagine? Her dutty baggy sliding down her legs before de Princess!*

"No know," said Tilda, moaning and furrowing her brow. What did she care about Missy's stinky underwear. All of the Blue Mountains rested on her shoulders. "Wat me fe tell Auntie?"

Missy who was doing another spin, stopped in mid-twirl. Not since her dada and mama left for England had she giggled like a careless colt. Skylarking never happened much with Auntie. Arthritis was lately hampering Auntie's body more and more. Sometimes, stooping, she could barely rise. Her *pinchy* fingers trembled when she made a grab for the children. More of Auntie's care was falling to Missy.

Her nose dramatically pointing upwards, Missy made a serious face, hocked, and cleared her throat. "Tell Auntie, Teacher say that by royal command, you. Tilda Webb. Of Maggoty Point. A back-a-bush-country-town in Jamaica. Have been issued. With a royal proclamation. To perform. Before the Princess Margaret Rose. Should you refuse? Off goes your head!"

Missy chortled. She clutched her side, where a stitch had struck. When she was once more sensible, she picked up her bag and continued her journey.

"Where you learn fe speak so good, Missy?" asked Tilda, impressed with her sister's almost perfect mimicry of Mrs. Reid.

"T'ink me some back-a-yard pickney? Teacher teach, *'To be well educated, you must speak like the Queen of England.'* Only. It hard fe keep it up de right side when everybody a-talk patwa."

To appease her sister and squash any more mockery, Tilda said, "You be better dancer dan me Missy. Wat if dem want me fe shake hands wid de Princess?"

Missy stopped again. She stared at Tilda. Bending low, she giggled until her eyes watered. "You? You? You shake hands wid de Princess," she spluttered. Tilda was such a moonshine baby! "Who you t'ink you be? Busta? Why Princess gwan shake you hand?" Unable to control her glee, she laughed uproariously. Then, wiping her wet eyes, she remembered their slackness in getting home. Still several miles remained before they would reach Auntie, who was certain to nip them for lateness.

"All me know is," she Missy, hurrying along the road, "dis prancing an' dancing gwan mak' more work fe me."

True to her word, after school, Mrs. Reid gathered the chosen eight for initial practices on the school platform. Two weeks later, they rehearsed at her home.

Mrs. Beryl Reid and her clear-skinned husband, Norman Reid, lived in a house he had inherited from his father. Four generations of Reid's had lived in the impressive three-storey whitewashed house. Hugging the side of a ridge, twelve steep concrete steps led to the front door; a lattice-bordered veranda overlooked the town. The backyard had a few cane pieces, four banana plants, three coconuts trees, and two papaya trees.

Tilda and her classmates followed their teacher through the cool, spacious, shuttered house. As she walked through the black-and white-tiled kitchen, Tilda's eyes widened in surprise. The kitchen had indoor water and a stove. Early that morning, she and Missy had gotten soaked through when they crouched before the makeshift kitchen to blow fire to make cornmeal porridge.

Mrs. Reid gathered her class in the long cool lounge at the back of the house. They rehearsed the song and dance. Watching their co-ordination, she said, "You are improving immensely. But, you need more polish. First, what will you wear?" She tilted her head, crinkled her eyes, and said, "Come here, Tilda."

She measured a white skirt, braided with black, yellow, and green ribbons at the bottom, against Tilda, then, pairing it with a white blouse elasticised at the sleeves and waist; she tried the combination on Tilda. A white cloth arranged into an African style tie-head around Tilda's hair, she turned Tilda around.

"Stand back, child. Let me see."

Tilda moved backwards.

"Good. Excellent. A perfect fit. Many hands have worked extremely hard to get the costumes finished. This is what you boys will wear." She held up a pair of long white pants with the same braiding sewn onto the flared legs. The boys would also wear white balloon-sleeved shirts.

When all the students were dressed in their costumes, Mrs. Reid sniffed. "Stunning. We are almost ready. But," she wagged an index finger at them, "we must practice and practice. Practice until we are perfect. We shall make our school and Jamaica proud."

Dancing For A Princess

When Princess Margaret's yacht docked at the Old Fort, the sea lapped gently against the moss-riddled concrete barricade that ran along the coastline. Jamaicans voiced their greetings. Children cheered and waved miniature Union Jacks. That evening, dignitaries and invited locals packed the large hall like trees in a sweltering forest. Excited women craned their necks. White handkerchiefs fluttered and fanned across hot bodies. A man eventually marched onto the stage and threw out his fat, brown, hand. He told them to hush up. Soon, their Princess would arrive. Did they want her to think they were uncivilized? They hushed up.

When the Princess entered and was seated, the man welcomed their royal guest and introduced the first act.

A plump man in a straw hat, white shirt, and skin-tight green-and-white-striped trousers ran on stage. A similarly dressed group settled behind him. Extending his arms like a Doctor Bird in flight, the man grinned, looked towards the Princess, and sang,

Long time gal me never see you, come mak' me hold you hand,
Long time gal me never see you, come mak' me hold you hand,
Peel head John crow sit upon treetop picking his blossom,
Mak' me hold you hand gal, mak' me hold you hand.

The group behind him shook maracas and twirled and sang,

Long time gal me never see you, come mak' us walk and talk,
Long time gal me never see you, come mak' us walk and talk,
Peel head John crow sit upon treetop picking his blossom,
Mak' us walk and talk gal, mak' us walk and talk.

Long time gal me never see you, come mak' us wheel and turn,
Long time gal me never see you, come mak' us wheel and turn,
Peel head John crow sit upon treetop picking his blossom,
Mak' us wheel and turn gal, mak' us wheel and turn,
Mak' me hold you hand gal, mak' us wheel and turn gal,
Mak' us walk and talk gal...

The second act was a dark-skinned, hefty man. He told a joke about a man who went looking for a wife. When the Romeo finally found his Juliet, Romeo could not decide whether to marry her or her mother. He told several more jokes then ran off.

Knowing her school would be on soon, Tilda's belly began to flutter with butterflies.

Mrs. Reid hovered beside her class like a mother hen. Face shining with hot sweat, she whispered encouragement. "Do not worry. Remember what I taught you." She lightly touched the curtain and took a quick peek at the audience. "Remember. When you are on, do not look at their faces. And do not forget the words." She softly hummed the tune and tapped her feet to the beat of the calypso they had rehearsed. "And, also remember." She paused to adjust a girl's tie-head. "Jamaica may be a small island, but there is one thing she excels in. That is dance. So go on and dance, dance, dance."

Maggoty School announced she flapped her nervous hands. "Go on. Hurry."

Tilda's tongue felt dry. Her heart hammered like a tom-tom. Remembering Teacher's advice, she stared over the audience, jumped to the right, and sang.

"One shift me got." She jumped left. "Ratta cut it." Then right. "Same place it cut." Then left. "Mum-ma patch it." Springing right, she sang, "Same place it patch." She jumped left. "Fire burn it." She flicked her right hand, so her index and middle fingers clicked the *Jamaican whip*, dropped low, and spun. "Teacher lick de gal an' she turn right over." Repeating the move, she swung left. "Teacher lick de gal an' she turn right over." As she came out of the left spin, her boy partner grabbed her waist with his left hand and spun her right.

"Hold 'im round 'im waist, Mother Tracey," the two sang. Clutching her waist, her partner spun her left. "Hold 'im round 'im waist, Mother Tracey." They swung right. "Hold 'im round 'im waist, Mother Tracey." Clicking the Jamaican whip, Tilda dipped low again and twisted right. "Teacher lick de gal an' she turn right over." Faster and faster she spun. "Teacher lick de gal an' she turn right over. Teacher lick de gal an' she turn right over."

Tilda bobbed, twirled, and spun, and the soulful calypso drew her from pain, sadness, and loss to a magical place where, for one moment in time, she happily performed for England's Princess.

Leaving Maggoty Point

Stagaback and stretcher sweets, half a hand of yam and dasheen, and two packs of salt fish wrapped in three sheets of the *Gleaner*: these sat between Missy, Tilda, and Roy's possessions in the special suitcase that Auntie had bought from Mitchell Mercantile. She had muttered at the extravagance of the new suitcase but reasoned that no grand-pickney of hers was going to a foreign country with rucka-rucka coconut baskets to disgrace the family. Brand new black silver-buckled patent shoes were the only ones Tilda would take to England. Auntie's words rang in their ears—plenty of new shoes were awaiting them in England, so Maggoty Point's poor pickneys would get their old ones. This was her reasoning as she fussed and busily prepared for their leaving.

The day before their departure to England, leaving Auntie sitting on the bed complaining and rubbing her bony knees, Tilda wandered through the shoebox sized room and into the yard. The shanty cooking outhouse looked sad and pathetic in the clear bright sun. Tomorrow, they would cook in the lean-to for the last time. Tomorrow, they would leave Maggoty Point for England. Tomorrow, at five in the morning, they would gulp down their cornmeal porridge and then Auntie would take them to catch the bus that left for

Kingston at six in the morning. After tomorrow, Auntie would return to her wattle house, with only cows and birds for company.

After a good sleep, Tilda scurried, ate, and dressed around a carping, agitated Auntie. "Hurry, haste," Auntie said, tottering. "Pickneys. Hurry so we get to bus station fe bus at 5:30. Else you no get seat an' stand all de way a-Kingston."

They arrived at 5:30. At 7:00, when the bus still hadn't arrived, Auntie straightened hats and clothes, warning that they must stay decent and not dutty up themselves. A warm breeze ruffled the wispy hair at Tilda's forehead that Auntie had valiantly worked on with water and Vaseline before they left for the bus. At 7:30, the aggrieved, teeth-sucking travellers swelled the waiting area. At precisely 8:00, a rattle and rumble announced the bus's arrival. Hiccupping, it spluttered, paused, and the door swung open. It seemed the entire population of Maggoty Point charged inside. Elbowing, shoving fellow sufferers, the hot bodies pushed Missy, Tilda, and Roy to the front of the bus, and they got seats. Uproar broke out on the bus. Too many bodies vied for a very small space. No matter what, they must get on the bus! The ruckus got so bad that Auntie's frantic, sad goodbye went unheard.

Pinned inside Missy's pocket was a letter Auntie had addressed to her youngest sister in Kingston. She would collect the three and get them on their flight the following morning. While the bus snored noisily, the passengers huddling together like beans inside a cocoa pod guarded their bodies from any feisty fingers that might want to nip their backsides. The driver called to a friend breezing along the road to buy him a bulla, a patty, and a bottle of Red Stripe beer. A man whose bottom was protruding outside the

186

door urgently called to the suffering bodies, "Move up. Mak' room fe me nuh."

A tall, stringy man, middle of the bus, his head surgically attached it seemed to another man's body, yelled back, "A jackass you be, man. To. Where. Do. You. Expect. Us. Fe Move?"

The strong brown hand of a woman clutched the back of a seat. A stumpy man stood over a crocus bag of coconuts. Beside him, a woman roosted over a bag of green bananas. A sickly looking youth, his nose glued to the window glass, was desperately trying not to vomit.

This was *squeeze-up-suffering*, Jamaican style. When bus comes, jump on. Squeeze up. Suck in your belly and hold on. Tight!

At precisely 9:00, the driver jammed back the long, vibrating, gear stick, and the bus shuddered into life. Horn honking, brakes cranking, it groaned, did a quick jerk, and pitched the passengers forward. A woman on the opposite side of the road craned her neck to check if it was safe to cross. She stepped forward then quickly jumped back as the bus raced past. Fist raised in vain, she sent a cuss to the bus driver. Was he some jackass who wanted to *dead her up*?

When Missy, Tilda, and Roy boarded the bus, Auntie had found a tree stump on which to sit and wait for the bus's departure. As the bus spluttered and sprinted from the square, Tilda turned. A white handkerchief fluttered a goodbye. Her belly tightened with loneliness; another goodbye, another loss. Tilda again remembered the Jamaicans proverb, *"First time you see monkey, 'im ugly. Plenty time you see monkey, 'im pretty"*. She had grown fond of the contrary, pinchy fingered old woman she called Auntie. She had protected, fed and worried over them. When memories of her mama and dada began to fade, Auntie became their security.

The bus speeding along Maggoty Point, Tilda fastened one final memory into her heart: the disappearing smallness of the old woman she called Auntie.

BOOK FOUR

England

It was a bone-chilling evening in London, the fog thick as gungu soup in a Dutch pot when Clifford and Sonny hopped off the double-decker bus and followed the road that led to the high street. Shoulders tight against the biting wind and deep in thought, Clifford was missing Clara and the children. Taking a drag of his Navy Cut, he thought of how the English had treated him when he landed in England.

By luck, his first night in London he had chanced upon a place to rest his head. A man from Barbados offered him sleep in one room that three others shared.

This was a new experience for Clifford. On the island Jamaicans rarely had dealings with people from the smaller Caribbean islands owned by Britain. The largest of these islands, most Jamaicans viewed themselves superior to the smaller islands. They referred to them as "Small Island" people.

When West Indians began to immigrate to Britain and whites refused to rent to them, necessity forced all West Indians to help each other. The educated and better off who at one time thought it unthinkable to associate, much less share a small room with an inferior, had no choice, whether a professor or a yard boy, Britain lumped West Indians together.

That first night, and for plenty after, Clifford suffered on the floor with a thin sheet and a moth-eaten blanket and no pillow. Every day, he told himself it was only temporary. Yet, he knew he should have considered himself a lucky man. For getting a room for only him was one difficult task. The men he shared with soon gave him the true score. Places that rented to coloureds were rare and hard to find. He must keep a sharp eye on the advertisements in newsagents' windows. If he spied a place advertised, he should write down the address and contact the name fast.

Just that he did.

Twenty-six Farley Place advertised a single room for rent. The three-storey house stood hip-to-hip with others on a narrow, treeless road. He straightened his hat below the house, where weeds grew between the cracked concrete steps. The bell rang, no one answered. He pressed again and held down his finger in case the bell had not worked. Eventually a blowsy, flush-faced, middle-aged English woman poked out her head and shrieked, "Yea, what you want?"

Head tilted left, he took a quick breath.

"Good morning, mistress," he said in his best English. "I see the advertisement in the newsagent that you have a room to let. It still available, mistress?"

"Don't rent to blacks," she said, screwing up her, tight, cruel mouth. "So you'd best clear off." She slammed the door in his face.

Such insults in broad daylight shamed him, made him view the English differently, made him want to batter down her door and ask where she had misplaced her manners. But, because it was her country, he swallowed his pride and took the bus to the next advertised place.

Here, smoke belched from the chimney stacks of the dingy houses that resembled jumby trees. A car sped by. A baby bleated from a nearby house. Chilled, miserable, and lonely, he checked his slip of paper again: *Room to let. 1 Morris Road. Cooking facilities. Contact Mrs. Ruby Gordon at the above address.* He rubbed his cold hands, tucked in his scarf, and eased back the squeaky iron gate. Raising the knocker of the red door, he gave it two sharp taps. A man on a bicycle and a woman pushing a pram, her two children straggling behind, gave him a strange look.

He hoped for better treatment here, so he would not have to keep sleeping in the rat-infested place he shared with the three men. When no one came to the door, he turned to leave. Just then the door swung open. An English woman checked her appearance before a wall mirror in the hallway. She buttoned her navy blue coat. A black handbag hung from the crook of her elbow. The last button completed, she turned, saw him, and puckered her bright red mouth.

"Yes?" she asked, walking towards the open door.

"Mistress," he began. He nervously pulled the slip of paper from his jacket pocket and fluttered it at her, to show proof of why he was there. "I...says here, mistress lady, that you have a room to rent?"

Once only did she look at him.

"I am sorry. I do not rent to your kind." She pulled the door behind her. When it banged and she hurried away, he stared after her like a jackass.

Humiliated again. What had he done to the English for them to treat him as if he were some nastiness under their feet? To ease his hurt, he gritted his teeth and silently cursed. *Damn. Damn de English. Damn dem prejudice. Why ask West Indians fe come a-England if you gwan treat us like dog mess?*

This was the sixth house he had tried. He had received the same damn treatment at each one. *Wat de matter wid you English? You no t'ink me got human sentiments in me heart like you? Wat you know 'bout me? Listen. All you English you. When war grieved you bad. When hunger bite you batty. Who you t'ink bend over American fields. An' haul crops. Fe feed you starving bellies? Plenty coloured like me. We dat you call 'nig-nog'. 'Coon'. We dat you refuse fe rent to. Or give a decent job to. Dis how you show coloureds you gratefulness?*

The same backside thing happened when he tried to find a decent job.

He knew how to look good. Two weeks after his arrival, wearing his smart grey suit, his grey hat straight on his head, he presented himself early at the biscuit factory. A job was available for a worker on their production line.

"Yes. May I help you?" the woman at reception asked.

"I've come in respecting your advertisement."

"Well. I don't know anything about that." Stiffening her marga neck, she checked him over. "Wait a minute. I'll get Mr. Stevens for you." She slid from her seat, walked stiffly towards a wooden door, and returned with a tall, bulldog-faced man. He sprouted bushy eyebrows and a thriving field of coarse black hairs in his nose holes.

"Yes. Yes," he barked. He touched his thick, curling moustache.

"As I've said to the mistress lady here, the job. The job was advertised. I've come early to apply."

When the man lowered his head and examined his shiny black shoes, Clifford grew timid. Clearing his throat noisily, the man glanced at the woman, then at him. "Well. What you say your name was, again?"

"Clifford. Clifford Webb."

"Well, Mr. Webb, I'm afraid only this morning the position was filled. A suitable gentleman came before you and applied. We offered him the position."

"But...but..." Clifford felt as if a John crow had looked him over and refused to eat him. "The people at the employment place. Said there was a job for me. Just come in. I come here, quick."

"That is as it may be, Mr. Webb." The man rocked on his heels and gazed at somewhere over Clifford's hat. "As I just informed you, Mr. Webb, that position no longer exists in this company. However, we do need a cleaner, if that would suit you?" He turned to the woman sitting primly on her chair. "Is that not so, Mrs. Curtis?"

"Yes," she stammered, flustered at the unrehearsed conspiracy.

"Well then. Would the cleaning position be suitable, Mr. Webb?"

His heart hurt badly. A feeling of nothingness swept over him. He felt as if he had taken a big dose of castor oil and it had drained away his bodily fluids.

"No. No t'anks. No t'anks." He stiffened his back, stared hard at the man, firmed his hat onto his head and marched from the place.

His mum-ma had always believed that in life, people had to choose good or evil. Often, when witnessing peoples' badness, she had said, "Let dem stay de. De Good Lord, He knows all wat going on. He will provide." She believed, no matter what people chose, that the final judgment belonged to the Almighty. Evildoers would eventually get Hell's roasting fire, and the good, Heaven's glorious salvation. It was a fact. His mum-ma was right.

Sonny had been in the same boat as Clifford. To save money, he also shared a room with three others. Two months after the biscuit factory experience, Clifford met up with Sonny. A tiny room in Sonny's rental house had become available. They grabbed it and moved in together. Cliford also got a job that did not require him to clean English latrines.

Almost at the high street now, Clifford stopped and said to Sonny, "No matter how we try fe fool ourself, Sonny. Dese English no want us in dem country, you know. It fact."

Sonny did not want to stop and labrish in the cold. He shrugged his shoulders and walked on. "Cha, Clifford. You must realise, man. Britain no want professional West Indians in dem country. Dem want Jamaicans. Fe sweep dem roads. Which white man gwan push broom. When a coloured can push it fe him? Dat de reason dem sail clear to de West Indies. Fe find road sweepers an' bus drivers. Coloured nurses dey want fe wipe white backsides in hospitals. Which white you ever hear say t'anks to us? Rawted man! 'Don't touch me wid you black hand' is wat coloured nurses get when dem lift white wrists fe check pulses. It's wat dem call de 'English bedside manner,' Clifford. Wat odder reason you t'ink dem let us in? Dem was desperate, man. Come build up Britain, dem tell us. She entice us wid lies." Sonny sucked his teeth and kicked a discarded Woodbine packet into the road.

Listening to his friend, Clifford thought how, not too long ago, Sonny had written about the good paying jobs in England. Opportunities were aplenty; a new and better life was in England. The mother country would welcome Jamaicans with warm arms. All she had given them was her bare white backside.

"Answer me dis," said Clifford. He wanted to get some heat from his friend, who always turned serious situations into jackass jokes. "Why write to me saying it good 'ere? Why tell me fe come?"

Vexed, Sonny shoved his hands deep inside his trouser pockets and pouted sourly. "Tell de English. Kiss me yellow batty."

Clifford's shoulders twitched. His head jerked back. His mouth opened wide as he chortled. His friend was solid. His heart lighter, he pulled up his collar against the biting wind and snuck his neck down.

A black car zoomed past. Sonny's eyes brightened. When it stopped at the red traffic light, he hurried to get a closer look. Admiring its sleek lines and sporty body, Sonny whistled, dipped his batty in a low swing, and clicked the Jamaican whip.

"Rawted, Clifford," said Sonny, grinning. "See dat baby? Watch out man. Someday soon. One like she's—me is getting." He clicked the Jamaican whip again.

"You dreaming, man. Plan fe rob Bank a-England?"

"Wait man. Wait. Big plans is wat I got."

A Shilling For The Light

An odour of sooty fog filled Clifford's and Sonny's nostrils when they turned towards the ten-foot brick wall that led to the tightly packed three-storey houses of Burton Street. Pushing back the iron gate shrouded in mist, they walked along the concrete path right of the pocket-sized garden and opened the front door.

If one of Hitler's bombs had shattered even a single pane of glass in Number 10 Burton Street, it would have forced the landlord to fix it up. Stinginess was part of the landlord's constitution. He collected rent but ignored all repairs. Any needed repairs he blamed on Hitler. Leaking taps were Hitler's fault. Un-flushable toilets were Hitler's doing. Vermin scurried under tenants' beds and into their food was because Hitler had warred with Britain. His philosophical excuse was, "Since Hitler didn't bomb her, she's as good as she is."

A brown-flecked linoleum on the narrow ground-floor passage led to the landlord's eight-by-eight coal-burning sitting room. His compact bedroom adjoined it. Next was a small kitchen with a door leading to the back garden; another door led to his daughters' bedroom. Eight steps up to a landing, a snug box room in a recess had a small cupboard with a curved, rusty tap dripping onto a deep, pock-marked porcelain sink. A few steps along, a bathroom had a gas wall-mounted *geezer* system for heating water beside a square frosted-glass window. A pull-chain lavatory was next door. A few steps further, a second room adjoined the third and largest room that faced the road. The third storey was a duplicate of the second. Each landing had a cooker connected to a gas meter.

Clifford and Sonny entered the box room and switched on the light. Nose wrinkled, Clifford sniffed. Usually, on entering, he immediately removed his jacket. This time, for some particular reason, unknown to him, he stood waiting but did not know why. The small, cold space squeezing at his body, he felt an eerie sensation that he could not explain. He had just started to undo his jacket when he heard a fizz. The room went black.

"Rawted light," Sonny said, bumping into a chair.

Clifford felt along the bed with his fingers and sat. "Watch out, man. Got shilling?"

"No know. Checking bureau." Sonny pulled open a drawer and slammed it. "Not one rawted t'ing man. Not'ing."

"Pocket?" asked Clifford.

"Empty too. Youself?"

"If me had, t'ink me ask?" Clifford eased off the bed and searched both pockets, just in case. "None." He eased back down.

"Wait," said Sonny. "Ask next door. Soon come."

Sonny left. He returned a few minutes later with a shilling. The light back on, both agreed. This meter business was one tricky thing to remember. In the future, they would always keep extra shillings, in case they ran out.

Dressed in pyjamas, Clifford said, "Dis English winter darkness too much, man."

"Winter soon gone, Clifford. Spring an' summer soon here. Country look better den. Flowers an' such t'ings fe cheer us," said Sonny, he had lived through the English winter before.

Clifford could not imagine anything growing in dismal England. When the dim electric bulb had flickered to life, it made no difference to the cold, cheerless room. Snow, fog, and rain seemed to be England's dress.

"How flowers thrive in dis place, me no know."

"Cheer youself up. No let England beat you down, eh Clifford. Man. We is Jamaicans. Freedom fighters. Even devil man 'imself can't keep a Jamaican in hell, you know! Drop a Jamaican in hell. 'Im find a way fe escape!"

Getting into bed, Clifford said, "You fool-fool, you know. Is stupid-ness you talking?" Yet, what would he do without Sonny to cheer him when he got the English blues?

The single gas ring in the room silent, its fetid odour still lingered as they shivered under thin sheets and tried to get some warmth. Sonny turned his head on the pillow. "Clifford," he said, "how you join up wid Clara?"

On the verge of sleep, Clifford heard the mumbled question. He pulled up his legs, stilled his body, slid his head under the musty sheets, and faked sleep.

"Hear me, man?"

Clifford's buttocks twitched irritably.

"Cha," he grunted, shuffling. "Why you no leave a poor, tired man to 'im sleep, nuh?"

That Clifford was proud of Clara was a fact to Sonny. It was also a fact that, if Sonny wanted Clifford to open up about her, he had to keep questioning him. He lifted his head and punched his flat, musty pillow. "She *is tallawah* an' hot wid passion? Is dat de reason you no want I mention her?"

"Want me come fist you like wat you doing to pillow?" Clifford said jokingly. He tightened the thin covers around his body to insulate it.

"Realise," said Sonny, "soon some mare gwan throw her harness round wild stallion man like me. How me fe know which bit fe bite? You an' Clara is good match. Wat tell you she right fe you?"

Clifford sighed and wiggled his icy toes. "You one idiot of a-jackass if you t'ink women a-some horse." He knew once Sonny got an idea, nothing would halt him until he got a satisfactory answer. Clifford decided to throw him a marga bone so he would leave him to sleep.

"We meet. Dat's all. Satisfy?"

The scrawny chicken bone did not satisfy Sonny's hunger for a hefty Jamaican cow foot.

"But where, man? Where you an' she meet? You pappy introduce both a-you?"

The room grew silent. Clifford begged for sleep in the frigid room, where a dusty brown curtain obscured a weak winter moon. Sonny's questions had rattled him. Why bring up Clara's name now? Life was hell enough when he glimpsed a woman's leg, or a low-cut dress. Whatever thing a Jamaican man told a preacher man on his wedding day, they needed their woman. Away from Clara his nighttimes were hell. *Clara?* "Hum," he muttered, his lips a dark purple. *Pappy introduced us. Wat a t'ing. De man wouldn't be so generous.*

Years before he met Clara, Clifford had been pressed by his pappy to take up with a *wire-waisted* woman from Black River. He had been out all day chasing the man's cattle. Hurrying to wash and change before eating his victuals, the man pounced on him like a marga dog spying a bone. Pappy told him he had been to Black River to sell stock. There he saw a woman just right for Clifford. The time was ripe for

him to marry. Clifford tried to silence his ears and not listen
to the backside talk. His pappy labrish on and on until his
mum-ma, who was slicing bread, quickly glanced at Clifford.
She silently warned, *Keep you mout' shut. Mak' man 'ave 'im say.*

Because she always tried to protect him from Pappy's
temper, he heeded her. Hungry and weary, he tried to eat
the red bean soup. He would have enjoyed it too if Pappy
had not continued his fool-fool labrish. His mum-ma tried to
warn him again as he forced down the food that now tasted
like a lump of hard dough bread in his mouth. Pappy
unbuckled his belt. Allowing his belly to hang over his
trousers, he belched.

His plate finally emptied, Clifford stood rigid and tall.
Legs hard against the bench and avoiding Mum-ma's eyes,
he thanked her for the food and cleared his dry, provoked
throat. "Pappy," he said. "No tell me who fe marry. Dat me
own business. Understand wat me a-saying, Pappy? When,
when me find a woman me want marry. Me give you her
name. Since den. No proposition me wid women."

That was the first time he had stood up to his pappy.
The memory heated his body against the cold sheets. "No.
Pappy never introduce us." His voice was a hoarse whisper
in the dark. "Choose her meself. Now you drag dat from me
soul case, let a man sleep, nuh?"

He did not sleep.

Why, no matter how hard he tried life always kicked him
in the backside? Yesterday, before entering a newsagent to
buy a newspaper a white man had hocked and spat in front
of him. First in the shop, others trailing behind, he was the
last to get served. A few white women showed coloureds
kindness and treated them with respect; the flooded abuse of
the majority washed away these kindnesses.

Britain's newspapers daily damned West Indians. Headlines stated they were flying to England for government assistance. What assistance? Who had assisted him when he stepped off the ship? What class of West Indian would go to a foreign country to live off the government? Lately, all he did was, shake his head and kiss his teeth. He supposed it was because he missed Clara and the children. It was taking longer than he expected to save money. There was enough for Clara, not the children. What if? What if Clara came first? She could work to help send for the children quicker. Kill three birds with one slingshot. The next day, he wrote to Clara.

Clara In England

The day Clara arrived, London was like a funeral. A depressing mist hovering, she shivered in her thin dress and cardigan as Clifford carried her suitcase to the box room on the second floor. Overjoyed to see Clara, when he asked about the children his heart ached for them. Their separation made him understand that Jamaicans were wanderers. Born on the island, Jamaicans lived there for a while before moving on to greener pastures. England would provide a better life for his family.

Clara woke in Number 10 Burton Street the following morning and did not remember where she was until Clifford threw his arms around her and pulled her close. Later, eating buttered toast, Clifford explained their situation. This small room he had shared with Sonny, who had moved into another room with friends, was their entire living quarters. Here they would sleep, eat, wash, entertain, and make love. When she asked where she could cook, he pointed his cigarette at the door.

"On de landing. Come show you."

He took her to the landing, switched on the single light bulb, when the bulb gave just enough light; Clara peered at the four-ringed gas cooker with a grill above and an oven underneath. Her nose wrinkled in disgust at the cooker wedged against oil-splattered wallpaper.

"It dutty."

Remembering how finicky she was, Clifford grinned. "It wat all de tenants on dis floor use."

They returned to the box room. He asked her to sit beside him so he could explain some facts about her new life. England for Jamaicans was rucka-rucka and *muckle-muckle* and make do until better came. He stood, walked to the door, and opened it.

"Going show you how cooker work. But, before it a-work, we need a shilling piece fe de gas. Come. Come. Show you." He took a shilling from his pocket, went to the cooker, bent before a metal box attached to the wall and said, "See dat." He pointed, glanced at her, and said, "Gas meter. Look."

She arched forward and peered at the metal box hidden in shadows.

"Dis shilling." He pinched the silver coin between his thumb and index finger. "Put in dis slot 'ere. Gets you a shilling wort' a-gas. No shilling in, no gas. No gas means no heat. No heat means you can't fix you food. Shilling go in 'ere so." He pushed the coin into the slot at the front, turned the lever, and heard a faint clink. Straightening up, he pointed to the cooker knobs. "Careful wid dem." He looked serious. "Turn gas on by accident. Is dangerous. Dangerous too if too much gas a-hiss out before it light. Can blow up house. Burn off you hair. Or kill somebody. So, as me say, go careful. Is dangerous. Show you." He gripped a knob and twisted it to the left. "Dis how gas turn on. Hear how it a-hiss? Soon as it a-hiss, strike match quick and set it 'ere."

Clara watched him turn the knob, heard the hiss, and saw a flame.

"Now it on. So, turn knob fe fiercer heat. So fe less heat. Depend how you a-cook. Show you." He twisted the knob a full turn, allowed it to blaze fiercely, and saw her eyes widen in alarm. "High flame is like when you put too much wood under Dutch pot an' food burn," he said, chuckling. "So fe slow cook." He turned the knob to a gentle heat. "So when you want gas shut off." He showed her again. Twisting it fully to the right, he stepped backwards. "If gas blow out by accident, gwan smell bad. Show you." He turned the knob again. This time he did not light it. Clara coughed and covered her nose with her hand. "See wat me mean? Smell so when it no light. Now try." He gave her the matches but warned, "Remember—gas can kill!"

Partner

Two months after Clara arrived in England, she and Clifford attended a West Indian party. Entering the smoke-filled double room filled wall-to-wall with coloured bodies, they spotted Sonny talking to a man. When he saw them, he untangled himself and hurried over.

"Clifford, man. Glad you both mak' it. How's t'ings?" Sonny grinned, slapped Clifford on the back, and then turned to Clara. "Man. Who's dis sweet-looking woman wid you?" He whistled.

Many turned to stare at a blushing Clara.

Sonny did not lie. Clara was stunning. Clear skin, straight, long dark hair, thick as a horse's mane, she made an unusual feature in England at that time. A rare beauty, she turned heads in the room that was mainly men. The few women in the room stole sly glances at her. Some kissed their teeth and wondered why Sonny Ford was favouring married Clara Webb when they were available. To get some privacy to talk, Sonny gestured for them to follow him into the hallway.

"How you faring?" he asked, resting his back against the passage wall. "You two been scarce dese days. Two settle good?"

"Yea man," said Clifford. "Only Clara putting idea in me head. Say for us fe buy our own place. No content how we live. Say to her. How dat gwan 'appen when we 'ave children fe send for?"

"Me own brain a-telling me same t'ing, Clifford. Me hear a house selling. May suit you." Sonny winked at Clara. "Find deposit. House yours. Plan buying one meself. Fe rent out. Substantial man I want be in England, Clifford. Why you no do same?"

Clifford shook his head sadly and squinted at the cigarette smoke that was watering his eyes. Single Sonny could roam where the breeze blew him, he was always hatching some new scheme. His latest was impossible for Clifford to entertain.

"Can't see how to manage it. But t'ank you kindly all de same."

They returned to the cigarette-smoke-fogged room and Clara settled into a corner to watch the dancers dipping to the ska music. In a far corner, a thickset man grinned into the face of a woman squeezed into a sleeveless dress. The man snaked his arms around the woman's waist. She giggled. Her yellow dress, tight as a banana skin, began advancing towards her balloon-sized backside. Clara's mouth puckered in distaste when the woman grabbed the man's smoke, placed it between her lips, threw back her head, and brayed like a hysterical donkey. She must have sensed someone watched, she turned her head, saw Clara's scornful look, glared back, funnelled her full lips, and cut Clara dead.

West Indian parties meant hard drinking, slack dancing, and labrish. Nursed on rum from birth, Jamaicans avoided beer. It *big up dem belly* they complained, and sent them to piss. A side table held the usual: Johnny Walker, Captain Morgan, and soda water, peanuts, and Walkers crisps. While the music thumped, pounded, and heaved, Clifford thought over Sonny's proposition.

Sonny had done some hard drinking before Clifford and Clara arrived. The Captain Morgan infusing his brain, thinking how to help Clifford and Clara buy their own house, he grabbed Clifford's arm, righted his body, and point at the man hugging the woman.

"See 'im," said Sonny, sliding into tipsy patwa. "Got some'ting goin' on. Eh, remember 'ow dem in Britain come a-Jamaica. A-beggin' fe us coloured boys fe come 'elp fight her war? An' we fly fe 'elp." He shook an admonishing finger at Clifford, challenging him to contradict him. "Af'er. Af'er all a-dat. Try. Try fe borrow money from a-English bank? See 'ow dem mak' up dem face. Like we gwan t'ief dem. Man. Dat de way dem show dem grateful t'anks to us coloured boys."

His first weeks in England, white doors had slammed in Sonny's face. With his own kind now, and oiled with rum, his contempt for Britain gushed out like water from a standpipe. Yet, true to his nature, he kissed his teeth and regained his usual jackass composure.

"Clifford man," he said, his lips curled, "Wat de backside. Just breezing fe ease hotness you know. But to business. See 'im." He pointed to the man again. "Got likkle t'ing going on. Dem call partner."

"Partner?"

"Yea man." He shook a finger at Clifford.

"Wat dat?"

"Sort a trust."

"Trust?"

"Yea man. West Indians got big plans a-England. Wid money scarce, it 'ow partner invent. 'Ow you t'ink Jamaica an' her people survive after Britain bleeds her dry? Scratch fe worm like fowl is 'ow."

"Still you no making sense, man," said Clifford, furrowing his brow he tried to find wisdom in Sonny's slurred words.

Sonny grinned. "Easy man. So-so it a-work. Say, say." He began explaining by knocking his left hand into his right, missing with every other knock. "Say. Say you want a quick ten pounds. Ten a-you get 'gether. An' fe de ten weeks. Each a-you put one pound in de pot. All decide 'ho want firs'. Second. An t'ird draw. An' so-so. Say you wan' de firs' ten pounds? Tak' firs' draw a de ten pounds. But keep putting in you pound till ten weeks up. Simple."

Clifford listened intently to understand the workings of the partner system. Based on Sonny's slurred patwa, Clifford determined that it involved a number of people agreeing to pay an agreed amount of money for an agreed number of weeks. The partners would agree on who would take the first, second, and third draws, and so on. To buy a house, Clifford needed a deposit. This was one quick way to get the deposit. Sonny explained that if the members wanted a higher amount of money, say one hundred pounds, the partners simply increased the weekly payment, or extended the weeks.

"T'ink me understand, man," said Clifford.

"Only way fe get house, Clifford. Else you always gwan live a-England like ratta."

Three weeks later, checking who would be the banker of an upcoming partner, Clifford joined. A month later he took the first draw of three hundred pounds with trembling hands.

Estate Agents

A few months after the party, Sonny told Clifford that a house was selling for reasonable money. If interested, Clifford should see the agents. He gave Clifford their address.

The estate agents' office was like many of its kind located in West London. On the ground floor of a brick building, the glass windows displayed a variety of properties for sale. The interior was small and functional, two desks and four chairs were strategically arranged to face the entrance. Another door led to a storage and tea area at the back.

Clifford pushed open the door, a bell pinged, and immediately a lone male sprang from a chair like a jack in the box. Tall, thin, and pasty faced, the man sported an excellent curled moustache. His pinstripe suit, sharp as his body, placed him in the clan of estate agents that treated their customers with courtesy and professionalism.

"Good morning," said the man. He hurried to greet Clifford and Clara. "And what can I do for you today?" His smile was what could be termed friendly, yet officious. Clifford removed his hat, clutched it, and explained in his best English that they were looking for a reasonably priced house and had heard one had just come onto their books.

The man arched his eyebrows and coughed, three rapid coughs, as if he were thinking deeply.

"Well," he said. Brow furrowed, he tapped a right index finger on his chin. "Recently one did come in. Yes, yes. But under unusual circumstances..." He left his sentence hanging and stroked the hair curling above his thin upper lip.

Clifford glanced at Clara from the corner of his eye. Her mouth was open, as if she urgently wanted to question the agent about what he meant by "unusual circumstances" but could not spit out the words.

Sonny had not mentioned any unusual circumstances when he told them about the place, that fact Clifford was certain. Was this man trying to send them on a janga chase in a river—trying to trick them so he could *high up the price*? Clifford had heard of a Trinidadian who tried buying a place on an all-white street. The owner heard that a coloured man wanted to buy it and changed his mind. Another coloured family bought a house on an all-white street. Whites slowly moved away. Only run-down places opened their doors to West Indians. If the man was playing *poppy show* on them, he wanted none of it. *Why worry brain fe a mash up place?*

"What unusual circumstances?" Clifford asked, he sounded agitated, his voice high as a woman's.

"Well," said the agent. He paused, opened a file on his desk, and stabbed a sheet with his thin, pale index finger. "Here it is. This one. Two-storey terrace. In reasonable shape. Structurally sound. Only needs a touch of decorating."

"If. As you saying house OK," said Clifford, "then what you mean when you a-say 'unusual circumstances'?"

"What I should have said was, ah, Mr.... ?"

"Webb. Clifford Webb. Here is me wife, Clara."

"Well, Mr. and Mrs. Webb. My fault entirely. Perhaps I should have clarified better. What I should have said was, the property has tenants."

"Tenants?" mouthed Clifford. Now he was even more *tunted* than ever. What else would the man fling at them? "Wat you mean?"

The man pulled out two chairs, asked them to sit, eased into a third, and crossed his legs. Hairy white shanks showed above shiny, laced-up black shoes and black socks.

The agent told them that the house was owned by a landlord. In fact, the landlord owned several rental properties. Two white families rented this particular two-storey house. Needing to sell quickly, the owner had given both tenants notice to vacate. The lower tenants immediately complied. The upper did not. The agent rattled on and on about the merits of the house. It was a bargain, a good investment. It was cheap for its size. Tenants were above to pay rent. Brushing delicate fingertips across black, Brylcreemed hair, he said, "The property, Mr. and Mrs. Webb, is situated in a very good neighbourhood. Near schools and buses. Very handy for work. There is even a library nearby, if you have children. Do you have children?"

When they stared at him in mummified silence, he continued. "Well. Not to worry. There is a library. This is not a chance to be missed." He extracted a snow-white handkerchief from a breast pocket, mopped his flushed face, and kept jabbering on.

"In conclusion, Mr. and Mrs. Webb, my opinion is, this is a bargain not to be missed."

Clara stared at the grinning, tobacco-stained teeth. An image entered her head: the Cheshire Cat. The story she had once told the children about the idiot girl who jammed her fat backside through a rabbit hole.

211

The agent finally, dried up. Still unconvinced, they thanked him and said they would discuss it and let him know.

A week later the agent arranged a viewing. He showed them the ground floor and back garden, but they did not meet the upper tenants. They were out. In their box room that night, Clara could not sleep. She felt uneasy. The agent's discoloured Cheshire Cat's teeth haunted her dreams.

The Evans Family

For three years, a Welsh family, Owen Evans, his wife Flora, and their three young children had rented the upper floor of 54 Newington Road. The landlord had originally purchased several properties as investments and converted them into rental accommodation. The idea was to make a lucrative income from rent payments. That dream he achieved for several years until a series of unwise investments turned sour. Frantic to obtain a large amount of ready cash, his only option was speedy disposal of the properties. He consulted his solicitors. They issued letters to the tenants to vacate 54 Newington Road.

The first letter addressed to Owen Evans, slid onto the rust-coloured mat. Flora picked it up, turned it over, pursed her thin lips, and took it upstairs to await her husband. Owen's evening meal ended, sprawled out in his favourite armchair in the sitting room with glass of Guinness at his feet, Flora timidly approached him and gave him the envelope. He slid it open, scanned the contents, threw it onto the coal fire, and reached for his stout.

A month later a second letter arrived. It almost met the same fate. Owen ripped it up and used it as toilet paper.

This war of wills continued in the ensuing months, save for one slight variation. One day the doorbell rang and a young Evans opened it. The postman asked for an adult Evans. The child called its mother. Flora stared apprehensively at the Royal Mail employee's hand. With no option, she took his pen and signed her name. Knowing that her husband detested interruptions at dinnertime, with much trepidation, she placed the envelope beside his plate. Owen secured his large frame onto his chair, gripped his knife and fork and was about to take a stab at his fish and chips when he spied the envelope. He nudged it with a ketchup covered thumb, took a swig of tea, placed his cup on top, as well as all subsequent food, drinks, and smokes, the envelope mysteriously disappeared.

For months, the landlord agonised over his dwindling finances. Why did the upper tenant not vacate his property? Desperate to know the reason, he asked his solicitors to conduct a thorough investigation—see if Her Majesty's postal services had indeed dispatched the letters to the correct address. Digesting the news later that all letters had been dutifully delivered to said address, the frustrated owner decided to visit the property. A move strongly advised against by his solicitors.

The landlord knew the exact time the pubs closed. He also had a good idea when families were in bed or about to retire for the night. In the evening, around nine, he drove to 54 Newington Road, parked his car, and placed his finger on the bell. He kept his finger down until Flora Evens, ashen faced and in pink flannelette dressing gown, opened the door.

"Yes?" she said. She blinked timidly and peered at him from the dark archway of the door.

"You Mrs. Evans?"

"Yes."

"Husband Owen in?"

"Yes. What you want him for?" Flora looked agitated. Her fingers clutched at a button on her dressing gown.

"Got business with him. Tell your husband his landlord Mr. James would like a word with him."

"Well, well, suppose you'd better come in." She opened the door just enough for him to slide his body inside. "Wait here. I'll get Owen."

The landlord's late arrival unnerved Flora to such an extent that she forgot to switch on the light when she scurried upstairs. Cyril James pulled off his hat and clicked on the light switch. Curses rumbled above, and then a bull like man eventually stomped down two steps.

"You asking for me?" the man barked angrily, he arched slightly forward on the stairway.

"Yes. Mr. Evans. I'm Cyril James. Remember? Your landlord—"

"Needn't introduce yourself. Ruddy well know who you are." The blue and white-striped-pyjama-clad body stomped down two more steps. "Well. Don't have all night. Spit it out." Owen made a circular movement with his thick, hairy arm.

The landlord had made a mental note long before he entered the house. He would stress to his tenant that his patience had worn out like a well-used vinyl record. He sidestepped the verbal attack and hardened his voice. "Have you received *my* letters to vacate *my* house from *my* solicitors, Frazer & Knowles?"

"What?"

"Letters addressed to *you* Mr. Evans. To vacate *my* property."

"Letters you say?"

In the dim, shadowy hallway, Cyril James wondered if his eyes were playing a trick on him. Did he detect sly craftiness creeping onto his tenant's face? Shaking aside the impression, he said, "Yes, yes. It's been almost five months now since my solicitors began sending you letters to vacate. Not once have you so much as acknowledged ever receiving them." He wanted the unpleasant business over, finished. For as sure as his mother had named him Cyril James; he was in for a long squall with this knucklehead. He rotated his shoulders and straightened his body. "Now. Evans. Are you going to comply? Reply to the letters and leave my property?"

Owen blinked. He tilted his thick neck. He scratched his right ear.

"Letters you say. Say you've been sending me letters. Have you?" His face took on the appearance of deep pondering.

"Yes."

"Say it's been almost five months, has it?"

"Yes. Yes."

"Have to ask the wife about that. I work you see. I works long, long, hard hours. Whereas she——." Evans paused and gestured with his thumb towards the upstairs landing behind him, in full knowledge that Flora's ears were glued to the kitchen door. "Sees to the letters and such. Flora does. Flora never told me about the letters. Never tells me nothing, she does." He stretched his neck and, like a fox surveying a hen house, studied his landlord. "Day or night, soon as I gets home, Flora hands me post. She does. Never seen no letters. None. How long you say it's been, you say?"

"Nearly five months."

Owen shook his head regretfully. "Five months? Tut, tut, tut. Long time for post to go missing. Enquired at the Post Office, have you? See if posties delivered them, did you?"

Cyril James could not believe his ears. His pinched lips slacked in disbelief. *The audacity of the Welsh buffoon.* He wanted to say, "Postie ruddy well delivered ruddy notices," but thought better of it. He kept silent. Was this a smirking imbecile or a sly, conniving liar? The sole reason he had come, was to settle the matter civilly and amicably. *Instead, look at what I get. A pack of lies and insults.* Knowing he was wasting his time, he dispensed with politeness.

"Let me assure you, Evans, that thorough investigations were made at the postal services. They categorically informed my solicitors that all letters were faithfully delivered to this address. Including registered ones."

His tenant gave him a sheepish grin, it almost appeared apologetic.

"Strange that," Owen said. "Very strange it is. A deep mystery if you ask me. Like one of them Sherlock Holmes mysteries, it is. Know Sherlock was a Welshman, did you? Tell by that pipe he smokes, can't you? And that violin he plays. Yes, Welsh. Definitely Welsh, he is. Very musical people us Welsh are, aren't we?"

When the small, weasel-like eyes gazed innocently down at Cyril James's furious arched eyebrows, the landlord knew; the crafty Welsh buffoon had won. This was what he got for renting to any Tom, Dick, or Harry; or, this sly Welsh fox. Ready to explode, common sense overrode his anger. If he lost his temper, that would give the lumbering lout the satisfaction. He whirled round, pulled open the door, and banged it behind him. More letters arrived at the house, and these too were ignored. When they petered out to a trickle, Cyril James made a last generous gesture. He found Evans alternative housing. They refused. For the first time in Cyril James's life, he felt like plotting a murder. Unless he took them to court he could not get them out. Courts cost money. His small pile was quickly dwindling. The courts might rule in the Evans' favour. With no other alternative, he placed the property into the hands of agents.

"Get rid of it. Sell it cheap. It's costing me too much money," he told the agents. He pulled open the door to leave, but turned back and added, "Those damned Evans. I'll be glad to see the back of them."

54 Newington Road, London

Clara still could not understand why she felt that the estate agent had tricked them when she and Clifford settled into the front room of the ground floor of 54 Newington Road in October. England's red-, gold-, and yellow-leaved trees were at their most spectacular.

They purchased second-hand furniture, only bought essentials, paid the mortgage, and saved. Clifford placed a notice in a corner newsagent to advertise the rent of the lower-floor back room. A busy day or so went by before they had the opportunity to meet their upstairs tenants. During a quiet spell, hearing movement above, they went into the hallway and looked up. Owen's and Flora's shocked faces stared down. Their expressions said, *What are these black people doing in the house*? Before Clifford and Clara could speak, the bulky man clutched the banister and lumbered down four steps.

"What you people doing here? Who let you in?"

Clifford's mouth dropped in dismay. He ignored the man's rudeness, smiled and said. "I'm Clifford Webb. This me wife Clara."

"How do you do?" said Clara politely.

219

"All right. All right," said the man. He knitted his brow and scowled. "Now I knows your name. I do. As I said, what you doing here?"

The man's unprovoked aggression shocked Clifford. He heard Clara's intake of breath, and soft "Backside." "I Clifford Webb," he said, deciding not to allow the brute, whose name he already knew, intimidate him. "I *own* this house now. I'm your new landlord. Now you pay me you rent."

The man froze. A muscular leg hovered in midair. His body buckled, as if hit by a sledgehammer. Fists tight on the wooden banister, he swung his head behind him. "Hear that, Flora? Got ourselves niggers for landlords. We have. Niggers! Because that bloody sod couldn't get us out. This his way of getting even with us. If I could get my hands on that bugger, I'd wring his bloody neck."

Clara's mouth opened into a silent "aho," and Clifford's neck popped up like a startled chicken's.

The red-faced man swung his body around, stomped back up, and left Clifford and Clara's ears tingling with "Nigger," and, "Whoever heard of a black man lording it over a white man!"

Beer to Owen Evans was like the only waterhole in a desert to a parched man. West Indians, who were brought up on hard liquor, had cut their baby teeth on Captain Morgan or Johnny Walker rarely got stoned, much less violent. The same was not true for the beer-swilling Owen. Three glasses made him surly. Four, mean. Beyond four, he was dangerous.

When Clifford and Clara heard the occasional rumble overhead, they ignored it. Wisdom said that cooped-up children must somehow fling off their liveliness. They also tolerated the curses that echoed above. For, was life not tricky enough for everyone? And, was not "*word a-wind dat soon blow away*"?

A Friday evening, tired and hungry, Clifford picked up his fork, about to stab at a chunk of beef sitting in a pool of gravy and heard a scream. He assumed the Evans children were playing a game and ignored it. A quarter of his cornmeal dumpling skewered with the beef, he raised the fork to his mouth, and heard another scream. This time it sounded like the gurgling wail a pig made when it was having its throat cut.

Pig killing, Jamaican style, was eventful and brutal. The squealing pig's trotters were secured with a strong rope and hoisted onto the sturdy limb of a tree. Its throat was then sliced with a sharp knife and a large tin bucket placed underneath to catch the blood.

Clifford threw off the horrific image of the bloody pig and chewed on. A third bloodcurdling screech penetrated his brain. This was *not* a child playing. He dropped his fork, hurried to the passage, and looked up. Searching the dim upper landing, he heard a woman wail, "Mr. Webb, help me." His heart almost stopped.

The loud wail drowned out Clara; she had hurried up to him and was asking about the commotion. When her voice finally registered with Clifford, he told her to go back and finish her food.

He hurried up, two steps a time to the dim landing above and almost tripped over Flora's body on the worn, chequered linoleum. Soft moans came from her waggling head that seemed attached to a rubber neck. He stared down in horror. She was desperately trying to unseat her husband who straddled her chest.

Not believing his eyes, Clifford wondered if they were engaged in some sort of sexual pleasure and wanted the entire house to witness their lovemaking. He flicked on the light switch. The bulb came alive. Owen's muscular hands were clamped around Flora's neck.

"Man," Clifford rasped his throat tight and his heart rattling. "Wat you doing to you woman?" Owen did not seem to hear. He continued squeezing. "Man. You deaf? You no hear wat me a-say? Get from you woman!"

His tenant looked dazed. He seemed determine to strangle his wife. Her eyes bulged. No sound came from her lips. Certain the woman was dead, Clifford lunged at Owen, rammed his body into him, and knocked him off Flora.

Clara had heard the commotion and ran up to the landing. Her husband was bending over their tenant. Owen was slumped against the wall. Worried Clifford had boxed down the man, she clenched her fists.

"Clifford!" she cried. "Backside! Wat..."

Trembling, his eyes fast on Owen, Clifford said, "Me okay." His voice came in short gasps. "Go. See to dem childs." He pointed at the room two steps above, where the Evans children hid. "Deal wid dis meself."

"But—"

"Go, me say," he almost shouted at her. "Me settle dem."

Owen Evans was slowly recovering from his drunken rage. Blood oozed from a cut on his right cheek. He raised his head and squinted at the coloured whom he knew was *not* man enough to take him down.

"Keep your nose out, Webb. Not your business. Between me and her." Owen stabbed a kick at Flora with a thick leg. It just narrowly missed her head. Clifford's jaw clenched in disgust. Raised to respect womankind, he could not understand the man's brutal dealings with his wife.

"Hear dis, Evans," said Clifford, his temper at boiling point. "You disgrace to mankind. Why treat you woman so?" Yet, even before he asked the question, he knew. The way Flora was pathetically trying to protect her head with her hands, he was throwing good words into the wind.

"Damn blackie," said Owen, shifting his elephant-sized backside on the linoleum. "Think, nigger, we're like *you*? Can tell *me* how to behave? Who asked *your* lot to come to *our* country anyway?"

Wisdom advised Clifford to ignore the racial taunts, but they stung—took him to the hill—to a suppressed need, to strike the brute—box him bad. The need pulling at Clifford's gut to box down Evans, his mum-ma spoke wisdom in his ear, "*De rank backside white man no wort' a quatty, Clifford. Cool you temper wid hot words me buoy. Why you want commit wrongness a-England fe a white man, Clifford. Listen to wat you mum-ma a-saying.*" Clifford shook his head and silently prayed that he would not lose his temper, then he would talk raw patwa. Then the *hasounou* would think him ignorant. Yet, try as he might to control his temper, the Jamaican in him won.

"Stinking rat like you," said Clifford. "Abusing you wife. Before you pickneys. If cutlass in me hand. You see some'ting dis evening. You rass clawt."

His tenant's eyelids flickered. He stared blankly at Clifford. He seemed to silently taunt, *Trust the black man to start his jungle talk.* It was then that Clifford understood. This was no decent white man. No good husband would treat his woman like so. This was one of those low-class whites he had heard about. And the only way to reach his class was to give him some Jamaican straight talk.

"Evans. Since me own dis house. It is me duty fe question you. It me dat pay mortgage. You is only me tenant. If you murder you wife in me house. It me police gwan question. So, dis is me business."

It was difficult for Clifford to detect whether his straight talk got through to Owen's beer-soaked brain. The man began to drag his body against the faded green wallpaper decorated with white swans floating serenely down a river. His back propped against a join in the wallpaper, Owen decided to tell this coloured boy that *he* was *his* superior. *That guttersnipe Cyril James sold up to nigger boy without even telling me. How was I to know when I threw away the letters that this wog would become my landlord. What's it matter anyway. No nig-nog's going to dictate what I do in my country.*

"I'm British, I am," said Owen. He stabbed a sausage-like thumb into his chest. "This my country, it is. Fought for it, I did. Don't want none of you nig-nog darkies coming here, telling me what to do. Understand, do you?" *Who do these darkies think they are anyway? Coming here. Living like rats. Buying up British houses? Think they're white and British, like me, do they?*

Strangling the urge to box down the man, Clifford said, "You? You're not'ing. Not'ing but a rass clawt. Hear so, Evans? Say you fight a war? It must'a be a woman dat you fight in war. Dat wat dem train you fe do, Evens? Fe batter you wife?

"It me. Me and me coloured wife's backside dat fight fe buy dis house. When me ever see you drop a few pounds into me pocket an' say, ''Ere, help wid mortgage'? All you do is squat on your fat, white, backside when landlord want 'im place. Since you hate coloureds so. Why mak' black man house you? Why no buy you own place? 'Cause you too damn lazy? Want play big shot at somebody else place widout lifting you rawted backside?

224

"Look at you. Crowing. Saying you fight fe you country? Well. Put dis in you pipe an' smoke it. It may surprise you Welshness. Dis. 'Ere. Jamaican. Fight. Fe. Britain. Too."

Owen's head jerked back. When it hit the wall, he widened his eyes in disbelief.

"Yes *me*. West Indian. Coloured. Jamaican. Clifford Webb. Bust *me* 'coloured' backside. As you call it. In America. 'Ere too. Fe feed you Welsh craw. So. Glue down you damn Welsh mout'. You *batty man*."

Never had Clifford before spoken so to a white man. This man's wickedness needed harshness. His cruelty and prejudice had pushed Clifford to call him, "*Batty man*", the unkind name Jamaicans labelled a cowardly man.

"Maybe it only woman you can fight, Evans? Maybe you no man enough fe fight man to man."

Owen flushed face scowled daggers at Clifford. He swung his head to his wife, who lay whimpering at his feet. "Deserves it, she does. Don't know when to keep her trap shut, does she."

Clifford sighed. Why waste his gums on the man? He bent, touched Flora lightly on the shoulder, and felt a tremor run through her body.

"Sorry Mrs. Evans, mistress." He touched her stiff brown hair. It felt newly permed.

Flora did not respond. She seemed petrified, unable to move.

To witness this treatment to a white woman rattled Clifford. He did not know how to act with her.

"Sorry you man treat you so, mistress," was all he could say. "Want I call police fe you?" he asked gently. He hoped she would get help for herself and the children so her man would never brutalise her again.

The word "police" brought a different reaction than he expected. Flora trembled. She moaned. Her terrified eyes rolled, she shook her head. She seemed to have shrunk inside her frock, then, dragging her body along the linoleum towards the room east of the landing, she pulled the door, slid inside and pushed it shut.

"Knows best, does Flora," sniggered Owen. "Knows best to keep her mouth shut, does Flora."

Clifford knew. Flora would do nothing to protect herself or her children.

"You wife may cringe an' hide Evans," said Clifford, he glared at the cowardly sack at his feet. "Not me. Not dis Jamaican. So tak' warning. Dis time me no calling police. But start any more of you rawtedness in me house again an' me call police. Understand?"

Clifford's threat to call the police seemed to harness Owen into a resentful truce. If Clifford or Clara encountered their tenant in or out the house, a stiff neck, tight lips, and a blank stare were all they got before he marched off. Clifford said to Clara one day, "Wat de backside. De less me see a-dat hasounou de better."

As long as Owen's son Ivan brought down the rent, Clifford tried to blot the Evans from his brain. Yet, facts dictated. Former habits often force a dog to return to its vomit. Many times Clifford and Clara heard Owen's tipsy body stumble across the floorboards overhead. Muffled curses also caused many anxious moments. Clifford would then cock his ears and listen, ready to fly upstairs.

Soured by his experience with Owen; Clifford began to keep an eye open for a larger, reasonably priced house. The children soon to come, he would need more room. Coloureds also badly needed a place to rent.

226

Several months of looking, he heard a three-storey house was for sale in the area. It had nine rooms in total. Three rooms were on the ground floor, a bathroom, adjoining latrine, and a kitchen. The six upper rooms had a bathroom with cooking facility on the landing. When he told Clara about it, she asked how they would pay the extra mortgage. He told her they would live on the ground floor and rent the six upper rooms. The little money from the sale of the present house would easily pay for the mortgage. In his excitement to tell Clara about the house he had forgotten the Evans. He groaned. If the former white landlord could not get these white people out, how could a coloured man they hated?

For once, the Almighty smiled on Clifford.

Having a smoke one evening, Clifford heard a hesitant rap on their door. He opened. Flora's timid eyes stared at him. Stuttering, and twisting her pale hands, she told him that they had always wanted to return to Wales. Between stammers, she said that the council in Wales where they once lived had offered them a place near their family. They were giving Clifford a month's notice. He almost grabbed Flora's hands and shook them. Now they could see about buying the other house.

Six months later, Missy, Tilda, and Roy arrived in England.

BOOK FIVE

Englishness

Her nose hard against the misty glass of the taxi, Tilda searched the murky sky for the sun as it dodged its way from the airport. All looked gloomy and wet. A man waiting at traffic lights pulled his coat collar up to his ears. Hunched under his umbrella, rain pinged like marbles on the road and concrete pavement. The taxi turned onto a high street. Two women in headscarves clutching umbrellas skirted over puddles. Quickening their steps, they merged with the silhouetted bodies swirling in the grim, depressing world.

Tilda rubbed at the fogged-up glass with her hand so she could get a better look. Where were the lush green trees—bushes, the vibrant, colourful flowers of Jamaica, the bright, hot sun that cooked and sweated the body—the ever-vibrating throb of Jamaica that was as constant as a heartbeat?

The cab eventually stopped at what looked like prison barracks. In reality, they were houses stuck together, they gave the illusion they were hugging each other to keep warm. Stepping from the taxi, her Jamaican clothes were no protection against the chilly, damp English weather. She shivered and ran inside the house.

Tilda had been one week in England before her mama told her, Missy and Roy to finish their corn flakes and milk, change out of their nightclothes, and return to the kitchen. She would then educate them about Englishness. They dressed, brushed their teeth, returned to the chilly kitchen, and awaited their mama.

Clara soon joined them at the table. She pulled out a chair and sat. Only a short time in England, Clara had learnt some of the English ways. She drew in her breath, folded her arms, and tilted her head.

"English ways," she began, "a-different from Jamaican ways."

Her hands firm on the mottled black-and-white Formica tabletop, like a general preparing troops for battle; she starched her shoulders and prepared herself to place Englishness onto her children's patwa tongues.

"Now you be in England. It serious t'ing dat you learn good English. So. Better leave all you patwa talk a-Jamaica."

Tilda gazed intently at her mama. Her puckered month and serious face told Tilda one fact: learning this Englishness must be one serious business. She had better learn well so as not to disgrace her island. Her dada and mama were already getting better at the speaky-spokey English. Patwa words still slipped out, especially when they got heated up, but they were better at it. And, since this was England, it was her duty to adopt this speaky-spokey way of talking and thinking. For, if dada and mama could learn this Englishness, so could she.

She pulled her chair in closer, crinkled her brow and focused.

Clara pinched her lips together. What, she wondered, was the most crucial ingredient of this Englishness to arm her children with before sending them amongst these English people?

"Englishness a-first dis," she said, having purposefully selected her armament. "Always say 'Please' an' 'Thank you.' You want some'ting? Say, 'Please may I have.' You no say, 'Me want dat.' Or, 'Dat t'ing give me.' It's no how it a-go in England. 'Please may I have' is wat de English say.

"Some more. Say, say you no understand wat dem a-say to you de first time dem a-say it. An' you want it say again? Wat you say is 'Pardon?' It go like so. Suppose, suppose..." She jiggered her head, heating up. "Suppose dem say to you, 'Do you want this?' And you no hear dem right de first time dem a-say it. Wat you say is 'Pardon?' Not, 'Backside,' 'Rawted,' or Jamaican, 'wey-you-a-say'. So, remember good."

Confusion clouded their young brains. Their eyes glazed over. Their mouths opened and closed like chicks gulping fat worms from their mother's beak. For, since their mama had lived longer in England than they had, they believed all she said.

"Eh, eh. Dat not de finish a-it. Next is politeness. English people favour dem politeness more so dan Jamaicans. If a-English people no like you. Dem polite wid dem mout'. But hate you in dey heart. If a Jamaican no like you. Dem box you down."

Tilda lowered her head when she heard her mama's condemnation of unruly Jamaicans. Had her dada sent for her quicker, she would have learnt this English politeness, and not have fisted Minna.

Clara saw their puzzled faces. She wanted to educate them more, but decided for now to keep silent. Her children had been armed with enough Englishness so they could hold up their heads proudly in English society. Newness was still with them. She would see how they settled, then, if needful, teach them more. *"No feed a chick old fowl corn,"* was her motto. First, ease them in gently.

Pushing to her feet, she said, "So remember. Follow dem. Do as English do. Learn at dem schools. But always remember dis. Jamaica is where you born. An' Jamaican is wat you is."

If only Clara could see into the future. Soon Missy, Tilda, and Roy would *really* understand what it was *really* like to be a Jamaican in England.

Meadowlark School

Had it not been for the shame and scandal, Clara would have walked out of the school outfitters shop when she learnt the cost of school blazers, pants, skirts, blouses, shirts, ties, cap, and berets for three. She took comfort in the knowledge that Tilda would inherit Missy's school clothes. The bell tinkled as she pulled the door open to leave.

"Did madam also want P.E. kits?" the school outfitters assistant asked, hurrying to her.

Clara straightened her neck and asked what those were.

Schoolchildren wore P.E. kits for physical education, the woman explained—whenever they participated in sports or games. When the assistant told her the cost, about to revert to patwa, Clara closed her unruly mouth and reluctantly paid for three sets of P.E. kits. Outside the shop she said, "Backside. Paying fe all a-dis gwan kill me."

She registered Missy and Roy at their schools and climbed the ten concrete steps up the dimly lit, enclosed space to the reception area of Tilda's new school. Along a narrow corridor at a door marked "Reception," she tapped on it. A female voice told her to enter. The woman wrote down Tilda's details and told Clara to bring her daughter to school the following Monday. Clara was also told, as the school would provide Tilda's lunch, each Monday morning

Tilda must bring a week's lunch money.

Monday morning, satchel in hand, a week's lunch money in her pocket, Tilda was left with her young Greek Cypriot teacher, a Miss Andrea.

"Hello Tilda," said the young woman in her Greek accent.

"He-hello," stammered Tilda, testing the word on her tongue for the first time. This was the first non-Jamaican she had spoken to since coming to England. Nervous, she tried hard to remember her mama's table talk so that Jamaican patwa wouldn't slide from her mouth and shame her.

"I am Miss Andrea, your class teacher for the remainder of the school year. Come along and meet the class."

Tilda followed the dark-haired woman dressed head to foot in black. From behind, the teacher reminded Tilda of a young John crow. Jamaicans rarely wore black. Loving lively colours, they kept black for funerals.

Muffled sounds trickled from the closed doors into the corridor. Large, panelled windows at an open, roomy area, right of the classrooms, rose from Tilda's height to the ceiling. At the back of the open area, dark, red curtains screened off a raised platform. The platform Tilda later learnt was where teachers sat when school assembly was conducted. Teachers also sat here and ate their lunch whilst monitoring the children lunch hour.

Miss Andrea pulled open a door at the end of the long wooden corridor, entered, and a wave of sickness bubbled from Tilda's belly to her legs. Curious white faces stared at her.

"Children," said Miss Andrea. "This is Tilda Webb. She has just arrived from Jamaica and will be in our class. Since she is very new to England, I would like two volunteers to be her monitors until she becomes familiar with our school."

Two girls fluttered excited hands into the air—a tall, stocky wispy-haired girl with grey-blue eyes and a petite girl with brown eyes. The petite girl reminded Tilda of the mannequin she had seen in the window at the school outfitters shop. Neat and perfectly turned out, her dark brown bobbed hair had a perfect fringe across an olive-skinned brow. Tilda never felt so alone and out of place among all the white faces.

The first thing Tilda learnt at school was, when she arrived each morning, all her class went to Miss Andrea's room. As their class teacher, she took attendance. The class then filed along the corridor to their next class period. Miss Andrea taught geography. If Tilda's class had a geography lesson, they stayed in Miss Andrea's room. If the next lesson was English, they went to the room of that teacher that taught English.

Happy at last be with her dada and mama, Tilda still felt unsettled and strange. England was damp and cold. The houses—everything was stuck together. She missed her island home. Everything was different in England.

Those first few weeks in the shadowy building, under the watery sun that refused to heat up, where hazy and unreal. Words and phrases sounded strange. She barely opened her mouth except to timidly mumble basics words: "Please," "Pardon," or "Thank you." She grew excited when given a pen, rubber, pencil, ruler, an exercise book, and her own reading book.

Some weeks later, walking down the cold concrete steps towards the playground, a girl jumped onto the same step.

"Where you say you from?" the girl asked, turning solemn brown eyes onto Tilda.

"Jamaica." Tilda shyly stared at her shoes and guided her hands down the brick wall.

"Where's that?"

"Jamaica."

"Oh. How'd you get here?"

"Aeroplane."

"Cor! How exciting. Never been on one," said the girl, hopping from the last step onto the tarmac.

"Me no remember much 'bout it meself. Me sleeping all de time me on it."

"Blimey, you do'n' 'alf speak funny,"said the cockney speaking girl. She giggled and ran off, leaving Tilda feeling foolish, never to open her mouth again.

Her cardigan pulled across her chest and buttoned, she scanned the playground. Four girls were playing a skipping game. Further along, a group of boys kicked a ball. Five girls and boys chatted under the seclusion of the bicycle shed. The girls week of monitoring ended, they returned to their friends leaving Tilda alone with no one to play with. She and another boy were the only coloureds in a school of almost three hundred students. Over time she learnt to rely on herself. This period of adjustment formed her character into a loner.

There was one thing that amazed Tilda at school. There was some shoving and name calling by students, but nobody boxed anybody down.

School lunch was the highlight of her day: Steak and kidney pudding with mashed potatoes on Monday and gravy and roast beef on Tuesday—Wednesday, Toad in the Hole and boiled cabbage. Thursday, minced meat with vegetables and mashed potatoes. Friday, crisp battered fish and chips with baked beans. Treacle tart and custard—jam tart and custard, Spotted Dick and custard. Chubby, silver-topped milk bottles and, for a few coppers, a McVitie chocolate biscuit individually wrapped in silver paper. She soon adjusted to these plain, staid, un-spiced British fare, devoured in the dim, chilly hall under the watch of the keen-eyed teachers sitting on the platform eating their lunches. To Tilda, food was food.

Library

One windy day, Miss Andrea took her class to the library. Trooping along the pavement in pairs towards the red brick building, Tilda excitedly gazed at the books through the library window, missed her footing and tripped over the front door concrete step. Blushing, she jumped up and followed her class. Inside the library, the teacher gathered the class and cautioned them to treat the library books with respect. Select one, find a seat, and read quietly. If they needed assistance, they should ask her or the librarian.

Tilda did not know where to begin. Had she died and gone "*where the blessed shall find eternal rest and peace to their souls*"? Her grand-mama Webb had often quoted this line from her Bible. She walked down the rows, looking at the titles. Tiptoeing, she touched a book and a tingle surged through her body—a peculiar thrill she could not explain. The book seemed to say, "Hello Tilda. Welcome. Come closer. Open me. Quench your thirsty soul." Some unseen force sucked at her soul. She pulled a book, opened it, read the inside page, and ingested a substance not known for its intoxication: the power of words.

Her mama's welcome-home meal of fried chicken and the rare vanilla ice cream treat never invited her into a magical world like books. Books spoke to her soul. Books made her spine quiver with a giddy hunger. How could she explain an intangible new emotion? Words explained a hurt leg, tummy ache, toothache, or head pain. The moment Tilda walked into the library, she felt word power.

She took *Grimm's Fairy Tales* to a seat and read until the teacher told the class to hurry and put their books tidily away. Tilda was disappointed because she had only read five pages. The teacher said they could join the library—all they had to do was ask their parents to register them and get them a library card. They could then borrow any book they wished. Tilda could not believe her ears. Lifting her head from the book of fairy tales, she mouthed, "Borrow any book? Any book? I could take books home to read?"

As Tilda slowly adjusted to her new life in England, school life brought unexpected challenges. Her school, Meadowlark, paired its students by sexes: two girls or two boys at each desk. If there was an uneven number, a boy and girl sat at a desk. Tilda sat next to a girl. A boy was directly behind Tilda, his girl partner, by the wall.

"There are several kinds of nouns," said the male teacher that taught English. He turned to face the class, pointed at the words on the blackboard, and asked, "Who can tell me their names?

Tilda knew one of the answers but would not put up her hand. Then the class would snigger and say she talked funny. If she did give the wrong answer, she would disgrace herself. She stilled her hands on her lap, shifted on her seat, bent forward and pulled her skirt over her knee. There was a tug on her long pigtails. She arched her body back, rotating her head; she felt another sharp tug, followed by giggles. Swinging completely around, she caught the boy behind her hurriedly untying her ribbons from the top bar of her chair.

She could not remember why she did it. Perhaps it was because the class tittered and whispered. She did remember her face heating and feeling embarrassed. She did remember swinging from the feisty-faced boy to stare angrily at the pen groves uniting the two inkwells on her desk. She did not remember swinging back to the boy. Nor pulling back her right arm and boxing the boy's face so hard that he pitched backwards. Legs flying and arms flaying, he crashed into the girl seated next to him, and the wall. She did remember the deadly hush in the room—the astonished looks on the white faces—the echoing gasps. The angry voiced teacher when he said, "Tilda Webb. Come here this instant."

She remembered her legs trembling, nervously advancing to the flush-faced teacher dusting chalk from his long, bony fingers.

"Why did you hit Roger Wilcox?" he asked, stern faced and tight lipped.

"He, he tie me hair to chair back, sir."

"Silence!" he barked at the giggling class. Tilda tried to stand bamboo-stick straight, arms stiff at her side.

"Tied hair or no tied hair, Tilda Webb," he said coldly as if his teeth were icicles, "I will not tolerate such unruly behaviour in my class. Do not hit any pupil in my class, or anywhere else in the school. Do I make myself clear? Do you understand me? Now put out your hand."

If only the ground would swallow her up. When it did not, she obediently extended her hand. He pulled open the top drawer of his desk, removed a checked cloth slipper, and raised it in the air. The thwack of the rubber sole on the palm of her hand stung.

"Now. Return to your seat."

Cheeks red and burning, ears as if bees swarmed inside them, fists clenched, arms and back stiff, she stared stonily at the wooden floor and shuffled to her desk. She did not immediately sit. Eyes defiant, glaring at Roger Wilcox's smirking face, she vowed with all the intensity of her young Jamaican heart—soon, somehow, she *gwan* box him down.

The Red-eyed Man

The children, household duties, and tenants kept Clara busy. Only sometimes could she peer through the front windows. Then she might see a moving shadow behind twitching white nets that made her ponder. To think—white people watched the houseful of coloureds that had moved onto their all-white street. She understood these suspicions, placed it down to *faasness*. For, was it not a fact—some people had nothing better to do than spy? People were the same the entire world over. Black, yellow, brown, or white, it made no difference. This also happened on the island. *Island people would wait till you dasheen, coco, or yam is a-boiling hard in you Dutch pot before dey pay a visit. Dese people 'ave no consideration. Just as you juicy, mout'-watering salt fish an' ackee. Is a-simmering. Dem decide fe draw dem foot a-you house. Dem backside on you chair. Dey try fe shame you up. Not one conscience dem 'ave. As dem wear out you patience so you force fe feed dem. Dem eyes a-wander round you house like a camera. Click-clicking you business fe scatter later to busybodies like birdseed.*

If out walking, she passed the English, they stared past her as if she were some janga in dutty water. Not even so much as a "Good day, Mistress Webb" would they say. She believed at first it was because she was new, they felt timid. When it rolled on regularly, from morning to morning, facts finally said that this was no shyness. The English hated her. It was then that a hot pain hit her under her breastbone, like indigestion. The English only saw her colour. She bore her burden and kept to her house.

When they bought the new house, and Clifford advertised, *Room to let for single coloured person, Enquire Mr. Clifford Webb at...*, the advertisement was answered by a tall, slim St. Lucian woman. She came to the house on a Monday evening. Clifford looked her over. Although she seemed quiet and respectful, he would have preferred a Jamaican. But, knowing it was difficult for West Indians to find a place to rent, and knowing all of them were paddling the same canoe in England, he rented her the middle room on the second floor. A month later, her male friend began calling.

Clara first saw the man when he walked up the concrete path and placed his finger on the bell. She peered at him through the white net and, for no reason she could explain, took an instant disliking to him. Whenever the gorilla-like small man lumbered into the house, she felt a shrinking, crawling feeling sweep through her body. It was as if a lizard had slid down her naked back. His creased navy blue suit hung limply on him, like a shrivelled-up piece of cow carcass. His mouth smelt of stale fish. The shuffling, swaying walk reminded her of a man dodging a boxer's punch.

She tried hard to do what the Good Book said; she frequently chastened herself for her un-Christian thoughts. Often she reminded herself to live and let live. For, since the Good Lord had turned sideways when He fashioned him, who was she to mock? As long as ugly looking people had good hearts, who was she to criticize what they looked like? But, it was the man's eyes—they grieved her. The things wouldn't stand still in their sockets. Wandering up and down, like a mangy dog snuffling for food, onto the linoleum, the stairs, and back onto her face, it worried her plenty. That was not the least of it. He had eyes like a blackbird's. Rings of red around the small, black, button like things made them seem like fire was a-blazing in them. Each time he looked her way, her teeth stood on edge. His eyes made her think that Beelzebub himself was a hiding inside the man.

It vexed her when he rang the bell; eyes jumping like a jig, he drawled in his snakelike, Small-Island way, "Miss Pearl. She in? Come pay she a-visit."

Her heart pounding, she would cement her lips and clutch the side of the door, reluctant even to look at him, much less let him pass by.

"She expecting you?" she would hiss through clenched teeth.

"Yea."

The snake would slide his batty past; she would turn and watch the dark shadow shuffle up the stairs.

Because Clifford worked shifts at odd times of the day and night, most times Clara opened the door to callers. As the man's visits grew regular, his manner towards her changed. One day, opening the door, the man fixed his eyes upon her. She felt certain twenty live lice were loose upon her skin. She had encountered plenty of feisty men like him before. She cut her eyes at him, sucked her teeth, and slammed the door after his backside as he walked into the house.

Some time passed before she saw the man again. When she did, he was leaving the house.

Early one evening, preparing food, she heard a key turn in the front door. She craned her neck to see who was coming in. From the open kitchen door, she had a clear view of the passage. A man pulled a key from the door and shut it. Her heart hammered when the crumpled cow suit disappeared up the staircase. She hurriedly closed the kitchen door. What was happening in their house? The man had a key. Yet he was no tenant. Who had given the man a key, his woman?

Suppertime came. Fried fish and rice on a white plate beside Clifford's tea and cigarette, she patiently waited until he had chewed his fourth mouthful.

"Clifford," she said, swallowing the burning vexation in her gullet.

"Hum."

"Dat woman. Pearl. Dat St. Lucian. She above us. Her man open our house door wid 'im own key."

Clifford was only half listening. His fork rested onto his plate, he stabbed a fingernail at a provoking fish bone lodged in his teeth. Testing his tongue on the tooth, he asked, "Got toothpick?"

"Eh?"

"Toothpick. Fe me teeth. Got one?"

Clara sighed, stood, opened a drawer, removed a slim packet, and gave it to him. Clifford jabbed and wrestled with his tooth. The fish bone dislodged, he placed it on the side of his plate, squeezed his belly, and belched. Clara tried hard to spice up the bland English food, but it still disagreed with him.

"Wat all dis 'bout?" he asked, groaning and screwing up his face in pain.

"Miss Pearl's man." Clara threw back her head and snorted, almost like a distressed donkey.

Clifford, who had silently watched the savage attack of her knife on her fish, knew the signals. Something vexed her, and though he was tired, bloated, and in pain, to resist what was coming was futile. Best he patiently waited for it to gush out.

245

"Pearl Williams's man," she said angrily, slicing into her fish. "Before. Always press bell. Now her man own 'im own key to our house. Me no like dat, Clifford. Suppose... suppose man sneak round our house like a mongoose. An' t'ief us? How we fe know? It no right, Clifford. No right."

An agonizing stitch struck Clifford's side again. Grunting, he furrowed his brow and slowly sipped his Tetley tea in the full understanding that further disruptions to his nerves would boil up his belly.

"Me go talk to woman," he said, trying to soothe Clara's raised feathers. "Man too, if me encounter 'im. But me can't stop man visiting."

This galled Clara, badly. All day Pearl Williams and her feisty red-eyed man had swarmed in her head like angry bees. She wanted action—now—not to have her grievances brushed off as if they were some soft sea breeze. Her chest braced like an afflicted fowl's, she told him that both of them owned the house: "So no tak' dis business so cool-cool." He was not the one who had to open the door so the Small Island's backside could slide inside the house. Only she had to endure his nasty looks.

Groaning and wanting his peace and his bed, Clifford eased himself to his feet and tenderly touched his belly.

"Cha, woman. Stop you labrish. I'll tell woman fe tell her man to no come a-me house. Tell her too fe get back me key. Only. Fe mercy sake. Leave a tired man alone, nuh?"

Why, he wondered. *Why soon as me sits fe eat, woman must drop tenants' business on me head? Especially after me long fatiguing round a-shift work. She still no understands. Unburdening troubles on me at food time causes 'ruptions to me belly*

* * * *

246

Clifford read his newspaper, finished his tea, stubbed out his cigarette, and trudged up to the second floor. He switched on the light and approached Pearl Williams's door. Pulling in a long breath, he knocked. Two minutes later, a key turned. Pearl opened the door and stood in the doorway.

"Maas Webb," she said, looking surprised and smiling. She touched her hair lightly. "Wat me fe do fe you?"

He did not return her smile. His tenant must understand he was her landlord and she must obey the rules of his house. "You man 'ave a key to me house, mistress?"

"Yea," she said, her sparse black eyebrows arched into a question mark.

"If dat true, mistress. Me a-saying plainly. I never recall giving you man a key to me house. Or renting me place to 'im. Mistress. How you man gain me house key?"

Her reaction was so swift and so savage that Clifford almost jumped backwards.

"Me give man key!" she said, pushing her mouth at him. Head waggling, she rolled her eyes.

Clifford bowed his head and studied the linoleum. When he finally raised his head, he fixed a steady stare at her. "Mistress Williams," he said, air whistling through his vexed teeth, "since dis me house, an' you is me tenant, an' since it me dat hand you key fe open me front door, an' since me never rent me place to you man, set me head straight. Who give you permission fe give me key to me house to you man. Answer me dat?"

Pearl's lips twisted, her nose flared at the tip, but, to Clifford's surprise, she kept silent.

"Since I 'ere, mistress. Might as well give you rest. Me wife Clara say when you man visit, he disrespect her. It's the other t'ing why I no want you man in me place." *Backside!*

247

*Wat a-t'ing dat is 'appenin' before me eyes. De woman heat up like
someone set a fire stick up her marga backside.*

She rammed her long arms against her bony hipbones;
her flat chest heaved.

"Maas Webb," said Pearl. She swayed sideways like a
limbo dancer under a bamboo pole. "Me no telling man
not'ing. You can't stop me man visiting me in you place. Dis
a free country."

Since his youth, Clifford had seen how West Indian
women quickly flared up. In case she decided to jump at
him, he stepped backwards and stiffened his neck.

"Well, Mistress," he said in his best English; he studied
her face. "Since I come peaceably to you. I leaving
peaceably. De day you come to me house. A-begging me to
rent to you, I explained the rules of me house to you. I give
you a key to me house. An' stress to you dat only paying
tenants can 'ave a key to me door. Tell you man so. An' get
back me key. No mak' me see 'im backside in me house
again. I bid you good evening, mistress."

* * * *

Two wardrobes are in Clifford and Clara bedroom.
Clara's double was by the door, and Clifford's single at the
far window that faced the back garden. Clifford's held two
suits, three pairs of trousers, four long-sleeved shirts, three
short-sleeved shirts, a brown and black jumper, a grey
cardigan, a blue dressing gown, and pyjamas. A hairbrush, a
tube of Brylcreem, and a small bottle of Soir de Paris
perfume (a Christmas gift from the children—he did not
have the heart to tell them it was a woman's scent) were
neatly arranged on a shelf. On a shelf below were a shaving
mug, (another gift from the children), a shaving brush, and a

strop and cutthroat razor. When Clifford shaved, he would clean his razor and return it and the brown leather strop to his wardrobe.

A month after his encounter with Pearl Williams, Clifford opened his wardrobe and removed his razor and strop. He took them to the empty kitchen, pulled out a chair, daubed water onto the strop, and began sharpening the razor. He rubbed it back and forth on the strop, sometimes stopping, he would lightly test his index finger on the blade for sharpness and then honed again. It was only when he was absolutely positive his razor was sharp enough to slice the throat of a pig that he replaced razor and strop inside his wardrobe. He then went to the front room, uncorked a bottle of Johnny Walker, and poured himself a large dose.

For a while, the children had sensed something was wrong with their dada and mama. At dinnertime, Mama constantly complained about Pearl Williams and her man. Dada looked troubled and smelt of rum.

One day, tidying her school books in her bedroom with her sister, Missy said to Tilda, "Somebody's making trouble for dada and mama."

"Who told you that?" asked Tilda. She slid a book inside her brown satchel and fastened the buckles.

"Somebody."

"What else this somebody say?" asked Tilda, frowning, feeling a nervous tug at her tummy.

Missy went to the wardrobe and hung up her school blouse.

"Not our business," said Missy. "But, think dada's going to stop the Small Island man from coming to the house. Hear dada say he still visiting his woman in the house. That's what worrying them, I think."

A rustle sounded outside the door. Missy opened up and Roy ran inside. Annoyed that their nosy brother had interrupted their conversation, Missy frowned, placed her finger on her lips, and warned Tilda to keep silent.

"What you want?" she asked Roy angrily. "Coming to snoop?"

Roy's eyes were two bright globes of excitement. He was the first to know this important stuff before his bossy sisters. They always ganged up on him.

"Oh, give over Missy," he said, with more confidence than he felt. "Only come to say there's going to be a fight."

Missy did not believe him. She wrinkled her nose, stomped up to him, grabbed his shirt, and shoved him in the chest.

"How d'you know?"

"Leave off," squealed Roy. "Stop, Missy. I'll tell, I'll tell." He tugged at her hand and tried to pull it from his shirt.

"So?" said Missy. She pulled him closer. "Who told you?"

Roy wiggled and squealed some more. When she finally released him, he clenched his fist in readiness. She had better not try *that* stunt on him again.

"Dada sharpen him razor," he said. He rolled his eyes importantly.

"So? Dada always sharpens him razor when he shaves, clever clogs. So there." She poked her tongue at him and gave him a hard shove in the chest.

"Stop it," he shrieked, fisting her arm. "Telling truth. Dada didn't sharpen it to shave. Been drinking too. Mama frighten. Hear them."

Tilda's heart fluttered. She knew it. She just knew it. Dada was in trouble. He might get hurt.

"True, Roy?" she asked.

"Course. Heard them. In their room. When passing. Suppose the Small Island kill dada?" he said in a matter-of-fact way.

The sisters glanced at each other. This was serious stuff, something their snitch of a brother was incapable of making up. Missy flopped onto the bed. She bit her upper lip. Tilda plonked herself down beside Missy and hugged her chest. Both sat in silence and tried to make sense of Roy's revelations. Grown-up business or not, what happened to their dada and mama was their business. Although Missy was reluctant to include her annoying brother in any of their plans, she knew she had no choice. She immediately took charge.

"When's this going happen?" she asked.

Roy could not contain his excitement. His annoying, bossy sisters were finally paying attention to him. He shuffled close and explained. In a high-pitched excited voice, he told them what he had heard. Dada said Pearl Williams's man was still opening his house with a key, even when he told the woman to get back the key. Dada said, since Pearl was feisty and hard of hearing, he would stop the man himself. The Small Island usually visited in the evenings, about five or six o'clock was what he had heard Dada say. When the man came, Dada would be ready for him.

He paused to try to gauge his sisters' reactions. Bowing his head, he sneaked a quick peek at both from the corner his eye. They looked quiet and glum.

Tilda's belly was full of fluttering butterflies. Though young, she had learnt—the only way to conquer enemies was to stand united. Dada would stand alone to protect his property and family. Suppose...suppose. Remembering what had happened on the hill, she spoke first. "What you think,

Missy?" she asked, frowning. "Can't let him kill dada. Can't."

"What you talking about?"

Tilda thought fast. Missy might be the oldest, but she had not faced the foes she had. Toughened in Jamaica, Tilda knew marga dogs would always yap at them.

"Well, we must do something. But what?"

Missy smoothed out her skirt and told Roy to check outside the door. Roy beamed. This exciting stuff was like those spy films. He was a special Jamaican spy. Eager to start his first mission, he carefully cracked open the door, pressed his back against the wall, peered out, and quietly closed it.

"All clear," he whispered.

* * * *

That evening, at five thirty precisely, a key turned in the front door of Clifford's house. The Small Island man, who had never tangled with a Jamaican before, stepped onto the mat in the dim passage and closed the door.

Clifford, fortified with several slugs of Johnny Walker throughout the day, was secreted behind the sitting room nets. Spying the small, dishevelled body shuffling along the garden path, he hurried to the front room door, glued his ear against the wood, and waited. Hearing the sound of the key turn, he slid into the unlit passage, just as the Small Island man dropped the key into his trouser pocket and turned.

"Backside, Webb," cried the man at the sudden appearance of his woman's landlord. "Wat dis 'bout?" The man's eyes darted as if madness were upon him.

Clifford's eyes narrowed. Booze boiled his blood. Lips pressed flat as a leaf, he flared his nostrils and pulled in sharp, harsh breaths.

"Small Island man. Before now. Me did ask you woman politely fe get back you key to me house. Me also tell her. Fe tell you. No bring you backside to me place. Is hard-a-hearing you hard-a-hearing man?"

In the many months that the six tenants had lived under Clifford Webb's roof, never had they heard their soft-spoken landlord raise his voice. They paid their rent for their little nests and were shown kindness and respect. Their landlord worked hard. He was a faithful husband, and a strict, loving father. If his friends visited, he kept them sober and orderly. When the commotion below stairs which had pulled the tenants from their rooms onto the landing increased, they scurried back. To conserve electricity, switching off lights and radiograms, they rushed back to listen.

The St. Lucian, recovering from his shock, jabbed a finger at Clifford.

"Look, Webb. Law says you can't stop me."

Backside, thought Clifford's boozy brain. *De feistiness a-de man.* Shoulders squared, he planted his feet wide and firm onto the linoleum.

"Well," said Clifford. He licked his lips. "Since. As you a-say. Law can't stop me. Let. Me. See. You. Place. One. Rass. Clawt. Foot. Pass. Dis 'ere me foot. Den. See if law. Gwan assist you black backside."

Clifford was ready. Tensed, arms loose and heavy at his side, his right thumb stealthily flicked off the razor's safety catch. He swung the blade up.

The St. Lucian's eyes widened, bulged in terror. "Webb, man," he cried. He stepped backwards. Hands flashing across his face to protect it, he said. "It no fight me come 'ere fe do. Only come fe see me wo'man."

"Small Island," cried Clifford, he flashed the razor at the man. "Me no wasting extra breath 'pon you. Wat me want is. You neyga backside, out me house."

The man did a quick dodge to bypass Clifford. Anticipating the move, Clifford sprang forward, pinned him against the wall, and slashed wildly with the razor. Warning, next time he would not miss.

"Rawted, man!" The razor narrowly missed his ear. "Easy me a-sayin'. Careful wha' you doin' wid dat, Jamaican man."

Clifford was not finished. Like a boxer about to fell an opponent with one deadly blow, he quickly stepped back, crouched, arched forward, and swung the razor up.

"Step one. Neyga. Foot. Pass. Me. Den you see wat gwan 'appen."

The man's Adam's apple jiggered. He scrubbed his moist face with trembling fingers. He stared at the razor like a stunned fish. Then, glancing over Clifford's shoulder, seeing three staring faces, he blustered, "Wha' you pickney doin' behind you, Webb?"

Clifford glanced behind him. Missy, Tilda, and Roy stood left of the stairway, Clara by the open kitchen door. Swinging back, he fixed his face into a scowl.

"Me business is wid you, Small Island. Tak' you neyga batty. From me house. No come back."

The man's face creased into a false, sickening smile. He nervously shuffled backwards, fumbled for the door, pulled it open, slid out, and slammed it shut. Clifford hurried forward and pushed up the lock. The door bolted, no key could open it from the outside. First thing, come morning, he would change the locks and give each tenant new keys. He would also warn Pearl Williams. If she cut another key for her man, she would leave his place.

Clifford felt a shiver run through his body. Suppose the man had put up more of a fight? Still, he would not have backed down. He was glad that blood had not been spilt. Remembering the children, he turned. Clara slipped into the kitchen and returned the knife hidden in her apron pocket into a drawer.

"Wat you t'ink you t'ree doing? Dis a-dangerous man, you know."

"Yes, dada," said Roy bravely. "We know. But we ready for the St. Lucian!"

The children returned their weapons to the kitchen—a black pepper shaker to fire up his eyes, a rolling pin to knock him out, a box of salt to fling at his head, and a bag of flour to *white him up*. As Tilda replaced the salt she caught Missy's eye. They giggled. The Small Island was like that nose-ringed, red-eyed Devil that snorted and stomped in Hell.

Roy ran into the passage, stuck his index fingers against his head, and chanted, "Red-eyed man, devil man, red-eyed man, devil man!"

Guy Fawkes

Roy had heard about the English tradition Guy Fawkes Night and was anxiously awaiting it. On his way home from school, listening to English boys labrish about their preparations for the night, he grew envious. From what the boys said, Roy knew he could easily make his own Guy Fawkes. All he needed was an old jacket, a cap and newspapers. He asked his dada to give him a jacket.

"Is you mad, buoy?" said Clifford. He sucked his teeth. "Where you expects me gets spare jacket from? Galang 'bout you business." He flapped his hand at Roy, a signal to leave him in peace.

Roy did not "galang 'bout his business." Denied the early years of parental nurture and structure, suffered Auntie's pinchy fingers and carping tongue and the dominance of bossy older sisters, he had become resilient and independent—unusual traits in a boy so young. Roy was wilful. Roy would get his Guy.

He checked to make certain neither Dada, Mama, nor his nosy sisters were watching, sneaked upstairs, timidly knocked at a male tenant's door and asked the man if he had an old jacket and cap he did not want. The tenant told Roy to wait. He returned with a sorry looking cap and a tweed jacket. The jacket he told Roy he had inherited from a

Jamaican the first time he came to England but had never worn. Roy thanked the man, crept downstairs, and hid both behind the pull-out bed in the front room. He gathered old newspapers, took his collection to the back garden and stuffed the tweed until its arms stuck out and its chest grew fat.

Since Guys also sat upon prams or pushchairs, Roy entered the old wooden shed in the back garden. Among cobwebs, broken flowerpots, rusty garden tools, and piles of mouldering newspapers, he found a sad pushchair, hauled it out, and ran to get his dada. Clifford listened in mild amusement, winked at Clara, stabbed out his smoke, and followed Roy. Smiling at the sorry specimen at his son's feet, Clifford returned inside for tools, rags, and an oilcan. He adjusted, cleaned, and adjusted again. When the dust, rust, and cobwebs had been brushed away and the wheels oiled, he gave the pushchair a nudge. It wobbled and limped. He made further adjustments then tested it again. His back against the brick wall, Clifford chuckled when Roy placed the fat tweed jacket on top of the dirty plastic seat of the pushchair and stuffed more paper inside. A cap upon its head, it resembled a *dutty*, legless drunk.

"Wat you gwan do wid dat, boy?" Clifford asked.

Roy's shoulders and head drooped. He did not reply. This was boys' stuff. If Dada did not understand, he would not explain.

Clifford did not press him. If this foolishness kept the boy happy and out of trouble, why churn up the water. He was glad he was adopting some English customs.

Roy had a plan. Why beg for the jacket, make the Guy, find the pushchair, fix it up, and only push it around the pocket-sized back garden? Dada, Mama, or his bossy sisters would never find out. He watched and waited. When positive everyone was busy and would not notice his absence, he tiptoed through the passage of the house with both Guy and pushchair. Outside the house, racing along the pavement, the Guy wobbling, he turned at the thick hedge at the end of the road that met with another road and hid his prize inside the hedge. It would stay there until he found a good spot to beg. Roy heard that money could be made from this English tradition. Find a good place to beg, stand beside your Guy, and call out like the English boys, "Penny for the Guy, mister. Got a penny for the guy?" and people would give him money.

On his way home, his conscience began to bother him. He quickly dismissed it. He must think of the best way to carry out his operation without his family finding out— especially his mama!

Mama was peculiar. She may not whip his batty with the strap like Dada, but still her mouth stung. And she always acted as if she were superior, more so than the Queen. Should Mama even sniff that he was begging on the street with his Guy, she would lash him with her tongue to make his head hang in shame. He was not ashamed. She would *hot up*. Roll her eyes, raise them to heaven and ask, "Buoy. Wat you t'ink you doing wid dat dutty sin'ting?" She would then turn her scandalised eyes upon him. "No child a-mine gwan set foot out a-street fe disgrace me by begging like some tramp." She would place guilt upon him. "Lawd-a-massy. Just witness de cross me 'ave fe bear a-Englan'. See how me only pickney buoy no 'ave no ambition," she would say, sucking her teeth. How was a small boy like him to have ambition when he did not know what having ambition meant? That was not even the last of it. She would call Dada and ask him to see how his one and only son, who did not have any ambition, were turning into a beggar man on English streets to disgrace them.

He wanted freedom and fun like the English boys, not to feel guilt or disgrace, or to worry about ambition. He was fixed. He would never let Mama, Dada, and his nosy sisters learn his business.

School not long over, Roy changed out of his school clothes, sneaked to the front of the house, ran to the hedge, and pulled out the pushchair. Tensed and alert for spies, he raced along the pavement, found a safe place, and made his pitch. Two shillings and six pennies later, the Guy back inside the hedge, he ran home and stashed his loot in a mint humbug tin under the pull-out bed.

The Friday before the big day, Roy begged Clifford— please, could they celebrate November 5th—until Clifford's ears tingled. Cussing, Clifford warned the boy that he had better leave him in peace or his batty gwan bawl. Roy kept up the pressure. He hung his head. To ease his conscience, Clifford said that Guy Fawkes was nothing more than setting fire to good money. Roy did not give up easily. Watching his son shuffling his feet and looking sad, Clifford finally relented.

Rockets were the best, but they cost more money. Rockets whooshed and zoomed way up high in the bleak, grey night sky. Clifford bought four rockets, a few bangers to make noise, and three catherine wheels. On Guy Fawkes Night, only he and Roy in the back garden, Clifford placed the rockets in turn inside a tin and lit them. He chuckled when Roy jumped and screeched as fiery, smoky trails lit up the fog-bound sky. Once all had popped and fizzled, acrid odour added to the already oppressive pea-soup air, both returned inside. Clifford, who soon had to leave for his night shift, drank a cup of tea, buttoned his coat, tucked his scarf around his neck, and placed his hat on his head. After a goodbye to Clara, he entered the misty outside world, where houses stood like shadowy ghosts.

Police

The foggy night progressed well past midnight. An occasional car headlight pierced through the brown and orange patterned curtains hanging ceiling to floor in the front room where Roy was fast asleep on the pull-out bed. At precisely one o'clock, the cuckoo clock with alpine flowers painted on its face, and hanging on the wall by the bay window, sprang to life. Its small door swung open. The bird attached to a wire swooped out, gave a single throaty *cuckoo*, and was sucked back inside.

Roy slept on.

Fast asleep, lying on her back in the room next door, Clara flung out her arms in wild abandon. As her arm struck the empty pillow beside her, a muffled sound echoed in the dark, sleepy passage outside. A faint shuffling of bodies was followed by the pound of heavy boots.

Quiet commands followed. A torch clicked on. A bright light searched the hallway, travelled along the wall, curved around corners, and stopped midway between the front room and the kitchen. Slithering up the snakelike arm of the wooden banister, the light marked the middle door. This was the one.

A male hissed, "Try that door."

In the treacly bedroom, double-lined curtains blocked all light for Clifford's daytime sleep Clara pulled up her legs, turned over, and did not hear the door handle turn—nor saw the bright beam search the cluttered room. It hit her face, full on. She cried out in terror, flung her body sideways, twisted onto her back, grabbed Clifford's pillow, and jammed it over her face. Trembling, she shrank into the bed.

Dark, invisible voices—rustling clothes surrounded her, they seemed so real. Was this a nightmare? Haunting jumbies? Who or what was in here? Her breath a shallow heave, she clutched the pillow and waited. Teeth chattering and icy cold, she sensed something. A bright light hovered just above her head. Her mouth opened for a scream. A rough, heavy hand grabbed her shoulder. She shank backwards, flung away the pillow, and clawed at the hand. The hand had a voice. It cried out, "Bloody hell," and shoved her chest, hard, into the bed. She grabbed wildly at the sheet, pulled it over her head and covered her entire body.

"Get up," demanded a man.

Her body heavy, unreal, she tried to speak. No words came.

"Get up," the voice repeated.

"Who...Wat you want? Who you a...?" Her heart pounded. It would fly to her throat—choke her.

"The police."

"Police?"

"Yes. We are the police, Mrs. Webb," a second man said.

"Police? Wat...? Wat police doing in me bedroom?"

She eased back the sheets and peered out. The light blinded her again.

Shielding her twitching eyes with her arm, she asked, "Wat, wat you want?"

"Are you Mrs. Webb?"

"Yes. Yes, I she." Her mind raced. It swirled with a cesspool of questions. *Suppose dem no police? Suppose dem somebody else pretending dem de police? How me fe know dem police? When dem a-blind me wid dem torchlight. Hiding dem faces from me?*

Doors opened and closed overhead. The ruckus below had woken the tenants above. Disgrace had come to her house.

"Get up, Mrs. Webb. We want to talk to you. Now."

Get up dem say? How me fe get up. When only thin-thin nighty is on me back? Since dem say dem is law. Why treat a respectable woman like me so?

"I no decent," she said, almost in tears. "Need fe put some'ting decent on."

"Well," a gruff voice conceded grudgingly.

"Me no decent me say," she pleaded, her voice a whisper.

"We'll wait outside your door, Mrs. Webb. Till you are dressed. Don't be long. We need to question you."

The light left her face. The switch on the wall clicked on. Her bedroom door snapped shut. The bulb flickered into life. Groggy, disoriented, and trembling, Clara turned her head to her shame—her damp drawers she had left to dry were still draped over a chair. She sucked her defiant teeth. Why worry her brain about her baggies? She had done nothing wrong. If British law had manners, they would have knocked first before bursting into her room to *blind her up.*

She slid off the bed, threw her red candlewick dressing gown over her nightie, and tied the belt. Before taking them to the front room, she told them to wait, her son slept in the front room. She took Roy and quietly laid him at the foot of his sisters' bed.

The navy blue–clad trio sat straight and stiff on the edge of the pull-out bed. They reminded her of John crows perched on the topmost branch of a gynep tree, patiently waiting for a dead dog to rot and stink up good so they could pick its flesh clean. The heftiest and oldest, his chamber-pot-looking helmet lying on the floral rug, held a spiral notepad and pen. She wrinkled her nose: white man sweat, stale tobacco and beer. Arms protectively across her bosom, she awaited their interrogation, while her head scorned. *Eh. Eh! Dis some'ting fe behold. T'ree British lawmen. An' a t'irty-five-year-old Jamaican woman. Is plenty-plenty police force. Dat come fe root me out a-me bed. In de dead a-night. Fe treat me like me-a-escape criminal from Wormwood Scrubs.*

"We've come about your son."

The mention of Roy surprised her.

A neighbour had called at the station, they continued. Reported that her boy had fired a rocket into their house; it landed in their front room and singed their curtains.

Roy was only a little boy, she told them. He hadn't lit any rockets or fire jacks. Her husband Clifford had lit them, before the old trees, out in the back garden by the fence. Her husband had lit them out in the back, not out in the street, not out front, she repeated, twisting her hands in her lap. Roy hadn't lit any fireworks. He was only a little boy, not a criminal, she told them. But what she really wanted to say was, "Why you no go terrorise an' put in prison all dem English dat insult West Indians?"

"We must investigate all complaints, Mrs. Webb," the one nearest to her said. Folding his officious arms, he accused her with cold, blue, eyes.

Investigate? She glanced at the clock. It was almost one
thirty. *Eh. Eh. Investigate. At dis time a-night. Wat kinda
investigating dese police need fe do? In de middle a-de night. Wat so
vital? So crucial. Dat law bust in me room. A-saying dem must
investigate a stray rocket. An' a small boy.*

The closest to her read from his notes: "A complaint
came from a neighbour." He turned a page. "Says, rocket
came from this direction. Could have caused serious
damage. Injury to life and property."

Her aggrieved heart thumped. "Me tell you plenty time
already. Me saying it again. Me son Roy never had no
fireworks out front. Never light no fireworks in de street. His
dada it was dat light dem out back."

"A neighbour reported it, Mrs. Webb. And we must, by
law, investigate all reports of this nature."

*Law? Eh, eh. When since British law troubled dem backside 'bout
coloured people? British law is fe dem dat white. How come dem a-raid
me house? In de blackness a-night. Like me some t'ief. Why no wait till
decent morning light? When me dressed an' sensible? Doing dem damn
duty, dem a-say. Aho. Well. Mak' dem take dem damn white backside
duty someplace else.*

Her lips trembled. Jamaican cuss words crackled in her
head like rumbling thunder. She wrapped her dressing gown
tighter, and prepared herself to answer their questions. *Watch
dem scratch dem pen over de paper. Asking. Prodding. Poking. Like a
finger tormenting de scab on a sore foot dat refuse fe heal. Same fool-fool
questions. Over an' over. As if me no understand wat dem-a-ask de first
time. Must t'ink because me coloured, me backward.*

They repeated the questions. She gave them the same
answers over and over, until finally, they seemed satisfied.
The pad closed and returned to a jacket pocket. One stood.
The rest followed. All soldiers on parade. Said they would
file a report. *File wat report? Dat dis many police bust in me room fe*

265

humiliate an' terrify me? She was glad when she shut the door behind their backsides. She bolted it while her belly churned with dislike, as if she had eaten too many mangos and gotten a bellyache.

She perched on a chair in the front room, like a Doctor Bird that had had its wings clipped. The cheerful cuckoo clock ticked. She felt as if she would never sleep again. Clifford was usually the thinker. Busy with child minding, cleaning the house and such like had robbed her of time just to sit and think. Alone with her thoughts, she pondered her life in England, and a woeful moan pushed though her dry lips.

"Mother country," she said with a sneer, kissing her teeth. "More like a mother dat abandon her pickney on someone doorstep." She stood, went to the drinks cabinet, poured a quarter measure of Johnny Walker, and drank it down in one quick gulp.

Clifford's Reaction

Clifford pushed the door; it lurched awkwardly. He closed it and made a mental note to check the screws and hinges before he returned to work the next day.

Streaks of early light brightened the stifling kitchen that smelt of stale fish. He pulled off his hat and switched on the light. Clara was slumped over the table. Her head rested on her arms. He thought she had fallen asleep whilst working late in the kitchen.

"Clara. Clara," he said, touching her arm gently. When she did not respond, he shook harder. "Clara. Clara."

Clara's head swung up. She stared at him as if woken from a drunken stupor, she then lowered her head onto her arms again.

Perplexed, he bent over her. "Woman. Wat you doing 'ere, dis time a-morning?"

Her head jerked up again; it tilted backwards. She opened her red-rimmed eyes and looked at him. "Clifford," she moaned. "fe de love a-God. Tak' me back a-Jamaica."

"You sick?" he asked, getting alarmed.

She shook her head.

"Children sick?" She kept shaking her head. Exasperated and getting worried, he raised his voice. "Well. Since you no sick. An' children no sick. Wat de dickens wrong, woman?"

267

Her midnight ordeal, now Clifford's rough questions, was too much for Clara. She swung her head around, rammed it into his belly and bawled patwa into his belly-button.

"De English hate us, Clifford. You no see how de white ignorant hasounous all a-hate us? Tak' me home, Clifford. To Jamaica. Before white people turn me head!"

He touched her hair gently. "Clara. Wat de trouble? Tell me before whole house hear our business."

Her head swung backwards, she glared at him with troubled wet eyes.

"Aho. T'ink tenants no know?" Sniffing, she rubbed her eyes with the back of her fist. "Clifford. It in de dead a-night. Police force demself in de house. Dem musta t'ink a-criminal-a-hiding 'ere."

"Woman. Wat dis stupidness you saying? Tell me plainness."

She told him all that her silent heart had endured from the first instant she stepped onto English dirt—her loneliness in a house full of tenants. White women's cold, silent stares when she tried friendship. She would not force herself on them.

Then she said, "Clifford. Me sleeping. Only in me thin-thin nightie. Dem bust in me room. Flash flashlight in me frighten face."

"No take it so," he said, trying to sooth her. "Settle youself."

Clara did *not* want to settle herself. His pacifying words fired her temper. Her right fist clenched, she banged the table and asked him why. How come, all this long time they had been married, good times never visited her. When they moved to this house, she thought peace and plenty had finally arrived. Instead, the British police had invaded their

268

place as if they were criminals. Hard as they tried, badness always drove them from their security.

"Why we come a-England, Clifford?" she asked, wiping her eyes with her fist. "Me can't bear living dis type a-life no longer, you know. Youself know how me come from decent, high-up people. Dis nasty English life is no fe me, you know. Me a-beg you. Tak' me back a-Jamaica." Her grief overcame her, pulling from him, dropping her head onto her arms on the table, she howled.

He silently watched her; heart almost jumping from his chest, he scooped her into his arms, and gently rocked her. They had battered life together, endured grievous heartaches, and many separations. She had had her own house in Jamaica—sometimes a maid to assist her. "Coloured," the English called her. They had stripped her of pride and position.

"Dry you face, Clara. It be okay."

"How it be okay, Clifford?"

"As God's me witness. Dis de last time dis 'appen. Oath me a-make. Visit station tomorrow. Issue complaint. No care if dem listen. Still doing so."

"Wasting you gums" she muttered, drying her eyes on her nightie.

"Still going. An'"—his voice became harsh—"from now on promise. None of dem rass clawt sin'ting gwan t'reaten you or me children again. Hear so?"

He left her. Returning with a bottle of Johnny Walker and two glasses, he uncapped the bottle, poured a finger for each, and gave her a glass.

"Drink. An' remember wat me a-say."

$$\infty \qquad \infty$$

BOOK SIX

Racism

Notting Dale, nicknamed, "the Dale", located in the area of Notting Hill, could be described as a rotting corpse. Crumbling brickwork, peeling paint, squalid, mildewed houses, and dark, sinister alleyways entombed its residents in a world of poverty, for which it was termed the "duckers and divers" of Notting Hill.

On the top floor of one of the many grim, three-storey tenements, a small bedroom faced a weed-and-junk-covered back garden. Greying, half-white nets behind dingy green flowered curtains hung at a dusty window. Three teenaged boys lounged on the lower half of a bunk bed placed against one wall. All wore identical creepers. Another rested against the door to their right. On a decrepit five-drawer chest, just inside the door, leaned a sullen fifth. Above it was an oval mirror. The five Teddy boys wore identical togs—long jackets, restricting drainpipe trousers—and all had slicked-down Brylcreemed hair and sideburns.

The Ted at the chest of drawers pulled a comb from his hip pocket and raked it though his oil-slicked hair.

"Well, Colin," he said to the youth by the door as he slid the comb back in his pocket. "What you think 'bout meeting?"

Colin, a grey-eyed blond, cigarette dangling from his lips, looked up and shrugged his shoulders. "Well. What he says true, ain't it?"

"That all?"

"What you expect me to say? Got things in me head tonight, ain't I?"

Dave Watson had just turned eighteen. The eldest of two sons, Dave shared the cubby-hole of a room with his snotty-nosed snitch of a brother and resented it. Yet, where else could he live so cheap? Dave resented most things. He resented his job. As soon as he settled into one, he was always the first to get the bleeding heave-ho. Yet never once did he question why.

He resented niggers: black bastards that came uninvited to his country to live like bleeding kings. They took all the best bleeding jobs from blokes like him. He had had a brush with one at work. Clifford Webb. Thought he was oh so bloody clever, that Nig. Polite he was, sucking up to the foreman. Did he think he was one of them? Made Dave sick, it did. Never in a million years would Webb be one of them. Nig thought if he worked hard, they would pally up to him. Never! Slaves they were once, weren't they? That was what his uncle Jim had belted out in the Elgin last week as they downed pints. Laughed their heads off, they did. The Dale was sick to its guts of blacks. The way they carried on, as if they owned the bleeding country. Look at the way they bleeding well armed up to their white women. If only the chimney sweep could hear what they said behind his bleeding back. Right nasty it was. Maybe he should stick it to his bleeding face. But, then, they didn't have no feelings, did they? Like monkeys, they were once.

Dave resented cops. Who asked Blue Bottles to stick their bleeding noses into the Dale's business, anyway? Best day ever was when he and Colin slacked off school. First, they tinkered around yards, did odd jobs then nicked stuff to release around the Dale for a quid or two until he landed the job at the factory.

First thing when he opens his pay package, he gives the old woman his keep. The rest went to pay for his Ted's gear, for flash. Leftovers went to fags, drinks at the pub, and a night at the Palais dance hall. He had roamed the Dale as a nipper and learned her ways. Arguments he settled with his fists. Hanging around streets, he chatted up birds and got into fights. This was his turf. He bloody well resented any bleeding wog taking it over. Latimer Road was full of them. Why were they here anyway? If they laid him off at work instead of that bastard Webb, he would have something to say about it.

Dave lit up a cigarette and drew on the weed. "None of you get nothing from the meeting?" he asked, scowling.

The posteriors snug on the cot clenched nervously. Why bother throwing out suggestions? Their leader never took a blind bit of notice to what they said anyway. Dave led. They followed.

When no one spoke, Dave grunted impatiently. "Well?"

Colin wanted to add something intelligent but did not know what. He punched his right fist into his left palm and added cautiously, "Was interesting."

"Bleeding well was," said Dave, squinting through his cigarette smoke. "More than bleeding interesting, if you ask me. Gotta do something big though. Can't let Nigs take over our country."

Now Dave was back on track, they no longer worried they might say the wrong thing. The three murmured their consent and lit cigs. The small space was now a fog-filled boiler room. The companionable silence drew a tentative and unexpected question.

"What can we do, Dave?"

"Soon see, Carrot Tops," Dave told his red-haired friend. "Go check outside. See if ears listen."

Carrot Tops unglued his body, checked the landing, and sauntered back. "Quiet as the grave, Dave."

"Right. Me folks at pub. Nipper's next door with Auntie Jean. Listen." Dave dropped to his knees and switched his smoke to his left hand.

"This's what we'll do. See. Go to the next meeting, right? Hear what they say, right? Then we'll..."

* * * *

Clifford was bent over a piece of machinery, when he heard someone call his name. Looking up, he saw his supervisor weaving through the clanging machinery. When the man beckoned to him, Clifford grew puzzled. What did he want? He hoped it would not take long or he might miss his bus home. He wiped his oily fingers, walked to the boxlike cubicle at the far end of the factory floor and entered. The foreman was seated at his desk. Arms linked across his chest, he studied Clifford and seemed to be trying to decide how best to approach a problem. He pursed his lips and, leaning back, cleared his throat.

"Dave Watson's been stirring up trouble for you." He arched his sparse eyebrows. "Know what it's about, Webb?"

The factory banned hats, loose clothing, or anything that could catch in machinery. Clifford felt vulnerable without his hat. Brow furrowed, he brushed his hand over his bare head. When the man fired the stray bullet at him, he stilled his body and said, "Know not'ing 'bout wat you saying."

The foreman knew the upcoming layoffs would cause friction between the few coloureds and mainly white workers. To ease the tight mask on the coloured's face, he pulled a pen from the collection inside a chipped mug.

"You're a good worker, Webb. Keep to yourself. Do your job. No complaints there." He dropped the pen back. "Watson's an agitator. Idle talk's been going round the factory floor. Men worry. Get touchy. Cause resentment and fear. Think they'll be next to get the push. With all that going on, they're bound to pick on someone different. Just the way it is."

Clifford tightened his arms around his chest and sucked air into his heaving lungs. Lips ironed into a hard, purple line, hot humiliation shot up his neck. Spine stiff like a steel corset nailed to a wall, he cussed in his head. *How many times must England tell me dis damn backside t'ing? "You good worker, Webb. But you coloured." Or, "It because you West Indian are different from us whites." Rass! Dem no t'ink me got feelings like dem?*

Clifford's dark brown eyes sunk into expressionless sockets. He gulped, licked his tongue over his dry lips and tried to buy time. Cool his temper. Act like them. Speak polite, hypocrite Englishness.

"Can't help it if I coloured," he said. His voice shook. "It how I born. Dave Watson and all his kind been after trouble for a long time. If it no me, it next somebody else he pick on. I'm a grown man. I no tangle wid boys." In speaking so,

Clifford wanted the man to understand in plain Jamaican patwa, "Tell Dave Watson fe tak' 'im marga white backside out-a-me face. Else!"

Not understanding coloureds or their lingo, the foreman grunted.

Clifford had heard rumours of the layoffs. But, since he had worked longer at the factory than Dave Watson, he thought they would brush over his head. No one complained about his work. Those who got their cards were the uneducated and lazy; turning up late, they clocked off before finishing their pieces of work. He never did that. Yet the foreman called him in to chasten him for what—his colour— being West Indian?

The foreman stood and rubbed his stubbly chin. "Webb, what I'm saying is watch out. Go careful. I'm no racist, but many out there are."

Although the foreman's interview had troubled Clifford, he kept his worries to himself. The hill had taught him well. Work hard and you eat. Shy away from work and either your belly bawls for hunger or you become a thief on other people's property. He lived by a strict law: do a job well so people respect you. This harsh early training had cemented his character. Yet, hard as he tried to live these principles, badness always seemed to box his face. The foreman's interview made him realise that he often underestimated people. The world was full of more evil-minded people than he had realised. He became more sensitive at the factory. Whispers that had never bothered him were now amplified on the factory floor. Every whispering white seemed to be talking about him. Jokes were about him. Any insults about coloureds were directed at him. He passed Dave Watson drinking tea with another worker during a tea break.

"Who want to work with a blackie?" said Dave.

His friend sniggered. "Soon they'll be more nigs here than white. They're taking over our ruddy country."

Prejudices before had been silent, he had been treated civilly. But what could he do? It was their country.

Bernard Newton

A month later, no sooner did Clifford enter the house than Clara called for him to come quick. He sighed and pulled off his hat. What troubles was she now dropping on his tired shoulders? His belly growled for food, a cup of tea, his newspaper and peace when he entered the hot kitchen.

"Clifford. It Tilda." She flapped her hand at him.

He smelt fish again. Glancing at the pots on the stove, he opened the door leading to the backyard to release some of the smell.

"Eh," he said, easing into a chair. "Mak' man sit before you worry 'im brain, nuh. Tired." Seated, he said, "So," and released a heavy sigh. "Wat dis 'bout Tilda?"

Clara walked to the back door and closed it. "So people no hear our business." She sat opposite him at the table. "White boy box her."

Clifford thought he had heard wrong. He stared blankly at her until the full meaning of her words registered in his brain.

"Woman. Wat dis you saying? Wat you mean 'white boy box her'?" The shut-in heat wetting up his neck, he ran his fingers around his damp collar and undid two buttons. "Box her?"

"Yea."

"She inside?"

"In bedroom. She an' Missy."

Clara was strict with her children. They must respect people, show good manners, and not turn nuisance on neighbours who already thought badly of West Indians. After school, Tilda was allowed short periods of outdoor play.

Now it was the holidays, Clara had wagged her finger at Tilda and told her that so long as she did her set work, she could go out and play. Tilda loved hopscotch, skipping, hula hoop, and most ball games and had made friends with some of the children on her road. She could outrun most of them.

Three doors down from theirs lived a pale-skinned, anaemic-looking girl in a house exactly like Tilda's. Jill had become Tilda's friend. As their friendship grew, and because Tilda was a year older, she became Jill's protector.

Six months before, a bulky, dark-haired, blunt-nosed boy had moved into a house on the next road. Ruddy-faced and pimply, Bernard Newton was a year older than Tilda. He always scowled. Tilda first saw Bernard whilst drawing hopscotch squares in the middle of the road. The second time she and a group were playing *catch ball* and a boy asked Bernard, who leaned against a wall and watched, if he wanted to join. He shrugged his shoulders and grunted. That was when Tilda heard his name. Later, whenever they included him in any game, he insisted he must win. If anyone scored higher, or opposed him, he complained, sulked, and bullied. They tolerated his rudeness for a while but gradually began avoiding him. He still tried to control the group.

When he first saw Tilda, he narrowed his eyes, and she instinctively knew he disliked her. She ignored him, played with the group and went home when the game ended. She never hung around the streets.

＊ ＊ ＊ ＊

Her work completed, Tilda dashed from the house towards the group gathered at the end of the almost car-less street. Her slim arms pumping the warm air, legs flying over the oozing, sticky tarred road, reaching the group and out of breath, she searched for Jill. Her friend hid behind the others, sniffing. Thinking Jill was hurt, Tilda asked what was wrong. Jill shook her head but kept sniffing and rubbing her eyes with her fist. The others stood by silently, their heads bowed. A few shuffled their feet nervously. When Tilda asked what had happened to Jill, no one answered. She was about press Jill for an answer when a loud bark almost shattered her eardrums.

"Keep your nose out, Tilda Webb."

Tilda was so concerned for Jill, that she did not hear Bernard sneaking up to her. She jumped when he bellowed in her ear.

A thin, curly-haired boy, still eager for a game, raised his head and asked, "What shall we play?"

"How about tag?" a girl suggested.

"Not playing if he's playing," said Jill. She made a snuffling sound and scrunched up her red nose.

Bernard looked furious.

The group had been waiting for Tilda when Bernard joined them. Jill, who had run to meet them, had unluckily bumped into Bernard. He had growled and given her a shove. Now he walked up to her, his mouth scrunched in dislike.

"Who asked you, pasty face?" He clenched his right fist and again shoved Jill hard in the chest. She pitched backwards onto the pavement. The unprovoked attack triggered a ripple effect amongst the stunned children. Their mouths opened wide. Each cried "Oh," and shuffled away from Jill.

"Look what you did," Jill said with a whimper as she valiantly tried to pull her ripped skirt over her bloody knees.

Jill sobbed and hugged her knees while Bernard smirked.

Over time Tilda had grown used to the civility in the English schoolyard—no one boxed anyone down. Bernard's unwarranted attack on her defenceless friend on a hot August afternoon turned on the taps. Anger pumping through her veins, Tilda automatically clenched her fists as hard as cricket balls. She swung around, delivered a punishing right into Bernard's belly, a left, a right on the same spot, then jumped from his reach.

The swift, unexpected blows winded the boy. He slumped low, shook his head, and faked a faint. Tilda knew he was pretending but was not quick enough when Bernard quickly pulled back his right arm and slugged an upper right into her belly. The punch hurt Tilda, bad, but she drew deep on her Jamaican schoolyard training. Her slender shoulders tensed, hands balled into fists again, eying Bernard's long arms, she jabbed, dipped, shifted, and then walloped a punishing right and a left into his manhood. She quickly bobbed backwards. A forward leap, another quick right at his chin, downed Bernard again.

Bernard bowed low; he rested his body. Cheeks red, puffing with fury, he raised his head and glared at the girl's determined face. Fists clenched, Tilda stood ready for the next attack. None came. Livid that a coloured girl had whipped him, Bernard straightened up, hocked, and spat a wad of slime at Tilda's feet.

"Nigger," he cried. "Go back to the bush where you belong. Wog. Go back to your jungle home, nigger."

A sick feeling swarmed inside Tilda's tummy. She dropped her arms, glanced at the bewildered faces huddled to the side, turned and ran home. Clara was coming from the front room when she met Tilda hurrying through the front door.

* * * *

"Me tell you, Clifford," said Clara, waggling her head and rubbing her right knee. "No know wat fe do wid she. Even white boy a-press us down now."

Life wearied Clifford. He had left the troubles of the hill for a new life in England; still stink wind followed him. "Mak' me hear wat she say fe herself," he said dully. "Call her."

Moments later, Clara brought in a reluctant Tilda. Head lowered in shame, she shuffled up to Clifford. He studied her bent head. Two thick plaits dangled across her chest. Sensing her sadness, he asked gently, "Wat dis 'bout you an' white boy?"

"I, I fight, dada."

"Why?"

"He, he pushed Jill. Hurt her."

Clifford had heard about Tilda's friend who lived along the road. He was glad she had found a friend in England. She raised her head and stared at him with sad, timid eyes.

"I box him, dada," she stammered guiltily.

Clifford's lips twitched at the corners. They would have spread into a full backside laugh had Tilda stopped there. When she added "He, he call me a nigger. Wog. Say, say, say" and stopped in mid-sentence, his lips tightened into angry lines.

Tilda had no comprehension of what she was trying to explain. Her innocent young brain understood one meaning.

Jamaicans were black, white and all the colours in between. They called their own all sorts of names. When a Jamaican called another Jamaican "neyga," it meant many things. "Tak' you neyga backside from me face, house, yard, pickney, woman, donkey, etc." simply meant, "Go away. Tak' you backside away. Get. From. Me. Face. Get lost."

"Natty-bump-head" was a phrase that Jamaicans used to show contempt for other Jamaicans.

They flung "dry-land tourist" at anyone who thought he or she was better than another person.

"Dry foot" was another term Jamaicans indiscriminately threw at anyone not liked for whatever reason. "De dry foot woman come a-me yard an' want fe feisty me" was simply a way of saying, "A bare-faced, dried-up, stick of a woman had the audacity, the unmitigated gall, to come to my property to cheek me!"

When English Bernard called Tilda "nigger," she identified the word as the Jamaican "neyga", and understood it to mean that Bernard was "bleeding furious she had whipped his backside." It was when she saw his hateful eyes and heard his venomous, guttural tone that something struck her heart and wounded it. She didn't know that it was not only insulting for a non–West Indian to call a coloured a "wog" or "nigger," but also highly degrading. Bernard had not just insulted Tilda's race—he had sealed his contempt with his spit.

Her dada's frozen face dropped icicle sticks down her back. She was definitely getting the strap. When his fist struck the table hard, she jumped.

"Didn't mean to hit him, dada," she blubbered. "It. It only, only, Jill's knee bleed."

Humiliated, thinking she had brought shame to them, babbling through tears, Tilda told her parents that she had not meant to box the boy. It was only that her temper flew into her fists.

Clara reached out to comfort Tilda, but Clifford pulled her onto his knees first.

"Tilda. Dry you eyes," he said stroking her hair. "Wid you. Me no angry. Wid England. Me angry. She dat train de boy fe hate. He saying only wat 'im hears. Learn it from big people. Eh, eh," he said sadly. And, like an old fowl scratching for feed amongst a yard full of pullets, he tried to pick comforting words from his weary brain to salve her hurt.

"Tilda," he said finally. "Listen hard. An' learn. When someone box you. Time mak' dat hurt wash off. But. Wicked words. Words like wat dat boy say. Well. Dat sort. Harder fe scrub free. Stay in you head. Gnaw at you soul. Me no angry wid you. Me proud a-you. Go back to you room," he said, softly easing her off his knees. "It all right." He touched her arm.

He waited for her to leave before saying, "Damn England. Damn dem all!"

Notting Hill Police Station
A Few Weeks Before Riots – August 1958

Sergeant Michael Stone of the Notting Hill Police cradled his jaw in his right arm and studied the top sheet of the mountain of paperwork on his desk. For two hours he had dug through the pile, and still it was stagnant. Tired, his back and eyes aching, and dying for a cup of tea, he rotated his shoulders to ease his aching muscles, puffed out his cheeks and glanced behind him at his underling.

"Any chance of a cuppa?" he asked.

"Not brewed yet, sir."

"Well, till then, any more of them reports come in? 'Bout them troubles?"

"Few sir." The minute the young constable spoke, he regretted it. Had he forgotten that his superior was one pigheaded dolt? Any hint that might ruffle the man's tranquil word was best kept silent. Appear totally neutral, always. He tried to make amends, shift any spotlight away from himself. "Lads on the beat said a few sir. They're getting worried."

"Well. They'll ruddy well have to manage with what comes in. Can't let no shortage of officers stop us doing our job."

"Right you are, sir. But. If I may be so bold, sir, think we're in for a rough time."

"How so, constable?"

Within Notting Hill's seedy boundaries, Timothy Evans had been unjustly accused and hung for murdering his wife and daughter at 10 Rillington Place in 1950. Five years later, in 1955, Timothy Evans was vindicated of the crimes. Mild-spoken and bespectacled John Reginald Halliday Christie, also of 10 Rillington Place, was hanged for the horrific murders. Prostitution, pimping, thieving, murdering, brawling, and gambling—all flourished around Notting Hill's boundary like fleas on a mangy dog.

When whites in the better off London areas refused rental to West Indians, Cypriots and other immigrants, they were forced into the run-down areas of Notting Hill.

The imposing red-bricked police station that served this grim, crime and poverty riddled area, had one fly in its boundary: Notting Dale, nicknamed "the Dale". Not only were the people of the Dale extremely poor, they were also clannish. Resenting anything and anyone foreign, they married their own and supported their own. All others they viewed with suspicion and contempt. When immigrants began renting near them, resentment festered.

The young constable had come from a small country village. Home life too tame, yearning for a meatier patch, he had jumped at the chance to transfer to the Notting Hill area. After witnessing some of the horrific cases that was dragged into the station most nights, he began to question whether he should have stayed local. Especially when he saw officers at the top, like his superior, cruising around in cars, or warming their arses as they shifted paperwork. Deskmen had no clue what *really* happened on the beat.

Tommy Budd reluctantly threw his superior tentative bait, in hopes he would bite. "Been rumours, sir."

Stone was glad for the interruption, he capped his fountain pen, placed it at his elbow, and swung to face his underling.

"What sort?"

"Troublemakers. Teens. Lads and girls. That sort. Teenagers acting like thugs, sir. Teddy boys."

"Teenagers? Thugs? Teddy boys?"

"Yes, sir."

"Thugs, teenagers," mouthed Sergeant Stone thoughtfully. He stretched his arms high above his expanding, middle-aged body, yawned, bowed his head, and, rotating his neck, chuckled. This here, was one very ignorant young constable. Bright sparks like him thought they knew everything. Two a penny in the force, they were. He'd soon settle his hash. He pushed himself to his feet and marched towards the fair-haired copper.

"Lad, lad," he said. "This here's ruddy Notting Hill. Area's ruddy teeming with criminals. Can't leave the ruddy station without bumping into one. Now we *must* deal with a new crop of criminals you say? Teenage thugs you say? Call themselves Teddy boys."

Stone felt he must explain facts to this country bumkin. New to the patch, this one thought every teen was a criminal. Budd should concentrate on the real hard cases and not bother him with trifles like teenagers. He'd put him straight.

"Want educating, lad?" said Stone stabbing a grubby, ink-stained finger at the station door. "Out there's every thief, con man, wife beater, and murderer. Every kind of vermin infesting our beat's out there. Hand you a fiver if you can find one honest crook among that pack. This, Budd, is ruddy Notting Hill.

"Young lads are always out to cause trouble. It's in their nature. The word 'teenagers' never existed in my young days. Bah!" He snorted and cleared his riled throat. "All that tommyrot 'bout teenagers started after war. Youngsters got more money now-a-days than sense. What they need's ruddy conscription. Take the starch out their arses. Mould them into men instead of boys who dress up like ruddy tarts. Take them drainpipe things they wear on their bums," said Stone, warming to his subject. "Tight as a Scotsman's purse, they are. Do themselves a ruddy mischief. Long jackets. And them queer shoes. And hair. What they playing at, I'd like to know. Right proper charlies they look like. More like pansy boys, if you ask me."

"But sir, this time it's different."

"How so?"

"Hatred, sir. Race. Racial name-calling. Attacks on coloureds."

Stone stopped in mid-rant. He grudgingly acknowledged that his junior might have a point. Head tilted, he considered the ifs and buts. Yet for some reason, he could not fathom the seabed that was the coloured race. "Well," he said, finally. "Yes. See what you mean." But Stone really did not, and certainly would never admit this failing to his junior. "Coloureds, eh? Racial stuff, eh? That's what you mean, eh?"

"Yes, sir."

Michael Stone made a gruff hocking sound in his throat. It almost sounded like a dog's yap.

"Well. Ruddy well can't see what all the ruddy fuss is about myself. Harmless horseplay if you ask me." He flicked the ridiculous notion away. Like an insignificant white fleck marring his impeccable navy blue jacket, race played no part in crimes in the area. He ruddy well knew what the ruddy problem was. Too many oversexed teenagers, with too much ruddy money, who had nothing better to do than hang round streets and cause ruddy trouble. Having sorted out the constable, he marched to his desk and picked up his pen.

It was Michael Stone's blindness to the unusual that so exasperated the young constable. The man seemed unable to see further than his nose. Entrenched in his narrow world of hardened criminals, blinded him to what was really happening to coloureds. Complaints by coloureds of harassment by whites had come into the station. Most had been ignored. Stone just did not want to know.

What a numbskull, Budd thought. Only last week, a mate had chanced upon fifteen Teds hanging around the coloured area of Colville Terrace. He approached them and enquired what they were about, the dark-haired lout straddling a souped-up motorbike got snarky, he had sneered at the officer. Asked what it was to a copper. When the officer cautioned the Ted to watch his lip and the rest to move on, they ignored him. As he pulled out his pad to take down their names, they swarmed him, knocked off his helmet, swore at him, and raced off laughing. Stone might choose to ignore the signs, but coppers like Budd on the beat were the ones who got it in the neck.

The Sly Fox

Two weeks after Dave and his mates had met, making certain his parents and brother would be out for the night, a lanky, pasty-faced man joined Dave and his mates in his room. The man's thick chestnut hair was slicked down and parted in the middle. He wore a smart light-grey suit and matching hat. Stooping, he entered the small bedroom reeking of sweat, smoke, and aged cheese.

"This yours?" the man asked, whipping off his hat, he scrutinised the faded wallpaper.

"Yea," said Dave proudly, he hugged the closed door with his back. "Me and me little brother's. Soon get me own pad." Dave gestured to a chair he had borrowed from the kitchen that was wedged beside the bunk bed. "Grab a seat."

"Thanks." The man edged around Dave and dropped his long frame into the chair.

Colin was by the window and Dave by the door. The three, shoulders touching each other, sat on the lower bunk bed. After some shifting and nudging, all settled. The room grew silent. When the silence became unbearable, the blue-eyed, long-faced man pulled his hat off his knee.

"So what do you lads think you can do for our cause," asked the man. He fanned his face with his hat.

"Bleeding lot," said Dave, stroking the tip of his nose. He grinned, recalling the hypnotic power at the fascist meeting he had attended a few days before. The hall had been full to bursting. Mostly men and the few women, they listened spellbound as the Hamm bloke spoke.

When the fascist Jeffrey Hamm stopped halfway through his spiel, Dave craned his neck to get a better look. A tall man had entered from the side of the building. Dressed head to toe in black, he wore some sort of armband. Three young *geezers* in similar togs followed the man. Proud as a peacock the man was when he strode up to Hamm. It was only when the crowd shouted Oswald Mosley, and he threw out his hands to quieten his admirers, that Dave realized who he was.

Colin, always as thick as two planks, nudged Dave in the ribs. "Who's he?"

"Don't you know nothing? That's Mosley. Our leader."

"Oh," replied Colin, unimpressed. Colin then bellowed in his lugholes that "Mosley was just another of them tin pot blokes what wanted power."

Dave could have murdered Colin there and then. Better still, let the crowd do it for him.

Oswald Mosley, Dave had heard, hated blacks. He was out to get them. The man was also trying to get votes for his party. He had been in the spotlight for years, even had a swanky "Sir" before his name. In 1955, some of Mosley's lot had tried to get elected in Brixton. They published a pamphlet entitled "Keep Brixton White–Stop the Negro Invasion". Many West Indians lived in that area and the party went all out campaigning among the Brixton whites. The ultimate goal of the party was to repatriate all coloureds and put a total ban on all mixed marriages.

In 1958 London saw a series of fanatical gatherings as the fascists' vigorously tried to recruit members. Because the Notting Hill area teemed with immigrants, they hoped for success among the disgruntled whites.

While Dave listened to Mosley's speech, one part became forever embedded in his skull: *Britain cannot be painted black. We must stop the invasion now as we did with Hitler's army. Do you want a black Britain?* The voices in the hall had boomed. The crowd went raving mad when Mosley said, *"No!"* And, *"Look what's happening to our jobs."*

Dave agreed, right on! Mosley spoke truth. He gave Colin a wicked jab in the ribs. "Mosley's damn right. 'Cos of blacks, can't even get a decent job after leaving school."

"Thought it was 'cos you never qualified for nothing, Dave?"

Colin's jibe right narked him. Put him in a right nasty temper, it did. Whose fault was it, he'd like to know, that they'd never attended school proper but spent most schooldays skiving down the bombsite? Teachers were to blame.

"I'm qualified more than any black. So shut your fat trap. Else, I'll shut it for you." To let Colin know he was dead serious, he clenched his fist and pushed it into Colin's kisser. This didn't scare the thick head, he grinned like some silly tart.

"Just 'cause I left school at fourteen don't mean I don't know what's what. This me country, isn't it? So why shouldn't I get the pick of the jobs, before some wog? Place's swarming with 'em. Like to drown the bleeding lot."

"Belt up, Dave," Colin said. "Listen. What's he saying?" He jabbed Dave's ribs again. "Ah. Missed the last bit."

"What you care what he says, anyway? Never do nothing 'bout anything anyway."

292

Mosley's electrifying rhetoric excited the crowd so much that it brayed for coloured blood.

"Kill them! Kill the black bastards!" it roared.

"Remember. I never said that," some heard Mosley say as hands eagerly snatched pamphlets to pass on to interested parties. After grabbing a pamphlet labelled "The Coloured Invasion," Dave saw an urgency to learn more. He pushed to the front and asked to speak to a head bloke.

Dave and Colin had to leave the dance at the Palais early so they could meet up with the fascist bloke.

* * * *

The man with uneven teeth brought Dave back to the present with a jolt when he grinned and said, "So. As I said. How can you lads help us?"

"What you suggest?" Dave asked. He flicked his cigarette ash into the cracked saucer on top of the bureau.

Dave heard that the movement paid blokes like him to stir things up. So why blab unnecessary information to the geezer? Try squeezing something from him first. If he got nothing, he'd still do it free for Britain.

"There are ways and means," the man said.

"Such as?" said Colin irritably. Colin was bored. Edgy and right narked, not only did he have to leave the dance early, but the twittering tart he asked for a dance at the Palais had rejected him. The rejection still smarted. This chit-chatting bloke was taxing his limited intelligence. Chatting up birds and mucking about on street corners was more his style. The man came to tell them how to kick the hell out of blacks, so why not get on with it. All he was giving them was a bleedin' polite merry-go-round.

"Our movement never advocates violence," the man said. His cultured voice sounded strange in the dingy room. He swept a calculating eye over Dave, seeing defiance and rage; he bowed his head and chuckled inwardly. No matter what, he must never reveal his disgust for these low-class morons who lived like pigs. A fit term indeed for these uneducated Notting Dale louts. He had heard that years back, Notting Dale was a place that housed pigs and human? Both was rumoured to have wallowed in filth and squalor? From the look of this dump of a hole, nothing much had changed: the great British unwashed. He must tread carefully. Never show even a hint of contempt for the idealistic fools needed for the movement. This ignorant lot hated anything and anyone different. With hundreds of these in the movement, Englishmen would be able to proudly hold their heads high again. Britain would again be the greatest nation on earth, like the old days, when the upper class ruled louts like these.

"Sometimes..." said the man, thoughtfully stroking his chin. He paused to search his brain for words that would never incriminate him or his party.

Dave shifted restlessly against the door. Why didn't the man dispense with all the dilly-dallying? Why not put the bleeding truth on the plate.

"What you mean is, do the bloody black bastards in?"

The man's head jerked backwards. He coughed nervously into his hand when his head narrowly missed hitting the wall. He flicked away an imaginary fluff from his trousers and nursed the flannel with delicate fingertips. "Lads, our methods are diverse. If one proves unsuccessful, we vigorously pursue another. There are several methods available to defend our mother country. Knowing the dangers threatening our motherland, we must all do our part. Do you not agree, lads?"

"Damn right there, mate," said Dave. He punched his right fist into his left palm.

The three on the bunk nodded their agreement. As soon as the toff cleared off, Dave would plan. He was a good planner. Look how many punch-ups they'd had together.

Certain that his indoctrination had sunk into the ignorant skulls; the man stood and donned his hat. "Remember," he said, looking almost apologetic. "And I must emphasise this rigorously. At no time did I ever advocate violence. Remember that. Those who profess our movement encourage violence. Err. What we do is stir people up. Put ideas in their heads. Get them thinking. That's all." He hoped he had given them enough delicate hints of his movement's true intent. If ever challenged, his little talk must never be interpreted as anything else but innocent party business. Softly-softly,—and then with a big stick. These louts know exactly what he meant, even if he had wrapped violence up in cotton wool.

He pulled open the door and left.

Dave was parched for a beer. He paced the small space for one full minute before dropping into the empty chair.

"Colin," he said. "You thinking what I'm thinking?"

"What you thinking, Dave?" asked Colin in his usual clueless way.

"Prepare. Fast! That's what I mean." Dave leapt excitedly from the chair. "Got any weapons?"

Dave's question caught the three off guard. They jumped up. One whacked his heads on the bunk above. Lowering onto the cot again, the one rubbing his sore head asked, "What?"

"Weapons, dolts. What you lot think I mean? Knuckledusters, knives, coshes."

"Oh. See what you mean. Well, got a few," said one.

Coshes and knives and such would require a bit of planning and thieving, but not impossible to get. Excited and raring to go, Dave's face lit up like a Christmas tree.

"Been 'bout," he said, his voice hushed. "Been talking to others." Then, glancing at the door, he mouthed, "Go check, Colin."

Colin reported that all was clear.

"Know fifty willing to join us," Dave said. "Been nosing around 'bout weapons. Know how to get plenty. Knuckle dusters. Knives. Bicycle chains. Belts for weapons. Stuff for bombs." Flushed, his heart racing like a runaway train, Dave envisioned leading them against Britain's black invaders.

Colin, however, was not so sure. Friend or no friend, he would not bloody up his forty-guineas Ted gear for no Nig.

"How d'you know they'll fight with us?" he asked sulkily. He felt betrayed. His best mate should have first discussed his plans with him.

Dave could not believe his ears. Teeth gritted, he resisted the urge to lay one on his friend.

"All English like us, aren't they?" he said. "Want to do this for their country, don't they? That's how I know, thick head."

For the hundredth time, Dave was right narked. He was bleeding fed up with Colin's stupid effin' questions. Had they not been mates for so long—how long, he didn't know—he'd kick the hell out of him.

"We'll do a trial run before the bank holiday," said Dave. "A symbolic gesture for Britain."

"Symbolic of what, Dave?"

296

"Solidarity," said Dave, puffing out his chest. "For the white cause. Keep Britain White. That's what."

"Oh, yea. See what you mean," said Colin. Lowering his head, he wondered if Dave really knew what he was on about.

The three on the bed untangled their legs and stood. One flipped open his fag packet and pushed it at Dave, who pulled one out, stuck it behind his ear, and swaggered. Tomorrow he would see the others. Tomorrow he would recruit his army.

"After tonight," he said, his eyes glittering mischievously, "know just where to start."

Sonny Comes for Help

Since the police and the British government allowed fascists to flout racial propaganda against coloureds around Notting Hill, what were the poor West Indians to do? To whom could they turn for help?

Clifford noticed subtle changes at work. Before, the young Ted Dave Watson, who strutted like a greasy young cockerel, had kept his dislike under wraps. Now, he wantonly flung racial slurs at Clifford, who tried ignoring them. Then one afternoon, walking outside the factory for a smoke, he passed the Ted.

"Webb," Dave Watson shouted. "Hear what Mosley saying 'bout you niggers? 'Keep Britain White.' That's what fellows like me going to do. Keep the likes of your lot out of our country." Dave flicked his smoke at a patch of dusty grass at the side of the building and hocked.

Fists clenched and face tight; Clifford whirled around and strode into the factory.

In his sweltering dark room, blacked-out windows helping Clifford to sleep during the day, he lay fretting in bed. *Some whites at de factory is okay. But wat dem really t'ink 'bout me. All me gets from dem is "Webb do this," or "Take this there, Webb," or, "Foreman wants a word with you, Webb." None ever sit wid me at tea or lunch break. Or invite me fe a smoke or drink at de local pub. When since one ask me family to dem house? Me years in England never give me one glimpse inside dem place. Now dis English yard boy a-crawling under me skin like ringworm. If me didn't need de job, I'd walk out.*

Restless and worried, he twisted over and pulled up his legs.

He slept for four hours before waking up. Searching the space beside him for Clara, he found it empty, shifted his body, punched the musty pillow, kicked the sheets off his hot legs, and fell back asleep. An hour later, a faint ring woke him. His bedroom was the nearest to the front door, and the continual ring drove away his sleep. He slid out of bed, fumbled for his dressing gown, tied the belt, and went to the front door.

"Sonny," he said, blinking at his friend who stood under the door's archway. "Wat you doing 'ere dis time a-day?"

"Ring bell. But whole house must-a-be dead," said Sonny.

"Dead sleeping is wat me doing till you wake me, man."

"Sorry. Escape me you on owl shift. Crucial business only t'ing dat bring me."

"Come in, man. Come. Sit in kitchen till I ready." Clifford ushered him through the passage and into the kitchen. Sonny sat down at the table as Clifford picked up the kettle.

"Want tea?"

"Need some'ting stronger dan Tetley, Clifford."

"Dis early?" asked Clifford, placing the kettle onto the cooker.

"Need liquor. Bad man."

"So you a-say. So you a-say. Go get it."

One of the first pieces of furniture Clifford had bought when he moved to the house was his drinks cabinet. Six months into the move, he placed a down payment on it. Three months later, it arrived. No ordinary piece of furniture, it stood on four shiny black legs, thick at the top. They tapered onto four gold disks. The cabinet was two tiered. A sliding-glass covered front section held glasses and china, and a three-door veneered section with ornate gold handles held Clifford's alcohol.

Clifford placed a bottle of Johnny Walker, a soda, and a small glass before Sonny. He poured a shot, sipped, glanced around the kitchen, and said, "Place fix up nice."

Clifford kissed his teeth and smiled. "Clara been pestering me since de move. Saying place too small wid no decent space fe eat. Wat me fe say to dat?"

"Women," said Sonny. He grinned weakly and ran his right index finger over the rim of the glass.

"Me mash out under de stairs. Fix it up good. An' still de woman no satisfy. Want new sink. Draining board. New table an' chairs. Dat cost me plenty. Me tell you." Clifford shook his head in mock distress. "Married life eat up you money. So," he said, studying Sonny's troubled face. "Wat so urgent so you wake me?"

Sonny took another sip and flattened his hands on the table. "Trouble man. Big trouble."

"You woman wid child?"

"No man."

"Police?"

Sonny blinked and shook his head. Sliding his hands onto his lap, he puffed out his cheeks. "Hum, police," he grunted.

The kettle sang. Clifford filled the teapot and left the tea to brew.

"Big trouble a-coming, Clifford. Fe West Indians."

"Kiss me neck back. Wat you a-saying?"

"Gangs. Mosley bully boys."

"Dat all stale news. De idiot been long time blasting off 'im dutty mout' 'bout us. Usual t'ing."

"Man, it different now. Serious t'ing is wat 'appenin'."

Clifford continued to study his friend. Sonny's short-sleeved green shirt and dark green pants looked expensive. So did his black leather shoes. His gold watch, bracelet, and thick gold ring spoke of money. Thickly oiled, crinkly brown hair, parted on the left, hugged Sonny's scalp like sealskin.

Clifford remembered the run-down Revenue Office in Maggoty Point and Sonny speaking excitedly of his plan to conquer the mother country. Enterprise and determination had earned him an expensive car and two houses. So why had he come to the house with his face looking like a *choco*?

"Clara an' de children in?" asked Sonny, his mind far away.

"She must-a tak' dem to de park. So me sleep. Else dem open up fe you. Back soon, me expect."

Clifford poured his tea, sweetened it with condensed milk, and sat down opposite his friend.

Sonny pulled a cigarette from his Navy Cut pack and lit up. After a drag, he said, "So. You no hear 'bout rioting? Whites an' coloured in Birmingham an' Manchester?"

"Wat dat to us?"

"'Appen dere. Going 'appen 'ere too."

"Who say so?"

Sonny sighed and squinted at Clifford through his cigarette smoke. Did his serious-minded friend, whose only interest was his family, really understand what coloureds faced in London? He played dominoes and frequented blues clubs with other West Indians. Clifford worked, went home, and shut himself up with his tenants.

"Plenty t'ings a-troubling me, Clifford," said Sonny, dabbing the tip of his smoke on a china ashtray. "British newspaper an' television saying not'ing good 'bout us, man. Say we de problem. Say, soon Britain be multicoloured. It, it as if we some sort-a contagious disease infecting Britain." He glanced up when a toilet flushed overhead. "Effects you tenants too. Just come from me cousin Alfred's place. White boys box down 'im an' friends. Dem in hospital."

"Kiss me neck back. Man. You joking? Serious?"

Sonny stood, walked to the back door, swung around, and threw out his hands in anger. "Walking. Dat all dem a-do. Walk. When, say, ten Teds jump dem. In bad shape. Hospital." His eyes seemed to sink into their sockets when he fell back onto the chair.

"Sorry, man."

Sonny explained. Alfred and two friends had been on their way to a blues party by bus. Jumping off and turning a corner, white thugs circled and attacked them. Putting the boot into the three, they left Alfred for dead on the pavement.

"Never stand a chance, man," said Sonny, his lips twisted in contempt. "Know wat de dutty mout', black-haired sint'ing an' friends say as dem lash at Alfred? 'Going carve up the rest of you Nig boy. Going keep likes of you out. And Keep Britain white. Take this for starters.' Dat's wat dem dutty mout' shoot off, Clifford. Dat wat Alfred say 'appen. War is 'appenin' on us, man."

Clifford could not believe what he was hearing. If being coloured was why Alfred and his friends had been beaten up, who was next?

"Police know who dem be?"

Sonny mashed out his smoke angrily. "Police? When since police worry dem backside 'bout us? It white boys wat do dis, Clifford!"

Dave Watson immediately jumped into Clifford's mind. Confrontation would come soon. He would lose his job. Why was trouble always biting his heels? Only once had he visited the depressed, run-down areas around Notting Hill. It disturbed him. If coloureds complained about their rental conditions, onto the streets went their little belongings. So, they suffered in silence in the hope that better would come. Degrading conditions forced a few, like Clifford and Sonny, to sacrifice to buy a place of their own.

On the island some Jamaicans that had a sore that refused to heal administered blue bloodstone as a treatment. Used to treat cattle with infected sores, blue bloodstone was a last resort for humans. Though it hurt like living hell, it eventually healed putrid sores. And so it was with West Indians in Britain. Enduring painful racial prejudice, they hoped for a better life for their children.

England did not know Jamaicans; she was wringing their patience dry.

"If wat you say is fact," said Clifford. "An' dat me no doubt. Wat you say we do?"

"Come Thursday evening," said Sonny. "Few West Indians a-meet at Alfred's place. Want you dere."

"Me? Why?"

"Hear you respectable, sober family man wid cool head sense."

Once, Clifford would have chuckled at the praise. Not now.

"No know wat good dat gwan do."

"We go. We talk. We plan. Den wait see if England come burn us inside our house."

Sonny joked. But what else could he say. Somehow he must survive in white man's country. He talked jackass foolishness to try and wash over the burden coloureds must bear in England.

"Come fe you a-seven."

Getting Fried

After Sonny's visit, at dinner that evening, between mouthfuls, Clifford told Clara of Sonny's visit and his decision to attend the Thursday evening meeting. Clara patiently listened for a while. When Clifford mentioned the meeting was for coloureds to plan how to stop the attacks, she stopped chewing. Staring daggers at him, she stabbed her hard cornmeal dumpling with her fork and sliced it in two. She divided it into quarters, dipped a portion into the thick gravy, and pushed it into her mouth. Even with gravy, the dumpling tasted like a lump of clay on her tongue. She was chewing another quarter of the tasteless flour ball, gumming up her teeth, when she heard a *slap-slap*. Someone was eating with his mouth open.

"Buoy," she said, turning irritably to Roy and pursing her lips."Why you mout' full up so? T'ink you a-animal? Want I tak' food from you?"

Roy bowed his head.

"I was only..." he began. Clutching his knife and fork for protection, he tried to explain. And he did explain—succinctly. He gave her good evidence. She had falsely accused him. His mouth had *not* been full up. It was not his mouth's fault if, whilst it chewed, it sounded like a pig's. For this was the only way his mouth knew how to chew. Yet, try

305

as Roy might to explain sincerely, with an innocent face, when he saw his mama's sour mouth, he bowed his head.

Not once, during the entire ruckus, had Missy or Tilda raised their heads. They quietly ate their stew and cornmeal dumplings. They knew what their mama's vexed face meant. Shut up. Eat up. With your mouth shut. For no matter how innocent you may look, no matter what you say, as sure as England fogged over in winter, when mama's face turns sour, she will drag out the chastisement until your head hangs low like a donkey's.

"Buoy," said Clara again, swallowing her lump of dumpling. "If. If you know wat good fe you. You shut you mout'. Want me use somebody else fat fe fry you?"

Roy gulped. He glanced at Missy's bent head, then took a quick peep at Tilda, who was delicately biting a piece of dumpling.

Both knew their annoying brother had slipped up. Still young and raw, Roy did not yet know the danger signs. Mama was vexed about something and he was getting fried for it.

Oblivious, it seemed, to the battle raging around him, Clifford finished his food, paired his knife and fork on his plate, and left.

Clara had had a provoking day. Their tenant Nora Nugent had dragged her onto the third floor to complain in her whiny Barbadian voice about sheets. Clifford's table news about coloureds' trouble, and his Thursday evening meeting, had pushed dry tinder under her simmering temper. It craved release. She ordered Missy and Tilda to wash and dry up and Roy to help. Her apron, off, she marched in search of Clifford. He was reading a newspaper in the front room. Closing the door behind her, she blurted out, "Man. A mad, you is mad?"

Clifford and Clara had a rule: never disagree or quarrel in front of the children– if a dispute startes simmering, hold fire for private war later. Clara felt that the mango was now fully ripe for picking. She positioned her feet beside the pull-out bed, jammed both hands onto her hips, and tilted her head backwards to give wind free passage to her words.

"Is England you a-come so you gets dead, Clifford Webb?" At all cost, she thought, *no mak' me talk raw patwa.*

Clifford's eyelids twitched. He scanned page two of the newspaper, turned it over, read the top section of page three, and then said quietly, "Woman. Stop dis nonsense."

He continued reading.

Arguments and unpleasantness troubled Clifford. His evening meal over, he liked to retire to the front room with his newspaper, a cup of tea or coffee, and a smoke at his elbow. This was his only solace in his troubled household. Clara's outbursts were as unpredictable and devastating as a hurricane. He called her "woman" to protect against her peppery tongue. It was a signal—she must hush up her mouth and leave him to enjoy his quiet. She ignored it.

"Eh, eh. Aho," said Clara. "So. It stupid-ness I saying, eh? Clifford Webb. How come. When me say good, sensible t'ing. It stupid-ness you a-say me a-say? Eh?"

Clifford shook the newspaper and raised it as a shield before his face. "Woman. Reason wid youself," he said. "Is cuss an' bad mout' you want English people fling 'pon us. An' we swallow it? Eh. Dat you want?"

Clara could recite chapter and verse the words he used to pacify her anger at English nastiness. *It dem country. Act polite. We dem guests. Soon we go home. So cork up you ears an' bear till den.* Now he was throwing different corn to smooth her feathers.

"Clifford," she said, walking up to him. "Youself a-say. Dis a-white people country. So why put de English on practice, eh? Long time now, as youself learn. White people is ignorant an' *out-a-order*. Dem got no liking fe us. 'Ere, we is strangers. We go home soon, you a-tell me. So why you no leave de English alone, nuh? Why you want fe stir up ants' nest?"

His quiet enjoyment now ruined, Clifford kissed his teeth and placed the newspaper on the side table.

"Clara. T'ink me want go?" Rising, he made to take her hand. "Look in me eye!" But when she pulled away from him and soured up her mouth, he cried angrily, "Woman! Understand dis. I no coward. Is *juck* you want de English fe juck knife us in our back? An' we say. 'T'ank. You. Mr. Englishman?' Time come fe Jamaicans fe understand dis. Britain no care one backside 'bout dem. So it we dat must find ways fe care fe our own business."

"Still it no mak' me change me mind," she fired back. "Suppose dem a-lick you down? Box you senseless? Who gwan cry fe you in dis pitiless country? Do dis t'ing, Clifford Webb. An' only God alone know wat gwan 'appen."

"Hush you mout', woman. No try fe make batty man out a-me. Not'ing gwan 'appen. Only meeting."

"Eh. Eh, Clifford Webb," she said, shaking her head sadly. "You is one fool-fool duppy. You t'ink coloured men can stand up to white man in 'im own country? T'ink you can change English t'inking? Lick down is wat you gwan get."

A feeling of loss and hopelessness engulfed her, she slid onto the bed and hugged her body with her arms. *Why, soon as a little sunshine a-come me way, storm clouds always a-settle over me head?* "No go, Clifford. Dis no you business."

"Soon may be."

308

She stood, defeated.

"Me a-beg you, Clifford. No bring white people trouble 'pon us. Already you self know how dem stay wid us."

"Listen," he said. She must understand he was serious. Vexed, he reverted to patwa. "All me a-doin' is see wat dem a-say. But dis fact understand. It no right wat 'appenin' to coloured people. T'ink. Till Englan' drive us out. Dem no satisfy. Wat 'bout our pickney, eh? Missy. Tilda an' Roy. Answer me dat?

"Wat 'bout dem? Eh. Want when dem big dem can't hold dem head high in Englan'? Shame who dem be? Eh. Dat you want? Our childs feel inferior to whites? T'ink dem no know wat a-'appenin' a-Englan'. Youself know dem got ears an eyes fe notice how de English feel 'bout dem. Notice how Tilda a-get quiet. Like she feel shamed. Me pickneys never fear who dem be till dem land a-Englan'. Englan' want dem fe turn shy puss. If me suffer fe dem. It good price payment fe dem future." His voice sounded high, sharp, like a whip on her bare back. Wincing, she stared at his angry mouth.

"You de one fe tell Missy she inferior. Hear wat me a-saying woman? Backside." He stormed from the room.

Clifford gone, Clara dropped back onto the bed.

Where had all the gladness in her heart gone? England's betrayal had soured her spirit. She lifted her skirt and fanned her hot legs. When Clifford wrote to her while she was in Jamaica, he had told her they would have their own place in England, and a front and back garden for the children to play in. He would have a good, respectable job. She could invite friends for tea and cake. Visit all the places she had read about at school: Buckingham Palace and Windsor Castle. The kind English would invite her to tea. She would make plenty of friends. All the fool-fool dreams had evaporated like water in a desert. That English people did not like coloured people was fact. That they did not want them in their country and did not have good manners was fact.

She felt no prejudice or hatred for the English. She was tender-hearted to all the Almighty's children. What grieved her, burned at her heart, was what she heard the English say about coloureds. She had thought her English next-door neighbour Alice was a friend. Alice was polite and friendly whenever they spoke. She had even asked her where she was from and how many children she had. It was only whilst hanging her washing in the back garden one day that she came to understand what Alice and her friend Mavis really thought about her. It stayed in her head like a constant moving picture show.

* * * *

"Tell you, Mavis," said Alice. "Could move today. Would. Pack me bleedin' bags. Off like a shot. But with my brood, where would I get a place as cheap as this?"

"Know what you mean, Alice. Bloomin' cheek gover'ment 'ave. Lettin' coloureds swarm in like flies. Take jobs. Houses. Got no say in matters, we don't. Me old man, Cyril, bless his bloomin' 'art. When not at the pub, or knockin' kids about, says, says to me, other day he did, says 'ow he'd like to send the bleedin' lot packing back to where they come from."

Alice hitched up her sagging bosom and settled her slippers beside a red rose bush. Simple Londoners, united by road and class, Alice and Mavis knew no other life than rearing their families. Husbands, friends, radio, and newspapers fed them information about the workings of their country.

"Seems to me, Mavis," said Alice, reflecting on what she had heard on the BBC, "Us lot's got no say 'ow the bleedin' country's run." She gestured at a distant house with her thumb. "Lil Brown. 'Er down the road. Can't stand wogs. Take the lot next door to me. Packed to the rafters with Nigs place is. Lil Brown says they're floodin' into Paddington Station like a bleedin' tidal wave."

"Joking, aren't ya? Where'd she get that from?" asked Mavis.

"Newspapers. Radio. Says soon there'll be no whites left in Britain. Says soon we'll all be bleedin' mixed like. Like some bleedin' mul-a-wa-toos or some such bleedin' jungle name. That's what Lil says we'll be soon. Reckons, reckons by then, with luck, we'll all be safe in our bleedin' coffins."

"Alice," shrieked Mavis. Lips puckered, she turned her horrified brown eyes onto her friend over the fence. "Me? A granny to a bloomin' half-breed? Not bloomin' likely. Does that mean my Mary? My Norm? Going to marry a nig nog? And create this new hybrid? What-you-may-call-it, Alice? Mul-a-wa-too race?

"Cor blimy, Alice." Then, eyes rolling, Mavis added, "Be like matin' bloomin' racehorses?"

It was at that precise moment that the penny finally dropped into Alice's brain. Rattling on and on, joking with her friend Mavis about what might happen to other Brits, she had not considered the ramifications in regards to her own family. If Britain became awash with coloureds, her children might be guinea pigs in this breeding. For to get puppies, a bitch must mate with a dog. The fact of the matter was, dogs didn't care whom they mated with. Alice's brain steamed with the dire consequences.

"Your Norm datin' a bleedin' black girl yet?" asked Alice, puckering her lips. She wondered if her friend Mavis was liberal minded?

"Not bloomin' likely." Mavis chuckled. "Knock 'is bloomin' block off, I would." To reinforce her disgust, Mavis borrowed several swear words from her husband. Her man might have bigger fists, but she wore the trousers in the house.

"Warned, him I did," said Mavis, her cheeks hot with indignation. "Good and proper, I did. Soon as lad steps in, I says, 'Norm,' I says. 'Norm. I'll have none of that funny business in my house.' Asked him straight out, I did. Says, says to Norm, 'Don't bring none of them nig nog girls home, my lad. I'm havin' none of it.'"

Alice got a fit of the giggles. Unable to control the stabbing stitch in her right side, she bent low, guffawed, and chortled at the idea—Alice's Norm mating with a coloured girl? Another bout of giggles struck her. Clutching the fence, she sucked hard at the air. She would have recovered sooner from her giggles if the image of her lifelong friend Mavis bouncing a woolly headed black baby on her knee had not jumped into her head. Roaring uncontrollably, gasping for breath, Alice dropped almost to her knees and clutched her side. "What. What'd Norm say?" she panted.

Mavis tugged at an escaping roller, tucked it under its net, and patiently waited for her friend to sort herself out, so she could explain.

"Barmy," said Mavis, giving her pink roller a pat. "Said I was stark ravin' mad. Looked at me strange, he did. Sniffed me up and down. Asked if I'd swilled the whole bleedin' bottle of cough mixture his brother's been takin' for his condition."

"How's the little bleeder by the way? Condition better?" asked Alice, who was now more or less composed.

Mavis's four-year-old son Billy had made an unexpected appearance when she was forty-five, ten years after she thought she was done with that sort of thing. Billy had almost died from croup the previous winter, and it had kept him hacking into spring.

"Right as rain now. Ta," said Mavis. "Gave me a right turn, it did. Pulled through though, glad to say."

"Hear 'bout them Teds attackin' blacks?" asked Mavis, suddenly changing the subject.

"Larks? Did I?" Alice licked her thin, dry lips. "Was younger I'd join them, would."

"Joking, aren't ya?"

"Why not?" said Alice. A whistle came from her kitchen. Turning to listen, she said, "Kettle's on. Better half's home. See ya. Ta-ra."

"Yeh. Ta-ra," said Mavis.

Driving to Notting Hill
Thursday Evening, August 28, 1958

As promised, Sonny picked up Clifford the following Thursday evening for the scheduled meeting. It was sweltering hot in the car as they headed towards Harrow Road. Clifford began thinking about the children. Now that they were getting big it was difficult to keep disagreements from their ears.

Strong-willed Roy was due for a licking on his backside. Three days ago, although Clara had warned him plenty of times not to kick the ball near the back window, hearing a crack, she dragged the boy inside and demanded to know why he hadn't listened. The next day, at the same cracked window, the *hard-a-ears* boy kicked the same ball.

Missy, she was always into her own world, never say much, just get on with her life. Tough and resilient, she was doing well at school.

And Tilda, lately she had been creeping around the house like a timid puss—acting strange and peculiar. Had she heard the labrish about the coloured trouble and was taking things to heart She was one peculiar pickney. He never knew how to take her. Look at the way she flew at the white boy Bernard.

Not long ago Tilda asked him what a Jew was. He asked her why. Dropping her head and going all shy-shy, she said that a girl at school had asked her who was her favourite singer.

She told the girl Frankie Vaughan. He sang well and was handsome. She was surprised when the girl screwed up her mouth and said, "Don't like him. He's a Jew." Tilda then asked him again what a Jew was. How could he answer her? Staring down at the questioning eyes, his heart sad, he told her that the Baby Jesus was a Jew. And the Baby Jesus was a very special person. She looked at him, blinked but said nothing. If this was what the English taught their pickney, what sort of life would his have in Britain?

He peered through the window. "Man. Why you a-go dis way?"

"Precautions. Case we meet trouble. No want Clara fe put obeah 'pon me," Sonny said jokingly. He checked a side mirror. "Hear 'bout wat 'appen to some coloured boys last evening?"

"A little."

"Teddy buoys out fe get us Clifford. Bad blood out dere, man. Trouble fe us."

"Suppose it isolated incident?" asked Clifford.

"Clifford." Sonny sighed. "De English a-out neyga hunting, man. Doing safari on us. Jamaicans dem want fe dem tiger trophy." Sonny chortled and jiggered his shoulders.

"It no joking matter you saying, you know," said Clifford, wishing he had listened to Clara and stayed home.

"Sorry, man. Wat you expect me fe do? T'row frock over me head? Bawl like woman? Consider, Clifford. We are subjects of Her Majesty de Queen. Yet her people out prowling her streets fe box us down. T'ink dem care one backside 'bout us?"

Clifford studied the roads. The car swerved left at Chippenham Road, back onto Elgin, and headed towards Maida Vale. Entering the secluded area of Maida Vale, Sonny cooled his speed and cruised along the leafy avenues where mature elms and well-kept lawns hid luxurious homes. Maida Vale was a distant world from the squalid box room that Sonny's cousin Alfred rented.

"Dis no de way. You lost?" asked Clifford, craning his neck to get a better view.

"No, man. Out a little. Back route I taking. Like me a-say. Case a-trouble. Cut through Randolph Avenue, den back a-Sutherland." Sonny pushed his hat from his forehead.

Clifford did not own a car. He thought he might start taking driving lessons after tonight, using what little savings he had. He could buy a reasonable second-hand car; take Clara and the children on outings. As he thought on this good idea, a grey cloud soured his happiness. How many places in England would welcome coloured people on an outing? One of Clara's relatives lived some place up north. She had not seen her for a long time. He could take her there.

A gardener pushing a wheelbarrow in the humid evening came into view. Clifford gazed in wonderment at the huge places of the well-off whites. What Clara would say if she glimpsed one of these? A queen she would be, living here. Missy, Tilda, and Roy would play hide-and-seek among the trees. Roy would have *trickify* adventures. As his fanciful thoughts enlarged, reality quickly halted him. *Cha man*, it said. *Why t'ink such stupidness? Places like dese cost big money*. Clifford chuckled quietly at his jackass pipe dream. Where would the big money come from to buy one of these

316

mansions? It was madness to think he could live beside these people.

"Wat de fun for, man?"

"No want fe hear it," said Clifford, regretting he had allowed his dream to see daylight.

"Try me?"

"See where we is?"

"Yeh man. Money places. Rich white people. Wid plenty money."

"Remember now. I only imagine it, me a-say. See meself buying one. Children playing 'ere. Clara on lawn wid her china set. Entertaining."

"You serious?" Sonny glanced at his friend, and then turned to the road.

"Remember. Me a-say. Me-a-imagine it. Plenty t'ings 'appen when I dream, you know. Imagining all a-it. I ask meself. How I pay fe it?"

Sonny's eyes became hard bullets of concentration. Hands tight on the wheel, he silenced his lips so as not to dampen his friend's wild fantasies. Would England ever turn into a place where hard-working coloureds could get on? Live where they wanted and not be forced into squalid slums? Left to their ingenuity, Jamaicans would hustle to rise up. Only slack people sat on their backsides to let others feed them

Visualising opportunities aplenty in the leafy avenues, Sonny's shoulders itched to bounce with laughter. Unable to control his jackass thoughts, he said, "Clifford. It easy fe afford one a-dese. Rent it out. Plenty West Indians want place fe live. Dese houses 'ave twelve, sixteen rooms. At least." He stabbed a finger at a large mansion. Four stories high, it was over twice as wide. The huge grounds, large enough to fit six of Clifford's houses and plenty of spare space; Sonny saw prospects.

"Eh?" Clifford said. Swinging his head, he stared at Sonny.

"Clifford. Man. T'ink. Place like dese. Full up wid West Indians? Fulfil you dream. Mak' plenty money. Fe retire to Jamaica. Live like a king. Clifford. Dese people is *desperate* fe 'ave us fe neighbours."

Sonny could no longer contain the backside laugh bubbling in his belly. Shaking with laughter, he almost lost control of the car when it nicked the kerb.

"You one born idiot, you know," said Clifford after Sonny righted the vehicle. "Want dead us?" Yet, was Sonny's suggestion such a jackass one? Rent it out. That was what some West Indians did in Britain to improve themselves. Rent it out. That's what he had done with his two houses.

More like renting out trouble.

* * * *

In Jamaica, only Clifford and his family had lived in their house. In England, tenants and trouble always locked him up.

He thought on the bottle-necked, Small-Island woman and the red-eyed devil she had brought to his house. After her, the quiet, slim man from St. Kitts who crept around the house like a jumby.

The sky had been cloudy all day. It looked like rain. A man pressed the bell. Invited in, he asked if he could rent a room. Clifford saw desperation in the man's eyes to rent a room. Checking him over, he saw a well-dressed, quiet, and respectable man. He thought he would make an ideal tenant.

He rented a room to him. *Backside.* Look what had happened. Nobody knew a thing.

Two months after the man moved in, Clara, never able to abide nastiness in her place was always cleaning. She pulled the hallway rug off the floor, opened the front door, banged the rug against the low brick wall and laid it back. A capful of Dettol into a bucket of hot water, soap added, and a mop dropped inside, she wrung out the mop and began pushing it over the worn linoleum. At the foot of the stairs she smelt something bad above the Dettol odour. Had a rat died inside the house she wondered. She placed the mop against a wall in the passage and scoured the main floor. She climbed up the second. Both were vermin free. The smell was more distinct on the third floor. The tenants in the small and middle rooms questioned, the bathroom and latrine checked, she rapped at the door of the largest room. No reply. She pressed her nose against the door, hurried to the railing, and bawled for Clifford to come quick. Said it was urgent.

Her insistent summons hastened him to the bottom step. He looked up and asked what she wanted. Hurry up, she said. Bring his spare key. The Small Island's room had a stinky smell.

Hoping he had not been smoking ganga or trying to burn down the house, he hurried up. Her troubled face made him touch her arm. He asked what the trouble was. Pointing to the door, she repeated herself. A nasty, *dutty* smell was coming from inside. He asked if the man was in. She shook her head. Said she did not know. All she had done was knock on the door and no one answered. She suspected something bad had happened to cause such a stink smell.

"Mr. Collins, Mr. Collins," he called. He knocked loud and long. "Mr. Collins, open up, me say. Open up." When silence greeted him, panicking, he quickly inserted his spare key, knocked again, turned the knob, and pushed. The smell almost sliced off his head. A flesh-rotting stink floated out of the room. It pitched him backwards. Fear gripping him, he covered his mouth with his hand and pulled the door shut. Hands trembling, heart rattling, he knew. Something was dead. Something inside the room was dead, and rotting.

"T'ink some'ting dead in dere," he finally stammered. "Hurry. Go. Telephone fe police. Gwan lock door till dem come." Seeing fear and dread in her eyes, he cried, "Go, me a-say. Quick!"

They came. Police and ambulance. All treated him like a criminal. He who always tried to avoid trouble—scandal and disgrace had come to his house again. How was he to know the man planned on killing himself? He never told anyone. Never placed a label on his forehead that read *Me gwan dead meself.* Sirens blared. Tires screeched. Dirty boots trampled all over his house.

Tilda heard the commotion of the English voices and saw the stretcher carrying out the man's body. "Dada," she asked. "Is Mr. Collins sick?"

What could he say to her? Pickneys didn't understand such things. Disturbed, he stared at her troubled eyes. Clara rescued him. She told her and Missy to go to the back room with Roy, to stay there until called.

Police swarmed his house like blue bottle flies at a cow's backside. Whites on his street who before avoided him like the plague were suddenly attentive. They swooped onto his doorstep, gawked and needed to know his business. Some spied from behind the comfort of white nets. All wanted to know whom the coloureds had murdered.

How eager the flush-faced, navy-blue-suited white boys were to question him.

"Mr. Webb," they asked their eyes suspicious. "Have you any idea why Mr. Collins took his life?"

Backside! Wat sort a-rawtedness a-dat? How me fe know dat? Me no de man's confessor.

"No. I have no idea." The question rattled and shook him bad. He had never interfered in his tenants' business. They paid their rent, never *jumped poco* over his head, and he was contented. Did these white boys not understand? That the man killed himself in his place was a bad disturbance. But they still wanted to winkle meat out of an empty crab leg.

"Did you see any indication of this happening, Mr. Webb?"

Were these police boys some fool-fool jackasses? Except for when the man paid his rent, their paths barely crossed. Most times, the man had handed his rent to Clara. If he were feisty, or nasty mouthed, he would have told them facts their ears would not want to hear.

Facts said: the man grew downhearted because of the prejudice heaped on his head. Facts said: lonely, anxious, and frightened, he had depression set in on him. Facts said: man dead, Britain no care one batty. It was one less black man in the country.

"No," he told the British law. "None."

* * * *

Then there were those sisters. From Grenada or from Trinidad, he never remembered which. Comely and friendly, they smiled and nodded at all his questions. He rented one room to both. Backside! Luckily the police did not visit then. Why had the Good Lord not warned him these were two-time trouble? What had he ever done to deserve the trouble that always a *heighed* him? All he had ever wanted was just to provide for his family.

Missy had just walked in from school. "Dada," she said, passing him and wrinkling her nose. "What's that funny smell?"

He showed her his smoke. "Me cigarette."

"Not that kind of smell, Dada. This different. It stinky."

His nose holes already full of his Navy Cut and Clara's fried fish and boiled cabbage, he could not detect the different smells. Fresh from outside, Missy could.

"Since you mention it," he said, crinkling his eyes as the smoke hit them. "Best me go check upstairs. Case tenants set fire to de house."

The second-floor landing smelt strongly of smoke. He knocked on the first and second door of the third floor. No one answered. The third door eased open at his knock. A sister pushed out her head.

"Good day, Maas Webb." She smiled and fluttered her eyelids as if she had been blowing fire under a cooking pot and the ashes had flown into her eyes. "Wat me fe do fe you, Mass Webb?"

"Mistress," he said politely. "I ask you. Please step out 'ere a minute. Have some'ting fe ask you."

She pulled the door closed behind her. When she turned her innocent eyes upon him, he could damn well tell. Her innocent look was a sham. She took him for a jackass.

Feisty as a mangy dog sniffing at a meat bone, he asked, "A weed you an' you sister smoking in me house, mistress?"

His forwardness seemed to shock her. Face tight, she opened her mouth as if to answer. But snapped it shut and lowered her head and stared at her slippered feet.

"Mistress," he said again. He sucked air into his vexed lungs and studied her bowed head. "Since you no answering me. An' since you an' you sister a-tak' me fe some jackass. Plainness is wat me now saying. Dis a-respectable house. It both a-you mistake fe t'ink you can conceal ganga from me. I born where it grow plentiful a-bush. Since both a-you favour it. Best you find someplace else fe live. I give you both notice fe leave me place."

A month later, they left.

* * * *

The car left Maida Vale for Randolph Avenue. A sharp turn at Sutherland Avenue almost pitched Clifford onto Sonny. Checking to see if white boys were out looking for them, Clifford carefully scanned the road. Turning left at Ladbroke Grove and entering St. Helen's Gardens, the car suddenly jerked and Sonny cried, "Backside. Clifford look. Look up front!"

Clifford bent low and peered ahead. Hundreds of screaming white teens wielding iron bars and sticks covered the entire pavement and road. Swearing and ranting, they hurtled towards coloured houses. Acrid fumes belched from a lone car turned onto its side. A petrol bomb whizzed through the broken window of a house. Exploding, it lit up the teenager's gleeful faces as they pounded houses, trampled gardens, broke down fences, and smashed windows.

"Rass," said Sonny, frantically swinging the car right. "Hold tight, man!"

Throat tight, legs trembling, Clifford clutched the door handle and yelled, "Backside! Move. Man. Move car outta here. Quick."

Sonny crunched the gears, spun the wheel, hit the curb, swung the car left, jammed the accelerator to the ground, and roared back the way they came.

Heart racing, fists fastened to the wheel, Sonny stared ahead. "Check. Road," he gasped. "See. If. Dem. Following. Side. Roads. Too."

Barely breathing—to do so might conjure up the mob—Clifford checked the roads and alleyways. The car roared through Oxford Gardens, turned right on Portobello Road, zoomed onto Lancaster Road, right on St. Luke's, and pulled up outside the three-storey building where Alfred lived.

Sonny and Clifford hurried up the six concrete steps and rapped hard on the door. A man opened it, peered out, opened it wider, and hustled them in. Sonny did not greet the man. He pulled off his hat, strode to the foot of the stairs, looked up, and asked the man if everyone had arrived. The man slackened his lips and studied Sonny. He then said that all invited were inside. Sensing something was up with Sonny, the man said, "Rest up Sonny. Some over dere too." He pointed at a group of eight men and women chatting left of an open door. Two single mattresses rested upright against a wall.

"Cha Benny. Glad fe see you man," said Sonny. "Only. Hurry dem inside room nuh. Quick. It serious t'ing me telling dem."

"Hear so. So you say." Benny threw Sonny an odd look. He was about to question him further, but seeing Sonny's grim face, changed his mind, cupped his hand over his mouth and called up, "You. All a-you up top. Come down nuh. Sonny say hustle. Want you down quick. You by door." He flapped his hand at the group by the mattresses. "Shuffle inside. Sonny got urgent business fe talk."

Benny turned to Sonny. "So. Wat dis 'bout, man?"

"Tell you all now."

Dark-skinned Jamaican Benny Wilson was from St. Mary Parish. He shared a room with Alfred. Clifford and

Sonny followed Benny into the double room where, to make more space, a wardrobe, single dresser, and small round table had been pushed against a wall. Discoloured brown and green curtains covered a dirty sash window. England's cold and damp had slowly peeled away the edges of the discoloured wallpaper in the room that had been warmed by paraffin heaters. Its elephant-like ears hung below the ceiling. The room was bare, stark, and impersonal. No pictures, no ornaments. No photographs, no mementos from home. Linoleum floor, no rugs, no carpet, men slept and ate here. For, scarce they had come, and scarce they lived. Save and send money home. Survival was their ticket.

Sonny threw out his hand and told them to listen. Where he just came from hundreds of white teens were attacking coloured places.

Patwa panic drowned him out. Sweating, and deeply agitated, a broad-faced woman fought her way to him.

"Sonny," she cried, panting and rolling her eyes. "It near where me live. Me husband in same place. Lawd-a-massy. Sonny. Tell me before me head bust. Me man okay?"

Sonny tried to console her. So as not to worry her unduly, he lied when he told her that the riots were not where she lived. He told her he was certain that the police would soon settle this backside trouble before it splashed over the newspaper. Britain might not want coloureds in her country, but she also did not want all the world to see that her clothesline was full of dutty washing.

"T'ink dem coming dis way?" a nervous man asked Clifford. Jamming a smoke between his lips, he lit up.

"Dat we no know. We never wait fe find out. But all me-a-say is. Afore night's out. No surprise some coloured gwan gets dead."

325

The room exploded into another patwa-fuelled panic. Another woman whose husband lived in the area made a dash for the door. Benny grabbed her arm, pulled her back, patted her on the shoulder, and told her to calm herself and stay.

Clifford grew nervous in the confusion and panic. He had come with Sonny to talk and calm fears. Perhaps settle on a way for coloureds to survive in Britain. That had changed. Frightened faces stared at Sonny for a solution. His hand brushing sweat from his face, Sonny looked worried.

Sonny told them that trouble was close by. That was certain. No one knew where and if it would dry out. He advised those living in the house to stay indoors and offer a night's rest for those from the troubled places.

"Mistress Toole live dere," he said, turning to the distressed woman. "Who can put her up till morning?" When a few volunteered, he said, "Aho. Good. Rest. Mak' space fe odders. See Mistress Toole sleep so till morning. Few men walks her home. Den see she okay. I t'inking. Best we stay tight tonight. So t'ings settle. Dis a-serious business dat a-'appenin'. It crucial we act wisely. T'ings 'appenin' a-London streets. Dat makes me t'ink. Plenty a-us gwan gets dead. It urgent we meet. Say. Early afternoon. De Bank Holiday. Monday. Den plan how fe settle dis backside business."

Later, driving east on Tavistock Road to drop off Clifford, Sonny kept silent. Perched on the black plastic, his body taut and alert Clifford left his friend to concentrate on the drive, while his mind conjured up vengeful teenagers at every turn of the wheel.

"Man. Wat in you head?" he asked Sonny after a long silence.

"Trinny. De half-caste Trinidadian," said Sonny. His flattened his lips as he recalled the puffed up, light-skinned man who had tried downplaying the concerns at the meeting. The man had told Sonny he was afraid of no one. After Sonny said that all coloureds were in this together, and must assist each other, the Trinidadian fanned Sonny with his grinning teeth. He called him a "yellow-skinned Jamaican man." It wasn't whites the man said that worried him. It was coloureds who thought they could take on Britain. Suppose Britain heard what they were planning, and shipped them back home? Blasting the room with this argument, the man tried to undermine Sonny. He caused more dread amongst the people.

"Last week. First time I step in man's place. Ask 'im fe come tonight. Man show resistance," said Sonny, who was still vexed with the man.

"Wat you tell man?" asked Clifford.

Sonny grinned for the first time since leaving Benny's place. "Backside, Clifford. Plenty t'ings fly in me head fe tell man. I ice it. Burn me bad when dese light-skinned West Indians come a-England an' play like dem no coloured. T'ink English care which island we from? Light skin or dark. We all negative to dem."

Clifford grunted. This was something he had never considered before. Jamaicans had their own prejudices when it came to skin colour, hair, and family. Yet he had never expected this sort of rawtedness from coloureds in England.

"Trinny's de sort you can't rely on," said Sonny. He turned the wheel. "Soon drop you home."

"Hear 'bout whites dat bruck up de West Indian business in Shepherd's Bush? Wid milk bottles?" asked Clifford.

"Fact man. Bad. Question is, who gwan be next?"

Sonny parked the car and followed Clifford into the front room for a drink to calm his nerves. After laying a sleeping Roy in the room next door, Clifford returned to the front room where Sonny and Clara waited. He poured two shots of Johnny Walker for him and Sonny and gave Clara a glass of cream soda.

"Want tell her?" he said to Sonny, who was staring dully into his glass.

"Man. Where me fe start? Still trying fe puzzle it out meself. We meet trouble on de way to meeting, Clara."

Clara who sat opposite Clifford with a coffee table between them, almost dropped her glass.

"Eh, eh!" she cried, flying around the coffee table to get to Clifford and almost pitching into him. "Wat me a-say to you? Eh?"

"We safe," said Clifford. In trying to soothe her with his sensible response, he only caused her further distress.

"Clifford," she said, arching towards him. "It no in dis very same room. Me say no go? It no me dat say. Dis gwan 'appen? It no me dat say. No go. Else fire stick gwan turn round an' lick you batty? But no. You is man. An'. As man. Is hard-a-ears. Cork you ears to good advice. T'ink you know better. Eh. So? Wat 'appen? Tell me."

Her singeing condemnation made Sonny glad he did not answer to a pepperpot woman. Yet strangely, he also envied his friend. England was one lonely place if a coloured man did not have a woman to care about him.

Clifford, silenced by Clara's tongue left Sonny to explain what had happened. The mention of the woman anxious for her husband made Clara even more alarmed.

"T'ink dem come 'ere?" she asked, almost grabbing Sonny's arm.

"Dat me no know. All me say is. Now Notting Hill is negative fe coloureds. We wait an' see where Notting Hill washing dis to. Me no know. Before me sleep going visit some boys. Give dem de score."

Clifford reminded Sonny that he was off shift until the following Wednesday. He hoped the trouble would be dead by then.

Sonny drained his glass and told Clifford he would visit him Monday morning before the afternoon meeting. He stood and told Clifford he would drive him to the meeting. Turning to Clara he told her not to worry.

She toucherd his arm. "T'anks fe bringing me husband home safe."

Sonny grinned. "Pleasure," he said, trying to lighten the mood.

Clifford followed him to the car, and they went over some of what should be discussed at the coming meeting.

"Till me come. Keep tight, man," said Sonny. "Else Clara worry. Pray dis no spread. Pray some kind English stop dis madness."

Prowling
Early Friday Evening, 29 August, 1958

The hazy moon followed the cat as it padded along the squat, squalid houses that straddled the road like a jaw of diseased teeth. It swung left and entered a dark, sinister passage. At an overstuffed dustbin, back arched, it gave the bin a quizzical stare, tapped a delicate paw on the, hot, dull, metal and sprung onto the lid. Both cat and lid flipped off. The lid clanged onto the gritty ground. Fetid odour belched from the bin's gaping mouth into the sweltering night. The cat padded away.

The hour was almost eight, the evening moody. No cool breeze relieved the sweltering souls in Notting Hill.

"Told ya, didn't I?" Dave said. He and Colin were sauntering towards a friend's home. A fag dangling from his lips, he nudged his blond companion in the ribs as they swaggered along the pavement. A match flicked at a pile of rubbish beside the road, Dave said, "Good punch-up that was. Gave 'em a right beating. Won't mess with us again."

Right chuffed with themselves, reaching the curve in the road, they turned left.

A few nights back, they'd kicked the living hell out of some Nigs. That was bound to send a bleeding message to coloureds. Good odds though. Fifteen to three, but what did it bleeding matter. Got the job done, they had.

At a brown door, on the sixth house from a black lamppost that hadn't seen a lick of new paint since only the Lord knew when, Dave pressed the doorbell with his index finger. His impatient body propped against the bricked entrance, he waited while Colin light another smoke. Dave murdered the doorbell again.

"Took you bleeding time, didn't ya," Dave barked at the sandy-haired youth who finally opened up. He pushed himself off the bricks, ambled into the dingy passage that smelt of boiled cabbage and damp clothes, and skirted an old bicycle propped against the wall. Taking the stairs two at a time, he threw over his shoulder, "Hurry up. Ain't got all night."

In spite of the squalor below, "Rodge the Dodge," Dave's nickname for Roger Boyd, led them into a surprisingly clean room. The top-floor flat of the three-storey tenement had no inside water, bathroom or lavatory. Roger's parents and four siblings shared a communal toilet, sink and tap in the back garden. This lack of indoor amenities did not defeat the Dodge's mother. She refused to submit to her lot in life, to "wallow in filth." Rare for her breed, she kept strictly to the commandment "Cleanliness is next to godliness" and applied Dettol, Vim and Ajax liberally.

Roger had been with Dave and Colin on their "nigger hunt." Since his family was out that evening, he agreed they could meet at his place.

Dave reported. What had happened after their punch-up was inevitable. Cops nabbed a few, but released them later without charges. They had achieved their first objective.

Dave began pacing the small space. At a four-drawer-chest unit, he dropped low and squatted onto the balls of his feet.

The Ted was an odd sod. Whenever close to the ground, sensible logic seemed to flow free and unrestricted into his head. If clipped on the ear as a nipper, he would slink to a dusty corner, scowl, curl up, suck his thumb, and fantasize about wonderful happenings. No sooner did he stand; they evaporated like water on desert sand—never saw the light of day again.

"Had our first trial run," Dave said. "Good start. Wound a few wogs. Got to go careful though. Parents may turn a blind eye. Law won't. If nabbed red-handed, that is." He linked his fingers over his knees and looked to his deputy, Colin, who hugged the windowsill with his drainpipe trousers.

"Keep what's said here quiet. Right? Don't want coppers to get wind of it. Right? Tell only the loyal few. Right?" He touched the tip of his nose with a finger and winked wickedly. "Next time it'll be big. Word's out. Hammersmith mates. The Bush. For it."

He pulled his right earlobe and tapped his pimply nose. "Next time we won't be short of bodies!"

They all laughed.

Energized and alert, Dave stood.

"Mosley's right. Leaflets stirred things up for niggers. We'll get the numbers. Don't lose sleep 'bout cops. Hate wogs too. Let's go down Latimesr Road and get some wogs."

* * * *

That Friday night was the worst in Constable Tommy Budd's career. The station had been "quiet." Not that it ever was. An urgent telephone message came in. It reported a disturbance near Bromley Road. Apparently a West Indian pimp and a Swedish woman living at Bard Road had caused the disturbance. Budd and a few officers went to investigate.

When Budd arrived on the scene, a right old barney was taking place. Screaming whites were pelting the Swedish woman with bottles. Smoke belched from her flat. Fire engines screeched onto the scene to douse raging flames. They carted her off to the station for her safety. Then Budd and the others charged to a blues club on Blechynden Street—another incident had been reported. This time, they needed reinforcements. Hundreds of whites had stormed the club chanting, *Keep Britain White*, and, *Kill the niggers*. Right nasty it was. What the world was coming to, he'd like to know. So-called civilized British were acting like savages. Desperate to dampen the brawl, Budd and the officers told everyone to go home. The mob turned on them. He rushed to apprehend a white yob attacking a coloured man lying on the pavement and got a milk bottle on his head for his trouble. Four officers were injured that night. He narrowly escaped with a minor cut to his left eye. When they reported to Stone later, Tommy Budd remembered their previous conversation.

Dave's Big One
Saturday Morning, August 30, 1958

Notting Dale, once called "the Piggeries" had moulded and toughened Dave Watson to think like a thug, and to dream big. When coloureds crowded into the Notting Hill area, his dream became his crusade. The upcoming bank holiday would make his big dream a reality. Blacks in Britain would be totally exterminated.

Yet, cocky and pig-headed as Dave was, he understood one truth: his gang alone could never totally cleanse the area of wogs. Something this big and this important needed outside help. That was Dave's problem.

For years bad blood had flowed unchecked between the Notting Dale lads and the gangs on the other estates around Notting Hill. Scraps, revelry, knife fights, and arguments over turf control had inflamed feuds that had festered into untreated sores. Dave knew he had to do some serious low-down heel thinking. When the barn door flipped open in his brain, Dave finally cottoned on. Extermination of wogs in Britain went far beyond clan grievances. *This was white against black.* Total extermination of blacks in Britain would unite and heal wounds. Dave sent out feelers and was deeply touched. Former enemies gladly came on board. Even the hated Harrow Road and Paddington boys were willing to unite and form a fighting force to take back their country.

They came by invitation. Gathering around a bombed-out site and wary as a pack of wolves, they eyed each other up. Muscles flexed and teeth bared, all tested the terrain. Most smoked. A few huddled on motorbikes. Former feuds and allegiances were reminisced about before they got down to brass tacks. They discussed weapons. Most had the usual arsenal of switchblades and coshes. All knew where to get more.

The few skirts present were eager to join. They complained that the coloured chimney sweeps leered at them. Made them feel unclean and threatened. Listening to them, Colin got right narked wanting to know what they were doing around coloured men anyway. He bellowed, "What you effing lot doing anyway. Why you hanging around Nigs?"

Excitement rippled through them. What they were going to do to wogs. The air turned blue. Dave had a right old time trying to calm everyone down. He told all gathered to simmer down and hold their hate for the big one coming.

* * * *

That evening Dave's face shone like a torch as he chatted and drank in his local pub with Colin and some mates. He had tramped the streets knocking on doors to get blokes to support his cause. *Time well spent if it pays off,* he reasoned. Unpredictable Colin, as usual, went with him. In the many years he and Colin had been hanging around together; Dave still couldn't fathom the effing mind of his friend. But, what did all that matter? For, no matter what, Colin was loyal. They had survived the education lark together. Unable to control or teach them, teachers gave up and booted them out with neither a skill nor certificate between the two.

"Keep Britain White" was their motto. The fascist bloke Mosley knew truth. His men had slipped them a bob or two to hand out leaflets. But what effing satisfaction did blokes like him get, just shoving pieces of paper into people's kissers? Pansies did that. Papers didn't smash faces. Inflict pain. Let blacks feel his hate. Feel cold knuckledusters against their black mush. Dead chuffed he was with them nigger-hunting geezers that did wogs in. Coppers might have nabbed them afterwards, but not before they'd inflicted some serious hurt.

His way would finally put them on the map.

He had met up earlier with his gang to give them the script about his encounter Friday evening—it still smarted to no end.

Friday evening gone, he, Colin and some of the lads had been out prowling down by Latimer Road Station. They chanced upon that Swedish tart and her darkie husband. The two were having a right old barney. Damn right disgusting it was. She white and him black. But, what'd he expect from foreigners? Different weren't they—he a darkie, she Swedish? They had only tried saving the ungrateful cow from the ugly Nig. She turned on them. *Slagged* them off, she did. Shouted—told them to clear off—mind their own sodding business. She did. Some of the chimney sweep's mates turned up. Thought they would intimidate him and his mates. Well they didn't. Nigs didn't scare them that easily. Next time, they'd get her right and proper, no mistake.

After the Friday night incident, word had flown round the Dale like racing pigeons. Niggers it was said were getting cocky.

Now it was Saturday night, the pub was bursting full with comrades. All were stupid drunk. Great old singsong and larking about was happening. Bragging over pints all agreed, the Dale was going to carve coloureds up.

At closing time, the over full pub emptied onto the streets. All gathered under the blackened arches of Latimer Road Station like vultures that was taking shelter from the rain. The night was suffocating hot. Like a bleeding tart's sweaty armpit. That's when they saw the Swede again. She was without her Nig. Strutting pass she was. Not so much as batted an eyelid and cool as a cucumber. It was like she owned the bleeding place. That narked them—her attitude. Some slagged her off. A few pelted her with stones and milk bottles. Good and proper. Then the interfering cops arrived. Blue Bottles didn't scare them. They did nab the one smashing an iron bar onto her. Cops hauled her off for her protection. If they hadn't, the whole Dale would have finished her off. The vultures soon got edgy. Cops had stolen their meat. Where else could they release their steam if not at the chimney-sweeps' club down Blechynden Street? They gave the place a good old battering with milk bottles and iron bars. The law came and stopped their fun, but all agreed. Next time would be big. Next time they would settle the Nigs, once and for all.

Storm Clouds
Monday Morning, Bank Holiday, September 1, 1958

Politically and weather wise, the summer of 1958 was scorching, sweltering, and unsettled.

The first inkling that the British public had of clashes between whites and coloureds around Notting Hill came from radio and television newsflashes. Blow-by-blow reports of the riots was broadcasted while many parliamentary and government personnel holidayed in sunspots.

West Indians had helped Britain fight her war with Hitler. They had also helped feed her starving people. Fourteen years later, by invitation, they also helped rebuild her country. When overcrowding, lack of housing, and unemployment threatened Britain, she began to bite the hands that had helped her. Why did Britain not explain to her white inhabitants that she had begged her Caribbean children to come? Why keep silent? For whatever reason, the Bank holiday week of 1958 would stain Britain's reputation forever.

Clifford was not enjoying his morning read. Shaking the newspaper he flung it onto the square rug covering the linoleum.

"Damn dem!" he cried. "Damn dem all. Not one good word England saying fe us."

338

Clara sat quietly securing a button onto his shirt. She bit the thread, weaved the needle through the tail of the shirt, and laid it on her lap. She sympathised with her man. He had been restless lately. Since Thursday night, barely a word had passed between them. His silence warned; she must leave his deep thinking to sleep. She sneaked a quick peek at his troubled brow, tight mouth, his faraway frown. Asking what worried him would get her silent stares. She must try a different bottle of rum.

"Clifford," she said, her eyes as innocent as a newborn babe's. "Newspaper print gwan dutty up rug."

"Wat me care? Wat in it is dutty. Wicked."

She bent, gathered the pages, and was sorting them when she noticed the headline: "MUST BRITAIN KEEP LETTING THEM IN." She searched for the date. The newspaper was two days old.

"Clifford," she said. "Why you reading stale news?"

Clifford did not reply. Rising, he strode to her, snatched the newspaper from her hands, pursed his lips, and kept folding the paper until he held a fat wad.

"Paper keep printing wat dem want white people fe believe 'bout us. Give dem excuse fe hate us."

She was about to reply when the doorbell pinged. Opening up, she was surprised to see a worried Sonny, who, on entering the front room immediately said, "Big trouble 'appenin', Clifford."

Clifford threw the paper wad onto the pull-out bed.

"Man. Wat now?"

"Hell a blazing in Notting Hill, man." Sonny closed the door behind him. "Reason I early."

Anxious for news, Clifford allowed Sonny to drop onto the bed before settling beside him.

Sonny told them that since he was last with Clifford, the attacks on coloureds had intensified. Whites were out mashing up coloured places around Notting Hill. Coloureds could no longer walk the streets alone. They travelled in groups. Most feared to leave their houses to shop or go to work. The police offered no protection. They only searched coloured boys for weapons so they could arrest them. Sonny told of a gang of whites who attacked a coloured house. When the husband rushed out to confront the attackers, the police charged the coloured man with breaking the peace. The white attackers got off free. Shaking his head, Sonny said, "Clifford. How we fe protect ourself. If law an' government do not'ing? We defend ourself. We is guilty party."

So shocked was Clifford and Clara at Sonny's news that only the cuckoo cock ticked in the silent, gloomy room.

Sonny was the first to speak. Stroking his knee with his strong brown hands, he soured his lips, sucked a long draught of air, and kissed his teeth. "England want fe trample us, Clifford. Me own eyes no believe t'ings dat 'appenin'. Me hear say. Whites a-coming from all over England. Dem want fe pick us clean like John crow. Teddy boys 'ave flick knives. Cosh. Bicycle chains. Knuckle-dusters on Notting Hill streets. Dem is looking fe carve us up."

He glanced at Clifford and sighed. "Clifford. White boys send message to us. Saying. Tonight. Is dem final burnings. Tonight. Dem gwan cleanse out us niggers. Buoy." Sonny's voice was guttural, low. "Never. Never, in all me born days. Me ever t'ink dis t'ing gwan 'appen to us a-England."

Clifford rubbed his hands together. He shook his head. What could he say to Sonny? If British law refused to protect them, what chance did they have? Feeling helpless to stop the attacks on coloureds, something ignited in his head.

340

Coloureds no mean one backside t'ing to Britain. Piss water is wat dem is to Britain. Piss water. Dat me old pappy shrivelled-up janga squirt inside de chamber pot. Dat mum-ma dash down latrine in morning. Now Britain used up Jamaicans. She wants fe dash dem from her country. Just like piss water. Is fact.

"But, Sonny. Police?" said Clara. Distressed, she wanted to break the tension.

"Police?" Sonny sneered, his head jerked backwards. "Dis-a whites you talking 'bout you know, Clara. It English police you a-saying. When since you ever see dem help us? Few may try. De majority is ignorant. How many coloured cases you see police carry before a judge fe prosecution? Evidence conveniently disappear. Clara. Even when coloureds report offence. Police say white boys a-having harmless fun. Hum. It fact, Clara. Wat police a-mean is. English can box us down. Burn us in our place. An' it all harmless white fun."

He rose abruptly. "Time passing quick. Decide how best fe protect youself. We meet soon. Beg you fe some rum, Clifford."

* * * *

The Bank Holiday Monday, 1958 saw sweltering Londoners praying for rain to relieve the steaming heat and dampen the weeping tar pockets on the roads.

While breakfasting, Britain scraped marmalade onto toast and sipped Tetley Tea, lies about West Indies were forced down their throats by radio and newspapers. To boost sales, newspapers bold headlines reported Notting Hill's racial unrest. Comic strips predicted the most likely places race riots might erupt. Titillating and sensational stories of black men living off white women and social assistance was also touted.

To fire up hatred, Oswald Mosley's movement pushed ahead with street meetings to recruit membership. His "Black Invasion" pamphlet drivel, reported that coloureds were flooding into Britain in ships and airplanes to rob whites of jobs, housing, and women. Grabbed by eager white hands, it ignited hatred in the ignorant and misinformed.

While this toxic, racial, mania, simmered, the government or police did nothing to snuff the fuse.

The proverb "Every cloud has a silver lining" could now be literally applied to Notting Hill. Its tourist industry immediately flourished. Whites that once flocked to Butlins, Battersea Fun Fair, or the seaside for their holiday now desired a different venue. Many opted for an "on-hand experience" of the real meaning of the "iron fist of Britain's thuggery" against West Indians. Masses of whites clambered onto trains, busses, and cars; they rushed headlong into Notting Hill's dismal slums—to assist their fellow Brits to fight wogs. Never had Notting Hill seen the like. One could wonder—would souvenirs be especially crafted for the event?

Calypso Club
Monday Afternoon, September 1, 1958

In the muggy heat of that early Bank Holiday Monday afternoon, a sombre group of West Indians entered a club in Notting Hill. They had survived the mother country's cold, damp, miserable winters; it almost froze their Caribbean blood. Had even endured insults about their colour and island home. But what had finally stuck in their craw—had finally forced them to meet—was one fact. Britain had systematically set out to place depression upon their souls.

A man shuffled in, he stole a quick peep at a woman to his left. Lips parted weakly, he found a seat. Another crouched on a chair. Head bowed, he seemed to be deliberating. One collided into a friend. He timidly bade him good day. Quiet, respectful, yet iron willed, they had come for a solution. Some settled onto chairs and stools. Others leaned near the bar, where a sound system played seductive *jump-up music* at night.

Barred from English dance halls, clubs, and restaurants, this dingy, smoke-filled club offered drinks, sweet music, and a dark, secluded corner, where, for a few hours each night, coloureds could socialise with their own kind.

Clifford drew on his smoke and followed Sonny into the club wedged between buildings. A man hailed Sonny. From the smiles and slaps Sonny was getting on his back, Clifford guessed he was a regular. He left Sonny and the man to labrish, pulled out a stool from the bar and sat in the shadows to listen.

Sonny walked to the bar, threw out his arms, and called them to order. "Plenty fe settle afore tonight. So let's mak' a start."

He reminded them—Mosley, whom Britain called "Sir," was on street corner with his man Hamm whipping up white hate for coloureds.

Contemptuous rumblings and teeth kissing broke out. Sonny quickly silenced them. They must hustle and plan, he said, for Britain's prime minister had bigger fish frying. Why then would he care about Notting Hill?

A man perched on a stool complained. He could not walk the street without police searching him up and down. One officer had locked his arms around his friend's neck. He was shoved into a police car, all on suspicion.

Sonny nodded his sympathy, pulled out a stool, and hitched his bottom onto the edge.

A large, big-bosomed woman, her swollen feet encased in a pair of white strapless sandals, waddled up to Sonny and parked herself before him.

"Wat me fe do, Sonny? Fear a-eating at me. Even fe set foot outside me place. How me know which a-dem gwan box me down? Eh. Tell me dat. How long we suffer dis, Sonny? An' do not'ing. Pickney boy me never fear before me come a-London. Me hand a-itch fe box white buoys' backsides. So dem know how it a-feel."

Sonny stood.

"Myrtle, Myrtle," he said, taking her hand and gently squeezing it. "Answers me no 'ave. Dis me only a-say. Trust nobody. Till dem prove friend."

He released her, sat, and arched forward. Puffing at his smoke his brain fried to come up with a sensible strategy that would not fail. As he mashed the butt of his smoke with his shoe and lit another smoke, a man approached him. He studied Sonny with black eyes.

"It's de backside way dem treat us," the man said, his voice deadly serious. "Like we no even dog mess under dem foot. Last evening. Tak' train fe home. Gets off. Hands inspector ticket. Walks out station. Wat me witness? Line a white boys. Do me usual. Walk pass. Dem cuss me up. Jostle me. Like dem want fe dead me up, man." He paused, rubbed a dark brown hand over his mouth, and continued. "Rattle me heart bad. Like hell a-hotting me backside, Sonny. How me pass dem widout wetting meself. Me no know. English knows. Authority knows. All a-dem knows wat 'appenin'. But not a rawted one a-dem cares dat Teddy boys saying dem gwan dead us up."

Clifford's neck heated in anger. Every damn day coloureds suffered. No white listened or helped. Here only could they let out their steam; tell of their frustrations. Soon what was happening to the others would happen to him and his family. When the man sat, sympathetic eyes followed him.

Only white voices thundered in print, radio, and television. In Britain, coloureds had no voice. No one spoke for them. No one took their part. Lies about coloureds rang throughout London Town like its stagnant sewers. "Coloureds are bad for Britain." Was Britain not bad before coloureds came?

What the man said helped Sonny understand one fact. Staying home and bawling like a woman would not stop the attacks. *Backside*, he reasoned. *Jamaicans been always feisty. When Britain tried conquering Nanny an' her Maroons. Jamaicans been feisty.*

When slaves rebelled over an' over. Jamaicans been feisty. England musta t'ink. Because coloureds endured all she drop 'pon dem head. We turned coward.

Jamaicans like fe feel t'ings out first. Watch an' see how it a-go. Before testing de river water. Jamaicans never act like a tourist. Widout batting an eye. An' even widout a boat. Tourists jump into de blue-blue sea. Fe swim clear over to Navy Island. Island people know plenty nasty things in sea fe mash us up. Man-of-wars. Hammerhead sharks. Stingrays. Such likes hide between Jamaica an' Navy Island. Safely on de beach. Island people watch while de idiots offer demselves up as shark bait.

Now coloureds finally understood. Only they must defend their future in Britain.

This was a fact.

Clifford had been content to sit and listen in the shadows. When Sonny turned to him and said, "Clifford, give us some a-you wisdom?" he almost fell off the stool. Heart pumping, settling back, he bowed his head and thought on his past.

For most of his childhood and early manhood, his pappy treated him like the bonded Indian or Chinese workers that laboured for chicken feed in Jamaica. When the Good Lord took Pappy, his children had fought for his land. While they plotted and schemed, Clifford patiently waited. What good did that do? It only gave them time to thief his birthright—his land and the house he had built with his own hands. Driven to Maggoty Point, he then heard Britain needed her coloured children again, this time to rebuild her country.

His reward on London streets was humiliation and disillusionment. He endured it all, sacrificed, worked hard, bought his own place, and sent for his children. Now, the English said they were coming to kill West Indians, burn them out. Drive them from their land.

His head hurt—bad. His heart thumped. It would fly out of his chest. He needed clarity, clear thoughts. He went to the hill, Webb's land where mountain peaks, plentiful trees, bush land, and clear air sweetened his soul. Sun-speckled trees warmed by tropical rain that sprinkled the earth in refreshing, dazzling bursts. The rain disappeared as swiftly as a fleeting mirage, leaving damp footprints among thick, wooden forests and exotic blooms.

They studied the slim-bodied coloured with his head bowed. Some heard tell that Clifford Webb was a nice, respectable man. He was married to a good-looking, clear-skin woman, and he had three pretty *pickneys*. He was hard-working, with no scandal to his name. He was a Jamaican man.

Clifford raised his heavy head. The eyes bored into him. A woman coughed. Touching her lips, she stifled another. He pulled off his grey hat and cupped it over his trembling knee. Leaning forward, he felt his body shudder.

He was no talker. Johnny Walker was the only thing that loosened his tongue. Johnny Walker gave him courage. He licked his dry lips, pushed himself onto his weak legs and sucked deep at the hot, musty air. He must untangle his tongue. It felt like a pound of salt fish in his mouth. His head thumped. Struggling for sensible speech, the faces swam before him—like *janga* in a stormy river. Even his mum-ma's face joined them. He fumbled with his hat and placed it on his head. Was this the obeah Mum-ma had predicted when she prophesied he would go foreign? What else she had said, he couldn't remember. He parted his lips into a sarcastic curl, and miraculously, words flowed. Free, not stumbling, but thundering and forceful, like Dunn's River's mighty waterfall.

"Dem charge us double. Fe rent dem stinking place."
His voice was raw, his patwa harsh. "Double me a-say. Wat
choice we 'ave. But fe pay. Force us fe sleep two. T'ree. Four
to a room. An' dem condemn us. We labour 'ard. Do
widout. Save. Buy our own place. Still dem condemn us.
Saying to us. 'So. How come you West Indians come a-
England an' live like kings?'"

His words rumbled, roared. They filled the club with
power and vindication.

"Only work *us* gets. Is wat whites no want dutty dem
hands on. Dem a-say. Is all *us* coloureds fit for. Still dem
condemn *us*. Now." His dry tongue lashed out in harsh
mockery, like a whip flaying a bare backside. "Now dem a-
say. Dey a-coming. Fe kill *us*. Burn *us* up. Mash *us* up. Grind
us up like cornmeal. Drive *us* out-a-England. Eh, eh. Well."

A heavy sigh echoed. It was a sigh that said, "Enough.
Time come!"

Now they finally understood. This Jamaican had plainly
stated one fact: Britain had abandoned them to her
bullyboys.

"Enough me a-say," cried Clifford. Knees dipped, he
threw out his arms in anger. "Dis wickedness *must* end. West
Indians *must* now protect demselves. De only time English
police rouse dem white backside. Is when black man fall
dead on English pavement. Britain no care rawted 'bout us.
Teddy boys an' such say. Dey is coming. Fe kill. Burn *us* out.
Us say. Beat dem back. *Us* say. Prepare. Now!"

Rawted teeth sucking and *eh-ehing* filled the air as heads
nodded and shoulders stiffened in vexation, sorrow, and
determination.

When Clifford said "Me never come a-England fe see
murder done to me family," the room held its breath. "Is
criminal wat is 'appenin'. White yard boys tell us. Dem is

348

coming! Fe burn down me house. House me an' me wife bust our backside fe buy. An' law. As usual. Gwan stand by. An' do not'ing? How we fe let dat 'appen. Dis no America. Wid lynching. An' de Klu Klux Klan. Dis a-England! Our mother country. We her people. Good as any white!"

"See 'ere," Clifford continued, stabbing his smoke at the sombre, staring eyes. "Show a hand all dat Jamaican." Fifteen brown hands flew up. He glanced around. "Trinidadian?" Five shot up. "Barbadian?" Three more. "Rest a-Small Island?" As he counted three more, a sweet peace claimed his soul.

"We come England. Fe a new life." His words were sorrowful, guttural, and slow. "A better life. Fe our children. An' ourselves. An' dis how Britain treat *us*? *Us* dat fight fe give dem freedom? *Us* dat fill dem coffee cups. Sweeten dem tea? *Us* dat mak' Britain rich. Fe centuries. Wat our reward? Fe all a-dat? Closed doors. Turned backs. Nasty sour faces. England no 'appy wid only beating *us* wid iron bars. Cutting *us* up on dem streets. England is coming. Fe finish us off. England is coming. Fe burn *us* down. In. Our. Own. House. Batter. Kill *us*. Well. *We*. Say. Enough. *We*. Say. Now we mean business. *We*. Say. Now *we* prepare."

Sonny was astonished. Was this his quiet, peace-loving friend? Hurrying to Clifford, he grabbed his hand and pumped it vigorously. Head tilted slightly left, he studied Clifford with a grin, and then, grabbing his hand again, shook it before facing the stunned coloureds that now all stood.

"Clifford talk true," Sonny said. "It our right fe defend ourself. Dey is coming tonight. We get ready fe business."

Before doing so, Sonny said, all must consider hard. What they were planning was some serious ganga. Once in the crocus bag, there was no turning back. Any who wanted out should say so now. Afterwards, all would be tight.

They shifted, wiped hot faces, and shook their heads. "We 'ere. We ready. We plan."

Sonny explained what to expect on English streets. They must give him a list. What was in their house to ward off their attackers? Anything that they can fling or use as a weapon they must bring. But one thing they must remember. This was no picnic they were planning. Whites would show no mercy.

He didn't want to *dread them up*, but he again stressed. Once they left the club, it was war. Whites would bring switchblades, axes, bicycle chains, iron bars, firebombs, and such like. Whites would come to kill them. Whites would come to burn them out. This was a fact.

A honey-coloured woman approached Sonny. She told him she had an axe under her bed. Any white that threatened the house she and her husband had scratched like a fowl to save and buy would get it. Then let British policeman dragged her to jail. Sonny calmed her down. He told her to use any means to defend life and property. Now they must hustle.

He asked for volunteers to head up the women and men. Sonny told them that the word was out around Notting Hill. Teddy boys had sent a challenge to coloureds. They were coming to burn them out. So, since the planned attack would happen at Blenheim Crescent, they must fortify the two houses there that housed coloureds. The houses faced each other. There they would fend off the attackers. There would be their fortresses.

All agreed.

Volunteers signed on to collect and distribute weapons to the houses. Someone knew someone who knew someone who knew how to make petrol bombs. The ex-servicemen in the room volunteered to head up and plan the defence at Blenheim Crescent. Finally, Sonny began to relax.

"Remember," he warned. "No labrish none a dis. Is serious t'ing dat gwan 'appen. Dis t'ing never 'appen before a-England. Coloureds defending demselves against de English in England. It our stand against injustice. It dangerous. Before it finish. Some of us may get dead. Us can't fail."

Bye-Bye Black Birds
Monday Evening, September 1, 1958

The landlord of the Queens Arms in the Dale had not seen the like since D-Day. What a rollicking evening was happening in his pub. Whites from Peckham, Balham, and further a-field packed his gloomy, gas-lit, smoky tavern. They had come to assist their countrymen. Sweaty boozers smoked and sipped pints. Many slapped comrades' backs. Beer flowed freer than rain over Ireland. Patrons, eager for a good old knees-up, abandoned their usual singsongs: "Knees up Mother Brown" or a Frank Sinatra favourite. Stirring racist choruses of "Old Man River" and "Bye-Bye Blackbird" roared from lusty lungs.

The landlord knitted his bushy eyebrows above his sea-blue eyes and rubbed a rag over a spot of spilt beer as he kept an eye on the drinkers' antics. A greasy, dark-haired Ted, suddenly flushed with cash, ordered his third round. Taking the coins from the sweaty palm, the landlord threw them into the till. What did he care what they sang as long as they stumped up for their beer.

Dave was right chuffed with himself. He had told the rest of the gang how he had not long chased a chimney sweep near the station. Knocking the wog to the pavement, he was yanking at his leg when he escaped. He expressed regret to

352

his mates—the darkie had scarpered into a nigger-loving greengrocer's place. No great loss. Plenty more pickings were on the streets.

Full of beer, and edgy, Dave was ready for a punch-up when they left the pub with the revellers. They all gathered under Latimer Station bridge to await the fascist leader in the hazy heat.

"What you think he'll say when he comes?" shouted Colin, trying to talk above the din. He nudged Dave in the ribs.

"Same as before, thick head."

"Think he'll come straight out and say? Let 'em have it? How'd you plan getting more weapons?"

"Shush," hissed Dave. "All this lark and talk. Why don't you put a sock in it?"

The leader finally showed. He spoke of moderation. Britain's woes he blamed on a government that allowed coloureds in. He bragged and strutted, lamented Britain's fading glory, and said Britain could once more be great, if his comrades in the Dale helped his cause. Flattering them with his flannel, slyly dotting his spiel with racist innuendos, he finally shouted to the mesmerized crowd, "Get rid of them."

So electrifying and fanatical was his rhetoric that his frenzied worshippers sipped at it as if it were lager.

"Kill the niggers!" the bloodthirsty mass roared in reply. "Let's go burn the bleeding lot of them."

Beer-bellied men, youths with grudges, teenage girls, and pram-pushing mothers, hell-bent on exterminating wogs, stampeded from the blackened underbelly of Latimer Station. They swelled, heaved and howled, "Kill the niggers!" and the police watched and waited.

"Go get them, lads. Go show them blacks," cackled a woman watching from tenement windows.

Dave wanted his own war. He left the mob with his mates and hurried down a side street. Spotting a wooden fence protecting a house from the pavement, he dashed to it, yanked it from the dirt, and yelled, "You lot. Break this up. For weapons. Watch for more stuff."

They raced on. Felling fences and rose beds, Dave jumped over a low brick wall and grabbed a dustbin lid.

"Come in handy with me chopper," he said, brandishing the lid like a shield.

* * * *

Local officials, alarmed by the increasing racial tension and frantic calls from residents to do something about the unrest in Notting Hill, heard fascists planned a meeting in the area that Monday evening. They begged the police to help. As a token gesture, Tommy Budd and three officers were sent in a Black Maria van to keep tabs on the meeting. Budd was not happy with the order. His superior had made a right cock-up of the coloured problem and was blustering through his mistake. Of that, he was certain. Why else would he order the three out without their tea? It stood to reason— top brass had ignored the free flow of racial hate. Now it was exploding in their faces they were trying to cover their arses.

Coppers like him got mouthful of obscenities around the Dale. Police car windows and lights were frequently kicked in. Should the likes of him be seen helping coloureds around the Dale, they got labelled "Nigger lovers" and told to clear off?

Before he came to Notting Hill, Tommy Budd never saw a coloured much less spoke to one. A few officers at the station were sympathetic to the coloured problem. The majority were downright racist. He questioned their logic, but did not really understand the racial stuff. Right or wrong, orders were orders. He obeyed orders.

They parked the tin bucket Black Maria near the gathering crowd, wound down the windows, shed their regimental jackets and helmets and still the van boiled like hell. Hungry, frustrated, and disgruntled, Budd tugged at his damp collar. Why send them here; then order them to keep out of sight? It made much more sense to let the fascists see them. That would warn them to tone down their rhetoric and keep a lid on things.

It seemed a long, hot, bleeding hour before Budd spotted a man strutting towards the waiting crowd. He watched closely through the window. There was a lot of hand waving and mouthing. Pieces of paper floated into the sulky night sky. A powerful shout—"Let's go lynch the niggers. Let's get ourselves some wogs" —shattered the air. It seemed to shake the van.

Budd craned his neck. The massive crowd was gathering momentum. It heaved and turned—surged towards the coloured section in Notting Hill. Stretching and spreading over pavement and street, Budd heard, "Go get them lads, go show them blacks," and groaned, "Bloody hell." He shouted to the three, "Grab your stuff. Now!" His voice sounded hollow inside the van. It was like a furnace. The young officer frantically buckling on his helmet heard Budd yell at him, "Look sharp. Drive to the nearest police box. Now." Budd scrambled for his jacket. He pulled it on. His helmet buckled, he scanned the road. A crunch of brakes, the van roared off.

"Turn here," he yelled at the driver. "Next. Now. There. There. Police box." Gasping, he peered ahead, stabbed his finger at a blue telephone box. "There. Stop!"

The van screeched to a halt. Budd jumped out, sprinted to the telephone box, breathlessly reported, banged down the telephone and raced back to the van.

"Follow them...if you can," he said, panting. "Fast. Orders. From station. Keep them. Contained. Till. Reinforcements. Arrive."

The driver immediately revved the engine. Spinning the wheel to turn the van, he wondered, *How can we few coppers stem this bloody tidal wave?*

Preparation for War
Monday Night, September 1, 1958

As night's hazy shadows settled around the tenement buildings of the Dale and the surrounding areas of Notting Hill, 9 Blenheim Crescent was tight as a fortress. Doors were barred, windows were closed, and curtains drawn.

That early afternoon, a group of tight-lipped, determined coloureds had hurried from a club. Now they would carry out the first-ever West Indian defence in England. That thousands of whites outnumbered them was a fact. That Britain had consistently failed to protect them from her white children was a fact. That she had forced them to form a defence against fear and tyranny was a fact.

The plan was simple. Fortify the two tenanted buildings that housed coloured on Blenheim Crescent. Women would bring anything to fend off the attackers—bowls, buckets, bags of flour, rolling pins, pots to boil hot water, caustic soda, kitchen knives, and machetes—anything.

Sonny had reminded them at the club that from their pickney days, West Indians were inventive people. They must consider hard what to bring—meat cleavers, iron bars, machetes, bottles, axes, and such like.

"But," he had warned, his honey-coloured brow furrowed, he gazed at the anxious staring eyes. "No tak' youself to de same ironmonger. Spread out. Use caution. Else dem a-suspect. Dis a-war dem a-bringing to us!"

The ex-servicemen laid out their plans to the group. "Men," Sonny told them. "You is de lifeblood fe our survival, you know." His face, which had been a hard, serious mask, broke out into a grin. He straightened his hat. "Backside. It irony wat a-'appenin' to us in Britain, you know. You dat Britain train fe fight her war. An' fe protect her people. It de same sin'tings. Dat a-coming. Fe kill an' burn us out tonight! It fact!"

He lifted his Navy Cut to his lips and pulled a drag. "Britain must-a think West Indians a-some kind-a jackass. If we keep putting up wid dis wickedness."

The frantic preparations began. Hundreds of milk bottlers were secreted into the houses. Machetes, iron bars, axes and knives were hidden and ferried in. A nervous man took a basket of bottles from a woman and heard her say that Teddy boys had slashed a coloured man's face with a knife down Latimer Road. Whites had also flung lit paraffin rags inside a West Indian's house, just to "watch the Nigs burn."

* * * *

To avoid being seen, Sonny parked streets away from the houses. He and Clifford hurried to 9 Blenheim Crescent. They gave the signal. An anxious-faced man eased back the door, checked them out, and hustled them inside.

When Clifford and Sonny left the afternoon meeting, they had rounded up people, brought weapons and secreted them to the houses. They had also tried to buy five iron bars and axes at an ironmonger. The owner gave them a suspicious look. Quickly paying the man, they hurried out, drove to another ironmonger and purchased more weapons. They also bought ingredients for the Molotov cocktails.

"Everybody 'ere?" asked Sonny, trying to see in the dark, hot, hallway.

"Plenty in, plenty more fe come," the man replied. He quickly bolted the door. "Hustle, quick."

Clifford and Sonny followed him through the dark passage to the largest room on the third floor. Two large sash windows faced the road.

"House soon tight wid people," said Sonny. "First start fe organize weapons. Den place people in positions."

While Sonny talked to the man, Clifford tried to force his eyes to adjust in the stuffy, dark room. It was sweltering hot. He could barely make out the piles of bottles and bomb-making material stacked beside the windows. When the man said, "Sonny. No know when dem a-coming. But any time now. So must hustle," Clifford felt as if his heart had stopped.

"Men up rooftop already," the man continued. "Ready wid dem orders. Soon as dem spy de attackers. Gwan signal de houses. Den hell a-'appen."

He turned to Clifford. "Stay 'ere, man. More coming soon fe help you. See bomb stuff under windows?" He pointed. "You tak' right window. In charge a-dat. Gwan tell odders. When come. Fe tak' odder window. Plenty more coming fe help in 'ere. So. Hold tight, man. Gwan tak' Sonny. Leave you 'ere."

They left.

Alone, Clifford squinted in the dark. He heard movement in the house and began to imagine all sorts of things. Why, he wondered, did he allow his slack tongue to say all that rashness at the club?

359

He and Clara had tried to keep this business from the children. Yet he sensed they knew trouble was in the air. Lately Tilda kept looking at him shy-shy; especially at mealtime and lately been off her food, barely touching her victuals.

Clara didn't know he was coming here. He had left with Sonny without saying where he was going. How could he tell her he was mixing up in this? And might get dead? Should he let that slip, the children might hear. He couldn't bring such distress on them. Once Clara say to him, "Man. No tangle youself in dis. It no you business."

"Who to fight fe coloureds. If no me and odders," he had angrily said. Wisdom told him to speak so to Clara. Still, he questioned wisdom's sense. How could two houses full up with coloureds fend off the whole of Britain? Why were West Indians feisty enough to think this? Suppose the English got their wish and burned them up inside the houses? West Indians were planning some strong rum tonight.

His mind had argued and debated this until it finally conceded. What other choice did coloureds have? Either they kept suffering insults, discrimination, and injury, or they defended themselves. And if in defending their lives, some of them got dead, *rawted*. At least they would die with dignity. This was fact.

The decision had been made. There was no turning back.

He heard more movement. Like black, agitated beetles scurrying in a blue-black Jamaican night. Up and down the house was a restless bustle, whispers and *click-clicking—* nostrils flaring. He inhaled stale, clammy heat then exhaled it back inside the hot, barricaded house. He smelt the thick, musky odour of sweaty skins. And something else: dread, defiance, and determination. Before they left the club, all

360

had agreed: should they die tonight, they would die defending their right to live without fear, injustice, or injury in Britain.

From birth, West Indians understood one truth. Life only gave them breath-to-breath living. Survival meant haggling for every mouthful. Death was reliable. Death closed empty mouths and bawling bellies. Dying to defend their right to live with dignity in Britain was their one choice. No one questioned this. And, what the backside—West Indians were used to harshness.

His shirt glued to his nervous body, Clifford pushed his hand inside his trouser pocket for a smoke. Remembering, he withdrew his hand. Even the tip of a lighted cigarette might draw attention to the houses. Both must appear normal and settled for the night. Total surprise would hit the whites when they came. That was the plan. Denied the sensuous relaxation that Johnny Walker and nicotine brought to his nerves, he suddenly felt vulnerable. Brushing sweat from his upper lip, he wondered at his sudden loneliness. Why did he feel so isolated in a house bursting with coloured bodies? Why did he feel as though he were locked up with death, like that time on the hill, when life had kicked him in the backside?

Defense
Monday Night, September 1, 1958

Clifford heard a car screech. Easing back the curtain, he checked the road below. Only the flickering glows of the hazy street lamps. He glanced at the house opposite. Blacked out, it looked quiet.

Coloureds had come from all over to squeeze up, push up, sweat up, and await the call to arms. Pale, brown, dark-skinned—united by race, they were tight in their cause.

Ten minutes after Sonny and the man left, fifteen men entered the room. Three went to assist Clifford at the window; four took positions at the left window. The others waited behind these. All had checked out the weapons and was armed with two Molotov cocktails. Those at the windows would be the front defenders, the ones behind, the rear-guards. When the front defenders paused to re-arm, the armed rear-guards would surge forward, and keep up the fight. Fling anything at the mob below, they were told. Whites had come to kill them. Whites had come to burn them out.

Clifford felt his heart racing when he released the curtain. Nervous, his mouth dry, he pushed his hand inside his trouser pocket. About to pull out his handkerchief to mop his face, he heard a cry thundered through the hushed house: "Dem coming. Rooftop spy dem. But. Wait. Wait. Fe. Signal."

Fingers trembling, Clifford clamped the Molotov cocktails inside his left armpit, and pulled out his Ronson lighter. A silent fear rippled through the room. All faced death. All held their breaths. The suffocating room was silent as a tomb.

The terrified room heard a thunderous cry, "Now! Now. Let dem 'ave it." Clifford swung into frenzied action. He flung back the curtain, shot up the window, and looked below. The deafening roar almost choked him. Whites of all ages and descriptions packed every nook and cranny of road and pavement, like locusts on a ripe field of wheat.

"Let's burn the niggers out," they bellowed. "Let's lynch the niggers. Kill the wogs." So vengeful and tangible was the roar of hate that Clifford felt physically sick.

Me gwan die, his head howled. *England gwan kill me dead!*

Then his fear vanished. His mind cleared. He was on Webb Hill. The morning was clear—fresh, the sky a brilliant blue.

Calm and controlled, yet tight with rage, his right thumb flicked the wheel of his lighter. He lit two Molotov cocktails, and flung them below. He was back on Webb Hill. There, he had fought for his lifeblood—Clara and his children. There, his family had tried to kill him—they had thieved his inheritance and driven him off. Britain was doing the same damn thing—whites came to burn them up and kill them dead. Here, he must fight for his life—his family, and those in the house.

His twelfth bomb smashed near a woman's heel and ignited her frock. Screeching obscenities, she tried to run. The panicking mob held her fast until a man doused the flames with his jacket.

"Bleeding wogs trying to kill us," cursed a shoeless woman who was trying to drag her teenaged daughter to safety.

The faint clang of an ambulance echoed in the distance. It raced to collect the injured. The stray thwack of a policeman's truncheon knocked a woman unconscious. He was trying to control the mob. An ambulance screeched to a halt. It hauled her off to hospital. A lorry loaded with milk bottles also screeched to a stop. Whites raced to it, grabbed handfuls of bottles, and began pelting the two houses. Women in aprons, young children clutching mother's skirts, teens, young girls and boys, all raced to join the rioters. Baton-wielding police officers linked arms to try to stop the advancing mob. Teds leapt onto their backs. Helmets clanked onto the road. Flying glass punctured the arms and faces of teenage girls. Their screeches filled the air. A third ambulance clanged away with two injured whites and three coloured men with knife wounds. Two streets away, a gang of whites chased a coloured man hurrying along the road.

Police cars jangled and rushed to other trouble spots in Notting Hill. Black-booted Bobbies blew whistles. Helmets clutched, they leap over bricks, rocks, knives, knuckle-dusters, bicycle chains, broken bottles, glass, and footwear abandoned by rioters.

Amidst the pandemonium, two Teddy boys tried to escape the onslaught. Weaving through the mob, freed and about to make a dash for it, two constables raced towards them. One recognized the dark-haired Ted as one of the main instigators of the riots. He grabbed Dave Watson's arm. Colin saw the arrest and wound his converted bicycle chain around his hand. He slugged the constable senseless. Tommy Budd and the three officers hurrying onto the scene witnessed the attack. One raced to help the injured constable

364

who was bleeding from a head wound. Budd lunged at Dave, smashed his truncheon into him, wrenched his arms behind his back and cuffed him. Colin tried to run. An officer quickly leapt at him. Dave and Colin arrested, Budd said, "Nick for you two," and marched the pair to the Black Maria and bundled them into the back.

* * * *

The coloured in the barricaded house knew the mob came to kill and burn them out. Intent on defending his post, Clifford was isolated from the rest of the house and had no idea what was happening below, much less the rest of Notting Hill.

"More bombs. Bottles. Light more. Fling more. How much bombs left? Good. We licking dem back. Keep up de pressure." He heard and obeyed the short, sharp commands. His focus: defend, defend, and defend.

Sonny, who was stationed on the ground floor, had a better idea of their defence strategy. When he saw the mob panicking and scattering, he yelled gleefully, "Backside. De English a-run." He and three men yanked open the barricaded door, rushed out, and chased the straggling rioters with choppers and cutlasses, then raced back and bolted the door. Then their luck turned sour. Around the corner screeched a Black Maria packed with police officers. The driver saw the four coloured men race inside the house, revved the engine, slammed down the accelerator and rammed the van into the door. Pandemonium broke out on the ground floor. They arrested Sonny and the three men.

Sonny and the men arrested, the house grew ominously quiet—their job was over. They had beaten back the rioters, they were alive. Not one person in the house had suffered a scratch.

When Clifford eventually crept downstairs, he learnt of Sonny's and the men's' arrest. Shocked and concerned for his friend, he helped to fix the door. Bolting it again, he returned to his post on the third floor and kept a vigilant watch until 4:00 a.m. Tuesday morning, still alert for straggling rioters, Clifford and six men crammed into a car parked three streets away. Miraculously it had escaped the rioters' wrath.

Arriving home Tuesday morning, Clifford quietly pushed his front door shut, crept into bed beside Clara, and immediately fell asleep.

A Well-kept Secret
Tuesday Morning, September 2, 1958

Tuesday morning, while Clifford slept on, parts of Notting Hill looked like a war zone.

Clara heard the news of the Notting Hill riots on the radio that morning. All of Britain was in an uproar. The nation was in shock. Eye witnesses told they had never seen anything like it.

Her husband asleep, Clara switched off the radio and began her washing in the kitchen sink. *"Cha,"* she thought. *"Man come in late. T'ink 'im can fool-fool me. Dat 'im been in bed all night."* She knew the exact time he had slunk into bed beside her but decided not to question him. Her man worked hard on shift work. He never skylarked much with other men. If he stayed out late, once in a blue moon with Sonny, then what the *neck back*. The man needed some time away from his tenants and home life. She did, however, wonder. Had he and Sonny witnessed the riots? Suppose those wicked whites had boxed him down and killed him dead? But why should she worry herself with such wild thoughts. Clifford would never place himself in such troubles to cause her to worry. She would let the sleeping dog lie.

Clifford woke, washed, dressed, and, before his smoke and tea, he hurried to a newsagent and bought a morning paper. He took it to his kitchen, made tea, sat down, and lit a smoke.

Clara, still washing clothes at the kitchen sink, did not see his face tighten, nor saw his fingers tremble, nor his lungs draw deeply on his Navy Cut.

Heart pounding, Clifford scanned the headline of the blow-by-blow report of the riot the night before. Tired, his brain frazzled, he relived every minute of what the reporter at the scene had written. He listed them in his head.

Incident: Flaming bottles flew from 9 Blenheim Crescent's roof of a four-floor tenement building housing coloureds.

Incident: A brick thrown by whites knocked out a coloured man at Bromley Road.

Incident: A middle-aged woman hurried into the white mob that was plummeting a West Indian. Grabbing her son by the shirt, she screeched, "No lad of mine will beat up people." She slapped the youth across the face and yanked him after her.

Incident: A Ted lit several paraffin rags and threw them into the shattered window of a roomful of screaming coloured people.

Incident: A distressed Jamaican woman brandishing a machete shouted at her attackers, "Leave us alone. We've done not'ing to you."

Incident: Police with dogs pinned a line of Teds against a wall and frisked them from head to toe.

Incident: A Black Maria rammed into a house of coloured people on Blenheim Crescent. Police frisked a line of coloured men and hauled away nine-inch knives and pickaxes.

Incident: Whites tore down the front fence of a white woman's house and used it to smash up the window of her Jamaican neighbour's house.

Incident: Teds jeered at police and called them "Nigger lovers."

Incident: Four coloured men arrested at 9 Blenheim Crescent.

Incident: Two Teds arrested for assaulting a coloured man with a knife and assaulting another outside Latimer Station.

368

Clifford laid down the newspaper and took a drag of his smoke. One fact was clear. He would never tell any of this to Clara.

Two days later Sonny was released on bail. Soon he would appear in court. But, as he told Clifford, "Me alive man. It me duty fe defend ourself a-Britain. Let English court prosecute me. Me gwan tell English some good Jamaican truths an' cuss words. No care man. Mak' dem do wat dem want." Sonny had grinned and kissed his teeth scornfully.

It was then that Clifford begged Sonny to never tell Clara he was involved in the riots.

"Clifford man. Why not. We heroes."

He told Sonny. Telling Clara would be worse than facing the rioters. She would never let her mouth rest. His ears would burn till kingdom come. If Sonny valued their friendship, he must promise, never let his involvement slide out.

Some months later, scanning the newspapers Clifford, laughed. A Teddy boy, Dave Watson and his blond friend had been arrested. Each would receive hefty jail sentences for their part in the riots. The harsh sentences meted out to the two gave racial whites time for reflection. British courts, shocked at the unprecedented violence, wanted to send a strong warning to its citizens. Violent acts like the Notting Hill riots would not be tolerated. Unfortunately, these warnings did not stop prejudice. It became more subtle. Hateful looks, slights, and underhanded colour bars in the workplace replaced outright venom.

The years that followed, Clifford and Clara always planned to return to Jamaica. They kept putting bits and pieces into the trunk at the foot of their bed. Soon they would return to their island home. They never did. Visions of Jamaica faded. England became their reality.

Missy became one of the first coloured midwives in Britain. Roy never did bring shame and disgrace on his family. He became an engineer. As for Tilda, well that is another story.

Clifford kept his involvement in the Notting Hill riots a secret for over forty years. An aged, grey-haired grandfather, in a comfortable armchair, occupied with his favourite pastime—a newspaper—his tea—cigarette at his elbow, he turned the page and cackled, "Backside!"

The newspaper revealed details of secret papers that had been released—facts proving there had been a cover-up by the government and the police about the Notting Hill riots.

"What dem idiots know 'bout riots," Clifford said, chuckling and kissing his vexed false teeth. "Me was dere!"

EPILOGUE

The Notting Hill riots forever changed West Indians relationship with Britain. Once West Indians believed that, as Britain's children she would protect them. The Notting Hill riots changed that illusion. After the riots West Indians questioned their identity. Who were they—certainly not British. Then it finally dawned; they were Jamaican, Barbadian, Trinidadian, and St. Lucian—West Indians. Britain must now acknowledge them as her legitimate citizens. Not unwanted baggage to be thrown out whenever she pleased. As her citizens she must treat them with dignity and respect.

The ensuing years saw small steps forward in racial harmony, followed by giant leaps backwards. Racism was Britain's giant elephant in the room.

One bright spark did emerge from the embers of the riots—the birth of the Notting Hill Carnival.

In an effort to promote racial harmony, in 1959, Claudia Jones, a Trinidadian woman, organized a carnival. She was to become known as "The Mother of the Notting Hill Carnival". In the years that followed, the Notting Hill Carnival evolved into a world-wide event.

ACKNOWLEDGEMENTS

My thanks to the writers group which I have been involved with for over nine years, Moya, June, Joanne, Betty, and Donna.

To Melanie, she read my manuscript and made suggestions.

Barb Howard, Writer in Residence, kindly read twenty-five random pages and suggested that this story must be told, and to fight for the "voice".

To my editor Rachel Small, she had never edited a book quite like this. She encouraged me to put in more patwa. Her kind suggestions made this a better book.

Thanks to Sarah Kuehn for her kind suggestions for the cover.

Thanks, also, to John Breeze for turning the manusctipt into the book that you hold in your hands.

My thanks to all those who helped me along this journey.

To my dear children for their support, for listening and making numerous suggestions, to my long suffering husband, he was my sounding board, so many of you helped to make this happen, thank you all.

SOURCES

The Gleaner Geography & History of Jamaica, 22nd Edition, 1985.

Jet Magazine 25 Sept 1958.

History of Jamaica, Clinton. V. Black. 1988

Forbidden Britain, Steve Humphries & Pamela Gordon. B.B.C. Books 1994

Beyond the Mother Country, Edward Pilkington. 1988.

The Independent, Ian Burrell, Media and Culture Correspondent, Saturday 23, August 2003.

The Guardian, Saturday 24 August 2003. Alan Travis, Home affairs editor.

Kensington News, 5 Sept 1958.

Notting Hill History Time Line – The Clashes 1958 – Rotting Hill 1940's – The Ghetto Early 1950's.

Notting Hill Riot Special, ITN News, 5 September, 1958 – ITN's Reginald Bosanquet.

Daily Express comic strip - Tuesday Sept, 2, 1958, No. 18, 125 - Pocket Cartoon.

Tuesday, 2nd Sept, 1958 – Bombs in Race Riot. Wednesday, 3 Sept. 1958.

Daily Mail, Saturday 20th August, Sunday, 21st August, Monday 22nd August 1958.

Daily Express, Monday 1 Sept, 1958 - Express Staff Reporters, Notting Hill. Thursday, 4th Sept, 1958, 2nd Sept 1959 – Fight in Barricaded House. (Reporting team – L.Turner and A.   Brown).

London Daily News cartoon.

Tony Benn, diary extract from *The Gaitskell Years* 1955-60.

Colin Eales Monday evening 1st September 1958.

Keep Brixton White, Union Movement pamphlet, March 31, 1955, London County Council Elections.

London Tribune, News Chronicle, The Daily Mail, The Times and *The Star*, 1955.

The Notting Hill Riots and British National Identity – Mr. Tim Helbing, Indiana University.

1958 Remembered – Riot Reminiscence – Riot Reports.

Teddy Boy's Picnic by Mo Foster.

Kensington News, 12th Sept 1958.

Hansard, Parliamentiary Debates, 1958.

GLOSSARY

Anansi	Jamaican folk lore spider
Back-a-yard	ignorant yokel/ bumpkin/back garden
Baggy	panties/knickers
Batty	bottom/posterior
Batty man	homosexual/effeminate man
Black widow	deadly spider.
Blow-fire-a-bush	no good/common individual
Bruck	broke
Chocho	wrinkled Jamaican vegetable
Degge-degga	nothing/none
Dry foot	derogatory term for someone not liked
Duckers and divers	shady dealers
Dutty	dirty/nasty
Faas	nosy/interfering
Feisty	cheeky/arrogant
Filt/Pupu	excrement
Fool-fool-duppy	idiot/silly person
Gallang	go away/clear off
Gig	child spinning top
Hard dough bread	hard white Jamaican bread
Hard-a-ears	disobedient/wilful/proud

Hasounou	someone who acts like a savage /wicked person
Hurry-come-up	snob, a person that think he/she is superior to others
Jamaican whip	a clicking finger gesture that indicates "Yea, man"
Janga	small shrimp/Jamaican slang for male sexual organ
Juck	prick/prod/stab
Jumby/duppy	ghost/spirit
Labrish	idle talk/conversation
Marena	vest
Marga	very thin individual
Moonshine	long time/a dim witted individual
Muckle	any little bit that helps
Narked	annoyed
Natty-bump-head	derogatory word for an individual not liked
Neyga	Negro
Nyam	eat
Obeah	witchcraft
Out-a-order	disrespectful
Pally	become friends/make friends
Petti-pettied	pampered
Pickney	child
Poco/Pocomanian	religious Jamaican group
Ponsy boys	effeminate males
Poppy show	make a fool of an individual/an idiotic and stupid thing
Puppus	pet name for someone liked
Rank foot	derogatory term for any individual not liked
Ratta	fist/rat

Rass Clawt'	Jamaican swear word
Rawted/rawtedness	mild swear word/harshness/no mercy
Redibo	derogatory name for a light skin/fair haired Jamaican.
Rolling Calf	A fabled terrifying Jamaican Bull
Rucku-rucku	broken down/making do with almost nothing
Rundown	Jamaican delicacy made of salt fish and coconut
Sambo	mixed race individual
Sea wall people	wise individuals
Shamey darling	green fern, when touched closes its leaves
Snarky	cheeky/ aggressive
Soulcase	an individual energy
Stag-a-back	Jamaican sweet
Station	position in life
Stretcher	Jamaican sweet
Susumber Bush	Jamaican vegetable
Tallawah	fiery/spitfire/proud
Tallboy	tall set of drawers
Tunted	stunned/bewildered
Wash out medicine	herbal concoction to clean out the system.
Wire-waist	thin, sticklike individual
Wog	derogatory term for a black/coloured individual
Wattle house	house made from woven bamboo
Yardboy	servant
Yob	young hooligan

ABOUT THE AUTHOR

B.M.J. Gatt was born in Jamaica and emigrated to England with her parents as a child. She now lives in Canada. *One of Many* is her first novel. She is working on her second.

44208503R00236

Made in the USA
Lexington, KY
25 August 2015